The Mud
and
The Snow

A Tale of the United States Army

The Mud
and
The Snow

A Tale of the United States Army

By the author of *2084*

Chris Durer

www.ivyhousebooks.com

PUBLISHED BY IVY HOUSE PUBLISHING GROUP
5122 Bur Oak Circle, Raleigh, NC 27612
United States of America
919-782-0281
www.ivyhousebooks.com

ISBN 13: 978-1-57197-472-3
Library of Congress Control Number: 2006929916

Printed in the United States of America

*I dedicate this novel to the memory of my parents
and what they stood for.*

Book
One

Chapter 1

It rose some four feet above the water, all metal whitish-gray, slick and highly polished, and glistening in the morning air; twenty-four feet long and six feet wide, straight like an arrow and light at the base, with a delicately formed semicircular stern and a slender prow shaped like the point of a javelin. Right in front and back of the protruding cockpit a machine gun was mounted, one pointing forward and the other aft, and a foot above the water, forward and rear, a narrow aperture had been wrought in the hull, a ready egress for whatever was lurking within. On each side a set of narrow indented steps, enough for a single foot but no more, reached all the way from below the water mark to the edges above.

"*Ça y est?*" the French officer called from the bank. "*Soyez prêt!*" Then glancing at a sheaf of notes clasped in his hand and lifting the bullhorn, he spoke in English slowly and deliberately, enunciating with painstaking clarity. "Pont-Mobile AF (Armée Française) 147/155, what you would call Mobile-Bridge can be operated by an army driver," he paused, smiling complaisantly, "by any competent army driver, French or American. No additional training is necessary. This vehicle, which can move on land and in the water, has a sixteen hundred horsepower engine, and stretches its floating or supported ladders forty feet in each direction, vertically or horizontally, as the situation demands. This gives you eighty feet plus twenty-four feet—104 feet altogether, and the ladders are capable of sustaining the weight of two tons on either side; the supporting poles having the capacity to reach as deep as twenty feet, a considerable depth for a river or lake. Mobile-Bridge can perform many tasks—Ranger-style attack, facilitating in the climbing of mountains, prompt conveyance of troops on land and at sea, crossing streams and so on."

The French major paused and let his eyes roam with satisfaction over the lake and the surrounding hills. He straightened himself up, adjusted the bullhorn, and let his words fall even more slowly and deliberately than before. "In today's warfare we must expect our equipment to be diverse, to have many different uses, to be ready for any contingency." He paused again and folded his notes. "We hope the U.S. Army will adopt our Mobile-Bridge as standard equipment. We in the French Army have done so already." Then throwing the bullhorn to the side he shouted, "*Alors, commencez.*"

At his bidding two swarthy figures in French Army uniforms emerged from the hold of the Mobile-Bridge and began to work the controls. At once the ladders jutted out at ninety-degree angles and with every passing second they protruded further and further. When they had reached the half point, they formed an arc before they touched the surface of the water with a splash. The engine was revved up and the Mobile-Bridge began to shake, pushing icy crags away from its sides. Then the engine grew even louder as the two swarthy figures stood at attention and saluted. The French major reached again for his bullhorn. "This concludes the last of our presentations and Colonel Laberville and I, Major Fergusson, will be glad to answer any questions. Thank you, gentlemen." As he nodded the ladders recoiled and reentered the apertures, the engine grew less and less audible, and the two crewmen disappeared down below.

A group of American officers clustered around a two-star general on a knoll some distance away had been watching the French performance very closely. A coat of light snow covered much of the ground, and ice filled the gullies. The temperature was below freezing point, and some of the officers stamped their feet, others resolutely rubbed their hands, and others still tightened their scarves and adjusted the earflaps.

"You gotta hand it to the Frenchies," said one of them, a strapping, thickset man, pulling the cheroot butt from between his half-frozen lips and spitting with gusto. "Best pontoon bridge I seen yet." A younger man, standing next to him, stiff and aloof, was on the point of saying something when the general's voice was heard, towering over the private chatter.

"This was a very worthwhile occasion." The words were flowing out at an uninterruptedly regular pace without pauses or the pitch rising or falling, in a rich voice originating somewhere in the Deep South. "And I already visited with the French colonel. Very fine fella."

"General Vickers," a voice shot out, "those reports that you requested, sir, do they have to be in writing or can they be given to your office over the phone?"

"In writing, Captain. And let me add a cautionary word: give me the benefit of your judgments, that's what I expect, but try to be concise. I'm reminded of what my junior-high school teacher used to say more years ago than I care to count"—a ripple of approving laughter was heard around him—"'If you can't say what you mean on any given subject in a single page, don't bother because it probably ain't worth writing.' The substance of your reports on the French Mobile-Bridge will be sent to Washington and Washington is already waiting. I need your reports within a week as of today," he surreptitiously glanced at his watch, "the 14th. Washington will have to make a big decision, a very big decision, which relates to a major piece of army equipment. A very significant decision and a very significant matter if you ask me! I shall await your reports very soon—as I indicated already—and they will be studied with care, no matter how long or how short they may be. As you all know, I read every scrap of paper that passes through my desk! The buck stops with Vickers!" The general rubbed his chin and cast a cursory glance around him. "I believe that terminates this very significant occasion," and he made ready to go, but the strapping thickset man broke in.

"Would you care to try our chow for lunch at 16th Engineer Group, sir?"

General Vickers' face registered the question with approval and he turned towards the speaker with something like geniality, but his aide, a tall man with a boyish face and an easy manner, drew near and began to whisper in his ear, cupping his hand over his mouth and the general's ear. The general nodded.

"That's mighty thoughtful of you, Major Trainer, and I appreciate the gesture. But Major Simmons reminds me that I am due at a very significant meeting at noon in another command. Thank you again, Major."

But Major Trainer was not to be disposed of so easily. "General Vickers, any news of our replacements? Group Commander, Exec Officer, two sergeants? This is what 16th Engineer Group needs bad, very bad, sir."

Hearing this, General Vickers lowered his head and took several steps away from the assembled officers. He then made a rapid about-face, saluted, and said very quietly, "Thank you, gentlemen." The others saluted in unison and began to walk away. The general made another about-face, and he now stood no more than a yard away from Major Trainer, with Major Simmons right on his heels. His voice drawled out again as the flesh on his face and forehead contracted and then relaxed and the pig-eyes shifted this way and that. "I fully understaaand your conceeern, Major, and it is a legitimate concern. We at Aaarmy consider your replaacements one of our most pressing and significaant priorities, and we are doing all we can. You know that at Aaarmy we work around the clock. Yes, sir! A most unfortunate occurrence that Colonel Higginbotham paassed on so suddenly, very suddenly! I know the family. And Colonel Weiler was snatched away, transferred to Japan, before he could assume command. Mind you, this was the Pentagon's doing, not ours. I am told he had an advanced degree in physics. As for your Exec Officer and the sergeants, we have the matter in hand. You're the acting Group Commander, Trainer; you're the king of the mountain!" Vickers laughed and it was a jeering laughter. "Enjoy it while it lasts! Anyyything else?"

"No, sir!"

"Well then, we'll be on our way," and the general extended his hand. "Good-bye, Trainer, and good-bye to you, Captain . . . Captain . . ."

"Captain Ronald Spelling, sir."

"Oh yes, Spelling, Spelling, I remember the naaame. Reeecently promoted, eh?"

"Yes, General Vickers."

As the general and Major Simmons were stepping cautiously over a partly cleared path towards a waiting car, the former droned out,

"Tom, what in the hell's name is that very significaant meeting I'm going to at noon?"

/ / /

Major Trainer and Captain Spelling chose the shortest way back to 16th Engineer Group, skirting the north side of the lake, climbing a mound slippery as an eel, and then along the right bank of the Elsenz and from there all the way to the black barrier of pine trees which resembled an unbreakable wall guarding the bailiwick of some medieval prince-sorcerer. Once past the pine trees they could see the meandering River Elsenz, the range of hills further to the west white with snow but punctuated by patches of sheer black, the two colors standing in relief to each other and never intermingling. The air was clear, visibility near perfect, and not a cloud marred the far expanse. Only with the help of field glasses could one penetrate into another region, far to the west and almost to the banks of the Rhine, over which delicate patches of mist fluttered and danced.

The two men advanced to the edge of the gorge, turned left, came to another clearing, and made their way through the lowest part of the encroaching wood. Up another steep mountain pass, and they were atop an eminence. They stopped. Down below lay the barracks of 16th U.S. Army Engineer Group, hidden from the east and south by bulging rocks and craggy mountainsides. To the left nestled the town of Kirchenberg. A mile or so further to the right a temporary French camp of the visiting pilot unit of a French Engineering Corps was laid out.

/ / /

Major Trainer relit his cheroot. "You'd better get on that report for Vickers right away and coordinate with Hurstwood. He knows one hell of a lot about pontoon bridges, more than one should know."

Captain Spelling coughed and cleared his throat. "The French don't like when we call it a pontoon bridge. It isn't stationary, it's fully mobile."

"Yeah, yeah, whatever," Trainer mumbled, rounding it off with a belch. Then he looked fiercely at Spelling. "Why the hell couldn't we have constructed somethin' like that? The greatest country in the world and the Frenchies are putting us to shame. I'll tell you why," he went on with fury, "'cause all that them Pentagon boys can do is sit on their asses, finger up in the air." He raised his index finger high above his head. "To see which way the wind is blowing and how soon their buddies can be promoted."

He began to lick his cheroot on each side, spat, shook his shoulders, and then spat again, this time aiming as far as his tightened jaw allowed. Captain Spelling, his winter coat half-opened, displaying spotless and pressed fatigues rising above the spit-shining and symmetrically laced brown boots, shot a sideways glance at the major, turned his head, and moved several steps to the left. For a few moments he stood there in silence, his eyebrows knitted, and then raised his pallid clean-shaven face, his eyes fixed on nothing in particular. Presently a sardonic smile began to contort his features, culminating in a wide grimace.

"The Kraut winter hasn't started yet, not like last year, and it's already mid-February," and Trainer went about buttoning his coat and tying his scarf.

"That's right, sir, the worst is still to come," Spelling put in officiously.

"What I'd like to know is how does a Frenchie end up with a name like Fergusson?" Trainer's tone was lighter now, his manner more relaxed.

"It's very simple. Fergusson was telling us about it the other day, sir."

"Oh."

"One of his ancestors, Malcolm Fergusson, was in the retinue of James II and accompanied his master into exile in France in 1689."

"Got a girl in trouble and had to leave town, eh?"

"Not exactly, he was king of England, but had to flee."

"What in Heaven's name did he want with the Frenchies?"

"It's too long to explain, sir, but France offered him asylum."

"Did it now? And our boy Fergusson . . . ?"

"Is the direct descendant of Malcolm Fergusson who stayed on in France and married a French girl. The children were born in France, and from then on the family was French. Major Fergusson told us they have all the papers going back to the Glorious Revolution."

"You don't say!" Trainer was on the point of making another remark when something down below in the French camp caught his attention.

"Why are the Frenchies starting bonfires? Look, they've got six or seven going. What the hell for?"

"Four of their men were hurt while putting together the mobile-bridges. Treads and belts wouldn't budge on several of them, and there were also other mechanical defects," Spelling reported dutifully. "In some cases their mechanics had to go underwater to repair and test, and their winter clothing isn't worth much. Back home we'll be ashamed to give it to the Salvation Army."

"They were told they could use the Annex Barracks on base, right?"

"Right, sir. But the Annex was once a detention center, and it's got six layers of barbwire all around. The French colonel took one look at it and just about exploded. Major Fergusson did the interpreting."

"What was his beef?"

"Some of the men were POWs in Indonesia, they remember barb-wire. The colonel got all red in the face, and I thought he was going to clobber Lieutenant Hurstwood. Fergusson did his best not to translate what the colonel was boiling over, but the colonel hissed in his face, 'Translate word for word.' That was last week, you were away."

"Right."

"It went something like this: 'This is the way the Americans are treating the French Army? Putting us behind barbed wire?' This was just the beginning—what followed was a barrage of insults. Fergusson did his best, but he didn't get far. Hurstwood got the gist."

"So they are camping out under the Kraut sky."

"Their colonel ordered it. Those among them who aren't actually injured are probably frozen stiff. Their tents are tropical." Spelling paused and then continued steadily, "Pretty bad in this kind of weather, and furthermore," he was at his sternest now, "it's against regulations, theirs and ours! Bonfires are their only means of keeping warm."

"I see," Trainer said pensively, "but we have no other accommodations, have we now? The Frenchies should've taken what was offered." He stopped abruptly and let his eyes wander over the variegated expanse of the French camp. "They should've taken it, barbwire or no barbwire!"

"Anyway, they'll be leaving the day after tomorrow," Spelling added, examining his fingernails. "It's all arranged."

"Right, Spelling, they'll be leaving us. But, I still wish we'd built that fuckin' mobile-bridge, not 'em. You read me?"

"Yes, sir."

"Good, and now let's get back to base. We've had a bellyful of this goddamn fresh air."

As Major Trainer and Captain Spelling were hurrying down the hill, not a sound rose from the French camp. There round the bonfires clustered ragged figures dressed in ill-fitting, oil-stained khaki uniforms, some stretching their arms forth to the fire and others edging their way as close to it as possible without getting singed. The tropical pup tents were scattered on the plain, this way and that with no passages between them, some still standing and others half folded or lying shapelessly on the ground. At rare intervals a wrapped-up figure, rubbing his hands and wearing an officer's insignia and cap, would enter the command tent and then come out frowning and shaking his head. The mess tent with its pipe chimney swaying and the entrance flaps fluttering furiously in the wind was the site of the most intense activity. Shivering, unshaven men, their light overcoats buttoned to the neck with collars standing up, were making their way in and out, occasionally exchanging a word of greeting, but otherwise looking miserable and disoriented. The more energetic stamped their feet while the others stood resignedly in place, casting vacant glances to the right and left, or moving somnambulistically around. The camp resembled a detention center where most of the inmates are either sick or retarded.

All of a sudden Spelling ground to a halt.

"What's the matter, Captain? Old ticker acting up?" Trainer also stopped and was observing Spelling critically.

"No, sir, ticker's fine, it's the French camp, brings back old memories."

"Didn't know you served with the Frenchies 'fore you signed on with us."

Spelling gave out a quick nervous laugh. "At the Point I did a project on Napoleon's Russian campaign." He paused. "I got top marks. Old memories keep pounding in my brain."

"Good for you, but you'd better make up your mind if you want to hang back or do a little reminiscin'. Either is fine with me."

"I don't know how to thank you, Major."

"Get on with it, Captain, before we freeze to death."

Spelling took a few steps to the right and was now facing the French camp, his countenance an epitome of extreme concentration, his eye cast far.

"This comes under the heading of transient military glory."

"Sure, sure," and Trainer relit his cheroot.

Spelling leaned forward, and his arms thrust aggressively forward enclosed the camp from both sides. He spoke with extraordinary feeling.

"It was not always like this! The forebears of these ill-nourished and ill-paid French conscripts, downcast and no longer caring and posted for the duration to the West German town of Kirchenberg, had fought heroically at Marengo, Wagram, Jena, Austerlitz. Some rose to be body and soul of the Imperial Guard! At Smolensk in a single charge they carried the suburbs, stood ready to scale the city walls thirty feet high and fifteen feet thick, but at their sight the enemy slithered away in abject fear. In pursuit they crossed the Dnieper, caught up with him near Valutino Hill, and brought him to his knees. *Vive l' Empereur! Vive l' Empereur!*"

At Borodino at the first rays of dawn the emperor cried, "Behold the sun of Austerlitz!" Soon fighting became so furious there was scarcely any room for maneuvering, and the attacks were made frontally and desperately—rifle, bayonet, cannon; rifle, bayonet, cannon! "*Vive l' Empereur!*" *Vive l' Empereur!*" The redoubts were taken, lost and retaken, and each officer reporting to the emperor brought the news of some heroic deed—this was *furore francese* that nations trembled at! In the end theirs was victory at the cost of 28,000 French and 50,000 Russians killed and wounded. "*Vive l' Empereur! Vive l' Empereur!*"

In retreat they were heroes too, indomitable, the ever-dwindling half-starved army and later starving with no more horse meat left and the Cossacks charging at them from all sides. Mozhaisk, Vyazma where the First and Fourth Corps fought against impossible odds, Dorogobuzh where the Russians were halted and on to Krasnii and Borisov. Many had their limbs frozen and died in the snow, and the Russians took no prisoners. "*Vive l' Empereur!*" Some crossed the Berezina, but thousands were drowned, crushed by wagons, shot through, maimed and left to die. The Berezina crossing claimed over thirty thousand victims. "*Vive l' Empereur!*" When at last they reached Vilna they were just a few thousand strong. "*Vive l' Empereur!*" Their loyalty to him never wavered."

Trainer clapped and patted Spelling on the back. "Well, done, Ron, this was a nifty piece of country time." Then he turned towards the French camp. More and more fires were being lit, and clouds of black smoke hovered over them.

Chapter 2

Major Trainer was sitting behind his desk, his unpolished, mud-covered, sloppily laced boots covered with creases and cuts, resting on a large blotter in front of him. He was shuffling papers, picking up individual sheets with his stubby, dirty fingers by the corner from a pile on his left, holding them up to the light before casting them to the right where they formed an inflated, irregular surface, their edges and covers protruding in all directions. Presently he hoisted himself up, farted, and reached for the telephone. "Donkers, I want to see Honigklausen"—he hollered—"He there? Oh, okay! As soon as he gets back from the powder room, tell 'im to get his ass up here." He replaced the receiver and stared blankly at the walls, his brow knitted, his features exhibiting an uncomfortable concentration over something, which apparently weighed on his mind. He strolled over to the window, was about to mumble something to himself, his lips curling and ready, and then decided not to, shrugged and kept gazing at the light snow falling at different angles and blown hither and thither by the wind.

Presently there was a knock on the door. "Come in!" he shouted. Lester Honigklausen, Group Sergeant of 16th Engineer Group, a large, obese man, quietly entered the Acting Group Commander's office, smiling ingratiatingly.

"The Major wished to see me," he began expectantly, the smile becoming even more saccharine.

"Yeah, yeah, yeah," Trainer was starting to light up a new cheroot. He hollered in a commanding voice, and he was unhurriedly gazing at the sergeant head to foot, wondering as he often did with the help of what supernatural powers was Honigklausen able to fit in the door. *He must weigh 350 pounds at least, probably more, 375 or 400 pounds, he mused, and every time I hear 'im turning the knob I'm ready to swear he'll break the damned door. But somehow he always manages to squeeze through. How does he do it, I wish I knew,* he went on musing. But business intervened. "Listen, I want ye to keep after the officers re: reports on the Frenchie vehicle. Vickers wants 'em in seven days, and I want 'em in five. Them reports are to come to me, not be sent directly to 7th Army Headquarters. I want this understood, so tell the you-ng gen-tle-men"—he pronounced the last words mincingly, wetting his lips and emitting a continuous smacking sound—"to stop scratching their asses and do something useful for a change. I don't want nobody and nobody to be late."

"As the Major wishes," Honigklausen responded hastily, standing at attention and breathing heavily. "It will be done."

Trainer now stood away from the window, and the sun came through it illuminating his entire figure, the large head with curls of blackish hair scattered on top and getting abruptly shorter and thinner on the back and sides, the crumpled stained fatigues covering the bull-like neck and the massive chest, the slightly bulging belly, the enormous haunches, the short legs and the short arms straining the taut sleeves. He blew his nose.

"How's things with the Frenchies, Lester? Got it under control?"

Honigklausen swayed, shifting his weight from one foot to the other before answering with utmost unctuousness.

"I'd like to go on record with the Major's permission, of course . . ."

"Permission denied!" Trainer roared.

"Sir?"

"Nothing, Lester, go on . . . go on!" Trainer's guffaw was equal to his roar.

"Well, in the manner of speaking, and with the Major's permission, the situation with the Frenchies is as good as might be expected."

"Go on."

"I had a very pleasant talk with Sergeant Lavoyzeer and extended once again the invitation for them French troops to use our Mess Hall like what Lieutenant Hurstwood extended to them the other day. This was just sergeant to sergeant talk but it was approved like by a higher authority."

"And?"

"Their colonel, Colonel Laberville, forbade his troops to enter our Mess Hall, direct order."

"I see!"

"But the good sergeant said they'd accept hot coffee, so we sent forty gallons this very morning. And he also said our troops are very welcome in their field Mess Hall."

"That will be the day," Trainer muttered more to himself than to Honigklausen. "That will be the day," he repeated looking away from the sergeant. "Sure, the whole thing's botched up, anybody can see that," he continued irascibly. "Army gave me no notice at all, no sir, none, about the Frenchies coming here! First I know is a memo from Vickers six hours after they started squatting in my backyard. Don't blame me, Army! Did my best in the first two days to locate that French bird. But he was nowhere to be found. Maybe turned himself into a chunk of cheese."

Sergeant Honigklausen, a little more relaxed now and exuding respect for the major, sounded off in a tone which left no room for doubt: "It's like the Major says."

Trainer waved a hand.

"Shit, all this fucken di-plow-macey, that's what they call it, there ain't no place for it in this men's army. They want di-plow-macey, they oughta hire some jackass from Madison Avenue to practice their di-plow-macey. Anyway"—he added with an air of finality—"try to keep the peace, and keep me informed."

"Yes, Major Trainer, sir!"

"There's some other matters I want to talk with you about, those two Articles 15, and the two courts-martial with me as witness, one summary and a special, and other things too . . ."—here Trainer rubbed his forehead and snapped his fingers. "Something I forgot to ask: is that medication, pills, injections, and whatever else they're giving you, doing you any good, Lester? Weight-wise, I mean? You'll be reviewed again in six months."

"The Doc wants to see me in two months' time, that's what he said," Honigklausen replied evasively, looking at the floor.

Trainer took two steps forward and was now looking Honigklausen straight in the eye, his features contracted, his sudden stillness denoting something more than attention to daily routine.

"You'll let me know if there's anything I can do, before you see the Doc, I mean. Medical leave, per diem, this kind of thing, okay?"

"I will, sir." Honigklausen drew himself up again. "And I thank the Major, sir."

"Good," and Trainer lit up another cheroot, sounding relieved, his face brightening. "We have work to do, so pull up a chair, and let's go through this crap."

But before the two men had the time to sit down, there was another knock on the door, and a tall, slim PFC in his late teens or very early twenties, his mane of brown hair falling roguishly to the side, entered the major's office.

"What is it, Donkers?"

"I thought you would like to know, sir. A message came from Army just now regarding the French troops and their activities. Major Simmons gave it to me over the phone. No, sir, he didn't ask for you— he gave it to me. It's a fairly long message, apparently he's sending same to all engineer units. I have it all written down."

"I see. I'll be tied up with Sergeant Honigklausen for the next thirty minutes or so. I'll tell you what, Donkers, you report back in half an hour, and bring your notes with you. Thank you, Donkers, and stop growing."

When Donkers returned to the Acting Group Commander's office, Honigklausen had already left and was in his own office. Donkers kept on sniffing the air and threw his head jerkily up and to the side before reading the message. "'Major Simmons would like to stress that the French should receive every courtesy from the U.S. Army. They are our guests, and they will be treated accordingly. I want to remind you again of the reports, which are due here in General Vickers' office in seven days. These reports are crucial for us.'" Donkers stopped and again sniffed the air. "At this point the message gets kind of scrambled. I'd say Major Simmons' instructions were far from clear."

"Unscramble it then."

"I'll try." At a slow pace and articulating with care Donkers lay before the attentive listener the rest of the telephone communication: "16th Engineer Group should try, if it wishes, to obtain further information about the French Mobile-Bridge and more broadly about the French engineer technology of which the French are so proud. In order to facilitate the American understanding of the new French engineer equipment, the French High Command is sending qualified personnel who speak English to all Engineer units within 7th U.S. Army Command. This personnel may contact the American units directly or through the office of General Vickers. But if no direct contact is made by the French, U.S. Engineer Units are encouraged to establish contact with the French Engineer Command. In the case of 16th Engineer Group, the French liaison is Major Michel Fergusson, who earlier today was the honored guest of the 16th Group, and who can be reached at the newly established extension 2092 at 7th Army Headquarters. Should Major Fergusson be away on assignment, telephone messages may be left for him at this extension.'" Donkers stopped again, sniffed the air, and cleared his throat. "The last part of the message"—he began haltingly—"is even more unclear because Major Simmons would say one thing and then rescind it, say another thing and then rescind it too, and go back to the original version, or provide a variant."

"Go on, this is getting better and better," Trainer said, blowing enormous puffs of smoke onto the wall where, next to the map of what had been the American Zone of Occupation, a solitary and bare nail was sticking out. This nail now became the focus of Trainer's exclusive attention. He drew close to it, drew back, inspected it from a ninety-degree angle on each side, retreated, and then jumped straight ahead with both feet so that his lips were now on the level of the nail and not more than three inches away from it. Frantically he bit on the cheroot, inhaled, and blew out smoke as quickly as his lungs would allow, one exhalation after another, each one faster than the preceding one, faster and faster, all pointing to the solitary nail on the wall. Soon only the vague contours of the major were visible in the smoke, the nail and part of the wall lost to view, and the rest of the office a semidarkness.

"Go on, kid, can you see me?" Trainer called out genially. Donkers coughed, stood up, and began to disperse smoke with quick repeated arm movements.

"Sorry, kid, should've known you ain't no tobacco fan. Where were we?"

Donkers resumed his seat and looked again at the message. "Major Simmons says that should U.S. personnel speak to the French they are not to ask any questions, just note down what the French are saying and under no circumstances express any judgments. Above all, U.S. personnel are not to engage in a dialogue with the French as to the effectiveness of the Mobile-Bridge in hypothetical combat situations. We are just to listen."

The major began to yawn. "Okay, what's next? How much more of this garbage?"

"We are almost at the end," Donkers intoned reassuringly. He shifted in his seat, made a few more arm gestures to disperse the hovering smoke, and proceeded even more slowly than before, as if trying with each new sound to decipher the hidden meaning of which the words themselves gave but a pale rendition.

"At this point there was a short pause, and Major Simmons asked me to wait. When he came back he said that discussions with the French were encouraged by Army as long as they were confined to technical matters only and didn't entail the broader issues of effectiveness of the Mobile-Bridge, its technical use or its tactical possibilities, but that individual units were prohibited from establishing direct contact with the French and were mandated to direct their inquiries and comments to General Vickers' office. At the same time, and Major Simmons made a point of saying it twice"—Donkers continued doggedly—"that in a situation like this each engineer unit should be given a good deal of latitude in cooperating with the French forces, obtaining information, digesting it, and establishing avenues of communication and exchange of data which would benefit our army and that of our trusted and old ally the French."

Major Trainer was quite still now, firmly ensconced behind his desk, his feet on the floor, resignedly blinking now and then, a bored expression lining his fleshy face where the razor missed little areas of growing hair. He raised himself just a little from his seat and farted very loudly, following this expulsion of intestinal gas with other, longer and less sonorous evacuations.

"The final part of the telephone message, and Major Simmons emphasized it and asked me to read back word for word what I'd written, is that this matter will be handled with the help of individual U.S. Engineer Units, but essentially on the highest level: 7th Army

Headquarters and French High Command in Karlsruhe, NATO Headquarters in Brussels, the Pentagon, State Department, and the French embassy in D.C."

Trainer looked up, keenly eyeing Donkers. "Vickers' covering his ass," he smiled, making an assenting nod of the head. "And I think I know what you're thinking, Donkers . . ."

"Sir?"

"He's also trying to work both sides of the street, lowdown son-of-a-bitch!"

"I wouldn't've put it like that, sir, but the idea occurred to me."

"Good! We'll do what's best for us in our neck of the wood, and if Vickers is to lick the dust, well that's his problem. I'll be talking to Fergusson."

"I don't mean to presume," Donkers was straightening himself up in his seat and looking at the major intently, "but you should be circumspect and . . . Machiavellian."

"What the hell do them words mean?"

"To put it in high Miltonic terms, you too should cover your ass and keep it out of reach of General Vickers' boot."

The major grew pensive for a moment, then he turned to Donkers and said matter-of-factly, "Good advice, kid, good advice!" He rose from behind the desk and began to crisscross the small office now free of cheroot smoke, where army manuals, maps, outdated memos, court-martial folders, and various unsorted papers were lying pell-mell on the desk, on the bookshelves, and on the small folding tables in the corners and under the window. He stopped and began to scratch his head, looking significantly at Donkers.

"I wish they found the new Group Commander, so I can go back to being operational with my engineers—'stead of being 'acti-n-g' with that toy soldier Spelling playing the Exec."

"They are certainly taking their own sweet time about it," Donkers conceded, "but maybe this is to your advantage."

"How?" the Major asked, highly amused. "How is it to my advantage? It's a pain in the ass."

"The question is really very simple," Donkers went on, "and it boils down to this: do you want to be the Group Commander or not?"

"What kind of a fool question is this? Sure, I want to be the Group

Commander." There was more than a note of puzzlement in Trainer's voice.

Donkers sniffed the air, stood up, bent backwards, and unbent, rhythmically drawing circles with his arms, while the major watched him in silence.

"It occurs to me, sir," Donkers was back in his chair sitting more or less at attention, "that you and I are similar in at least one respect."

"You and I," Trainer smiled indulgently. "You and I?" he repeated.

"Yes, sir. Both of us were taught that if you want something you should be prepared to work for it."

"That's right, Pa was always preaching it to us kids, though what good it did 'im I couldn't tell ye."

"It follows that if you want a permanent command you should be willing to work for it." Trainer lifted his shoulders and raised the index finger of his right hand.

"Listen to me, Donkers. When that asshole Vickers appointed me Acting Commander of 16th Engineer Group four months ago he made it as clear as his forked tongue would let him that this was a strictly temporary appointment. It went something like this: 'I want you to be under no illusion that this temporary appointment as Acting C.O. will ever be converted to anything more permanent. We shall find our own man in due course, full colonel it will be, but for the time being you're in charge.' End of story."

Donkers shook his head. "Things change, and what General Vickers said is not carved in stone. The truth of the matter is that a short list of candidates for the command of the 16th Group exists at Army and your name is on it."

"You're sure?"

"Positive, sir."

"What are your sources?"

Donkers smiled, jerked his head this way and that, and stroked his chin repeatedly before answering, "I am afraid, sir, my sources have to remain anonymous. But they are reliable. I have buddies at Army."

"Ho-ho-ho, PFC! *Pardonnez-moye*," Major Trainer went on laughing, utilizing the full force of his lungs, his eyes glittering. "So the Rotarians and the Freemasons got their fangs in you too! Group Clerks taking over! Is that the ticket?"

"Something like it, but the point remains that your name is on that list, and if you play your cards right you'll be the new C.O."

"And how do I do that, schoolmaster?"

Donkers rose from the chair and took a position in the far corner of the office by the door leading into the corridor, touching it lightly with the palm of his hand to see whether it was really closed.

"I have to backtrack, sir. You know that less than a month ago General Stebbins was transferred to 7th Army from Italy."

"Yeah, heard about it."

"And you are acquainted with General Stebbins?"

"Sure. He handled my battlefield commission in Korea. Was a colonel then."

"It so happens that General Stebbins and some of the people around him support your candidacy for Group Commander. Other generals and some colonels and different members of the Promotion Board have their own favorites. The final decision can go this, that, or any way. It's touch and go."

"So?"

"So! It might be a good idea if you paid a courtesy call on General Stebbins whom you probably have not seen for a considerable period of time. A courtesy call," Donkers enunciated slowly, trying to render the meaning of these words understandable.

"Hell, Donkers! I know what a courtesy call is. I ain't that dumb!"

"No, sir. But time is running out, and the Promotion Board is meeting again and possibly for the last time this quarter in two weeks. You should go to Army tomorrow and pay a call on General Stebbins; he'll be there this week, but next Monday he's traveling to Hanover to confer with the Brits. He'll probably want you to meet other officers. Tomorrow! There's no time to lose!"

Major Trainer was standing with his back touching the window, silent, his eyes roaming the walls, his features cast into an aspect of firmness and resolution.

"Anything else, Donkers?"

"As a matter of fact there is. You should wear dress uniform, go in a staff car driven by a sharply dressed corporal, and carry a briefcase."

"Why a briefcase? I never carry the damned thing! That's for the pop-in-jays at Headquarters."

"Briefcase," Donkers repeated softly. "And one other thing."

"And what might that be if . . . if . . . if you permit me to inquire?"

"You need a haircut, sir, a decent haircut."

"There's no time for it before tomorrow."

"There is. Chuck Miller in C Company was an apprentice barber when he was drafted. He's got his equipment with him. Cuts our hair, pretty good at it. Regular haircut is a buck, what Chuck calls haircut with all the trimmings, two bucks, and shampoo is fifty cents extra. He can be here in ten minutes. Though, of course"—and Donkers' face was suddenly illuminated by an expression in which beatitude and the keen sense of disparity of all things in the universe were evenly mixed—"Chuck may have a different rate for majors. After all, we are a capitalist country."

Major Trainer advanced slowly from the window to the simple wooden armchair behind his desk and sat in it—his face stern and forbidding. "Donkers," he spoke brusquely, his fingers tapping the blotter on the desk. Donkers moved several steps, and he now stood in front of the major. "This is what I want: a staff car outside my quarters at 0700 hours, spotless and shining with full tank, and my driver a sharp-looking corporal, and he'd better look sharp if he values his life. I'll be going to Weiningen on official business. Tell Sergeant Honigklausen to make necessary arrangements. Captain Spelling will be in charge during my absence. I expect to be back tomorrow night, but if not, Captain Spelling will be notified . . . And tell Private Charles Miller, C Company, to report here on the double. That's all."

"Yes, sir." Donkers saluted, and Trainer returned the salute, throwing his right hand in a wild and expansive gesture the full length of his arm.

Chapter 3

After dismissing Donkers, Major Trainer sat in silence, gazing at the four walls. Presently he picked up the receiver, dialed, and spoke briefly to his wife. He replaced the receiver, and almost at once he became aware of voices and laughter faint at first and then progressively more and more audible coming from the corridor, several offices away and close to that of the Executive Officer. He swung the door open and stepped into the corridor. To the left, halfway or so between him and the far exit marked by a large red sign, he saw Captain Hastings, the Group Chaplain, talking to Captain Spelling outside the latter's office with Donkers hanging on idly in the background. Hastings noticed him, raised an arm, and called out, "Hi there, Ed, glad you're here so I can bid my adieus." He was still talking to Spelling, and Trainer advanced, swaying slightly to the left and right, looking at nothing in particular.

"I have high hopes for this retreat." Captain Hastings uttered these words quickly, his pale delicate face registering emotions instantaneously, the lick of sandy hair dangling capriciously over the high forehead. "We've got almost eighty men this time, though only four from our outfit," he added with regret. "Still, I have high hopes . . ."

"So you're leaving . . . ?"

"Tomorrow at the crack of dawn, carrying with me our four noble volunteers, destination Augsburg."

"Well, have a good retreat, Bob."

"Thank you. I was telling Ron that we really ought to encourage the men as strenuously as we can, and officers too, of course, to take advantage of religious retreats. They can make a difference, a real difference in a man's life."

"I am preparing a memo on the subject," Spelling broke in at once, "and a short lesson or pep talk, whichever you care to call it, will be read at formations by all the platoon leaders."

"Good man!" Hastings exclaimed. "Good man. If we start encouraging the men now, it'll make a dent when the next retreat comes around. It isn't so much the question of making it known to them"— Hastings was warming to the subject and the speed of his delivery was waxing—"They know the Army gives them the opportunity. What we have to do is convince them that they ought to make religious retreats part of their lives. No more, no less! Ultimately it's up to me, of course, as chaplain, and from now on I'll make it a point to bring up the matter of retreats before the Sunday services. It's up to me, but Ron's idea is very helpful."

"We'll do what it takes, Padre," Spelling announced obligingly.

Trainer nodded perfunctorily and was on the point of walking away when Captain Hastings spoke again.

"You remember I'll be away for a week after the retreat. Council of Churches meeting in Geneva this year . . . and we are very privileged to have Rufus Huddleston as our honored guest . . ."

Trainer looked at Hastings with a blank expression on his face. "The Right Reverend Rufus Huddleston, the Episcopal Bishop of Boston . . . he can only stay for a day and then he's flying to England to link up with his brethren-in-Christ at Canterbury."

"Oh!"

"He graciously and very promptly accepted our invitation . . ."

"I'm sure he'll add luster to the proceedings," Spelling commented officiously, casting an inquiring glance at Hastings and then at Trainer. "He must be one of the big guns."

Hastings raised his shoulders and moved his head to and fro, giving the impression of being noncommittal on the subject of big guns. "I've known him for many years and he was my teacher at Harvard, but I wonder if he'll remember me."

"It would be very odd if he didn't," Spelling countered helpfully, ". . . in view of your past association, that is. I'd be surprised."

Hastings laughed, the clear tinkling sound reverberating through the corridor.

"Let me tell you this, Ron, when a guy gets to be a bishop he often suffers from a partial loss of memory. Happens all the time."

"That means he ain't no different from any other bigwig," Trainer joined in, slapping Hastings on the back. "Is he now?"

"I guess not."

"You take good care of yourself and sail safely back to port, Bob. We don't want to lose you." He began to walk away when Hastings called after him, "After the meeting we'll take a few days off around Geneva. Courtney and the kids will join me. I'd like to give them a taste of the Swiss Alps. Courtney was on the phone to Beryl this morning asking if there is anything she might want brought back from Switzerland. And . . . I nearly forgot," his voice rose in volume as Trainer was farther and farther away, "Terence Robson at the 554th will cover for me in emergency. Fully reliable. Take care."

Trainer raised his arm and waved without looking back. He opened his office door and, surging out of nowhere, a sharp-eyed PFC stood before him, his thick wavy dark hair visible under the cap, still regulations but only just, wearing King Farouk sunglasses and holding a black shining case in his left hand. He saluted with a flourish. "Sir, Private First Class Charles Miller reporting as ordered."

"Ah . . . okay . . ." Trainer, his eyes narrowing, crossed the threshold and turned on his heel to face the visitor. "Come in, Miller, and close the door."

When Major Trainer had left the company of Captains Spelling and Hastings, Donkers drew nearer to them without interrupting the flow of conversation. But when the two men paused, their present topic apparently exhausted, he turned to the chaplain and asked: "You wanted to speak to me, sir?"

"Yes, yes I did." Hastings picked up the thread immediately at his usual high speed. "I'm glad you're here, Dirk." He glanced searchingly at Donkers and shifted his head, the sandy lock of hair dangling as capriciously as ever, while Spelling stood a few feet away giving every indication that he too wanted to be included in the conversation. Hastings apparently did not mind.

"Before I go anywhere else, I just want you to know how highly Pastor Günthers thinks of you. Every time I see him he can't sing enough praises of 'our American friend.' That's what he calls you. You've been doing some volunteer work in his church, and he is deeply, deeply grateful. You're just about the only GI who gets invited to German homes, you have German friends, you're trusted and liked. Dirk, you're our ambassador to the German community. I wish there were more like you. I thought I would let you know."

"Thank you very much, sir."

While Hastings was talking, Spelling was all ears, and he stepped a little closer to the two men. His lean face was tense, the deeply set eyes fixed on Donkers with prosecutorial zeal, the thin lips pressed together.

"Good job, Private," he said in a voice devoid of even a trace of emotion.

"Thank you, sir."

"Let me shift gears," Hastings went on. "My present assistant is not all I'd expect of one in his slot even in these deplorable years. Nothing drastically wrong, to be sure, but undependable at times, and curiously unenthusiastic about what takes place and, even more importantly, what could take place in the chaplain's office. Might just as well be tinkering in the Motor Pool or scrubbing floors. No dedication, no zeal, and in our holy office dedication and zeal are only outshone by God's grace." Hastings paused as if to organize his thoughts and Spelling, who was listening with exemplary attention and nodding silently at uneven intervals, lit a cigarette.

"Should you know of someone who'd like to apply for the job," Hastings was speaking much more slowly now, looking Donkers straight in the face. "As Group Clerk you come into contact with many of the men . . . any ideas, Dirk?" Hastings lay a hand on Donkers' shoulder, and his face was all expectation. There was a long moment of silence.

"I am sorry, Captain Hastings, but I can't think of anyone, not offhand."

"But, you'll think about it," he gave out a quick, nervous laugh.

"Certainly, sir."

"This is an important matter, Donkers," Spelling joined in, "and we want you to be of help. If the chaplain is away and you have something to report, you'll report to me. In any event, I expect the chaplain to be kept informed," he added with an even greater sense of authority. "Is this understood?"

"Yes, sir."

"Since we are on the subject," Hastings began resuming his rapid delivery punctuated now and then by a quick and muted cough, "since we are on the subject, I'd like to tell you both about what Günthers said to me the other day, in fact several times not so long ago."

Spelling stood erect, respectful, and expectant as before, living proof of treasuring the occasion; and Donkers moved to the back to be on the sidelines. "Günthers is very upset because there's so little . . . interaction . . . between us and the Germans. He said it's tragic that allowing for very rare exceptions the men have contact with the lowest elements of German society only—the *Gasthaus* clientele of doubtful repute and prostitutes. It's as if the Americans took a goodly sum of dollars and tossed it into the gutter every month. He's very upset about it. He talked about the outreach . . . ways of making friends, exchanges, visits and so on. And he's dead serious about it. As for me, I concur on religious, moral, and military grounds. Our men shouldn't be looking at the world outside the barracks as the out-there for boozing and whoring."

"As a matter of fact last year there was a circular from Army about this very issue, but the then Group Commander threw it into the wastepaper basket. I may still have a copy," and Spelling began to go furiously through the drawers of his desk. "I should have a copy, Padre, if you give me a moment."

Hastings nodded and smiled wanly as Captain Spelling's head and shoulders bobbed up, disappeared, and bobbed up again from behind the desk while the search continued. He turned to Donkers. "Again, congratulations on your excellent work with the German community . . . you know the language, Dirk, and that really helps." Donkers was on the point of thanking the chaplain for his kind words when the latter exclaimed, waving a hand in the air, "I enjoyed our talk about Nicodemus the other day. We have to talk again. We have to," he persisted. "We have to."

"Of course, sir," Donkers answered noncommittally, "whenever you have the time." Spelling's search for the circular was not crowned with success even though he now had most of the drawers stacked one on top of the other, three or four high, and he was going through the loose papers on the extreme end of the desk, which he had pulled out from the two filing cabinets. He was perspiring and his cheeks were red.

Hastings cleared his throat and said gently, "Thank you, Ron, I'm sure the circular will turn up one day, and besides I know what's in it. I greatly appreciate your efforts."

"You're welcome, Padre," Spelling answered with satisfaction. Still he persisted, "It's got to be here, got to!" And he went rummaging with passion among the papers and folders, rearranging them, and making new piles.

Hastings smiled again, the wan smile of understanding and resignation. "When the time comes," he said very quietly. Then a new resolution lit up his face. "Religious retreats have to be on the front burner, new life has to be instilled. And our men and the German population must get closer together, we must build bridges." He spoke these words emphatically, more to himself than to the others.

Donkers looked at his watch and started to walk away from the two captains who were engrossed in their own pursuits, but all of a sudden the chaplain stirred nervously, casting brisk glances here and there, swirling on his heel, and craning his neck to get a better view of the pell-mell in the Exec's office.

"Folder, my folder," he muttered through clenched teeth. "Did . . . did you see a folder, manila folder, did I have a folder with me?"

"No, Padre, not so far as I could see." Spelling was showing deep concern.

"I didn't see a folder either, sir," Donkers responded as Hastings' searching eyes converged upon him.

"It's my retreat folder, it's got the information . . . maybe I left it in the car, maybe in the Mess Hall, where the deuce is it?" he complained helplessly.

Donkers put all the latent energy into his legs and did not look back. In his flight he could hear the receding voices of the two men, one droning on about his predicament, the other about his willingness to help. He grasped the doorknob, swung the door wide open, and burst into the Group Sergeant's office where his own modest desk stood in a nook in the far right corner, light years away from the sergeant's imposing desk by the door. He grinned, slammed the door shut, and all was silence.

Chapter 4

In the evening Donkers sat down in his living quarters at a small portable typewriter. The wind was howling outside, but the room was cozy and no human sounds reached him. His roommate, a PFC attached to the Infirmary, would not be back until midnight and the third bunk, screwed on top of his own, was unoccupied despite Sergeant Honigklausen's periodic warnings that lack of space and uninterrupted arrival of new recruits would make it imperative for a third man be moved to 17L soon, very soon perhaps. Donkers glanced at his watch; it was barely 8:00 P.M., and he had at least two hours before the rowdy crowd would be checking in on their way from the Enlisted Men's Club and the surrounding *gasthauses*. There would be hollering, then a brawl or two, raucous laughter everywhere, and now and then the shrill and repeated sounds of the MPs' whistles. But, now he was undisturbed. He rolled a sheet of paper into the typewriter and began to type:

Dear Jonathan,

Yours of the 24th received, and it's good to know that your presentation before the Society of Music and Dance has gone off so well. Alessandro Scarlatti! There was a time, only a few years ago, when I sim-

ply couldn't have enough of the Scarlattis, father and son. I remember being consumed by Alessandro's operas Scipione nelle Spagne, Gli Equivoci nel sembiante, and the divine Il Tigrane and never wanting to listen to anything else. We were purists then, you and I, and your words that anything after Mozart is not worth listening to are still engraved in my memory. Those were happy days because we worshipped what we believed in our souls to be perfection, the latter part of the seventeenth and the eighteenth centuries marking for us the final limit to which human spirit could rise. Everything else was vastly inferior and we were communing with the highest, the unparalleled. What a wonderful state to be in! But, in the last few months I found new gods. I broached it in my last letter, and I can't but think it brought a frown of surprise to your brow. In short, I discovered Wagner. Isn't he extraordinary, and I started off with Tristan und Isolde! More about it later.

It's a little more than three months before your arrival in mid-June. You expressed some concern about coming to London rather than landing somewhere on the Continent, but once we've done London (a misstatement if ever there was one because one can never "do" London, there is simply too much to see there) we can go off to Italy, and later to Switzerland. Besides, there is always the matter of the airfare during the summer—London being the most economical. I wish those three months could be contracted into three hours.

I was looking the other day at Genesis 1:31: "And God saw everything that he had made, and, behold, it was very good." If the creation is very good, are we, you and I, very good too, being part of this creation? We love nature as God has spread it before us, but we are also responsive to our own natures as God has made them. We were granted a glimpse of the majesty of the Lord, and the word of the Lord is clear.

Are we to be damned, Jonathan? Are we to be damned because God gave us the capacity to love and experience rapture no other men experience? Are we the damned because we have loved beyond the scope of other men? Are we the damned?

This is the French week at the 16th, and their engineer outfit showed us a toy that travels on water, under water, and on land. I don't know if it flies in the air or burrows in the ground like a mole, but that remains to be seen. Aren't you lucky, having been classified 4F because of your abominable eyesight, to be missing perforce military high jinks?

Stay well,
Dirk

Chapter 5

At a long regulation table of the kind found in army installations, prisons, and some community centers, covered for the occasion with a spotless white cloth, sat Group Sergeant Lester Honigklausen savoring his daily morning coffee break in the company of his longtime friend and confidant Sergeant Larry Sampler, Master Sergeant in charge of the Mess Hall at 16th U. S. Army Engineer Group. Honigklausen usually arrived between 10:15 and 10:45 A.M., and his coffee break could be extensive. Most of the time he and Sampler were the only two sergeants sitting at this table, which conforming to the unspecified orders of the day was reserved for NCOs in general, but to which only Honigklausen and Sampler had access, the other NCOs of less exalted rank taking their places at a similar table, which was rarely if ever covered by a table-cloth, some distance away.

This morning, however, two Mess Hall corporals were allowed to join them, Tannenbaum and O'Leary, who were already noisily taking their seats on the bench alongside Sampler and opposite Honigklausen. Facing the Group Sergeant and clearly visible over the Mess Hall sergeant's shoulders was a short passage leading to the kitchens, on his right the wide expanse of the Mess Hall proper crowded with multiple regulation tables and benches for enlisted men, and on his left some twenty yards away a swinging door behind which stood another door, gate, and portal to the Officers' Mess. The various buildings of the caserne erected in the late 1920s housed in succession units of Freikorps and S.A., regiments of the Vermacht and the S.S. and one time, at the beginning of World War II, a school for Luftwaffe pilots and airplane mechanics. Taken over by the U.S. Army in 1945, the Kirchenberg Kaserne was thoroughly remodeled, refurbished, and enlarged, its rickety plumbing system ripped out and an ultramodern one installed.

The new governors could do little to change the architectural character of the buildings which reflected the Wilhelmian taste of the early twentieth century with their massive outside walls, turrets over the roofs, high ceilings, arches, vaultings in the halls, and the bulky masonry sloping from the lowest level windows to the ground below like the last line of a formidable defense against the foe who may have forced his way past the outposts but was now up against the fortress itself. What the new governors did was to transform the interior of the buildings: electric lines were overhauled or replaced and new ones added, myriads of new electrical fixtures wired and drilled in the walls, new tile floors laid, staircases widened, the large meeting halls divided into smaller living quarters or small and middle-size offices, with new thinner walls now separating them. Hundreds of square yards of woodwork were fastened to the inner walls and some windows broadened. On the outside the buildings of the Headquarters of the 16th U. S. Army Engineer Group still looked grim and medieval, but the interiors were filled with the marvels of the new technology, flaunting the American power and wealth. What caught the eye were long stretches of lights illuminating the facades and house lights everywhere suffusing all objects; everything was flooded with light. German old-timers who happened to be near would shake their heads and mutter angrily, "Not as in the old days!"

Of the six buildings enclosing the parade ground on three sides, three housed the men's quarters, one was the Command Building, the other the Mess, and the last a vast storage area full of equipment and supplies but allowing ample room for camp beds and sleeping bags. This was the building surrounded by barbwire which impelled the French colonel to damn American hospitality. Immediately to the left of the main entrance stood a newly built MP station, painted white and often repainted, accommodating several offices, and next to it a nondescript detention center. Two other buildings erected by the U.S. Army in the late 1940s completed the base: Motor Pool, a large sprawling light-and-brown structure rooted behind the Command Building, and far away on the other side of the parade ground a small wooden colonial church, strangely incongruous in these domineering surroundings, like a willowy New England maiden accosted by a squad of overbearing Teutonic knights. It is here that Chaplain Hastings conducted his non-denominational services.

"Nowadays," Sergeant Honigklausen was saying, taking another dainty sip of coffee and helping himself to another chocolate doughnut, "when a kid goes to college he loses all respect. And it don't matter what college, understand." He looked pointedly at those present. "It don't matter one iota because all them colleges preach the same gospel." He tapped the table with his forefinger. "And respect goes out the window. Just like that."

"Respect for whom, Sarge?" Tannenbaum asked skeptically.

"Respect for his parents, his elders, his betters." Honigklausen was raising the coffee mug to his lips, let it be suspended in midair and announced sententiously, "This country was founded on respect and it be . . . behooves us to bear it in mind."

"Gee, Sarge," O'Leary sounded off, "I thought this country was founded on a revolution. We showed so little respect for Georgie-Boy and his redcoats that we kicked their asses right across the pond to merry old England."

Honigklausen smiled bleakly, tilting his head to the right and left, weighing in his mind what he should say next.

"O'Leary, you should see things in . . . in context . . . you're kind of confused . . . gotta think things through and . . . aim at the better understanding of . . . of what stares you in the face. Respect is fundamental to our way of life."

"Respect? Don't talk to me about respect, Sarge," O'Leary chattered on with a shrug. "Why . . ."

"Lester's got a point," Sampler intervened. "Had a letter from my brother yesterday, he's on the police force stateside." He leaned forward and then to the left, renewing eye contact with his friend and the two corporals. "And he sure paints a grim picture of what's going on in our town. Crime is up, petty stuff, but also them burglaries and violence and worst of all, teenage crime." Sampler went on describing the situation, quoting figures, deploring the downside, naming neighbors who were as horrified as he was, naming public officials who did nothing to help except scratch their asses, contrasting the present with the past of five or six years before. "What you might call public morality . . . ain't there no more. Everyone's trying to make a buck fast, fast, fast and they don't care how they go about it." The two corporals looked bored, but Honigklausen kept nodding and raised his hand several times making jerky little upward movements with his fingers, egging his friend on.

"Respect is fast disappearing, God help us!" he said. There was a brief pause.

"On the subject of respect, Sarge," all of a sudden boredom vanished from O'Leary's face, "let me tell you this: my old man was drunk more often than he was sober, and my mother had to practically fight him to get money to feed the family. Respect, you say! Respect for that creep! Forgive me, Sarge, but no respect is forthcoming from me." Sampler's eyes were now fixed on Tannenbaum and he pointed to the coffee jug. Tannenbaum made a hardly perceptible nod and stood up to refill it. Then he turned to Honigklausen and spoke in a placid manner. "My old man and his woman—she's his second wife, mother died when I was born—cheated the owners of that dry cleaning and alterations outfit they managed, they cheated the customers, and they probably cheated each other, I wouldn't put that past them. On top of it they cheated on their income tax, I know it for a fact, and on just about anything else they put their grubby hands on. No offense meant, Sergeant Honigklausen, but we need less respect in this world, not more."

"Now, now," Sampler lifted both hands in a conciliatory gesture, "no need to get all heated up. After all, we ain't going to the mat. More coffee, Lester?"

"I'd like more coffee." They waited till Tannenbaum returned with the full jug, and Sampler refilled the four mugs.

"I heard you," Honigklausen began, "and I am fully aware of the sig-significance of what you boys put before me. Yes, I can truly say . . . like . . . I understand, I mean, I understand what you meant." Tannenbaum and O'Leary exchanged knowing glances. "But the fact remains we need more respect on all levels, not only in the family nest like . . . but on all levels," he repeated with emphasis.

"Lester's got a point," Sampler joined in expectantly. Honigklausen's head was now bent forward, his hand cupping the remains of the doughnut, a saccharine all-forgiving smile distorting his face, his lips curved and thrust forward and shaped like a piglet's snout.

"On the subject of respect," he began with his smile growing even more saccharine and all-forgiving, "on the subject of respect," he repeated, "it cuts me to the quick to hear President Eisenhower savagely attacked in the newspapers and on the radio. It ain't decent, it shouldn't be allowed."

O'Leary shrugged his shoulders. "Once Ike threw his hat into the ring he joined the ranks of all them two-bit politicians. If it's too hot for him in the kitchen, hell, he ought to get out."

Honigklausen shook his head. "It isn't seemly. He's the President and Commander-in-Chief. Those savage attacks are . . . are shameful. This is what I meant when I said our ins-ti-tutions are being destroyed."

"Eisenhower was a better general than he is President," Tannenbaum said yawning. "He should've stayed in the Army instead of getting kicked upstairs."

But Honigklausen persisted. "Those savage attacks are bad, real bad. Mark my word, they'll destroy us as a nation . . . and all 'em sick jokes about the President, that he's thinking only about golf, and when he's silent . . . dreaming about hole in one."

As if pricked simultaneously by a prodder Tannenbaum and O'Leary burst into uncontrollable laughter. "The papers and the radio may have something, Sergeant Honigklausen," Tannenbaum exclaimed, his convulsion of laughter half spent.

"Oh, it's more than that, Ernie, it's as sure as the eagle shits on the last day of the month. Maybe golf is the only thing under the blue sky that gives Ike a hard-on."

Sergeant Honigklausen's face now reflected disgust, and it grew redder far beyond its usual hue.

"So all college boys are bad," O'Leary went on, "and mind you, Ernie and me, we ain't college boys, so what's the remedy?"

"I don't know," Honigklausen replied, his voice ringing with sincerity.

Tannenbaum drew closer to the two sergeants. "Isn't that Group Clerk fellow, Donkers, isn't he a college boy?"

Honigklausen nodded. "What if he is?"

"Well, that kinda throws a monkey wrench into your argument."

The sergeant drew himself up, and he was now sitting on the bench stiff and erect. "Donkers' a good kid and works hard, can't help being saucy now and then . . . but he's okay."

"Still, being a college boy, how does he get his respect for people and institutions? What's the catch?" Tannenbaum was pressing the point.

Honigklausen snorted. "I tell you, Tannenbaum, Donkers is okay. Why his dad's a man of the cloth back in Minnesota."

There was a moment of silence, during which Honigklausen betrayed a sudden uneasiness, shifting in his seat repeatedly, tapping the table with his fingers, lifting the coffee mug to his mouth, and then lowering it down without taking a sip as if he were following some secret ritual.

"Lester's got a point," Sergeant Sampler said loudly, his voice vibrating with authority.

"Oh sure, I see it all, Sarge," O'Leary's voice was strident now, "all college boys are bad because they lack respect, but if a kid has a daddy sporting a dog collar then everything is hunky-dory, all sins forgiven—past, present, and future."

Honigklausen went on repeating, "I didn't mean it that way," but what he said was drowned in O'Leary's ongoing monologue which grew not only in volume, but also in the richness of expression, his vocabulary becoming more and more colorful, the images sharper, the punch lines wittier and more telling. Still, though the speaker obviously exhibited genuine passion there was little if any hostility in what he said towards Honigklausen or anybody else. Coming to the end of the peroration he added in a softer tone, "There was no offense meant, Sergeant Honigklausen."

"And none was taken, Corporal O'Leary," the sergeant uttered with a sigh of relief.

"Furthermore," O'Leary went on very gently now, "in no way was this meant to be a censure of Donkers; I know Dirk and he's a friend. So does Ernie."

An uncomfortable silence fell as the four men took another gulp of coffee, picked up the remains of the doughnuts, and cleared their throats.

"Well, it's been a lively coffee break." Sergeant Sampler blew his nose and cast a knowing glance in the direction of O'Leary and

Tannenbaum. "It's probably time for the two of you to go supervise those good-for-nothin' KPs."

"Right, Sarge," Tannenbaum said, standing up and beckoning to O'Leary. "Let's go, Jimmie, and thank you for having us at your table."

"We're most grateful for this gracious invitation to this here holy of holies," O'Leary intoned, "the truth of the matter being that we enjoyed it, and we thank you very much."

As the two corporals walked away, Honigklausen asked, "How they doin'?"

"Okay. They do their job, but have to be watched. The RAs we get these days ain't substandard, but they ain't outstanding either."

"I thank the Lord O'Leary is not working for me. Could be dangerous for both of us."

"Should we lose the next war, Lester, I'd recommend that O'Leary be sent to sue for peace. The enemy would either kill him out of sheer desperation 'cause they couldn't stand listening to him for another minute or else they'd accept our terms. As for Tannenbaum, he's taking correspondence courses, trying to improve himself. Told me Donkers helped him one hell of a lot, advising to whom to write, what courses to take, and all that jazz."

"Hmm. Improving himself, by way of OCS maybe?"

"Maybe," Sampler answered noncommittally.

Now the sun blazed down through the oversize windows of the Mess Hall, glaring from the shining pots and pans, resting on long wooden stands in the back, and stirring up flashes of irritating brightness for those standing in chow lines. More boots were stamping the spic-and-span tiles of the floor, there was more commotion in the kitchen, more voices were heard. Sergeant Sampler got up from the bench and stretched out his arms. He was of middle height, hollow-chested with unusually long arms and very big hands. He took a few steps towards the kitchen, exchanged words with several noncoms, and came back to where he had left Honigklausen.

"There's something I want to ask you, Lester."

"Shoot, Larry."

"There's a scuttlebutt going around . . . 'bout inspections . . . that from now on inspections will be unscheduled, a closely guarded secret, you might say. In the past we always more or less knew when the inspecting teams would drive up, though we were not supposed to know. But now . . ." he left the rest unfinished.

"I heard it too and from different places."

"Whose bright idea was this—Ryan's, Vickers'?"

"It's hard to say."

"Don't shit me, Lester, we go back too long."

"Well, there's been different directives . . . from Vickers' Office, they kinda want to tighten the reins, more discipline, higher efficiency, NCO Academy . . . all that stuff."

"Is this to impress the Krauts or for the folks back home?"

Honigklausen appeared conspiratorial and dead serious. "To the best of my knowledge Vickers is in charge . . . but it's Ryan's baby or may be even higher; they . . . they want to make us a better fighting force."

"Fighting force against whom?" Sampler muttered contemptuously. "We're fighting our wives, our schatzies, our superior officers. That's the size of it. I doubt we'll ever fight the commies 'cause they are scared of us, scared shitless. Who the hell wants to take on Uncle Sam?"

Honigklausen was listening attentively, but not saying a word.

"Vickers! I remember him, Lester, I remember the bastard. First I saw him was in North Africa, Operation Torch, November '42. He came to us after the landings when things were quiet like, that's what he usually does, he was a colonel then and strictly in the paper shuffling business; anyway he came twice to inspect the Mess Hall, me being a young sergeant assisting old 'Scarecrow' Johnson, Master Cook, you remember him? They used to say Johnson's Mess Hall always had left-over chow 'cause when the men came to eat and took one look at 'Scarecrow' they lost their appetite. Anyway old Vickers came inspecting, and nothing was good enough for him; he was rattling off to his aide about areas in need of improvement, gigs, penalties, the whole goddamn list which that jackass gave to Johnson. I'll never forget that Reb voice mouthing away: 'In this cliimate which may be neeew to maaany of youuuu refrigeeration is of speeecial impooortance', and so on, and then a 'brand new gimmick, some Mess Halls haave alreeady staarted using indigeenous labor, but I would remind eveerybody that sooo far the Army has not authorized it.' Anyway, he found fault everywhere and got Johnson real pissed off. Miles kept hissing out 'Yessir, yessir' whenever Vickers came to a pause, and at one point I thought he was going to smack him! Good thing he didn't! I've had my belly full of Vickers, what a clown!"

"Yeah, I remember Miles Johnson. He was a thirty-year man," Honigklausen said softly, a touch of sentiment breaking through. "He was with MacArthur in France in 1917, and again with MacArthur in the Philippines in the thirties. A thirty-year man," he repeated musingly.

"He got it at the end of '44 in what the geniuses in the reporting business called the Battle of the Bulge," Sampler said. "Been transferred to the Third Army, some time before and ended his life serving under the old Blood and Guts Georgie Patton."

"A thirty-year man," Honigklausen whispered to himself.

"What, what did you say?"

"Nothing."

"By the way, what the hell was Trainer doing a couple of days ago dressed up like a recruiting poster? Saw him with my own eyes 0715 hours outside the Command Building, pressed trousers, all the medals tingling in the wind, and carrying a briefcase, a briefcase of all things under his arm, climbing into a staff car. This must have been some jaunt, his driver being Kelly from the Motor Pool, you know he's another recruiting poster, the guy who used to work in that fancy department store in Frisco and knows all about the latest men's fashions and so on. He charges what he calls 'con-sul-tation fees' and he and O'Leary nearly came to blows, O'Leary claiming and swearing on a stack of Bibles that Kelly's no more than a damn cheat. Anyway . . ."

"The Major had to go to Army with reference to them French engineers, official business, and we don't know yet how it turned out," Honigklausen announced. "It's a touchy matter."

"Sure, anything that has to do with the Frenchies is a touchy matter. They may be a strange bunch, but I'll tell you this, Lester, I pity the poor bastards 'cause of their pisspoor pay, chow that ain't fit for animals, living conditions that would make niggers in Dixie rise up in arms, no damned good clothing, equipment, or anything else."

"That's the truth."

Sampler looked warily around.

"There's been some talk we're getting a new Exec. Anything to it?"

"I heard it too, and Spelling may be out on his ass."

Sampler concurred, showing no visible affection for Captain

Spelling. He next articulated some thoughts of his own which brought out vividly Spelling's martinet-like mentality and his general unpopularity among officers and men.

"I hear Trainer can't stand the sight of the little Kraut either," he chuckled, "and if the little Kraut who's only acting Exec anyway is out on his ass, the new Exec will be a major which is what the post calls for."

"And this . . . this means Trainer will be promoted to Lt. Colonel, which is also what is called for." Honigklausen smacked his lips, his eyes flashing with satisfaction. "We can't lose on that."

"Trainer is sure getting to the top of the heap on the double," Sampler commented. He paused, tilted his head, emitting peals of laughter. "If that North Korean attack hadn't happened near that hick place, Osau, or whatever it was, he'd be taking orders from us today. You know damn well there are different versions of what happened."

"The official account is the true one," Honigklausen countered with conviction, "and I know he was recommended for the Congressional Medal, but army politics being what they are he didn't get it. And remember, Larry, after the battlefield commission he got quick promotions for outstanding valor and initiative under fire. He earned it!"

"Yeah, yeah, yeah," Sampler yawned and pulled a face. "I got nothin' against Trainer, he's always treated me right. But one wonders."

As the noise in the Mess Hall grew louder and louder and ever growing swarms of men poured in through the two swinging doors, Honigklausen examined his wristwatch and embarked on the slow process of standing up from the table, heaving his legs over the bench one at a time, and finally standing clear of it, safe and firm.

"Major Trainer is the Acting Group Commander," he spoke brusquely with full consciousness of his rank, "and he merits our respect. And remember, Larry, this country was founded on respect. Without respect we don't amount to nothin', nothin.'" Sampler nodded several times and began to yawn, the successive yawns getting to be longer and longer, an apathetic expression painted all over his face. Suddenly, there was a glint in his eye. He half rose and called to Honigklausen, "You won't forget about that inspection business, me and my men sure don't want to be caught with our pants down."

Honigklausen raised his hand in acknowledgment and moved slowly away.

Chapter 6

Three and half miles northwest of 16th Engineer Group Barracks lay Omar N. Bradley American Village. Constructed in the early 1950s, it stood on a flat stretch of fertile land, which formerly had seen little vegetation and had been sparsely coated by yellow grass, thistles, and dandelions. Then the site became a U.S. project. The diggers had gone to work scooping up the dry layers of subsoil, gigantic sieves separated stones and pebbles from sand, chemicals and enormous amounts of fertilizer were dumped on three acres of wasteland, and countless seeds were planted. The result was close to a miracle. Within six months luxuriant vegetation, flowers of every description, thick blue grass, shrubs, bushes, and trees were germinating and then shooting forth in multicolored abundance. The event was written up in the local German papers, *The Stars and Stripes,* and American dignitaries on inspection tours of the U.S. Forces in Germany, as well as agricultural experts from several countries, were duly conducted through the fecund acres and given numerous brochures, illustrations, and statistical tables.

The project, which had been carried out by several American governmental agencies under the humanitarian auspices of "Feeding the Germans" and "Saving Europe," had been pronounced a sensation and an unqualified success. But in the spring of 1949 it abruptly came to a halt. In official circles this was referred to as the beginning of Phase II of the Kirchenberg operation. The planners of American villages in West Germany, housing officers, some NCOs, and their families, were given wide discretionary powers and the earlier humanitarian concerns were quickly forgotten. Without delay the planners set to work, and their first order of business was to convert the fecund acres into an area on which buildings could be erected and streets laid. Accordingly, mammoth tractors and bulldozers were employed, clearing the land and flattening it further, high-velocity cutting machines razed to the ground the rich panoply of smiling flora, and new chemicals were implanted in the soil to stump incubation and growth of any kind. When the last brick was laid and the last shutter painted in the fall of 1953, Omar N. Bradley American Village had a pastiche look of what realtors' booklets advertised as American suburbia, pure and simple, undifferentiated and unregionalized, the happy abode for those Americans whose closest ties were to the federal government, and whose rights and privileges were jealously guarded by the American Eagle writ large.

Still, this was "Little America" and this was home. The houses were all one story high, for one family only, or duplexes and triplexes, and others further subdivided into apartments for unmarried personnel—all in accordance with the military rank of the occupants. The wide streets bore the familiar names "Grand", "Pine", and "Spruce," and similar ones variegated by a few named after famous Americans whose mention would not spark off even a ripple of controversy. Those who lived at the Village and traveled to 16th Engineer Group as part of their daily duties, and to the American PXs in Heidelberg or Mannheim, to the American libraries at 7th Army Headquarters outside Stuttgart, or to American schools for dependents within easy drive from Kirchenberg, were twenty-four hours each day enclosed within the wall-less American compound protected by American might and immune to the winds of economic and political change. It was a well-regulated existence that befitted the victors, lately become partners in an American-European Union, who insisted on preserving their own way of life. Despite the concerted efforts of town planners and building contractors, the soil within the confines of Omar N. Bradley Village continued to be wildly fertile in places and some of the wives spoke about it with approval. The time for planting Victory Gardens had long passed of course, and in any event such a venture would be blatantly inappropriate; but flower beds were laid, again and again, in many parts of the Village. Some of these flowers—it was bruited—surpassed in size and loveliness those sold at marketplaces of German cities.

In a living room no different from many others in the Village, furnished in a manner strikingly similar to that in which living rooms in the Village were furnished, Captain Ronald Spelling, blue jeans and a sports shirt prominently displayed, was uncorking a bottle of scotch and filling two glasses.

"Helluva week, Ted, helluva week," he cried out in his high-pitched voice, handing Lieutenant Theodore Hurstwood, who was also wearing blue jeans and a sports shirt, a glass. "Helluva week," he went on.

"Cheers!"

"Cheers, Ron!"

"Still, there were some bright spots on the horizon, some bright spots you might say; told no one about it . . . because I kinda didn't feel like spouting. But I want to tell you."

"Greatly honored and all that . . ."

"Well, I met somebody . . ."

"Aha," and the two men gulped down the whiskey.

"I met somebody," Spelling continued bending and unbending, faithfully following the regimen of calisthenics and brushing intensively the back of his head, "and I am still under the spell."

"I take it the person you met is neither a man nor a hermaphrodite."

"She is something . . . she is something," Spelling burst out rapidly and nervously, refilling the glasses. "Never met anyone like her."

"Congratulations, I hope everything will go just right for the two of you."

Spelling slumped into an armchair, his face contracted, his eyes fixed on nothing in particular, then he jumped up and crisscrossed the room several times. Finally he stood over Hurstwood, glass in hand, his mouth wide open, saying nothing. Hurstwood was silent too, the folds of his cheeks growing a little deeper, a slight frown of concern marring the well-shaped face.

"You're not in any kind of trouble are you?" he asked in a level voice.

"No, no, no," Spelling exclaimed, more relaxed and communicative. "Sorry if I raised the alarm, everything is fine, but it's a thunderstroke."

Hurstwood's face lightened. "Well, I can only say you're a master of suspense." He laughed. "You should be on the boards cutting a sinister figure in one of our Western melodramas. They need histrionically minded guys like you."

"Listen to me, Ted." Spelling pulled up a chair and was now sitting astride it, his hands clutching its back, and very close to Hurstwood. "Her name is Claire, and she is the widow of a congressman from Ohio. He dropped dead all of a sudden on the campaign trail, I think . . . several months back. She is here, I mean here in Germany, I mean at the 7th Army Headquarters, or rather . . . staying with her sister who's married to a G2 Colonel at Army . . . I mean staying with them."

"Sounds fine!"

"Right! She's the most unusual woman I ever met, and her personality can only be described as . . . as scintillating . . . scintillating."

Hurstwood made a thumbs-up sign.

"But here comes the rub, she told me where she and her husband stayed when they traveled, where they ate, and this sort of thing. No way can I keep up with her on captain's pay, no way, d'you understand?"

"Maybe you and she can go dutch."

"Nooo . . . nooo . . . she's not a dame who goes dutch with anybody . . . not her."

"Perhaps she can foot the bills, this would simplify the situation," Hurstwood laughed.

"Make light of it, Ted, make light of it," Spelling exclaimed, striding towards the doorway and standing in it, tense and anxious. "Your parents are well-heeled, aren't they, you've got money to burn, money is no object, rich boy, right?"

"Hardly, I wouldn't put it that way."

"My dad's just a civil servant, and there's no money in the family."

Spelling picked up the bottle and again refilled the glasses.

"I think you ought to be candid with her, say that unfortunately your ancestors didn't leave you the downtown of teeming American cities as family heirlooms, she ought to understand."

"And if she doesn't?"

"She's not worth having your arm around her."

"Yes, yes, yes," Spelling kept repeating, ". . . there's something in what you say. Yes, yes, yes . . ." he intoned, tilting his head this way and that.

"How did you meet her?"

"At the party General Ryan threw for Secretary Brucker at Army. You were invited too; all the Westpointers were." Spelling made a point of it.

"Yeah, I remember I was in Hanover that day. Called in as prosecution witness against that slob of a Brit lance corporal who raised Cain down here."

"You missed a swell party, and General Ryan showed good taste by not inviting Trainer. It was strictly officers and gentlemen, officers and gentlemen and their ladies," he repeated, chuckling derisively and looking pointedly at Hurstwood. "Anyway, to go back to Claire. I saw her at the party, and we talked for a long time and she asked me to call her, which I did and some days later she called me. She is away now, traveling with her sister, probably hitting all the hot spots in Western Europe. But she wants me to call her when she gets back, which will be before long. That's the story!"

"Sounds fine."

"I know I said it before, but I want . . . I want to say it again," Spelling began with a sudden spurt of energy. "Claire's personality is something extraordinary, I've never met anybody like her, it's like being high on champagne twenty-four hours a day." He made a belittling gesture. "I'm not good with images and all that literary stuff, but you get the picture. Her personality, her entire presence, her just being there is . . . is . . ."

"Scintillating," Hurstwood put in.

"That's right, Ted, you found the right word. Scintillating! What a dame! What a dame!"

"You have my best wishes," Hurstwood spoke with confidence, taking his turn at refilling the glasses.

"Mind you, once again I didn't broach it earlier, but she is a little older than me."

"It stands to reason she would be."

"But she is still very young!"

"Of course."

"When I called her, the colonel, her sister's hubby, answered and . . ."

"And?"

"He sounded very nice, very friendly."

"Why the hell shouldn't he be?"

Spelling lifted his glass and was rotating it gently, sipping the whiskey and then rotating the glass again. He then gulped what was left in it. "Anyway, this is the bright spot," he called from the doorway leading to the kitchen. "I'd better get the other bottle, the one you brought."

Hurstwood half rose, stretching out his arms and legs, taking a deep breath, and shaking his head vigorously as if to remain fully alert. "Happy Days," he let the words out resoundingly.

"Happy Days," Spelling echoed from the kitchen and returned with another bottle of scotch, setting it down next to the nearly empty one.

"Well, what's new in this men's army?" he asked.

"Nothing very much. I hope this business with the French will be handled better from now on than in the past. The French are our allies and they have a standing army; there should be better communication."

At this Spelling laughed frantically, hitting the palm of one hand with the extended fingers of the other and hoisting himself up to assume the posture of a public speaker, but his foot slipped on the floor and he was back in the armchair reclining, his arms spread out.

"How can Trainer and Honigklausen handle anything, right? Why and let me tell you that . . . more than Trainer and Honigklausen I meant Vickers' 7th Army and that cretin Simmons."

Hurstwood interrupted, "I'm sure there's enough blame to go round."

Spelling concurred, "But this doesn't excuse the Acting Group Commander." He mimicked with gusto Honigklausen's ingratiating tones and then called out Trainer's title once more with flamboyant mimicry, "And his super-toady Group Sergeant."

"If we don't handle it in an adroit manner now, there may be political repercussions."

"I suspect the harm's been done already and can't be undone," Spelling commented with a shrug, and he instantly and zealously launched into his favorite topic, beads of sweat dotting his forehead, his eyes glistening with anger. "The Soviets can attack any moment, any moment, mark my words, Ted, and how can we fight a modern war with assholes like Trainer and Honigklausen?"

Hurstwood was silent.

"Look at Honigklausen, he weighs four hundred pounds, and he can hardly move about. What happens in combat? Are they going to carry him on a stretcher or push him in a wheelchair from one skirmish to the next?"

"Honigklausen has a glandular condition and he's on medication; his weight isn't his fault."

"So be it! But why keep the asshole in the service? Medical discharge is what he should be getting and not tomorrow or the day after, mind you, but now, this very minute."

"He has his uses."

Spelling snorted and waved a hand. "Do you know that asshole speaks to Trainer, I mean he addresses Trainer in the third person." He laughed uncontrollably. "Would the Major like to do this, would the Major like to sign this, what would the Major's decision be in this matter? And Trainer eats it all up. Who the hell does he think Trainer is, Frederic the Great?"

"I can't think of a better military leader to emulate."

Spelling went on laughing and then shook his head sadly. "Okay, Honigklausen's a medical case, but Trainer is just a pig, a subhuman piece of trash. I mean look at his manners, the belching, the farting, the spitting, the foul language, the soiled uniform—so this is a U.S. Army officer, a major commanding an engineer group! It wouldn't be all that sad if only his personal conduct was far-out, but he doesn't have the smarts to command anything, least of all a military unit. That man is a moron. His idea of warfare is a barroom brawl."

"Well, he got a battlefield commission, and they're kind of hard to get and usually mean something."

"I'll tell you what I heard at Army, not from just one guy, but from several and at different times." Conspiratorially, Spelling shifted closer to Hurstwood, and he was now speaking in an undertone. "When that North Korean platoon moved against the abandoned huts where Sergeant Trainer and his men were laid up, they hit a jackpot. Trainer and his men were in the middle of a party—Korean broads, booze, that kind of thing. The men were half-naked, the broads too, and the North Koreans just burst in, but they were under orders to take prisoners, interrogate them to get information that was vital. Well, Sergeant Trainer and his gang took to their heels, ran downhill like hell, long johns or no long johns, and down below they ran into a North Korean patrol, just a handful of hungry and utterly exhausted gooks. They disarmed them, forced them to give false signals to their buddies on the hill, and when the platoon reinforced by another platoon came down expecting to see friendly faces in the clearing they started shooting, massacring most of them and taking the rest prisoner. It was a fluke. The whole thing was a fluke."

"I heard a different story, much different, Ron. And later at Seoul . . . and . . . again at Heartbreak Ridge and . . . Pork Chop Hill, Trainer distinguished himself, saving his men, fooling the enemy, reaching objectives which the brigade commander thought could never be reached and keeping casualties to a minimum. These are facts, fully documented." Hurstwood spoke slowly, lifting the nearly empty whiskey bottle and reaching for the glasses.

"It's all a matter of opinion," Spelling countered. "Trainer's buddies are sure covering for him, if he has any buddies, which I doubt. By the way, he was seen looking as if he'd taken a shower and gotten some clean rags a few days ago, apparently on his way to Army. And carrying a briefcase—briefcase means papers and Trainer can't read. What's he up to?"

Hurstwood emptied his glass and different sparkles lit up his face, hints of contradictory emotions. "Trainer is a good soldier, I'd say an excellent soldier. But he's far from being orthodox," he said firmly.

"That's a stretch. Not orthodox! My, my! At the Point his designation would be cleaning latrines for keeps!"

Hurstwood was helping himself to what was left of the whiskey in the first bottle. "Sure he's not invited to cocktail parties and the brass doesn't like the way he talks, smells, and dresses. But when something big happens, forest fires near Mannheim, the Nuremberg floods, avalanches that buried U.S. installations in the Alps, who do they send for? Trainer! Trainer! Do you remember the War Games in Bavaria last year? It was Trainer who had done the planning, insisting that these games should be absolutely different from the previous ones, that they must contain actual combat situations—live ammo, the largest possible obstacles, unexpected use of additional troops, sudden changes in deployment, bad weather, and so on—and not be a goddamn marching exercise with cozy picnics along the river. By the way, there's a rumor he may be promoted to Lieutenant Colonel."

Spelling made a gesture of unconcern. "Maybe some of it is true, I don't know, but I am a professional army officer, and my goal is highest possible efficiency. We are not efficient and we are not combat ready, there's too much dead wood high and low! And don't forget the Soviets may attack any moment, and when they do God help us!" He got up to his feet, strode across the living room, and switched on the two lamps on the mantelpiece. There was an uneasiness in his manner, and he took a few aimless steps, adjusted some papers and books on the side table, looked idly out of the window. At last he rejoined Hurstwood. "This country is in deep trouble, Ted, deep trouble. Our last hope of saving it may well be the military, the military in conjunction with the F.B.I., maybe the C.I.A., and whatever good men are left in this godless liberal age." He smiled wanly, not really expecting an answer from Hurstwood, but letting his words sink in and simply waiting. Hurstwood remained silent, but tiny creases broke out around his eyes and mouth and he was looking absent-mindedly at the ceiling.

"That's why the military is so important," Spelling picked up the thread, "the enemy without we see with our own eyes, we know what he is up to, but the enemy within is a hundred times more deadly because he is invisible, because he uses every dodge, every ruse to deceive, to subvert, and ultimately to destroy."

"Go on," Hurstwood said in a flat voice.

"The commies have already infiltrated the federal government, many a state government, countless seats of power. They're just waiting for the right moment to strike, which will be synchronized with a recession of some kind or an economic slowdown. It's only a matter of time."

"And?"

"We may have to fight the four columns outside the city and the fifth column inside it right along, and it may be the day of doom. We have to be prepared!"

"Who are the fifth column?'

"All kinds of public figures, politicians, educators, journalists, and so on who scream about civil rights, the First Amendment, the plight of the colored people, the sins of capitalism and the rest. Some are just overripe fellow travelers, the others paid agents of the Kremlin. I'll give you just two names: Adlai Stevenson and Dean Acheson." Hurstwood was on the point of saying something but Spelling broke in, "Both are in the latter category—paid agents of the Kremlin." He laughed sardonically and stood there in the middle of the living room, desperate and determined. "And as we speak, the Democrats are murdering, yes murdering, the one man who can save the Republic! Joe McCarthy!"

Hurstwood focused his eyes on the floor and was quite still.

"Ted, I wish you'd see things for what they are. We are under siege. You and I are buddies, and I want you to be in the right camp. Do you want the U.S. to survive as a free country?"

"Sure, I do."

"Then join us. Our organization has chapters in every state. We all took an oath, and we are ready to put our lives on the line. It isn't the Soviets we are most concerned about, it's the enemy within, our own commies who before long will stage a coup and try to take over the government. They'll be resisted of course. Blood will flow, there'll be fighting in the streets, but if we good honorable men stick together the Republic will be saved." Spelling came up to Hurstwood and slapped him on the back. "Think about it, Ted. Think hard. We'd like to have you on board. It's men like you we need."

"I'll think about it."

"Do you mean it?" Spelling was unable to hide his satisfaction.

"Yes, I mean it and this calls for another drink," Hurstwood said jovially, as if trying to laugh the matter off. He reached for the new bottle and the glasses.

"Cheers."

"Cheers."

"There's another scenario," Spelling began sheepishly, "different from the American commies marching on Washington, less likely, but still a distinct possibility, and it has a silver lining."

"What's that?" Hurstwood asked without curiosity, keeping on coughing after a gulp of whiskey had gone the wrong way.

"If the Soviets gain the atomic initiative, they may want to wipe out American forces in Germany and American forces on American soil. If you and I survive, we may be generals overnight."

"What about those four hundred generals at the Pentagon?"

"Well the assumption is . . . the assumption being they would be wiped out in the first strike of the Third World War. The Pentagon is first priority for the Russkies. Can't deny it."

"I see, so you and I," Hurstwood went on coughing, "would be . . . would be . . . brigadiers."

"Or higher!"

"I'll think about it too." Hurstwood's cough was now under control, and he was sipping his whiskey with relish. Presently he tried to rise from the sofa, but lost his balance and was back on it in a semi-reclining position. He tried again and this time he succeeded.

"I'm very happy you met the lady . . . very happy for you . . . I'm sorry her name escapes me."

"Claire."

"Of course, Claire. How could I forget it!"

"Beats me."

Hurstwood straightened himself up, raising his glass and making an occasion of it. "Let me propose a toast, to Claire!"

"To Claire!" Spelling's face radiated with joy. He too straightened himself. "To Claire!" he called out. "That's mighty nice of you, Teddy."

The two men emptied their glasses.

"May the two of you be happy in the sack," Hurstwood broke the silence.

Spelling's face was still radiant as he shifted his feet nervously. "Let me scare up some chow," he blurted out, heading for the kitchen.

Chapter 7

The first jeep whizzed and ground on a mass of gravel, nearly over-turned hurling itself against an icy shoulder, then regained its equilibrium and forced itself onto the center tracks. "Careful, Donkers," Major Trainer snapped with a smirk. "You don't want to kill us all yet."

"No, sir."

The major threw the passenger's flap open, leaned out, and called to the jeep behind, "You guys be careful!" He saw Spelling and Honigklausen nodding vigorously, the latter's arm raised and hovering in the air. He closed the flap and lit a new cheroot. "Hell of a weather, even for April, but today it's sure winter. Are you hanging on, Hurstwood?" he asked, turning his head to the back seat.

"Yes, Major," Hurstwood replied. "I'm hanging on."

The barracks were barely visible to the rear, and in front lay a country road not often driven or walked on now covered with a veil of snow that fell during the night. A morning mist was still hanging over the craggy hills and the uneven grazing ground, lighter over the tops and thicker over the troughs and slopes. As they drove on, the hazy contours of Lake Weilheim came into view, darkish dots on the bank breaking the monotony of the all-encompassing whiteness.

"Yesterday I talked hell of a long time by phone with Major

Fergusson. We really touched base," Trainer said. "And I told 'im we in 16th Engineer Group support their mobile-bridge one hundred percent. Just about all our officers thought it was a nifty gadget. Isn't that so, Hurstwood?"

"Absolutely, sir. It should become our standard equipment; it surpasses anything we have in the same category."

Trainer pulled a pensive face and added, "I also invited Fergusson to come to the Group as our official guest. Told him if he doesn't want to bunk at the Officers' Club in Mannheim, Beryl and I would be happy to put him up. He was mighty pleased. In fact . . ." Trainer paused.

"Yes, sir?"

"He said something I didn't understand. When I invited the guy, he was silent for quite some time and then he said, 'Thank you, Major. This makes all the difference.' I still don't understand, but it don't matter."

Hurstwood smiled. "I am glad he said that."

Trainer was deep in thought for another moment and then became alert and watchful. "This was your idea, my calling him and the invitation. It seems it paid off. Thank you." They were all silent until all of a sudden the jeep lurched, narrowly escaping turning over.

"For crying out loud, Donkers, keep your eyes on the road. We want to get there in one piece," Trainer hollered, genuinely angry.

"Very sorry, sir."

The major's narrowing eyes were watching Donkers very closely, and his lips began to move as if he had made up his mind to say something else, but he didn't.

They were now within a stone's throw of the Lake Weilheim, and they could see three French officers on the bank, two of them bent over a large camera on a tripod, and the third a few yards away taking notes. Two small tents fluttered in the wind to the right, and a small citroén with military markings was parked some distance to the left. Further from the lake and behind the citroén a large tent stood firm, impervious to the elements. As they drew closer, Hurstwood leaned forward and said, "Those two around the camera are lieutenants, the third a captain."

"Thank you, Hurstwood." Trainer opened the flap and extended his arm, signaling to the other jeep to stop. Donkers, still behind the wheel, was mopping perspiration off his forehead and breathing heavily. Through the rearview mirror he could see Captain Spelling jumping nimbly out of the jeep and Sergeant Honigklausen easing himself down slowly and laboriously as if he were climbing down a scaffolding. From the corner of his eye he saw Major Trainer glancing at some notes, which he presently folded and put in his breast pocket. Trainer was halfway out of the jeep when he spoke again. "I want you to stay close to me, Donkers, 'cause I want the French officers to know precisely what I say to 'em and what they say to me."

He was out of the jeep now and saw puzzlement painted all over Donkers' face.

"Didn't Sergeant Honigklausen brief you about today's assignment?"

"I am your designated driver for today," Donkers replied, the expression on his face not changing an iota.

". . . and interpreter," Trainer added. "Your 201 says you speak them foreign tongues. That's why I picked you for the job."

Donkers had now climbed out of the jeep, walked over to the passenger side, and stood there facing Trainer with Hurstwood to his right. Still some distance away, Spelling and Honigklausen were slowly walking towards them. Donkers sniffed the air several times and moved his head to and fro, kicking the ground.

"My 201 is inexact, sir. It gives me too much credit. I speak only Dutch and German, no other foreign tongues."

"Shit," Trainer muttered under his breath. "God-mother-fuckin' shit."

"Perhaps one of the French officers speaks English. After all, it wouldn't be unusual," Hurstwood put in cautiously.

"No, they don't. Fergusson told me so." He turned in silence scanning the four of them, Spelling and Honigklausen now standing alongside the others.

"Does anyone here speak French?" he asked hoarsely, pugnaciously biting his lip. They all shook their heads.

"Well, let's go and meet 'em anyway, that's why we're here." He belched, spat with a vengeance, and advanced boisterously towards the French officers, Spelling and Hurstwood right behind him, Honigklausen and Donkers forming the rear guard.

The French had taken cognizance of the arrival of the American party and were talking to one another in brief, rapid spurts, gesticulating now and then. When they saw Major Trainer and the others approach, they fell silent and arranged themselves in a military fashion, the captain in the middle and the lieutenants flanking him one step to the rear. Major Trainer came to a halt, stood at attention, and saluted. The captain, also at attention, returned the salute. Trainer began to speak very slowly, very distinctly, obviously at pains to make every word understandable.

"We are here at the invitation of Major Fergusson"—a ghost of recognition shot across the faces of the French—"who informed me that you gentlemen would be here today, taking pictures and exploring further the terrain in connection with the display of your mobile-bridge some weeks ago."

He paused, swallowed hard, and was going to continue when the French captain interrupted: "*Vous etes bien venu, mon commandant, mais je suis desolé que nous ne parlous pas anglais.*" He smiled amiably. "No English, no speak English."

Trainer rubbed his face, grinding his teeth, and was at a loss for words when one of the French lieutenants asked softly, "*Mon capitaine?*" The captain nodded. The lieutenant, tall, light complexioned, and sporting a well-trimmed moustache, advanced a step and spoke very slowly in French.

"*Messieurs, puisque vous ne parlez pas francais, je me demande si un de vous ne parle pas allemand; deutsch; sprechen Sie deutsch? Je parle allemand. Ich spreche deutsch.*"

Trainer lifted his right arm high in the air and was drawing little circles with it, a sign of unmistakable progress and imminent victory.

"Donkers!" he roared. "You'll be the interpreter after all. You'll translate what I say into German and translate for me what the lieutenant says in German."

"Right, sir."

"Tell him."

Donkers duly translated the message and then translated back. "The lieutenant says everything is in order."

"I want to finish my pre . . . preliminary remarks. Translate as I speak."

"I am sorry there were misunderstandings several weeks ago, when you showed us your very fine mobile-bridge. The responsibility for these misunderstandings rests squarely with the U.S. Army, and not with the French Army. For this I offer my apologies." He paused. "Am I going too fast for you, Donkers?"

"Not at all, sir, just remember to pause after every three or four sentences to give me time and also remember that the lieutenant has to translate what I say into French."

"Right." After an interval the major went on. "I sincerely hope that this day will mark a new phase in the military cooperation between your units and 16th Engineer Group. The French Army and the American Army must work together and work harmoniously, because only in this way can we achieve our objectives, the defense of our respective countries, defense of NATO, and preservation of the free world." He paused for translations and then continued. "But even between the best of friends disagreements and misunderstandings arise. They arise also in the best and most ideal of marriages. This is life, and as a wise Frenchman once said, *'c'est la vie.'* Let us hope that these disagreements and misunderstandings will be few and far between. After all, France and the United States are very old,"—he emphasized the words—"very old allies. Thank you, gentlemen."

When the translations were finished, the faces of the French bore the expression of guarded gratification mingled with that of recognition that the sentiments expressed by the American major were just and they, the French, could share in them. The captain briefly consulted the two lieutenants and addressed himself to Major Trainer through the inevitable interpreters. "We thank you, Major, for your gallant words and for the thoughts which lie behind your words. Let it be known to you and to the American Army that we share your objectives and your hopes. We are honored by your presence here this morning." He saluted and the salute was promptly returned.

"And now"—the captain beckoned to his interpreter that he had still something to say. "Would you care to join us in the tent? We have some deck chairs there. We can talk more comfortably inside, away from the wind."

"Thank you, Captain, we'll be happy to join you in the tent. Please lead the way."

Inside the tent, Trainer introduced members of his party, and the French captain introduced the two lieutenants and himself. "Lieutenant Jean-Pierre Kieffer," he said, pointing to the French interpreter. "And Lieutenant Etienne Dujardins," he said pointing to the other lieutenant.

"I am Captain Edmond de Crecy." There was handshaking all around, and they sat down on deck chairs, portable army beds, boxes containing photographic equipment, and piles of sleeping bags and blankets thrown together. Major Trainer again complimented his hosts on the success of the mobile-bridge and wanted to know more about its speed and firing power. The captain happily obliged, stressing that Pout-Mobile could go as fast as thirty miles per hour and up to forty for brief spells. As for the firing power, the captain announced with undisguised pride, the key factor of Pont-Mobile could be summed up in two words: flexibility and adaptability. "We had two heavy machine guns mounted on it for the demonstration"—he continued—"because machine guns would be particularly useful in most situations; but mortars could be installed instead, or fire-throwers, or some other kind of small gun depending on the nature of the mission and the opposition anticipated. You see, Major, our Pont-Mobile is equal to just about any challenge."

Next both Captain Spelling and Lieutenant Hurstwood asked specific, highly technical questions. The French in turn were curious about the NIKE Ajax missiles, Army Corporal missiles, new engineering equipment, "flying jeeps," and new U.S. Army helicopters, and this information was provided mostly by Spelling and Hurstwood. At one point Lieutenant Kieffer turned to Sergeant Honigklausen and said, "You had coffee brought to the lake two weeks ago when our men were here. It was a nice thing to do. We thank you again."

Honigklausen, his chest swelling and his head high in the air sounded off, "You are very welcome, sir. Methought your boys needed something that would burn their bellies good and proper." They all laughed, and Trainer, barely visible behind clouds of smoke from his cheroot, drawled out, "Good job, Sergeant!"

Gradually the conversation shifted onto more personal grounds. Kieffer told the Americans about his childhood in Alsace, Dujardins about his tour of duty in Indochina. Trainer, Spelling, and de Crecy pinpointed on memory's map the places where they had served. Hurstwood and de Crecy compared notes on the life of cadets at West Point and Saint-Cyr. Honigklausen was questioned about his experiences in WWII and recounted them volubly, not missing a single detail, and Donkers was asked about his studies, about American universities, and why he had chosen philosophy and psychology as his double major.

As peals of laughter filled the tent it was decided that the men of the hour were the two interpreters, Lt. Kieffer and PFC Donkers, without whom the two republics, the French and the American, would most assuredly perish, and extravagant honors were dangled before them, fireworks of wit which evoked from Kieffer a half-suppressed yawn and no more, and from Donkers a curt comment that he'd just settle for a three-day pass.

Later in the morning, Major Trainer rose to his feet and announced that the hour for the departure of the American party had struck.

"It's been a very useful meeting," and he put out his hand to Captain de Crecy. "You'll be through this afternoon, I take it."

The captain nodded assent.

"In that case, you and the lieutenants are invited to dinner at the Officers' Mess, 16th Engineer Group. After dinner, arrangements will be made to lodge you for the night at the Officers' Club in Mannheim before your return to Karlsruhe tomorrow. We hope you will accept." He paused. "We would like you to accept."

A barely perceptible wrinkle formed itself on Captain de Crecy's forehead.

"It's very kind, but I have to consult with the lieutenants."

"Of course, but remember there's no barbed wire around the Officers' Mess and around the Officers' Club in Mannheim. I'm sure you understand why I'm bringing this up."

"Perfectly."

A rapid consultation followed between the French officers, words and phrases being tossed about and exchanged at breakneck speed. Presently de Crecy again faced Trainer. His face was radiating the morning light that was now streaming through the small windows of the tent, lending the meeting a new and more cheerful note and his manner was relaxed.

"We accept with pleasure."

"Great!" the major cried out. "Will 6:30 be convenient?"

"Perfectly convenient."

"Till this evening?"

"Till this evening."

Once outside, Trainer turned to Spelling. "Make all them necessary arrangements at once, and tell Sergeant Sampler to prepare something special. You have the booze?"

"Yes, sir, everything's under control."

"I want this to go without a hitch. Call Mannheim and if anyone, and I mean anyone, gives you any lip, tell 'em this is straight from General Ryan, direct order, unless they want to wave good-bye to their stripes or bars. The French are to receive V.I.P. treatment."

"Yes, sir."

As they climbed into their respective jeeps, Trainer shook his head vigorously. "Maybe we did some good work this morning. Maybe. I guess the future will tell." He spoke more to himself than to the others. And then his mood changed and he was laughing jovially. "How did I do?" He half-turned, craning his neck.

"Not bad, not bad at all. You departed from the script now and then, as they say in Hollywood, but all things considered, we are rather proud of you." Hurstwood spoke with studied detachment.

"Blessed are the speechwriters and the coaches," Trainer began and then stopped . . . "I can't remember how it goes on . . ."

"For they shall remain silent and anonymous," Hurstwood finished for him.

Trainer was still chuckling when he motioned to Donkers to start the engine. He leaned slightly to the left and with mock gravity urged Group Clerk to drive with care and avoid head-on collisions with blocks of ice, boulders, gigantic trees, and anything else moving or stationary which rose above the dwarf-like measurements of the jeep.

"Unless, of course, you have a hot date at noon, Donkers, unless you have a hot date," he drawled out, his face lit up by animal spirits.

Chapter 8

Donkers tossed his fatigues onto the bed, kicked off his shoes, and settled before the portable typewriter. He adjusted the black and silver banker's lamp and pulled out a folder from the desk drawer, put a sheet in the typewriter, and began to type.

Dear Jonathan,

There are a good many things to tell you since my last letter, but let me begin with the talk of the town. There are persistent rumors that Major Trainer will be named before long Group Commander and that his "acting" days will soon be over. Just about everybody has something to say about it, good or bad, for or against it, and it is also being bruited that we shall be getting a new Exec Officer, presumably a major, since this is what the post calls for. This might mean that Trainer will be promoted to Lt. Colonel, and Captain Spelling may have to find himself another banana tree to lounge under, and once again tongues are wagging. Conventional wisdom has it that General Vickers is strongly opposed to Trainer's appointment and promotion, but many are saying that our brave major still has friends in high places, notwithstanding. Apparently some other generals at Army favor him.

The guy I wrote to you about who works in the Adjutant's office at Army, and who is one of my most reliable sources, says that Trainer has a 50/50 chance, and that his supporters and opponents are more or less evenly divided. He also told me that the matter must be decided one way or another in the next few weeks because of deadlines, contingencies, etc. Most of the time my informant is wise as to which end is up.

Time passes fast, and as we are in the second week of April it's only a tad more than two months before we see each other in London. Only two months! Sadly two more months! But enough of rumors and rumor-mongers. The event of prime importance last week was the visit of the French officers to the Group. Trainer met them by Lake Weilheim where they were reconnoitering and taking pictures, and they are part of the engineering outfit that put that mobile-bridge of theirs on display some weeks ago. In the evening they were Trainer's guests at the Officers' Mess, and I was the interpreter on both occasions. It is only fitting that the complete account should be offered when I see you in London because whenever I put myself in mind of what had happened, I am overwhelmed by uncontrollable laughter and run the risk of bursting a blood vessel. Suffice it to say that the translation was in two parts: I translated from English into the German, which one of the French officers then translated into French. What the French said was translated into German by the same French officer and then by me into English for the benefit of Trainer, Spelling, Hurstwood, and Honigklausen. It all went off rather well, the only handicap being that the pauses and delays detracted from the natural rhythm of the situation, as it developed. Viewed from another perspective it all seemed to be a living caricature of our lack of preparedness in meeting even the simplest emergencies, but in the end topping it with a bit of luck. Spelling had made the official arrangements, but it was Hurstwood who was really in charge. The French drank their wine dutifully, but it was good ol' American bourbon they fell for. Their captain, Edmond de Crecy, said he had had very little American whiskey in his life, having drunk mostly scotch. And he said he liked bourbon. Yes, he liked it a lot.

There were some lighter highlights, one of which involved me; the French were very complimentary about my German and were duly impressed when I said that I also spoke Dutch. Rather puzzled, they asked how I'd come by it. I replied that Grandpa came from a village just outside Amsterdam, and when he lived with us after Grandma's death he insisted on speaking Dutch at home. So if I wanted to speak to Grandpa I more or less had to speak Dutch, hence my fluency in that language. Grandpa, who knew English very well and had used it in business, claimed, especially as he got older, that speaking English made his throat sore. For some reason this really amused the French and they were hooting with laughter. I attribute it to the latent hostility the French feel towards things American or English, in this instance, the English language. Still, these three French officers were less antagonistic towards us than they were towards the British. It was obvious they didn't care for their neighbors across the Channel, and their minds were set. I suppose mere fifty years of entente cordiale cannot efface centuries of hostility and wars. As for us, judging by the odd remarks they made and from the questions they fired at us, it was clear they considered the Americans as being still half-formed, half-developed—something like a caveman bravely straining to climb out of his cave to start a better life. However, they were courteous and in high spirits.

Several days after their visit we had another one from Major Michel Fergusson, who is in charge, so to speak, of the mobile-bridge. He and Major Trainer spent a good deal of time together. As Fergusson is fluent in English, my services were dispensed with.

Captain Hastings is back from his retreat in Augsburg and the vacation in Switzerland and is painting word-pictures of everything Swiss, especially the Alps, for the benefit of anyone willing to listen. His wife is apparently even keener on Switzerland than he is. Major Trainer has a great deal on his plate these days. The meeting with General Stebbins— and this was crucial—had gone very well; this was several weeks ago. In the interim, we've had several courts-martial, inspections, and other boring events. Sergeant Honigklausen is the same as ever, showing his unabated disgust for the declining morals and manners, especially of the young, and Captain Spelling is the winner of the Martinet-of-the-Month and Creep-of-the-Month Awards. He eats, drinks, and breathes Army Regulations, ceaselessly yapping about efficiency and fitness.

So much for the lords of authority! On the day following the dinner for the French, Hurstwood asked me to come to his office. He said he would like to know what general and particular impressions I had of their stay with us and did his best to put me at ease. I said I thought the French genuinely appreciated our trip to the lake, the dinner, and then being lodged at what, by their standards, was a very comfortable and luxurious club. I also said they were puzzled why we'd gone to all that length. To sum up, I thought their general reaction was a mixture of appreciation, puzzlement, and suspicion. Hurstwood was watching me very closely and asked, "Do you think our hospitality was overdone?"

I said, "No, sir, and if we'd served them only hot dogs and beer they would've been also puzzled, though in a different way, and probably offended."

Hurstwood was silent for a long time and then he asked again, "Why do you use the word 'suspicious'?"

"I had the impression the French half suspected that before the coffee and brandy, or immediately following it, we'd pull out of our briefcases papers ceding a part of a French territory to the U.S. or reducing so many honest Frenchmen and Frenchwomen to the status of indentured servants under the American yoke, or something similar, and ask them to sign."

"Should we have not asked them to dinner?"

"No, we did the right thing, and the way we did it was also right. But we mustn't expect that our hospitality on this particular day will bang out true and lasting friendship between us."

"This was in part to offset the way we treated them when they came here to show us their 'new piece of equipment.'"

"Yes, and I think they were aware of it. I don't think they are grateful, though. Above all, they don't want to be bought. For them this was a social occasion which unveiled again American power and wealth."

"Should we have acted differently?"

"No, I don't think so. We did the right thing, but we mustn't expect too many brownie points."

"So the result is not negative."

"By no means, no. It's simply that we mustn't expect too much from it. Major Trainer's prolonged conferences with Major Fergusson are likely to yield more lasting results."

Again Hurstwood fell silent. Finally he said, "PFC Donkers, I want to thank you again for your work as interpreter, and my thanks are on behalf of the 16th Engineer Group. You carried out your assignment well."

So that's that. And now for another piece of good news. I had a letter from Brent and another one from the law firm which looks after the money Mother had, her own money which came from her family, and *which she was going to leave to her two sons. Well, when Father found out about me, he tried to persuade her to leave everything to Brent and not a penny to me, and at first she consented. I still have butterflies when I remember Father's words, "It would've been better for you if you had never been born. You're a disgrace to the family and to the Church." He stood there in his black suit, wearing a clerical collar, a hymnal in his left hand, and he was on the way to church for the evening service. "It's only proper to tell you that I disown you and so does your mother. Don't expect anything from us." And then he came up very close to me, looked at me pointedly, and said, "Human beings like you have no right to live. Do you understand, Dirk? You have no right to live." I am surprised he didn't hand me a gun there and then. Anyway, when I went to see Mother the next day, she was already in intensive care and the doctors were shaking their heads—she looked not at me but through me, her face immobile and vacant, and at first she didn't know who I was. And then all of a sudden she cried out, "Dirk, Dirk, my son," and she opened her arms, and she was holding me and she kept on repeating, "Dirk, Dirk, my son." I was hugging her and she was crying and I was crying and she went on, "Oh Dirk, Dirk, you're still my son, you're still my son."*

To cut a long story short, after her death Father tried to change the legal provisions with regard to the legacy and this took time—this is what Brent says in his letter—but he was unable to do it. Apparently after leaving all the money to Brent at Father's behest, she reversed herself and went back to her original intent which was to divide it equally between the two of us, and she made a new will only days before she died. Brent says Father is still furious but unable to change anything. He had apparently exhausted all the legal means. At the end of his letter Brent says with characteristic succinctness that had Father prevailed he would still have shared the legacy with me. I have no reason to doubt what he says. Anyway, I feel jolly about it! The money will help with grad school—not that it is a grand sum, but it's better than nothing.

And now, back to my own unique psyche! I am getting sicker and sicker of the army and the moronic surroundings in which I am constrained to live. I could recite for you a litany of pointless, stupid, and incompetent acts which are the order of the day at 16th Engineer Group and which are repeated with deadly regularity every week, but it would make tedious reading. Fuck the army and all who sail in it, except myself, of course! I have seven months to go—and perhaps this is a seventeen-

month itch. Who knows! I was in Trainer's office when he was going through new directives and orders from Army. He began to swear as he often does, and then he said something that grew on me: Peacetime army is a contradiction in terms. He said, "The most outrageous imbecility ever puked out by a sick mind; it's neither fish nor meat, but we gotta live with it, and there ain't no way out!"

There's something in it, friend, but the night is no longer young. And so to bed.

Stay well,
Dirk

Chapter 9

Captain Hastings pulled the side door of the chapel shut, gave a cursory glance to the bulky sheaf of papers he was holding in his right hand, and stepped onto the gravel path which crisscrossed the parade ground. He began to walk at a leisurely pace, now and then covering his eyes with his left hand to shield them from the afternoon sun burning like a fireball and suspended just above the roofs of the barracks. He switched the papers from the right hand to the left, returned the salute of several enlisted men who in their meanderings found themselves within his field of vision, called out heartily by name to those he knew personally, and smiled broadly nodding his head, one slight nod followed by another in rapid succession.

But halfway to the reviewing stand he slowed down and began to look this way and that, eager to include within his ken all those present, irrespective of what their rank might be, irrespective of whether they were merely strolling or marching hurriedly to their destinations, irrespective of whether they were strangers or of his acquaintance, irrespective of whether their beliefs were close to his own or not, if they had any beliefs, that is. They were his flock, and he was determined to do good by them. He was ready to look each of them in the eye, take each of them by the hand, listen for hours to what they wanted to get off their chest, counsel, help, advise, see them again and again no matter what the hour, be at their beck and call, be at their service, because in so doing he was at His service, and nothing would stop him. Straining his eyes, he caught a glimpse on the opposite side of the parade ground of a PFC from A Company whom he had counseled at length several months earlier about his relationship with a German girl from one of the surrounding villages—a shoddy affair allegedly involving a breach of promise, pregnancy, and a possible lawsuit by the girl's parents—the affair which he had helped to shift onto less explosive grounds, calling on both parties to show understanding and fairness, and being at least partially successful in his ministrations.

He remembered vividly the scene in his office when he saw for the last time the PFC in question, and remembered that after the matter had been settled—as well as it could ever be settled—he tried once again to speak to the young man as his minister, tried to reach him not as his superior, well-wisher, friend, or one man speaking to another, but simply as his pastor. He remembered the man's vacant face during that last meeting as he remembered the vacant faces of the four of them— the parents', the girl's, and the man's—during the earlier meetings whenever he tried to speak to them not as a lay judge or counselor. Recalling the general course of events he became again painfully conscious, as he had been earlier, that his initial attempts to speak as a man of God deteriorated very soon into a juridical posture conforming to which he conscientiously weighed the legal pros and cons and lay stress on common decency, and what he perceived to be secular justice. Ever since the matter had been placed on his desk, he wanted to speak to the two parties of God's transcendent love, of sin and redemption, of God's infinite grace and forgiveness, and he felt that without any conscious effort on his part his ideals were supplanted by the black ink of equity, judicious compromise, and pragmatism writ of large. He had wanted to speak for the Church, but he ended up speaking for the State. This is what the Army expected of him without ever giving him a direct order, and this is what he himself decided to do because otherwise the opposing parties would simply cease listening. The Army wanted to avoid legal entanglements and referred the matter to him, by-stepping the Judge Advocate. He followed their unwritten instructions and did his utmost. Another recollection of the last meeting with this particular PFC flickered in his mind: he had begun by speaking once more of prayer and divine love, but the blank expression on the PFC's face, devoid of even the slightest interest in what he was saying, made him stop. After a few moments of embarrassing silence he said, "I like to keep in touch with my parishioners; could you come and see me in a month or two? I'd like to know how you're getting along."

The PFC said with manifest conviction that he would come to see him and took his leave, and now standing in the middle of the parade ground several months later, Hastings was suddenly struck by the sheer ludicrousness of his remark. "My parishioners, staying in touch with my parishioners!" He laughed raucously and repeated the words with a sneer. The PFC never came to see him, and now as Hastings was watching him in motion across the parade ground he realized that the man was changing course; instead of leaning slightly to the left so that in a minute or so he would be no more than twenty yards away from him, he turned sharply to the right and soon disappeared behind a building.

Hastings jolted in his tracks, shook his head vigorously to free himself from the gnawing memories, and resumed his walk. Ahead and to the right he caught the sight of Lt. Hurstwood emerging from the Depo Building. He waved and Hurstwood waved back, waiting for him to catch up.

"So," Hurstwood drawled out with a chuckle, "Switzerland was peachy, I hear, Bob."

"Before Switzerland was the retreat," Hastings replied, assuming a serious mien, "and that's gone off reasonably well, reasonably well," he repeated. "Only two black sheep this time, and so clumsy in their escapade, running straight to the local palace of pleasure and skipping prayer and meditation when they must've known they would be missed. But otherwise quite satisfactory."

"And Switzerland?" Hurstwood queried.

"Ah, Switzerland!" Hastings echoed, gazing at the ground. "I don't suppose you're all that interested in what went on in the Council of Churches, Ted. But there were many bright spots, Huddleston's address for one, really first-rate, on the expanding role of the churches in Western society." Hurstwood nodded sympathetically. "What you're really waiting to hear is how we took to the Alps and all that."

"Well, I was hoping . . ."

"We had the time of our lives. I don't remember the kiddies in such high spirits ever since we set foot down here, and Courtney's snapshots, literally hundreds of them, will probably take years to develop." He gave out a quick, nervous laugh. "She took pictures of just about everything and, of course, everything was worth the candle." His face lit up, and he rattled on about Geneva, Lausanne, and Bern and then with redoubled enthusiasm about the lakes, the Piz Bernina, the Matterhorn. Hurstwood pointed a finger at the Officers' Mess, Hastings nodded, and they began to walk towards it, Hastings rattling on excitedly, and Hurstwood listening to him with polite attention.

At the other end of the parade ground between the Command Building and the paved road leading to the Motor Pool, Donkers now on the way to his quarters stooped to tie a shoelace. The sun was no longer burning wildly over the rooftops. It had descended two stories and could only be seen far smaller and less luminous now between the buildings. Soon dusk would be falling slowly, very slowly as if the gods of the night were in no hurry to take possession. About to stand up, Donkers became aware of somebody looming near him.

"And how's the mighty Group Clerk, still up to his dirty tricks?" Chuck Miller asked nonchalantly, his hands in his pockets, his lips curled, and his faced contorted with histrionic mock-anger.

"Still the same and trying to put the bad guys away."

"Oh, it's like this now!"

"How could it be otherwise?"

Chuck took a number of steps in the direction of the Motor Pool and motioned to Donkers to follow. "Let's get out of the officers' favorite thoroughfare, so we don't have to salute the creeps."

"Okay."

"Haven't seen a trace of you for sometime, and no way to thank you for sending me yet another customer."

Donkers knit his brow, his face impassive.

"What customer?"

"The high and mighty Acting Group Commander, Major E.E. Trainer, soon to become permanent Group Commander."

Donkers whistled and smacked his lips. "Sure, I remember. Always ready to oblige a friend. By the way," he went on, "how much did you charge him for the haircut?"

"Five bucks."

"You normally charge a buck or two."

"This is for those I'm supposed to call my buddies. I give them cut rates so they don't break into my footlocker, slash my clothes, or strangle me when I'm asleep. When you live with animals, you have to make concessions."

"Okay."

"In point of fact, I'm surprised Trainer didn't tip me extra."

"He already gave you three times the prices you charge."

Miller yawned and tilted his head. "There's no need to go gung-ho on me, Dirk. Trainer got a super haircut and he gotta pay for it. I don't run a shelter for the homeless, you know."

"I see."

"I don't think you see anything, Mr. Group Clerk. The government's robbing me of thousands of dollars which are rightfully mine." His eyes glistened, and he was warming to the subject. "When I was drafted I was only an apprentice-barber, but I was already hired by Yachtsman's Trim, d'you know what Yachtsman's Trim is?"

"The most expensive clip joint in your town."

"There's still hope for you, boy. Anyway, no apprentice-barbers are ever taken on, but they made an exception for me, for me personally, and promised me a job. Mr. Clayton interviewed me and was very impressed by my work and references. Everything was set, and then a week later I get my draft notice. So now the government is robbing me of what is rightfully mine. Tens of grands."

Donkers remained silent, and Miller elated was speaking from the heart.

"Do you know who comes to Yachtsman's Trim? The best people: bankers, some politicians, successful M.D.s, and attorneys, CEOs, all top echelon. We cater to wealth and class."

"The two don't often go together."

"Don't give me that bullshit. We turn people away at the door; it's by appointment only, and we are kind of choosy."

"Good for you!"

"My girl Mavis is a manicurist-pedicurist, and she does an odd massage; we were a team already and better was to come." Miller paused and shrugged, his face furrowed with disgust. "The damned government, the goddamn government," he hissed out and then he lowered his head, his expression becoming softer, almost sentimental. "Mavis misses me something terrible—it must be hell for her to be without me; her letters tell the story, poor kid."

"How long do you have?" Donkers asked.

"Sixteen more months, sixteen long months."

"Well, it isn't eternity."

"It sure feels like it." Miller looked pointedly at Donkers and put a hand on his shoulder. "I'll tell you something I don't ordinarily talk about. All things considered, I didn't mind the basic all that much, being stuck in the mud like a goddamn animal, hikes with full pack, being yelled at by apes who couldn't earn a buck wearing civvies, and all the rest. No, sir, I didn't mind it that much. I figure the generals are entitled to a little fun. Something else got to me though."

"What was that?"

"Those dumb-ass movies and lectures before we were sent over-seas."

"So! We all had to see that crap."

"Yeah, but that crap got me riled up like nothing else in the military, 'cause of its goddamn hypocrisy; those turkeys telling us we'll be defending the free world, standing up against evil which threatens the American way of life and the rest of the shit. I remember one guy who had it bad, real bad . . . a civilian, the most hypocritical lectures came from civilians, probably high-up in the government or something . . . and this guy went on for more than an hour about our sacred duty . . . defending the United States of America, defending our European allies, and fighting the commies wherever they may be, under the bed, in the trenches, in high places. Gee, I'm surprised he didn't list other lairs where the commies might be hiding such as inside your pizza or at the bottom of your beer glass." Miller stopped, looked critically at Donkers, and then went on with fervor. "I'll never forget what he said at the end, it kind stuck in my mind, if you know what I mean, Dirk, 'cause of its goddamn hypocrisy and here it goes, best I can remember." Miller adjusted his sunglasses and assumed an official tone. "'When you boys go overseas you will act as American ambassadors to the other nations of the world, you will be looked up to and honored by the inhabitants of the country to which you've been sent because those inhabitants have a great deal to learn from you. Above all you will be freedom's pro-tectors.' Yeah, this was the punch line, "'freedom's protectors.'"

Donkers shrugged. "So, don't lose any sleep over it."

"Okay, okay, but let me just point out to you that I've been sent here at a great financial loss to myself, and to the detriment of Mavis' well-being and peace of mind, and whom in hell's name am I protecting and where the hell is the enemy? The whole thing's a joke. I haven't seen a Russky since I've been here; in fact, I've never seen a Russky in my life. I ain't no ambassador for nobody. I ain't fighting nobody, I ain't protecting nobody. What the hell are we doing here, what the fuck is going on? Why can't we go back to business as usual?"

Donkers rubbed his nose, drew up, placed his right arm across his chest, and recited with feeling:

Theirs not to make reply,
Theirs not to reason why
Theirs but to do and die.

"Lost your marbles?"

"No, I was reciting lines from *The Charge of the Light Brigade* by Alfred Tennyson."

"Who the hell was Alfred Tennyson, and what the hell was that Light Brigade of his? Was he the C.O.?"

Donkers smiled and turned on his heel. "Make the best of it, Chuck, it isn't for keeps. I hope Mavis survives the separation."

"I am not so certain she will; she worships me, poor kid." Miller took off his sunglasses and was surveying the activity on the parade ground—the steady movement towards the Mess Hall, the men entering their quarters, others leaving them. "What a hole to be stuck in for months on end," he sighed. "Still . . . you did me a good turn, and Chuck Miller never forgets a favor or an injury."

"I'm certain of the latter, doubtful of the former."

Miller chuckled and drew closer to Donkers. "Have it your own way, fella. You're well known in these parts, and some are saying you're a regular guy, straight shooter, always willing to help, but others are saying you're smart, just smart and nothing else. Most would agree you carry weight around here, what with a dumb bastard of a Group Commander and a prematurely senile first sergeant, it's only to be expected. You kinda run this outfit, don't ye?"

"Tell me more. I'm dying to hear it."

"As for myself, I'd say you're deep and a bit of a stargazer. You try to look beyond, trying to see what's there. Don't bother, friend, there's nothing there, just empty space."

"I'll bear it in mind."

Miller chuckled again and made ready to go. "Any prospective customers you'd like to send me will be well treated and sent away fully satisfied, and there may be something for you at the end of the day."

Donkers nodded and watched Miller walk away, but suddenly he snapped his fingers, a sly half-smile breaking out all over his countenance.

"Psstt, hot shot!" he called.

"What now?" Miller turned round looking bored.

"The chaplain is looking for a new assistant, interested? I'll put in a good word for you."

"I don't know about you, I really don't know about you, Dirk. Maybe this sickness of yours is just temporary, too much hot air inhaled under adverse conditions, but see a shrink anyway," and he was gone.

Chapter 10

Having listened at length to Hastings' accounts of his vacation in Switzerland and having later accompanied him to the mess, Hurstwood was glad to be back in his office in the Command Building. He sat down in the massive wooden armchair behind the desk, lit a cigarette, and blew out puffs of smoke intent on making them as large as possible without distorting in any way their circular shape. He glanced perfunctorily at the newly arrived supply and equipment manuals, at the latest issue of *Time*, put them aside and sat in silence still blowing out puffs of smoke, his elbow on the desk and his clenched fist supporting the chin. His eyes roamed the office: the three chairs, the side table, the half-empty bookshelf, the filing cabinet, the family photographs on the stand by the window next to the West Point mementos, more and more engineering manuals scattered here and there, the maps on the walls, the clothes trees, and on the almost bare desk, half of which was covered by an enormous blotter, several books squeezed between two marble dividers, *The Uniform Code of Military Justice* being the most prominent.

"Light baggage," he whispered to himself, "light baggage indeed, could it be in anticipation?" The question amused him, and he suddenly felt carefree and delighted at there being so few objects in his office, at there being so much room in it, and most importantly at his feeling no attachment whatsoever to what surrounded him, with the exception of the family photos and the West Point paraphernalia. Hurstwood rose, looked at his watch, stubbed out the cigarette, and sauntered over to the door. He opened it and was lolling in the doorway examining at close quarters his nameplate that read *Lt. Theodore H. Hurstwood, Supply Officer.* Laughing, he tossed his head, dusted the corner of the nameplate, tightened his tie, smoothed the Army Greens, and proceeded towards the Group Commander's office.

"Good evening, sir," Sergeant Honigklausen greeted him unctuously bowing his head from behind the desk, a sugary self-effacing smile adorning his face.

"Good evening, Sergeant."

Honigklausen reached for the large leather bound calendar on the desk and held it at arm's length.

"Your appointment to see the Group Commander is for 1900 hours, and it is only 1855 hours. The Group Commander will be back in a minute; he just stepped out; he's the most punctual officer I've ever served under . . . present company excepted," he added officiously.

Hurstwood laughed. "Of course, Sergeant, of course. You're up late. Determined to burn the midnight oil?"

"We in the military have to forgo time and time again the private comfort when duty calls, because duty comes first. With General Vickers en . . . ensconced in his new post, we got more directives, circulars, and such like than ever before. The general believes in thorough and detailed written communication between the Headquarters and the subordinate units, and it is my duty"—he raised his head high in a commanding gesture—"to see to it that it is duly taken cog . . . cognizance of and processed."

"Right you are, Sergeant, right you are," Hurstwood put in, looking out of the window.

"And I might add that all of us are very happy to have the chaplain back with us and looking so rested."

"Yes, it's good to have Bob back," Hurstwood muttered from the window.

"There's another item of news, sir, that you might be interested in." With some difficulty Honigklausen stood up and then walked to the large map of Eastern Europe on the wall next to an oversize filing cabinet. He picked up the pointer and went on. "There's a cold front and a storm, snowstorm, coming our way. Presently it is here in southern Finland and around Leningrad, but it's blowing straight at us and will be in Kirchenberg in a couple of days. I thought the Lieutenant might like to know."

"You bet. Have all the company commanders been notified?"

"Yes, sir. Donkers left urgent messages with all the company clerks this very afternoon before he went off duty. And, as you know, the Infirmary and the Motor Pool get their information direct from the weather station."

"Good, this is important. Thank you, Sergeant Honig . . ."

They both heard the door swing open and turned around.

"Ha, ha, ha." Trainer's boisterous laughter would've been heard far beyond the confines of his office. "So the good sergeant is briefing you on how to get to Moscow and get your paws on the Kremlin gold, ha, ha, ha."

Honigklausen's enormous figure stood at attention, exuding unquenchable respect and dutiful alertness.

"I took the liberty of informing Lieutenant Hurstwood of the approaching snowstorm," he spoke with great dignity. "We have to be prepared; information has already been dis . . . disseminated. We know how to handle them emergencies."

"Good man," Trainer sounded off. "Good man. You've done enough for today, call it quits, Lester. Go home and forget this goddamn place exists."

Honigklausen smiled, took his hat and coat off the clothes tree, and opened the door. He saluted and, his voice mellow and comforting, said, "May I wish the Major a pleasant evening and a good night, and may I wish the same to the Lieutenant."

"Thanks, Lester, and good night."

"Thank you, Sergeant, and good night."

Trainer fumbled in his pockets for the pack of cheroots, found it, took one out, and began to lick it at one end, fumbling at the same time for his lighter. Hurstwood held out his own lighter and lit the major's cheroot.

"Thanks, care to try one of my coffin nails?"

"No thank you, sir. I prefer regular-size coffin nails."

"Okay, light up if you wish."

Silence intervened, Trainer fixing his gaze uncharacteristically on the floor. At last he said, "Let's sit in my office," and he led the way. Leaning far to the back in his armchair, his fingers drumming unrythmically against the edge of the desk, he appeared to hesitate, as if he didn't know how or where to begin. Hurstwood did not take his eyes off him, waiting for the opening words. Presently Trainer banged his fist against the side of the armchair and hollered, "Let's have a drink." He pulled a bottle and two glasses out of a drawer, placed them on the desk close to Hurstwood, and moved a chair standing against the wall so that it now faced the visitor.

"It's bourbon, and I'm sorry to say there ain't no ice 'cause I drink it straight." He unscrewed the bottle and began to pour. "I'd bet a month's pay you're a scotch man, your Pa being a multi-millionaire and your coming from high above the common folks."

"I am not certain of that," Hurstwood laughed. "But bourbon is just fine, sir, you're very kind."

They raised their glasses and Trainer smacked his lips. "I hear the men nowadays don't say 'cheers' or 'bottoms up' or even 'shit' or 'drop dead' or anything like it no more. They say 'Nikita,' that's the new toast. Well me too say 'Nikita.'"

"Nikita," Hurstwood echoed, and they emptied their glasses, which Trainer immediately refilled.

"You're right, that 'Nikita' business caught on and spread like wildfire." Hurstwood was mildly amused. "Morale officers are a trifle worried, and G2 is looking into it."

"Just like the Army, the poor bastards don't understand nothin.'"

"Shall we raise the ante?" Hurstwood asked with spirit.

"Nikita!"

"Nikita!" Trainer cried out, and once again the noble brew disappeared from the glasses.

"I read your letter of resignation," Trainer began, "and I figure there ain't no way to make you change your mind."

"None!"

"When I got word that you wanna resign your commission, I got hold of your service record and gone through it careful like so that I could talk with you sensibly not forgetting anything. What happened outside Fort Dix?"

"Upon graduating from West Point in '52 I was assigned temporarily to Fort Dix. On July 14th I was struck by a cab just outside the main gate. The driver was under the influence. The ambulance took me to the hospital; I had multiple fractures in both legs, broken ribs, broken shoulder bones, dislocated spine. I spent close to a year in various hospitals, and later had to undergo two additional operations on my spine. I was returned to active duty in November of 1953."

"So you were never in combat?"

"No, I wasn't."

"And then?"

"I was assigned to Fort Bragg, as a supply officer, stayed there for more than a year and was later assigned to 16th Engineer Group."

"Bad luck, rotten bad luck," Trainer muttered under his breath, his eyes still fixed on the folder before him.

"I couldn't agree with you more. The Army pronounced me ninety percent rehabilitated, which means if there's a real emergency I'll be behind a desk, behind a desk permanently."

"That's right, it's all here."

Hurstwood lit another cigarette and placed his hand knowingly around the whiskey bottle.

"Would you like . . . ?" he asked softly.

"Damn right, pour it in," Trainer cackled through the clouds of smoke. He stood up and took a few aimless steps around the office holding his head down, and then eased his great haunches onto the chair.

"I thought if we spoke after hours we wouldn't be disturbed; in this business it's better we ain't disturbed." Hurstwood nodded, and Trainer went on, raising his glass in a silent toast.

"Your ratings, Hurstwood, have been excellent, from all commands including this one and written by me, just like your West Point record, something to be proud of, graduated third in your class."

Hurstwood smiled bleakly.

"Well, let me take you back a year or so, back to Bavaria last winter—U.S. Army maneuvers. You commanded a company of raw recruits, most of 'em straight from Basic, whom the Army in its infinite wisdom put up against the men from the Second Infantry Division, many of 'em RAs, many of 'em Korean veterans. I remember the occasion well, I was an umpire. Anyway, things didn't go the way the Infantry figured they would. You damn well knew if you advanced right on, or threw it in from the flanks you'd be massacred or captured. There was simply too many of 'em, you were the Reds, the enemy, on the attack, and the Infantrymen were the Blues, right! Defending the red, white, and blue. So what did you do? During the night you took your men some five miles west and then north till you reached that damned chain of mountains. You took 'em over the mountains, each man hanging onto the rope, single file at first and then on the way down two files, still hanging onto the ropes, till you got within a mile of the 2nd Infantry."

"There were some casualties on the way, regrettably."

Trainer shook his head slowly, sympathetically. "They couldn't be avoided. Three men almost drowned, two cases of broken legs, frost bite that was easy to deal with." He paused and refilled the glasses. "By this time it was 0500 hours. You told the men to rest or sleep for two hours and use their K rations. A line of trees at the foot of the mountain provided cover. Around 0730 hours, as dawn was breaking, you attacked. Those poor infantry bastards didn't know what hit 'em. They had no sentries in the back 'cause that way was considered impassable. They expected an attack from the front and had lookouts and watches in that direction. In fifteen minutes you captured three entire companies, the command post, two colonels, five majors, and I don't remember now how many captains, first and second johns."

"Quite a few."

"The general wasn't at the command post at the time, just as well 'cause if you'd captured a general you'd never hear the end of it. Pretty good showing for someone whom the Army dumped into a desk job." Trainer paused again and took a swig. "Correct so far?"

"Correct, sir!"

"Well, Hurstwood, you had a first-rate plan, and the company followed you to a man. I understand that some of the guys who got to be droopin' like were helped by their buddies, 'cause everyone wanted to be on it, everyone wanted to be part of the action, and no one would dream of allowing himself to be taken by the medics to the dressing station. The three men who nearly drowned were issued dry clothing, given something or other to make them warm again, the details of which I'm not going to inquire about, and they were in the ranks in the matter of minutes. The two guys who broke a leg were carried by their buddies so they could be part of the attack, and only after the capture of the enemy were they driven to the field hospital. Correct?"

"As you say, sir."

"These kids, raw recruits straight from Basic and ninety percent of 'em draftees who'd never been on any military exercise before, were soldiers, you made soldiers out of 'em. I understand when all was over—objective reached, mission accomplished and the rest—they didn't just go to sleep, they stood there chanting, 'Good ol' Ted' and 'For he's a Jolly Good Fellow.' This don't happen often. No, sir. This don't happen often. They trusted you, and in combat trust is everything. The men have an uncanny way of telling whether a C.O. levels with them or not. They may not be geniuses but they know, they can tell. If they trust you and you show some spunk, they'll do a lot for you. But if they don't, forget it, brother, they won't give you their best, and they'll just be thinking about their own safety. I've seen this in the War and in Korea. I've seen C.O.'s shot in the back by their own men 'cause the men didn't trust 'em. That's the way things are."

"Now, before I go any further," Trainer paused to fill the glasses, "I just want to tell you that this infantry general was pissed off, real pissed off 'cause some of his men had Ranger training and the whole operation was to be a cinch."

"Is that the same general who gave me my commendation?" Hurstwood asked.

"The very same, the poor son-of-a-bitch had no choice, he had to decorate you and say all those nice things to your face."

"I thought he was rather tense."

Trainer smiled indulgently.

"I'm guessing, but maybe I'm guessing right." Words were sticking in his throat and he hated every second of it, but he was also a trooper and knew there was no way around it. "Still"—he hoisted himself up in his chair—"that don't matter, the infantry general don't matter. What matters is that what you did in Bavaria tells me something about you. You're a born soldier, Hurstwood, and you belong in the army; you know how to command and the men will follow you. In peacetime as in wartime we get a lot of deadwood in this men's army, creeps who for the good of the service ought to be kept out, not in. But you're different. You're a natural. If U.S. Army is to amount to anything, you and guys like you should be in it. Why the hell do you want to leave the Army?"

"I thought my letter of resignation made the reasons for my decision clear. I would remind you this letter is four pages long."

"Yeah, yeah, yeah," Trainer reluctantly acknowledged the fact. "Sure I've read it, and it don't make one ounce of sense."

"Well . . . I can only say I am baffled, sir."

"Just shut up and listen, just shut up and let me talk. You say in that goddamned letter of yours that you don't agree with the foreign policy of the United States and that you don't want to be part of the force . . . which I take to be the U.S. Army," Trainer pulled a face of mock-heroic bewilderment, "that imple . . . implements this policy."

"That's correct."

"But you're not a politician, man, you're not part of the Washington gang that makes policy. You're just a soldier, fella, who may go far, very far in this men's army if he maintains his present record of excellence. That ninety percent rehabilitation can be appealed, I want you to know, to that same Washington and be nun . . . nullified. You can get 100 percent, and no sweat." When he finished speaking he kept looking at Hurstwood, uncertain, disoriented, not expecting the lieutenant to say anything let alone contradict him, and experiencing an uneasy feeling that he experienced seldom, that he was not equal to the task at hand. Hurstwood was also in an impasse, gazing vacantly about, and the silence welling up was oppressive.

It was a long time before Hurstwood got up to his feet, crossed the office, and stood leaning against the wall, his coat unbuttoned, his tie loosened, cigarette and whiskey glass in hand.

"Let me try to make my resignation understandable to you, Major." He began speaking in his usual level tone, but as he went on the calm and objectivity sounded more and more forced, like a calculated flight from emotions. "First though, I'd like to tell you something about myself which you won't find in my file. I've always wanted to be a soldier, ever since I can remember, ever since the fourth or fifth grade. No other occupation held any luster for me—locomotive driver, fireman, cop, secret agent, cowboy somewhere out West—none of them. By the way, all that talk about the Hurstwoods being multi-millionaires is horseshit. Father is managing director and part owner of a chemical company in New England, and yes we are well to do but hardly one notch below the Rockefellers. It never ceases to amaze me how rumors grow and multiply in the Army where men are supposed to have better things to do than gossip day in and day out. When I was appointed to West Point it was the culmination of all my dreams. When I graduated my resolve, if anything, was strengthened, and I wasn't thinking of promotion. I just wanted to spend my life soldiering, commanding, leading the men in combat and looking after them. The accident to which I fell victim did little to dampen my spirits. It simply meant my soldiering days would have to be postponed. Thank you for mentioning the ninety percent rehabilitation. I've been aware for a long time that this decision can be appealed and upon the presentation of satisfactory medical evidence annulled. When I was returned to active duty in November of 1953, I was once again happy as a sandboy because my true life could begin anew. But then starting in early '54, I became gradually beset by doubts about our role in the world and about the Army as its prime executant even though it's the Air Force that is named more and more often as playing this role. These doubts grew and grew." Trainer was sitting quite still, his arms on his chest.

"Go on, Ted, tell me what there is to know, and keep it simple."

"Right! We are now the most powerful nation in the world, a superpower, well and good. Europe is only just beginning to rise from the ashes, and the Soviet Union is no match for us. But lately we've taken to telling other nations what to do and we say, 'You do this or else we'll drop an atomic bomb on you.' We're getting to be pretty tyrannical ourselves, the tyranny of China, North Korea, and the Soviet Union notwithstanding; we believe that our country has to be defended on the Korean border, in Southeast Asia, and along the Elbe, and our belief is grounded in ignorance and hysteria. The most effective instruments of our foreign policy are our armed forces. We rarely resort to negotiations, and we prefer threats backed by our atomic capability." He stopped. "Sir, may I refill your glass?"

"So long as you refill your own."

"It's a deal." Hurstwood brandished the bottle before pouring out. "Under the circumstances I don't want to be part of this suicidal policy. I love soldiering, but the price is too high. This way madness lies. In my family we have always believed the United States to be very special, a unique nation, an eagle among the vultures, better and nobler than any other country on this planet. But now I am not so certain."

Trainer blew his nose and lit another cheroot. "You make dandy speeches, Ted, maybe you oughta go into politics."

"Not on your life."

"Well, I'm a little closer to grasping what you made all this god-damn fuss about, and maybe, just maybe you got a point. I don't know. One piece of advice though, if you're hell-bent on getting out, don't breathe a word about that political jazz to nobody. Give 'em the med-ical reasons, they'll understand."

"I couldn't do that; as an officer I have the obligation to defend my country; as a citizen I have the right to speak my mind."

Trainer lifted his shoulders. "Yeah, yeah, yeah. Anyway, this settles it. You still have some time to put in, and you'll have an appointment with the Commanding General, which should go smooth as silk if it's Ryan, and God help you if it's Vickers. He'll bore you to death, unless you plain sleep through it, which mind you, has happened on occasions." Trainer burst out laughing, and Hurstwood followed suit. Then anoth-er silence intervened, carefree and cheerful this time like a music inter-val at a dance hall when the dancers, having just ended a whirling round, look hopefully to the next. Trainer stood up and began to stretch his arms, Hurstwood still leaning against the wall, a cigarette and the glass between his fingers.

"Sit down, Ted, take the load off your feet, relax."

"Thank you, sir."

"You like being stationed overseas, more specifically in Krautland?"

"Yes, I like being here."

"It may surprise you but I like it too, and so does Beryl. In some respects we get better treatment here than stateside. You're not married, are you?"

"No, sir."

"Any prospects?"

"Well, after my accident Lucy and I had a number of very serious conversations." Trainer nodded conspiratorially. "And as my future was uncertain, we decided not to see each other at least for the time being. Subsequently she was going to marry someone else, but this fell through, and a few weeks ago we began to correspond. I'll be seeing her later this year."

"Good luck to you! Any brothers to carry on the military tradition when you pull stakes?"

Hurstwood took hold of the bottle and poured out the meager remains.

"This calls for another libation," he laughed and raised his glass.

"What's the joke?"

"Yes, I have a younger brother, Nathan, no sisters though. He's seventeen and still at Choate. Fancies himself as a pacifist and horrifies my parents telling them, when he condescends to come home which is seldom at the best of times, that he's going to burn his draft card, not for any political reasons mind you, but because he hates regimentation and the very smell of the army."

Trainer blinked several times and frowned. "What does Nathan want to do?"

"Ah! He's onto music, but not classical music, that would delight my mother who's a fine pianist, but jazz, ragtime, blues, that sort of thing."

"That's brisk, tangy stuff." Trainer exclaimed. "Makes your head swirl."

"Yeees," Hurstwood nodded. "You might say that. Anyway, Nat doesn't even want to go to college, he wants to play in a band. Father's rather upset; the men in our family usually go to Yale, unless, of course, they go to West Point."

"Understood."

Hurstwood puffed aggressively at his cigarette several times, emitting varied clouds of smoke.

"To tell you the truth, Major, Father was rather upset when I didn't go to Yale and then to law school, which had been his path." He paused. "He will be very upset when I resign my commission. I know he will, and I hate upsetting my father, I really do." He looked up. "Please believe me, but in this instance I have absolutely no choice."

Trainer, sitting in silence, drew closer to Hurstwood and patted him on the back.

"You'll do what ye think ye'll have to do."

Hurstwood was smiling bleakly, his eyes focused on the floor, his body motionless, his face a little more red than usual. Then as if large doses of energy had been suddenly injected into his organs, he drew up and looked sharply at Trainer.

"You're a married man, aren't you? Any children?"

"No." Trainer articulated very slowly. "Beryl can't have kids."

"But if you want children, you can always adopt."

"No, we wouldn't care to adopt, we just wouldn't."

"There's something I want to tell you, you may know it already, but I want you to know others know it too."

"Shoot."

"It's widely known that in Korea you were recommended for the Congressional Medal, which the majority opinion felt you deserved. You didn't get it because of army politics; there was apparently a group of officers in the right places who thought that a battlefield commission was all you deserved; a sergeant getting to be a lieutenant was in their eyes high enough reward, even though what occasioned the recommendation took place ten months later. It is also known, though not so widely, that the same group of officers tried to block your promotion to captain and later to major; I'm glad they were unsuccessful."

Trainer was looking into space, not responding at first as if what Hurstwood was saying was too petty for words. At last he said, "Yeah, I've heard about it too, and it don't surprise me. You might put it in fancy language, but I'd say boys and girls are at bottom just the same no matter where they come from, right side of the tracks or wrong side of the tracks, high up or down at the bottom, it don't make no difference." Hurstwood's eyes were now directed at Trainer, watching him closely.

"I hope you'll get your promotion to light colonel soon, you deserve it."

"Thanks, Ted, but it ain't my game. That's what all the buzz is about, you know that!" Trainer looked away, puffing at his cheroot.

"I want you to know I studied your military record closely, and I am fully aware of what you did in North Africa, in Italy, in Belgium, and later in Korea. It's an inspiring story."

Trainer smoothed his hair, sniffed the encircling smoke, and began to chase it away with rapid cutting movements. "Thanks again, Ted. Appreciate it." He turned to Hurstwood, and his face lit up with a broad, cheerful smile.

"And the best to you too."

"Thank you, sir; I told you about my love of soldiering way back when I was in short pants. Would I be right that you too had the same overwhelming desire ever since your toddling days?"

Trainer stood up and laughed boisterously, his eyes twinkling with delight as if he had just heard the most amusing tale.

"Hell, no! I had no such over . . . overwhelming desire. I just wanted a job, and this here is the only goddamn job I could find in the thirties. If you wanna hear about my unmilitary days, Lieutenant Theodore Herbert Hurstwood, graduate of the mighty Academy of West Point, where every self-respecting cadet carries a shaver between his legs for this here el . . . elimin . . . ination of pubic and other bodily hair the presence of which might be deemed common and uncouth, if this is what ye're leading up to, then we'd better break another bottle." With alacrity Trainer produced a brand new bottle and began to pour.

"West Point is not as sissy as you make out, Major Trainer, sir. We have tough boys on the roll."

"Damn it, it must be my ignorance."

"It's not for me to judge."

"Very commendable respect for a superior officer," Trainer drawled out raising the glass to his lips.

"You're from Kansas, sir."

"Never said no different."

"And you enlisted before the outbreak of the War?"

"There was nothin' else to do." Trainer paused and took another swig. "Pa bought a dirt farm in '27 some thirty miles southwest of Kansas City, where we hail from, while he was still working for Deere, and thought we might all breathe in fresh air like away from the brick and mortar of Atherton. We kids loved it, but in '29 all gone bust and Pa couldn't make no more payments to the bank. The farm was lost, and we moved back to Atherton to rented lodgings. They were laying people off at Deere and everywhere else right and left, and Pa too lost his job. Afterwards things were grim and we lived from week to week, from day to day, getting odd jobs that were getting scarcer and scarcer all the time."

"Large family?" Hurstwood inquired, looking uncomfortable.

Trainer nodded. "You might say that. There were seven of us, four boys and three girls, Wilbur, Lenie, Josh, and myself and Susan, Velma, and Katie, and we survived and somehow managed. I guess it's all behind us now; we're all settled, except for poor Wilbur and Josh, and God only knows where Katie might be."

"How so?"

"Well, Wilbur and I put our heads together and saw clear-like that things in Kansas wouldn't get no better, and it was already 1938. So we enlisted, Wilbur in the Navy and me in the Army, and the day was September 20th. Political situation in Europe getting worse, Mr.

Roosevelt decided that our armed forces should be strengthened like and more men taken in. We were just two kids in search of jobs, but there were no jobs to be had."

"You said, 'poor Wilbur?'"

"That's right, he got it at Pearl, December 1941, and Josh, well, Josh is a very different proposition." Trainer refilled the glasses. "He'd started with petty theft, nickels and dimes, and served several short like jail terms but then it got more serious and the last I heard, and that was several years back, he was convicted of armed robbery and sentenced to fourteen years. I guess he's still inside."

"And Lenie?"

"Lenie was the smart one. In '38 I think or thereabout, he somehow finagled his way into a dentist's office, and at first he was washing all 'em instruments of torture and probably sweeping the floor and the rest, but then little by little he became a kind of technician taking evening classes at the same time and spending nights reading all them dental manuals so when he was drafted in '42 he went in as a dental technician, if you please, and spent his war years gaping into men's mouths and taking stock of men's teeth. And then, guess what!"

"What, what?"

"After the war he got the GI Bill and gone to school to be a jawbreaker in his own right. Well, it took him a hell of a long time, twice as long as anybody else maybe, 'cause he had to have some preliminary schooling first, but he stuck to it, come hell or high water, got his piece of paper or whatever at the end, and hung out his shingle just before Christmas two years back. 1954 it was."

"Good for him!" Hurstwood exclaimed.

"We had one of them family gatherings when all the family shows up, far and near, and Ma and Pa stood there proud like the Shah of Iran that their son actually got to be a licensed jawbreaker." Trainer fell silent, a smile of reminiscence setting on his face.

"Let's hear it," Hurstwood urged him.

"Very well, when all the fuss was made over our very own success story, Pa said with a wink at us kids, 'Why,' said he, 'now that Lenie's hanging out his shingle as a jawbreaker he can make folks scream with pain and get paid for it too.' But Ma wouldn't have any of it. 'How can you say such a thing, Bill?' said she. 'How can you say such a thing of our own son that he'd give pain to others? Why, I'm very surprised at you, Bill, saying such a thing. Why, we are decent folks.' Pa kind of took the cue and was careful not to say nothin' like it again. Ma was proud of Lenie," Trainer went on in a reminiscing mood, "but it was Wilbur who was her favorite, and we all knew it. He was a handsome guy." Trainer tossed his head back and was actually sipping the bourbon. "Could've had any girl in Atherton, and probably had them all, and when he left girls would be calling all hours, 'Where's Wilbur, where's Wilbur, when's he coming back,' and Ma would answer very prim and proper, 'Well now, Wilbur is in the Navy, and you probably know U.S. Navy has a great deal to do these days, so why don't you leave your name and number, my dear, and I'll give it to Wilbur when he comes back.' She made it sound like he was an admiral or something, not a common deckhand. Well, he never came back." Trainer stopped and looked around the office.

"Go on," Hurstwood said, his grave gaze still set on the major.

"When the wire came from the Navy that Wilbur fell at Pearl, Ma was dealt a blow from which we thought she'd never recover. She would just lie in bed crying, or sit in the living room staring at the four walls. She wouldn't eat and kept repeating, 'Why did God allow the Nips to take Wilbur away, why did He allow it, Wilbur was a good boy, why does God allow such things to happen?' She lost lots of weight and was beginning to look like a skeleton. Pa feared for her life, and the Doc could do nothin' about it. He muttered something about a specialist in Kansas City, but there was no money for it, and Pa was in a blue fix. So finally he gone to see the Reverend Tyler, and the Reverend came with Mrs. Tyler and afterwards Mrs. Tyler would come regular like to see Ma, and she'd talk to her and read to her and now and then she'd cook a meal for her and Pa, and slowly, very slowly Ma got better, but it took many long months."

"Is she well now?"

"Yeah, she is fine, and Pa got his old job back at Deere, and he'll be retiring soon."

"Let's be grateful for small blessings," and Hurstwood held up his glass. "And the girls, your sisters, I mean?"

"You're a persistent kind of fella, aren't ye?" Trainer laughed. "Okay! Two girls got married, and I couldn't tell ye now how many kids they have between them; Susan got hitched with a sanitation inspector from Kansas City—that's a fancy name for the poor slob who picks up the garbage—but it's a regular job, good times, bad times, and you get your pay check every two weeks on the dot, rain or shine, and Velma married a policeman, took his sergeant exams as soon as he got the green light, and took to bein' a rising star of the Atherton finest; could be a lieutenant by now, or higher."

"There was a third sister, as I recall," Hurstwood said, shifting in his seat and leaning back. He extended his glass. "Could I have another drink, sir?"

"Sure, why not, and this goes for both of us." Trainer poured out. "Am mighty pleased this here expensive West Point education ain't wasted. You can always count on a West Point man to be able to count to three."

"Thank you, sir!"

"Right, there was a third sister, Katie, and none of us knows for sure where she's now and what she's doing, but someone told Lenie she's in L.A. and doing fine, being a nurse or something like it."

"Why all this mystery?"

"Katie didn't care for us, she called us kids 'pigs' to our faces and she just wanted out. On the day she graduated from high school she got on the bus and headed for L.A.; left a note for Pa and Ma, just a few words that she was leaving and didn't want to stay in touch. I guess," Trainer paused, his eyes roaming the dark walls. "I guess she was . . . she was ashamed of us."

Hurstwood remained silent, and Trainer got up, rubbed the back of his neck, belched, and sat down again.

"I hope to God these days never come back . . ."

Hurstwood leaned forward expectantly from the edge of the chair.

"I mean what took place before the war, folks by the millions out of work, some folks close to starvation, folks broken down in spirit, folks just lost, not knowing where to turn, like helpless kids in an immense black forest with no clearing in sight . . . sure there were all kinds of programs put on the road and maybe they helped others, but they didn't help Pa. Pa worked his fingers to the bone filling out forms after forms and taking 'em to what was called the Recovery Offices in Atherton and Kansas City. They had clerks galore in there, four out of five from out of state and they said there was hope Pa could get his farm back, but failing it he would have a steady job with the federal government. But it all fell through, and Pa and Ma would take anything that came along, temporary like, and it didn't come often, window cleaning, domestic chores, fixing gutters, washing cars. One day, Wilbur and I got a tip they were going to hire next day for the kitchen in a fancy country club in a resort not too far from Atherton—I must've been sixteen then and Wilbur fifteen, me being a year older, so at the crack of dawn we got a lift from a friendly driver of a county car and stood first in line. We got the job dishwashing it was, but it paid real money and some food went with it. Never were two kids so happy! But it only lasted half a day. I'd guess those fancy permanent employees didn't like the way we looked, the way we was dressed, the way we spoke, and the way we smelled.

Anyway, as we were washing pots and pans and the lunch dishes here comes this general manager. Man, he was somethin' to look at; tails, starched white shirt, blue tie, gold-rimmed glasses sticking out of a very commanding face. He turned to us and said—Trainer now began to mince and lisp simultaneously, his manifest enjoyment mounting with each new word—"'We appreciate your coming to help us in the kitchen, boys, but I wonder whether you really belong here, and it might be better for you and for us if you applied to some of the places at the other end of town.' This other end of town, as Mr. General Manager well knew, was where there was an abundance of shacks and one or two very greasy spoons." Trainer now broke into a self-congratulatory laughter, his eyes dancing with mirth, his head moving expressively this way and that to stress a point. "This was my first and only close-like with the higher order of society," he went on, "until I got my battlefield commission and became an officer and a gentleman by act of Congress." He laughed again. "To go back to what I was saying earlier, Mr. Roosevelt did not help Atherton or Jefferson County, Kansas. Maybe he thought he did, but he didn't. Them folks who were down and out in '33 were just as much down and out in 1940, and it wasn't until we were in the war that things started to pick up. That's God's truth!"

"You, sir, and my father might get along just fine," Hurstwood spoke cautiously. "Father couldn't stand FDR, and even today he rarely misses an opportunity of voicing his displeasure at his various policies."

"Is that a fact?" Trainer sounded genuinely amused. "Is that a fact?"

"It undoubtedly is."

"Well, I'll be damned." He crossed over to the window and was peering into the darkness. Then he confronted Hurstwood, exuberant, brimming with pent-up energy, supremely confident. "Drink up, Ted," he hollered.

"There's still some poison left." Hurstwood got up too and stood at attention, glass in hand, keeping one hand on the desk and swaying slightly.

"Nikita!" he babbled out, raising the glass.

"Nikita," Trainer echoed, following suit.

"Now you know all about me, Ted, and this and your previous sneaky re . . . research into my past make you an expert on E.E. Trainer."

"Hardly," Hurstwood gasped as they sat down. "Everyone says you're a happily married man."

"You might say that."

"I haven't had the pleasure of meeting Mrs. Trainer and . . ."

But Trainer waved, stopping him. "We're one of a kind, Beryl's from Gilmore, small town some twenty miles west of Atherton, and she had a real job in Atherton in a wallpaper and paint outfit. I gone there once in '46 being home on leave and kept looking at them rolls of wallpaper that Ma wanted me to check out. And then someone brushed against me on the way out and I stepped aside, knocking down all kinds of boxes and rolls, and the manager came out red-faced and all that and started lecturing me." Trainer returned to his mimicking and lisping manner. "'In the future, Sergeant, you should be more careful when you enter stores and other buildings where the property belongs to others and not to you. We are out of the war now, and we expect civilized behavior from all our customers; you are not storming the enemy where no doubt all kinds of conduct were tolerated. You are back in Kansas, and you should try to conduct yourself in a civilized manner. Hell! . . .' Beryl was standing there quiet-like, she was the cashier, but finally she said, 'Mr. Phillips, this wasn't the sergeant's fault. A customer was leaving in a hurry, and the sergeant just moved to the side to be out of the way and accidentally knocked down these boxes.' Mr. Phillips took another long look at me, hemmed and hawed, and went on again like a goddamn dutch uncle"—Trainer went back to the mincing and lisping—"'There may've been extenuating circumstances here, but I want to make it clear to you, Sergeant, that rowdy behavior will not be tolerated in this store, under any circumstances. We are having a lot of trouble with you fellows coming back after several years in foreign parts where common decency and good manners meant nothing.' And he was off."

"Beryl smiled knowingly, and I thanked her for sticking up for me. Well, I asked her out and one thing led to another. We soon found out we had similar tastes, and we kinda looked at things same like. Oftentimes we didn't even have to speak 'cause we knew we were of the same mind. We got married in August."

As Trainer was winding up, Hurstwood's demeanor underwent a sudden change. His lips were tightly drawn, his jaw thrust forward, his fists clenched, a wild grimace distorting his face.

"What is it?" Trainer asked, leaning toward him.

Hurstwood banged his fist against the desk and cried out, "I want Lucy back," and again at the top of his lungs, "I WANT LUCY BACK!"

"Take it easy, boy, take it easy." Trainer lay a hand on Hurstwood's shoulder. "You'll see her later this year, this is what ye said."

Hurstwood banged the desk again, shook his head violently, and shouted in Trainer's face: "But I don't want to see her in three months, I want to see her now. I want to be with her NOW, NOW, NOW!" And then he was speechless, his head bowed.

"Call her tomorrow, and in the meantime we'd better take you home. Besides"—Trainer glanced at his watch—"it's getting late." He picked up the phone and dialed. "Honey, we need transport. Who? Well it's Lieutenant and me . . . sure we are okay, we could walk all the way to Bradley Village no sweat, but it'd take too damn long . . . sure, we're fine, and we'll drop Hurstwood by the Bachelor Quarters . . . right you are, twenty minutes in front of the Command Building. Thanks, honey," and he hung up.

"My car is in the lot," Hurstwood said very quietly, his head still downcast. "I'll be glad to . . ."

Trainer smiled, fumbling in his breast pocket for another cheroot.

"Transport's on the way, you can pick up your car tomorrow."

The lieutenant straightened himself up in his seat, making every effort to compose himself.

"Sir, I'd like to apologize for my outburst, there is no excuse."

Trainer kept silent for a moment and then said, "You should see the young lady as soon as possible . . . the sooner the better . . . and I hope you'll reconsider . . . I'd like to have you in my outfit."

"Thank you, sir." Hurstwood was close to being his old self, calm, self-possessed.

The two men moved to the window, the lieutenant more unsteadily than the major, and through the cracks in the shutters peered at tiny snowflakes waxing with every second and being buffeted in wide symmetrical streams by the wind.

"I can't hear a robin sing, can you?" Trainer chuckled.

"It's the snowstorm Honigklausen was telling me about."

Trainer nodded, and Hurstwood began to tighten his tie and button his coat.

"I meant to ask you, sir, is Sergeant Honigklausen's health improving?"

"You mean his weight? No, it don't. That treatment he's getting ain't worth a ball of feathers."

"I see." Trainer emptied the ashtrays into the wastepaper basket, threw the empty bourbon bottles into a plastic bag, and reached for his overcoat and hat.

"Let me tell you something, Ted. Honigklausen put in eighteen years in this men's army. He fought in two wars, and he's got a good record. He paid his dues. If he had his way he'd re-enlist for another ten years, but more likely than not the Army won't have him 'cause of his weight problem. I want him to finish his twenty years and get what he's entitled to because that's common decency, and I sure don't want him to be kicked out on a medical before his term is up 'cause a bunch of weirdos with M.D. after their names have pronounced him unfit for duty."

"I understand."

"Got everything?"

"Yes, sir," and Hurstwood opened the office door. As they were walking down the corridor wrapped up in their winter coats, Trainer asked, "You're buddy-buddy with Spelling, ain't you?"

"Yes, our quarters are next to each other."

"He's all for regulations, isn't he Ronny-boy! Would put his own mother under lock and key if she broke the re-gu-la-tions. For him Army Re-gu-la-tions were drawn up not in a smoke-filled room in D.C. with armchair generals farting in their seats, but on Mount Sinai in the presence of the Almighty and all His prophets."

"He's conscientious . . . he means well."

Trainer chuckled. "Spelling would be just fine for some armies, for some armies," he repeated, "not for U.S. Army."

As Hurstwood swung the front door open, a gust of freezing wind blew in their faces. Trainer buttoned his collar and advised Hurstwood to do the same.

"I meant to ask you something, you know Donkers, he worked for you?"

"Bright kid, did excellent job in translating and dealing with the French, and I believe his general performance as Group Clerk is . . . just fine . . ."

"He does bang-out job in all areas, has been of great help to the Group . . . and to me personally. I'm trying to get him an early promotion to Spec IV."

"He deserves it."

"Right, but I've noticed and so have others . . . he's pale, drained-out like, and every time I see him thinner than before."

"Not undernourished, is he, unless he can't stand army chow?"

Trainer was silent and then went on. "Hurstwood, check with Honigklausen when was Donkers' last physical, and if he's just overtired, is he in line for some three-day passes."

"Yes, sir."

Through the fluttering of snowflakes, he and Hurstwood could see a pair of headlights drawing nearer and heard the screeching sound of the brakes being applied as in emergency, the headlights bobbing for a few seconds and then resting easy.

"It's Beryl all right," Trainer whispered, getting a grip on Hurstwood's arm and guiding him towards the waiting car.

Chapter 11

His office invaded by the morning sun through the half-closed shutters forming radiant squares and rectangles of all sizes on the floor and walls, Captain Spelling was busily adding several new books to the already overloaded bookshelves, tidying the papers on his desk, and dusting the furniture. Some months before he had hired an elderly German national, a partly disabled veteran of WWII with irreproachable credentials, to dust his office, polish the floor and furniture, and carry out whatever other tasks might be required to preserve and, if need be, enhance his high standards of neatness and cleanliness. But the man had been a disappointment. Entrusted with the commission of coming once a week for approximately an hour in return for what his employer thought was an adequate recompense, he at times skipped these appointments and at other times shortened them at will. When questioned he would hide behind the language barrier, stare vacantly at Spelling mumbling "No English" and shake his head vigorously whenever Spelling tried to justify his dissatisfaction by word of mouth in English, in pidgin German, or in sign language.

Spelling's irritation had been further exacerbated when he found out that the man apparently knew enough English to plead his case before the Mess Hall personnel to let him have free of charge a portion of the day's unconsumed rations. In consequence, Spelling was himself dusting and polishing on a weekly basis, always hoping that the man would mend his ways, being half-determined to fire him if he did not. He lay down the duster and stepped back. He was immensely pleased with the way his office looked. The desk was not regulation, but solid oak furnished with the coat of arms of the State Baden-Württemberg, engraved in black, yellow, and red on the sides next to the massive legs, purchased for a pittance from a German couple in Kirchenberg on the very day they were emigrating to Australia; in the middle of the tile floor lay an imitation Persian rug displaying "Cyrus routing the Assyrians." The three bookshelves now filled to capacity were neatly divided into sections on U.S. military history, world history, Eastern Europe, engineering lore, and various reference works, one section being particularly bulky: works of all kinds and sizes on communism and the communist conspiracy, most of whose titles he knew by heart.

The walls were covered by maps of West Germany, East Germany, the satellite countries, and the Soviet Union, and in the rare places unclaimed by cartography hung oleographs and posters of Mexico and Brazil. On the very top of each bookshelf stood the family photos—his parents together and some distance away separately, the larger ones showing his father in his Army Reserve uniform and his mother, shears in hand, flanked on both sides by shrubs and flowers, photos of family vacations, birthday and anniversary photos among which figured those of his sister Tricia about to graduate from high school who, he suddenly remembered, astonished her parents by announcing that she had abandoned her intention of going to the state university and had decided on a private college instead to which some of her high school friends were going. This, of course, and the thought was gnawing him now, would place an additional burden on the family financial resources, but Tricia's mind had apparently been made up. Still, he was in no mood to allow anxiety to spoil his morning.

Leaning against the door he now reviewed with immense satisfaction the different objects in his office: the nine West Point photos arranged in threes on top of the three bookshelves, standing in identical places, the less formal family snapshots numbering eighteen also meticulously arranged in threes between and to the front of the other ones, the straight lines of the books on each shelf with no single cover jutting out, the symmetrically arranged papers on his desk, and the two chairs for visitors in front of it at right angles to his desk and flush with its sides. On the walls the maps, the oleographs, and the posters were placed in such a way that the narrow spaces between them were identical in each instance, and no irregularity, however slight, was noticeable. The office had the look of being lived in, but neatly tidily lived in, and order and symmetry reigned.

Smiling joyfully, Spelling at a flash pitted his office against that of the chaplain with its perennial clutter often causing long delays in finding what was needed and against the absolute pigsty answering to the name of the Group Commander's office, which not even the concerted efforts of Honigklausen and Donkers could redeem, and finally against that of the supply officer, his friend Ted Hurstwood, which was sadly unlived in and anonymous. With mounting glee he recalled a scene from the past when the newly arrived chaplain first came to see him and exclaimed, "Why, Ron, this is the neatest and best organized military office I've seen for along time," as he was cordially shaking his hand. And then another image forced itself on his mind jarring but inescapable, of Trainer looming in the doorway, soiled fatigues and all, his red face puffed up probably from consuming a quantity of cheap liquor the night before, the folds in his cheeks thicker than usual, his eyes bleary, his lips inflated, obviously feeling out of place in the company of the two officers, and mumbling, "very fine, very fine," before he came to the point. Spelling winced in revulsion. "What a pig, what a goddamn scumbag," he called out with shrill emphasis, lit a cigarette, and headed for the Group Sergeant's office. As he was about to go inside, a private from Communications, whom he recognized, sidled past him saluting and then marched off double quick.

His enormous frame safely ensconced behind the desk, Sergeant Honigklausen greeted him unctuously, a saccharine smile—as if he kept some all-important vigil—adorning his face.

"I trust you are having a good day, sir," he began, casting a glance at the window. "The weather's getting worse and worse as we speak."

"Thank you, Sergeant," Spelling shot back. "Yes, we're in for it," he added abruptly. What attracted his attention was a narrow brown envelope of the kind used by Communications lying on the desk in front of Honigklausen and partly covered by his large fleshy hand.

"A teletype message I see," he muttered. He leaned over a little, ostensibly looking for an ashtray, and then leaned over in the opposite direction each time trying to catch the name of the addressee; but all he could see was Honigklausen's hand moving gently from left to right and the other way round, blocking the view.

"A teletype message, must be something important," he ventured, feigning indifference.

"It's for the Major, sir, marked urgent and confidential, and I'll deliver it to him as soon as he concludes this here telephone conference."

"Yes, yes, very good, Sergeant."

"Is there anything we can do for you, sir?"

"No, you can't, I dropped by to have a word with Major Trainer, but it'll keep. Thank you, Sergeant," Spelling said, thinking, *You goddamn mountain of putrid lard with the I.Q. of an overgrown louse, you have as much right to be in this army as a syphilitic skunk, and don't you think for a moment that I shall stand idly by. As soon as I become permanent Exec I will make it my business to run you out of this men's army for the good of the red, white, and blue. You will then clean latrines or drain off piss into bottles and sell it at country fairs as a cure for hemorrhoids, and this will be the extent of what you will be called upon to do. Until this time comes enjoy your ill-gotten gains, and the sooner you kick the bucket on account of the fetid toxin in your gut the better.*

"Your wishes are commands to us, sir, and we aim to keep everything shipshape," Honigklausen said, thinking, *You worthless piece of Kraut shit, you don't know your place, and very soon your place won't know you. You're off-beam, boy, and don't know what's in the works; all indications pointing like to there bein' in store a fast promotion to lieutenant colonel for the Major and what follows the arrival hereto of a permanent Exec with the rank of major. You'll have to vacate your position like to which you ain't entitled anyway, and if you're lucky you'll be sent back to the infantry rising in due course to the meritorious office of inspector of field and other like shithouses. But as things stand now do me a favor, Ron, and go and fuck yourself.*

Spelling crossed the Group Sergeant's office to where Donkers was sitting silently at his desk and tapped a finger against it.

"Don't forget those fifteen reports from the companies have to be transcribed and on my desk the day after tomorrow, Donkers."

"They will be, sir, I have the matter in hand."

"Good, I knew you would but thought a reminder wouldn't be out of place," Spelling said, thinking, *You're a bit of a smart ass, Donkers, aren't you, and I know your game. I know all about that mimicking of officers that goes on in the barracks, and they tell me, I have my spies mind you, that you, Donkers, are the ringleader; a bit of a vaudeville on rainy day, eh? Showing to the world your artistic sensibility, eh? You think you're so goddamn smart, college and all, and you take the rest of us—place of honor being naturally reserved for the officers—for nothing better than a bunch of cornballs! I have news for you, my friend; I have my eye on you, and when I catch you stepping out of line, which may be sooner than you expect, I'll throw the book at you. You think Major Trainer will cover for you, but let me inform your stinking little self that Major Trainer may not be with us much longer! So, if you want to stay alive, smart ass, shape up, SHAPE UP!!!*

"It's very kind of you, sir, I appreciate it," Donkers said, thinking, *You goddamn little sub-humanoid dredged out from the vast recesses of the mentally defective, the unbalanced, and those plagued with congenital and incurable forms of infantilism. I understand you click your heels at least a hundred times a day in front of a mirror both as a rite for which you would give your life willingly and as a narcissistic compulsion, that curious behavior defining to a tee your decomposed psyche. The kindest thing one can say about you is that you have the makings of the underling to the underling to the assistant to the assistant to the top boy in those sad periods of world history where tyranny and mayhem are riding high and quantities of little Spellings are clicking their heels and making a mess of things. Anyway, your spell of glory may be coming to a screeching halt because decisions are expected at Army which may land you on your bare ass. If there were even a remote chance of your being curable, I'd recommend solitary and hot and cold baths, but you are too far gone. So, little shithead, why don't you do the human race a favor and shoot yourself quietly in the corner.*

Spelling's hand was on the doorknob, and his head tilted in the direction of Honigklausen.

"Tell Major Trainer I was here, and I'll be back later," he announced curtly, and was gone.

Visibly relieved, Honigklausen half-rose, leaned forward, and cupped his hand around the ear, listening intently to whatever sound might be coming from Trainer's office. Presently his eyes lit up, and he announced both to himself and to Donkers, "That here telephone conference is over." He shuffled his way from behind the desk and, the brown envelope poised fastidiously between the thumb and the middle finger, he knocked on the Group Commander's door.

"What'd you say . . . teletype message from Army! Why, it would sure mean lack of respect if I didn't open it right now and on the double, right, Lester?" Trainer was fumbling for a letter opener, found it, and with one swift stroke ripped the envelope open, and then belched to his heart's content.

"What do we have here?" he sneered, while Honigklausen stood respectfully by.

As he was scanning the message Trainer gave every sign of astonishment followed by more astonishment and finally by sheer delight. "I don't believe it, I don't believe it," he gasped and ordered Honigklausen to bring Donkers in.

"Well, gentlemen, let me read you the latest teletype message received this very morning." He shifted in his seat and began to read slowly, his voice unemotional and subdued:

"FROM: General Patrick C. Ryan
Commanding General
7th U.S. Army

TO: Major E. E. Trainer
Acting Group Commander
16th U.S. Army Engineer Group.

My heartfelt congratulations on your intelligent and sensitive handling of the visits to our command by the French Engineer units in connection with their exhibition of the Mobile-Bridge. You have carried out your duties in a superior manner, and this citation now becomes part of your permanent record!

Signed: Patrick C. Ryan
Commanding General
7th U.S. Army"

"Good news," Donkers' eyes narrowed, "and congratulations, sir."

"The Major deserves every bit of that here citation and my very respectful congratulations," Honigklausen spoke with feeling.

"Thank you both." Trainer threw his legs on top the desk and was looking into space. "I wish once in a while I could figure out what Army is doin' and why it's doin' it."

"In this case it doesn't matter, because they appear to be on your side," Donkers broke in.

"Appear?" Trainer looked up. "That's a carefully chosen word, Donkers."

"It is."

"Is there something you know and we don't?"

"No, sir, I don't know anything concrete." Donkers turned to Honigklausen, "I don't know anything factual that would have a bearing on the matter; if I did I would've reported it to you at once, Sergeant Honigklausen."

"I know it, son, and I think well of your loyalty."

"So." Trainer retrieved his legs and stood up, his enormous haunches pressing against the desk and the wall. "All we have is speculation, and we don't even know if we speculate . . . with the wind or against the wind, right?"

"That's right, sir," Donkers threw in quickly before Honigklausen had the time to reply. "There is no doubt in my mind that General Ryan's citation is sincere and it means what it says. What should be borne in mind is that there's opposition to you, sir, at Army, and the question confronting you now is how strong this opposition will remain in the light of General Ryan's most recent action."

"The way I see it is, if I may put it like with the Major's permission, we just sit and wait, and put the Major's citation to every good use."

Trainer nodded and fixed his sight on Donkers.

"Sergeant Honigklausen understands the situation better than most. If there is an enemy, let him come to us."

Trainer nodded again. "Anyway, I'm mighty proud to be thus recognized by General Ryan." He was silent for a moment and then went on, "I want a memo sent to all those within the Group who helped in one way or another with the Frenchies, expressing my appreciation. Lester, give Donkers the necessary instructions."

"Yes, sir."

Trainer clapped his hands with gusto. "I'd be a liar if I told ye I'm not proud and happy to receive this citation." He beamed. "I am, and to hell with what you guys call the oppo-si-tion." Honigklausen and Donkers beamed in return.

"Say, Sergeant, don't I have a meeting to go to?"

"Absolutely, sir. The Major has a meeting with all the company commanders and their deputies in exactly five minutes."

"You don't say! And what about you, going for coffee and dough-nuts?"

"The Major no doubt remembers I have a meeting of all senior NCOs to attend. In fact, I am chairing it."

"Oh, and it starts . . ."

"In five minutes precisely." Honigklausen finished for him.

"Can we trust the Group Clerk to be left here without supervision, Group Sergeant?" Trainer posed the question, enjoying himself immensely. "Don't break any windows, and don't get pissed while we are away kid, promise?"

"And don't break any furniture either, Dirk," Honigklausen admonished him.

They both heard a vague and qualified affirmation coming from the Group Clerk's lips as they were closing the door behind them.

Left to his own devices Donkers discovered almost at once that he had absolutely no stomach for carrying out any of his duties. He pulled out from the drawer a recent German biography of Richard Wagner and began to read, but after a few minutes put it back. His mind wandered.

Next he became acutely conscious—these bouts of despondency came upon him seldom and irregularly—that for him life without Jonathan was simply not worth living and were he to be condemned to a perpetual separation from his friend he might just as well blow his brains out. The point is—he was asking himself—can I get through the next two and half months? He shrugged and let his mind wander back. He and Jonathan had entered the University in the same fall semester four and half years ago and before long they had become lovers. What followed were three years of bliss, of sharing pads, of living as a devot-ed couple, irked only by the exigencies of student life with its deadlines for papers and reports, the unavoidable midterms and final exams, and the advisability, if nothing else, of maintaining a respectable GPA. They graduated in the same year, and Jonathan—who had been classified 4F because of his poor eyesight—enrolled at once in the graduate school to work on his MA and eventually the PhD in modern European his-tory. There were times when Dirk regretted not following his friend's example and enrolling immediately after the completion of his under-graduate studies in the graduate school, but this was the time when his father found out that he was "a pervert and a criminal" and cut him off completely. Had he persevered he could have in one way or other obtained the money for at least the first year as graduate, but he was hurt and disoriented. His mother was gravely ill, and he wanted a reprieve from what the others were doing to him.

When the draft notice arrived he took it philosophically rather suspecting that he would be stationed in the Continental United States, and when in due course he was sent to Germany he accepted it, expressing to Jonathan and to others his firm belief that the foreign adventure on which he was now embarking would be a kind of merry escape into the unknown, salutary for both the spirit and the body. In Basic Training and in the second eight weeks he was in frequent contact with Jonathan, and in Fort Dix just before being shipped to Germany he finagled from an accommodating lieutenant a twenty-four-hour pass that allowed them to spend time together off base. Since that momentous day Jonathan flew to Germany only once, between semesters, eight months before—he now had an assistantship and his free time was at a premium—and though they wrote to each other regularly and on some occasions spoke by phone, the separation was proving unendurable to Dirk and from all accounts unendurable to Jonathan. "Two and half months to go," he whispered, his face contorted by a wild grimace. "Oh Lord, give me the strength, and give me the patience! But do not give me humility because humility is a worthless commodity in this world of Yours!"

A sharp ring of the telephone on Sergeant Honigklausen's desk interrupted his train of reminiscences.

"16th Engineer Group, PFC Donkers, Group Clerk speaking."

"This is Major Simmons from General Vickers' office at 7th Army Headquarters; I'd like to speak to Major Trainer."

"I'm sorry, sir, Major Trainer is at a meeting; he will not be back until 1300 hours."

"I see . . . is Sergeant Honigklausen there?"

"No, sir, the Group Sergeant is also at a meeting." With difficulty Donkers restrained a chuckle. "He too will be back at 1300 hours. Would you like me to connect you to the Exec Officer?"

"Who's that?"

"Captain Spelling, sir."

"No . . . that won't be necessary." (A short pause.) "Donkers, I'll leave a message with you for Major Trainer, and I'll like it to be delivered to him personally as soon as he is back in his office."

"Yes, sir."

"This message is direct from General Vickers, and it is confidential and has top priority."

"I understand, I'll see to it that the major gets it right away."

"Good . . . if you have pencil and pad ready. I'll give it to you now."

"Please begin, sir."

Donkers was writing now on a pad, and Simmons was going at just the right speed to allow him to get everything down. When he had finished dictating, he said, "And now I want you to read the entire message back to me. Go slowly."

"Yes, sir," and Donkers proceeded to read the message, pausing at the end of each sentence and identifying the punctuation marks.

"Good, very good," Simmons said. "That's all, thank you, Donkers," and he hung up.

Donkers placed the message in an envelope, sealed it, and put it in the back of the center drawer. He got up and, his mind straining to make sense of what he had just heard, he sniffed the air repeatedly and kicked the floor with the tip of his shoe, aiming at the nonexistent pebbles in his path. He walked over to the window and was contemplating the sleet and snow coming down heavily, his mind ceaselessly at work.

Chapter 12

He was back in the Group Sergeant's office shortly before 1300 hours, everybody else being still at lunch. He waited. Presently he heard the heavy stamping sound of feet hammering the floor at irregular intervals that spelled the advance of one man only.

"Hi there, young man," Trainer hollered, swinging the door wide open. He stood there exuding good fellowship, grinning like an over-size Cheshire cat and blowing the inevitable clouds of smoke.

"Why that long face, Donkers? Anything the matter?"

Donkers told him of the message.

"I see," Trainer said, scratching his neck. "You'd better come to my office and read me the damned thing."

"Major Simmons was stressing that this message is direct from General Vickers, that it is confidential, and has top priority," Donkers reported, now sitting in front of the major, the message pad in hand.

"Yeah, yeah, yeah." Trainer's response was one of boredom and indifference. "Let's have it."

Donkers cleared his throat:

"FROM: General Trenton Lee Vickers
Deputy Commander

7th U.S. Army

TO: Major E. E. Trainer
Acting Group Commander
16th U.S. Army Engineer Group

It came to me as a considerable surprise that you failed to seek instructions from my office in dealing with Major Fergusson and other French officers associated with the Mobile-Bridge project. You had been informed by messages under my signature that in undertaking any pertinent action it was incumbent upon you to consult with me and my office. Instead you took it upon yourself to deal with the French forces on your own and without proper authorization. While no doubt well intentioned, the steps you have taken were, in some instances, in direct contravention of the established policies of the U.S. Army with reference to the French forces.

End of message."

"Is that all?" Trainer broke out with a crack in his voice.

"That's all."

"What the hell is going on! What the hell is going on!" Trainer turned sideways in his armchair so that he now faced the floor and was biting furiously at his cheroot.

"What the hell!" he repeated. "Find Hurstwood and ask him to come here at once. I'd like to have him here when we . . ." he left the rest unfinished.

"Lieutenant Hurstwood is in the field with C Company; they are testing new equipment."

"In this weather?"

"The lieutenant wanted to test it in adverse conditions, they won't be back before dark."

A faint, self-protective smile formed itself on Trainer's face. "It looks it's just you and me, pardner! We'll see. First question: can this wait till tomorrow, or the next day?"

"No, it can't." Donkers was looking Trainer straight in the eye and speaking with finality. "This calls for immediate action."

"I agree, and I think you and I are on the same page, so there ain't no need to waste words." He was clenching his teeth and thinking.

"Does the citation of the kind you received from General Ryan normally call for an answer? Are you supposed to acknowledge, respond, thank?" Donkers asked.

"Beats me, I haven't seen too many of 'em." Trainer was painstakingly searching his memory, but it was clear he was genuinely ignorant on the subject. He looked startled and confused.

"If you were to thank General Ryan by teletype, sir, it wouldn't be a violation of the military protocol, would it?"

Trainer was still confused, and in addition he was sailing in uncharted waters. "I couldn't tell you, Donkers. I guess it wouldn't be." He clenched his teeth again, the wrinkles on his face deepening, and he held up a hand as a sign that he did not want to be interrupted. At last he spurted it out, his old vigor returning.

"No . . . it wouldn't be! Why the hell should plain thank you be what you call a vio-lat-tion of military protocol?"

"I have a plan."

"Go on."

"You should send the following message to General Ryan. I wrote it a short while ago, and send it as soon as possible. Every minute counts." At a nod from Trainer he went on:

"TO: General Patrick C. Ryan
Commanding General
7th U.S. Army

FROM: Major E.E. Trainer
Acting Group Commander
16th U.S. Army Engineer Group

I thank you for your kind words and the citation received today. It is an honor to serve under you in the 7th United States Army. We in the 16th U.S. Army Engineer Group fully understand that nowadays U.S. Army units face a variety of new tasks, among which cooperation with our European allies is of utmost importance. Rest assured that the 16th Engineer Group will always be equal to any challenge which may present itself. At all times we shall carry out our duties in a manner consistent with the glorious tradition and high accomplishments of the United States Army."

"Next, in an hour or so you should call General Ryan's aide . . . who is . . ."

"Lloyd Anderson, Colonel Anderson."

"Do you know him personally, sir?"

"Sure, I know Lloyd, and he's a straight shooter."

"You should call him and express your astonishment at General Vickers' message. But I wouldn't be too specific, and don't tell him too much, though you might say that General Vickers had given free hand to regimental and Group Commanders in various messages, and that you simply followed orders. But make certain that your teletype has been duly received and logged, and again through Colonel Anderson thank General Ryan profusely for his citation."

"What are we trying to do?"

"We are trying to neutralize Vickers' telephone message, better than that, we are trying to tell that world that it has never been sent, that in effect it doesn't exist, and should it give the appearance of existence its contents are to be considered questionable or untrue."

Trainer was for a moment lost in thought and at last he said, slowly stressing each word, "Send the message, and I'll call Lloyd in an hour or so." Then he turned towards Donkers, his face still tense and his manner rigid as if he were determined to keep himself on the alert, ready for any contingency, "Thank you, Donkers."

From the shuffling, sighing, coughing, hemming, and hawing next door it became obvious that Sergeant Honigklausen was back. As Donkers was leaving, the Group Sergeant put his head through the door and announced with mellow officiousness, "The Major wouldn't believe how drawn out those meetings of the NCO Council can be. Why this one went on for several hours, and it took a working lunch to bring it to an end . . ."

"Sure, sure, I understand, Lester," Trained laughed. "When I was a sergeant we'd stretch out our meetings till God knows when to get some shut-eye, or work in a poker game. Everything is understood."

"I meant to speak to the Major about Donkers' replacement . . ."

"Oh yes? Just a moment, Lester. I gotta take a leak, be right back," and Trainer disappeared in haste. Immediately and keeping a watchful eye on Trainer's office, Honigklausen waddled to his desk and picked up the telephone.

"Sergeant Sampler please, this is Sergeant Honigklausen . . . Larry,

Lester here, I couldn't tell you at the meeting . . . the next unscheduled inspection of your Mess Hall will be on Tuesday, April 12th. They'll come around 0900 hours and turn your place inside out, but the principal targets of this here inspection will be your electrical equipment, your refrigerators, freezers, and the like . . . You're welcome, and I'll be talking to you soon." Honigklausen replaced the receiver with dignity, his chest swelling, his exacting mission accomplished.

"Isn't it a little early to be getting a replacement for Donkers?" Trainer was saying a few minutes later, his feet in their habitual place on his desk, and betraying little, if any, interest in what Honigklausen was unfolding. "The boy has seven more months to go . . ."

"With the Major's permission it's now six months, and he'll be on leave for close to three weeks in June—taking his accumulated leave all in one lump, he's put for it already and it's approved."

"So?" Trainer was yawning and making no attempt to hide it.

"Donkers' job is kinda important and at times tricky like, if the Major catches my meanin', and we need a good man to take his place . . ."

"And you have a likely candidate?"

"Yes, sir . . . and I want him to come to us a little earlier so he can learn the job under my . . . and Donkers' supervision, fill in for Donkers when he is on leave, and take over when Donkers is gone."

"If you want him and think he'll do, fine, who is he?"

"Vallejo's the name, a Mexican kid now working in the Motor Pool, doing clerical chores; he's been to clerical school, and Carl, Sergeant Steiner that is, is giving me good reports on him." Honigklausen waved before Trainer a sheaf of papers. "If the Major would like to look at 'em?"

Trainer waved them away.

"He's a good kid, hard working . . ." Honigklausen paused, his head high in the air, ". . . and respectful, respectful . . . He told me his folks would be mighty proud if he got to be Group Clerk."

"Well, if you want him, that's fine with me." Trainer began to yawn again but checked himself. "Wait, but we can't have him filling out reports in Mexican. Does he speak English?"

"Sure does," Honigklausen had his answer ready, "he was born in Taos, New Mexico."

When Donkers came back to the office, he at once told Trainer that his message had been sent and, as he waited, had been received, confirmed, and logged. There was nothing else to do now but resume his daily duties, monotony of monotonies, drudgery of drudgeries, to which he turned with unmistakable reluctance. In the middle of the afternoon Hastings arrived unexpectedly, cheery as ever, full of small talk, chattering away about the forthcoming conference of army chaplains, his wife's shopping expeditions, Switzerland, and a hundred other topics, the very paradigm of geniality. As he was about to leave, he came over to Donkers' desk, and beckoning to him to remain seated, asked again whether the Group Clerk had found someone suitable to take the place of the present assistant who—Hastings made a very deliberate point of it—was turning out to be less and less satisfactory by the hour. With regret Donkers informed the chaplain that he had found no such person.

Shortly before 1700 hours as both he and Honigklausen were clearing their desks the latter, a fatherly smile ennobling his countenance, inquired about the leave.

"You've got somethin' of a leave coming up, don't ye? Almost three weeks long!"

"That's right, Sarge."

"Well, you deserve it, son, all this work you've been putting in."

"Thank you, Sergeant Honigklausen."

"Teaming up with a chick?" Honigklausen asked conspiratorially, his eyes atwinkle and delighted with himself at using the lingua franca of the new generation. "With one of them luscious Minnesota blondes?" he went on tauntingly.

"Nothing so exciting, I'm afraid, Sarge. I'm teaming up with an old college pal, and he and I will do some sightseeing."

The fatherly smile came once again to dominate the sergeant's countenance. "Very proper, the way it should be," he articulated sententiously, "your leave's still two months away, but you have my best early wishes on it."

Later, after Donkers had left, Honigklausen looked at some of his private correspondence, which he kept in his desk, and decided that certain letters had to be answered soon. He was very comfortable in his armchair, unwilling to move, but it was well after 1700 hours, and it was time to head for his quarters. Resignedly he began the slow process of standing up when the telephone rang, and soon he was rapidly scribbling down a message given to him by a fast speaking woman. Once on his feet he trotted as promptly as he could to Captain Spelling's office but found it locked. He trotted to the main entrance, and although it was snowing heavily he stepped outside, casting quick glances this way and that in search of a familiar figure. He almost gave up when he noticed Captain Spelling leaving the Motor Pool and making his way towards the Mess Hall. He began to trot in his direction, waving his arms, and shouting, "Captain Spelling, Captain Spelling," the thick snow wetting his head and getting into his eyes. He saw Spelling halt in his tracks, and drawing closer he detected a chilly expression on his face which he was now to confront.

"Captain Spelling, I've been looking for you everywhere," he gasped, utterly out of breath.

"Well, now that you found me, Sergeant, what can I do for you?"

"Not longer than a few minutes ago a message came for you from a Mrs. Claire Aldridge. She's been trying to reach you at your quarters but without success. The message is about travel. Please call her right away. She said it's very urgent—she stressed it. I wrote down the number, etc." Still gasping, Honigklausen handed Spelling a wet slip of paper.

Against the falling snow the telltale blush was hardly perceptible on Spelling's cheeks, but it was there. He stood stiffly about, at first lost for words, and then glaring at Honigklausen with a mixture of fury and contempt.

"I thought the Captain might like to have this message right away," Honigklausen put in obligingly, his entire figure getting whiter and wetter with every passing second.

"Right," Spelling shot back, "you did the right thing!" and he walked away.

Late the same evening Spelling called Hurstwood. "Ted, Ron here . . . Listen, could you lend me some green stuff till payday . . . ? Thanks, thanks a lot, old buddy."

Chapter 13

Robert Hastings flattened his face on the wheel, pressed the accelerator to the limit, and kept turning the dial on his transistor radio. The call for help from the driver of a German school bus came on again giving the bare facts and the location, just as it did three minutes before when he was jumping into an army truck on base. Using his very rudimentary knowledge of German he had nevertheless identified the location then, and now hearing it again he was convinced he was rushing in the right direction. Unexpectedly, the announcement was repeated by American Radio in English, once again giving pertinent information, and Hastings was no longer in doubt as to where precisely the accident had taken place. He made a sharp left turn onto a narrow unpaved road which was a shortcut to the river, and extracting the last ounce of energy from the jolting and swaying vehicle he raced forward. In a matter of seconds the high beams tearing across the evening darkness enabled him to recognize the river bank, and right in the middle of his field of vision a large unassorted mass, square or rectangular, was sticking out of the water. Hastings stopped the truck on the bank and jumped out. The front half of the school bus was in the water and was sinking fast, the unconscious driver slouched over the wheel, bleeding cut on his forehead. But the rear was held fast by a protruding rock, and through the dim windows he could see the children, some of them submerged in water and ice, some straining bravely upward, others clinging to the backs of seats, and still others in a state of shock lying immobile in the aisle or leaning against the sides of the bus. The windshield had been smashed, water and fragments of ice pouring inside and the two doors, one on each side, half open, their levers out of control, let more water and ice in.

Hastings jumped into the icy water and swam towards the front end of the bus, calculating that the time of impact, the bus plunging into the river after careening from the road to the riverbank, must have been only a few short minutes before. With the help of a jack from the truck he managed, after initial difficulty, to pry one of the doors open, and he climbed inside the bus, the water level rising dangerously. Speaking in English, incorporating the few German words he knew, and relying heavily on sign language and exaggerated gestures, he told the children to stand on the backs of the seats and hang onto the leather handles attached to the ceiling, exhorting the more energetic among them to try to open some of the windows. Most of the children, who he thought were between the ages of seven and eleven, responded at once, and he smiled at them and patching up a phrase in German uttered it in a quiet and reassuring tone of voice, "*Zuviel Wasser hier, besser auf dem Ufer*," so as not to alarm them.

At once he saw broad and subdued smiles on the faces of boys and girls, most of them shivering and coughing, and they cried out in unison, proud and delighted, "*Zuviel Wasser hier, besser auf dem Ufer.*"

Hastings addressed them again, but this time in English because his German vocabulary was rapidly being exhausted.

"Two at a time, one under each arm, and cling to me," and as he was saying it, a boy who was undoubtedly one of the oldest children in the bus translated his words into German and another boy joined in.

Hastings spoke again: "The youngest first, and girls before boys," which provoked a tumultuous reaction from the male sex, Hastings being unable to translate it word for word but understanding its meaning to a tee which rendered into the American vernacular was on the order of "Why do girls get all the breaks?"

With the help of the older children a door was immediately pushed open, and Hastings with a girl under each arm, slid into the river and swam and waded to the bank. Returning at once for another pair and then another and another, he heard the siren and saw four U.S. Army ambulances being parked on the bank, medics darting out of them with blankets and large thermos bottles. In a matter of minutes most of the children were safely on the bank, several of the oldest braving the waves by themselves, and the medics wrapping them up and distributing hot drinks. Hastings cast one last glance on the bus and saw it being submerged. He jumped into the river again and, followed by the medics, swam to the front. After numerous attempts the three of them pulled out the driver still bleeding but conscious now. He was also shivering and coughing and received immediate medical attention.

Hastings, once more on firm ground, wearily sat down and reached for a cigarette, but his pack in the breast pocket had been reduced to a semi-liquid lump with bits of ice embedded in it, and a medic lit a cigarette and put it between his lips. The sergeant in charge of the U.S. ambulances came up to Hastings and said, "We are going to take the children to the German hospital in Kirchenberg. They should be examined by doctors."

"Of course, Sergeant."

"And you need medical attention too, Captain."

"It will keep."

"No, it won't," and he pointed to a jeep heading towards them. "That's Dr. Evans. He'll take you to the Army Medical Center in Weiningen, and here are the blankets and more hot drinks."

"Thank you, Sergeant. Could I say good-bye to the kids?"

"So long as you don't keep them up half the night." The sergeant smiled. "Go ahead, Chaplain."

As Hastings waved to the children in the four ambulances, now comfortably wrapped up in blankets and savoring their hot drinks, he heard them sound off joyfully one set of voices after another: "*Zuviel Wasser hier, besser auf dem Ufer.*"

He smiled, waved again, and walked over to where Dr. Evans was standing. The American ambulances were already racing towards Kirchenberg, and as the two of them were getting into the jeep they saw two German police cars and an ambulance pull up.

/   /   /

Donkers, half asleep, was conscious of someone shaking him by the shoulders, of the overhead lights being turned on, and of a loud shrill voice droning on and on something he could not understand. He could not tell if this was a dream or if he was already awake. As the shaking and the droning continued he raised his head, yawned, and rubbed his eyes. Standing over him was Captain Spelling, stern and commanding.

"Get up, dress and report on the double to Major Trainer's office," he ordered.

"What's the time, what's going on?" Donkers was mumbling and yawning.

"This doesn't concern you, PFC, I am giving you a direct order!"

"Awe right," Donkers muttered.

"What!!!"

"Yes, sir," and he began to fumble for his clothes, one leg on the floor and bending forward, his long arms stretched to the utmost, groping in the air like a blind man cutting for himself a path through a field of invisible obstacles. In his office Trainer was sitting stiffly behind his desk and Spelling, Hurstwood, and Honigklausen were standing around him.

Trainer nodded at Donkers and cleared his throat, "Let me review the situation one more time for the benefit of Lieutenant Hurstwood and PFC Donkers who are joining us presently. At 2045 hours Captain Hastings heard a call for help on his transistor radio from the driver of a German school bus taking the children home after a rehearsal of the Easter pageant in Kirchenberg. Visibility and road conditions being poor the bus careened from the road to the riverbank four kilometers east of the town and plunged headlong into the river. The Padre was there within minutes after the impact. He jumped into the river, managed to get into the bus which was sinking fast, and got the children out, swimming and wading with them to the bank, two kids at a time. It's a miracle he saved them all, and God only knows how he did it. He also pulled out the driver, who'd been badly hurt and partly immobilized. I got a call from the O.D., and at once dispatched four of our ambulances. They drove the kids to the hospital in Kirchenberg, and a call was made to me from that Kraut hospital nearly half an hour ago that most of the kids are doing fine and only three are running a fever and will be kept in. Captain Hastings insisted on staying on the scene until the last German kid and the driver were taken away, and only then did he permit the medics to drive him to the field hospital from which he will be taken this morning to the U.S. hospital at Army. There were twenty-four German kids on this bus, ages seven to eleven. Any questions?"

"Not a question, but an information item, sir." Trainer nodded to Spelling.

"When Captain Hastings jumped into that truck in the Motor Pool and drove off, he failed to sign for it. Any officer taking a vehicle from the Motor Pool must sign for it, it's regulations, sir. Captain Hastings waved the sentry away and drove off at what the sentry reported was excessive speed. Not signing for the vehicle is a violation of Army regulations, sir," Spelling thrust his jaw forward. "I thought this should be reported."

For a very long moment Trainer was observing Spelling without saying anything, his face expressionless, his hands absolutely still and spread out on the desk.

"I'm putting Lt. Hurstwood in charge of this operation, with PFC Donkers as his interpreter, translator, and general assistant," he resumed in a level voice, and then leaning towards Honigklausen, addressed him with a straight face as one addresses a figure of importance. "Can you spare your clerk for a couple of days, Sergeant?"

"Might be able to, sir, might be able to . . . valuable as he is." Honigklausen was in his element, wheeling and dealing. "I'll borrow one of the company boys for a filler, we'll manage."

"Good. Tomorrow and next day there may be German newspapers calling, and Army will have to be kept abreast. A trip to that German hospital will be under consideration, speaking to the parents of would-be victims and the rest of the PR stuff will also have to be dealt with. All of it is now in Lt. Hurstwood's knapsack, and you'll let me know, Lieutenant, if you need me in one capacity or another during this operation."

"I certainly will, sir."

"From now on all inquiries, all matters pertinent to what happened to Captain Hastings and the German children on that bus are to be referred to Lt. Hurstwood . . ." He was going to add something, but Spelling interjected.

"Sir, as the Group Exec Officer . . ."

But Trainer cut him short, ". . . You have a good deal to do, and I don't want to drive you away from your regular duties."

"I understand, sir." Spelling's face was redder than at the best of times.

"Okay," Trainer smacked his lips and turned to Honigklausen. "Sergeant, I want a general formation on the parade ground at 1715 hours today. Every swinging dick, and I don't want to hear goddamn excuses, understand. I'll address the troops, tell them what happened 'cause they are entitled to know what one of their officers did, and how he did it. We are all in the same boat, and that's God's truth."

"It'll be done as the Major orders." Honigklausen bowed his head and then stood briskly at attention.

"This covers it, I believe," Trainer's controlled voice rose once again over the oppressive silence. He glanced at his watch. "It's almost 0300 hours. Try to get some sleep if you can, and all of us are on duty again at 0800 hours sharp. Lt. Hurstwood, you'd probably want a word with Donkers." Hurstwood nodded.

"Good night, gentlemen," and Trainer made ready to leave.

Chapter 14

His body lamely absorbing overdoses of caffeine, the scanty sleep of the previous several nights making his eyes dim and watery, and his bones aching from cold and physical exertions, Donkers all of a sudden became brisk and full of vigor, a roguish smile breaking out all over his weary face. He fitted a sheet of paper into the typewriter and began to type.

Dear Jonathan,

Your last letter received and let me speak first to what is on page one: I am coming round to the same view you hold, and although you may be ahead of me in the final analysis, we now share the same deep commitment. You may remember that over the years there has always been at the back of my mind a sense of guilt followed by something akin to hopelessness, much more so in me than in you because I felt we were beyond the pale and damned, yes, irrevocably damned. I was hoping to find consoling and encouraging words in the writings of St. Paul, in Luther and Melanchthon, and elsewhere, but I didn't find any. The verse from Leviticus was always hanging over me, a dire reminder of what God had ordained. But in the last few weeks my views on the subject have undergone a drastic change, and now we are one. Since we were created in this way, we should remain true to ourselves and take every advantage of our own heredity to progress towards the fullest realization of our individual potentialities. Gradually—there was no breaking point—I began to experience a sense of relief, of liberation, until I could say: here I stand being what I am, do not try to change me, and I'll do my utmost to lead the good and decent life. Currently too, the traditional biblical and religious injunctions in general, and the traditional societal injunctions with regard to what you and I are, became less and less relevant to me, until I saw them for what they really are—outdated and prejudicial notions, worthless yet capable of doing infinite harm.

On page one of your letter you also say that in the future we ought to fight for a better understanding, for tolerance on the part of others. Again I agree. This is our obligation because in so doing we shall be fighting for justice and decency and against the dregs of Former Ages which have a way of corrupting the mores and the laws of today.

I believe I mentioned it in the course of our brief telephone conversation the other day, namely that some time ago I sent all the necessary forms to the graduate school, and the application for the assistantship to Philosophy. It's in the works apparently, and if all goes well I'll be a grad student as of September. "Long live, Student Prince." My two-year contract with Uncle Sam about which I was not consulted beforehand expires on September 4, and I am counting the days. I have two charts on the wall, marking the passage of time, one for my discharge, and the other more immediate and urgent for our vacation which is due to begin in less than two months. That reminds me, we ought to get a decent pad beginning fall semester; something a little more . . . civilized than in the olden days. Do you remember that apartment on Elm we shared several years ago, with that odious woman dropping in at uncivil hours "to see how the boys were getting on?" Hopefully the bitch is in another world by now, but if not she ought to be eschewed. You can chew on it, ha, ha, ha!!!

And now for the local dirt: you have the gist of the Hastings story, our esteemed chaplain forcing his way onto the immortality sweepstakes. His saving the German children became no less than a cause célèbre. For the last five days Hurstwood and I have been issuing all kinds of press releases, answering scores of telephone calls, talking to our people and to the Germans—hectic days. The Stars and Stripes *sent a creep who went poking around the barracks for what he called "background material" until Hurstwood told him in no uncertain terms that the base was off-limits to him and the only information he was going to get was from him, Lieutenant Hurstwood, and from no one else. We had various American papers asking for facts and* The Boston Globe *already printed a nifty piece about Captain Hastings. We visited him in the hospital, of course. He has double pneumonia but his condition is stable as of this morning and, by the way, he was moved to the U.S. Hospital at Wiesbaden, which has better medical facilities. At Army hospital he received a stream of visitors, Generals Ryan, Vickers, etc. etc. and a no-nonsense nurse told us that if this continues she'll put her foot down because after all the captain is entitled to some shut-eye like everybody else. A deputation of German civic leaders and politicians had called on Ryan expressing their thanks and admiration, and our own Major Trainer received the grateful Bürgermeister of Kirchenberg together with the parents of some of the saved children. Everybody has jumped on the wagon, and continues to do so, irrespective of nationality, and not meaning to sound cynical, right now this is the thing to do.*

Hurstwood is good at dealing with people. When he spoke to the generals and the colonels I thought he struck just the right balance between military courtesy and his own self-assertiveness as the man in charge. Most of the Germans liked him, and many regretted that they had to communicate with him through an interpreter. Hurstwood told me that he possesses what amounts to an anti-talent for modern languages. He had tried his hand at various times at French and Spanish, but in each instance the mission was aborted. On the other hand, when he was at Choate—a shelter from the rain for young gentlemen of fortune—he took a good deal of Latin and developed a passion for it. One evening this week standing on a chair—he explained that according to the classical precepts the orator should be poised above the crowd—he delivered nearly half of a Ciceronian oration and followed it with lengthy excerpts from Virgil. I'd like to see him use his Latin lore on Trainer one of these days, of a Saturday night preferably!

By the way, Hurstwood is the one who is resigning his commission. To go back to page one of yours: a new dawn is breaking, and to hell with Leviticus 18:22!

Stay well,
Dirk

Chapter 15

In the next few days the celebratory activity attendant upon Captain Hastings' heroic rescue of the children and his hospitalization has somewhat abated. Long telephone conversations were still being held between Hurstwood and Trainer on one side and Army and the U.S. Embassy in Bonn on the other, but there were fewer questions to answer and fewer visitors and reporters. Chief U.S. Army Chaplain sent a congratulatory telegram to Hastings, which was duly printed in *The Stars and Stripes*. Colonel Lloyd Anderson had called Trainer the day after the rescue reviewing the possibility of promotion of Captain Hastings to major, and Trainer expressed himself strongly in its favor. Above all, and to everyone's satisfaction, the bulletins from Wiesbaden testified to Hastings' stable condition and to his being on the mend. But as the good news came daily, the bad weather persisted. After the avalanches of wet snow came the torrential rains mingled with sleet and hail and puddles of water, rimmed with irregular white designs or semi-transparent fragments of ice, were seen everywhere. Shortly after 1700 hours Donkers said good-bye to Lt. Hurstwood and was walking along the corridor past Honigklausen's office. Through the crack in the door he heard two voices, unmistakably those of the sergeant and the major, and he came to a standstill.

"Bob's days as army chaplain are over," Trainer was saying. "He'll be sent stateside to the Pentagon most likely to minister to armchair generals and their half-witted wives . . . Courtney may like it . . . I don't know if Bob will. It'll be martini street for both of them."

"Well, that's the way the Army rewards its gutsy sons, kicking them upstairs, it's always been like this if the Major cares to go back in time," Honigklausen commented, warming to the subject.

"True," Trainer's voice was heard again, followed by a belch.

"I'd say all things considered like, Captain Hastings would be of greater use to the Army right here in Krautland . . ." There was a pause, "'cause of the goodwill he . . . has . . . ge . . . gen . . . generated."

"You have a point, Lester, but the Army don't think like that . . . that would be too sensible-like, that ain't the Army way."

Donkers moved on. As he was leaving the Command Building, a figure wrapped up to the gills, a black box held by a gloved hand on his side, was carefully placing his feet on the path leading away from the parking lot. Donkers recognized Chuck Miller.

"Well, if it ain't Dirk the magician," the barber intoned with some surprise. "What the hell are you doing in these parts? I hear you're hob-nobbing with the brass."

"Just waiting for a cab," Donkers answered modestly.

"Sure, sure," Miller picked up the thread. "But I can tell you this, fella, the business is picking up. When you gave my name to Trainer whenever it was, it may have started a winning streak . . . since then I've gained six new customers, regular customers mind you, all officers. I do them in their offices or in their quarters, and if it's the latter the wife brings me coffee and cookies after the shearing, if there is a wife, that is," he laughed. "If it's just a floozy, no coffee, no cookies, but I may be ahead in the tipping department." He laughed again.

"Well, glad to hear it, Chuck."

"That lunatic who jumped into the freezing waters, is he getting any better?"

"By all accounts yes, on the way to complete recovery."

"I'd like to ask somebody, not you because you wouldn't know the answer, but somebody else, what does make a regular guy go bananas, just like that?" And Miller, his thick scarf wrapped partly around his mouth, his collar upturned, and the winter coat buttoned to the last button, resumed his walk intoning again, "Stay in touch, Dirk, stay in touch."

After dinner Donkers read again the letters from his mother's attorney and Brent and made some calculations. Then he had a long conversation with Phil, the company clerk of A Company, mostly about baseball and the season ahead. It was now nearly 2000 hours, and he decided that he would spend the rest of the evening reading that new and much touted biography of Wagner but remembered that he had left it in Honigklausen's office. A raincoat draped over his head and shoulders, he ran to the Command Building, unlocked the office door and slumped onto his chair wholly out of breath, his face shining with rain. He reached for the book in the drawer. Yes, all the reviewers, German and foreign, had bestowed much praise upon it, and in addition some of them advanced the view that the author had ushered in a new era in the art of German biography by treating a national icon in a detached and slightly ironic manner, neither blindly encomiastic nor mercilessly censorious—the very via media of biography. He clutched the book in his hand and was about to make a run for it when the telephone on Honigklausen's desk gave its shrill, inimitable ring. He identified himself and took the message, his head bowed, his lips compressed. His eyes roamed the walls for no reason and then he dialed.

"Mrs. Trainer, I'm sorry to disturb you at this hour. This is Donkers, Group Clerk. Could I speak to the major? It's urgent . . ."

"Sure, Donkers, I'll get him for you."

"Sir, I'm afraid I have some bad news. A minute ago I took a message for you from the U.S. Army Hospital at Wiesbaden. Captain Hastings died at 1907 hours today. Further information can be obtained starting tomorrow at 0900 hours from Colonel Warrenburg, Chief of Medicine at that hospital."

Chapter 16

Donkers, a copy of the local paper *Kirchenberger Blatt* on his knee, was facing Trainer who was lounging behind the desk. He was translating, and Trainer was paying close attention to every word. Clearing his throat he announced, "Here's the last paragraph," and went on, "The name of Captain Robert Makepeace Hastings, the gallant American officer who saved twenty-four of our children from almost certain drowning, will not be forgotten in the town of Kirchenberg, it will not be forgotten in the State Baden-Württemberg or in West Germany as a whole; nor, for that matter, will it be forgotten in any part of the world where decency and honor still reign. Like a soldier that he was, Captain Hastings gave his life in the higher cause of humanity . . . a soldier who . . ."

Trainer was shifting uneasily in his seat making little drumming noises with his tongue and lips. "Why the hell do the Krauts call Bob a soldier, an officer?" he exploded. "Bob was a chaplain, he never fired a shot unless chasing jackrabbits in downtown Boston; his business was with sin . . ." He stopped and relit the cheroot. "Some armies have commissars and some have chaplains, and I couldn't tell which is worse. Back in Korea we had a young chaplain for a while, clean-cut, well-bred, mama's dream but his nerves were bad, and he couldn't stand the shelling, so he spent most of the time in the fartsack; we used to take him tea, he liked hot tea with extra sugar."

"Do you want me to go on, sir?"

"Sure, sure, I didn't tell ye to stop. Did I?"

"Not in so many words."

"Well?"

". . . a soldier who was not afraid of death and who put his own life on the line because . . ."—Donkers was slowing down, searching in his mind for the closest English words—"his sense of duty and the officer's code were for him inviolable." He folded the paper.

"It's more important for the Germans that Captain Hastings was an officer than a chaplain," he said. "You know, the European or, more specifically, the German outlook about the officer corps, it being the pride of the nation as it were, much more so with them than with us."

Trainer shrugged and pulled a face. "Yeah, yeah, I heard something like that once before."

"You know that the city fathers here in Kirchenberg want to name a street after Captain Hastings and the West German Chancellor was on the phone to General Ryan."

Trainer nodded. "I read your memo, Donkers; poor Bob, he kinda didn't take kindly to having a lot of fuss made over him," he added pensively. Then he turned towards Donkers, his rigid furrowed face keeping Group Clerk under unremitting surveillance, as if he wanted to extract from him the final and definitive answers about Hastings' death, answers to all his questions, explanations of all the reasons why Hastings had to die.

"What was Bob trying to prove by jumping into that icy water and savin' those Kraut kiddies, what was he trying to prove?" His voice was filled with fury. "He left a widow and two small children. What the hell was he trying to prove?" Donkers was silent. "What possessed you, Bob, to do a thing like this, ye should've known better Bob, it's a dog-eat-dog world, everybody for himself, and there ain't no occasion to ram your way through for others. What the hell were you doin', Bob?" He fell silent, and when he spoke again the anger had consumed itself and his voice was soft and sad. "We were different, but I liked Bob, I liked him a lot, he was straight; whether he liked me or not I couldn't tell you. Also, Courtney was just about the only officer's wife who was nice to Beryl, and that mattered to me. Ah." Trainer raised his forefinger, knitting his brow in sudden remembrance. "There is something I want you to give to Hurstwood. Captain Devlin called me last night, Father Devlin, he's one of the Roman Catholic chaplains at Army. It appears he was in the hospital room along with the others when Bob was dying." Trainer paused and muttered, "This mustn't go further, Donkers, you understand?"

"Yes, sir, it won't go any further."

"Anyway, when the end was near, and they were going on with their code blue or whatever they call it, sticking pins into Bob and doing their damnest to revive him, all the leeches being present and accounted for, Courtney got to be hysterical, they had to hold her back from the bed and then she passed out; when she came to she got to be hysterical again, interfering with what the leeches were doing, so they had to take her out and sedate her. In the meantime Bob was breathing his last and there was no hope, his heart was giving out. Devlin was standing very close to Bob and noticed his lips were still moving so he bent over and put his ear as close as he could to Bob's mouth. Devlin told me the voice was very faint, but the words clear as a bell and there could be no mistake. This is what Bob said, and these were his last words because he checked out as soon as he spoke them. 'Oh Lord, my God, forgive me for I have accomplished so little in Your service, forgive me Oh Lord.' Devlin wrote it down there and then, and then he spoke to the Protestant chaplain and they decided that I should be contacted first to handle this here matter of the last words." Trainer relit his cheroot. "Isn't there someone coming over from stateside?" he asked.

"Yes, sir, Captain Hastings' brother, Randolph Hastings, is flying over. He is in business somewhere in Mass; he should be in Wiesbaden tomorrow afternoon.

"I see. And the funeral?"

"Lieutenant Hurstwood was informed that the body will be taken back to Boston for burial, and there will be a memorial service at Army next week."

"Good, I want you to give this piece of paper to Lieutenant Hurstwood. I wrote on it what appears to be Bob's last words and the names of the two chaplains." Donkers put the piece of paper in his folder. "Hurstwood will probably want to speak to Randolph, and someone will have to decide whether them last words as we call them are worth showing to Courtney or not. Anyway, this is Ted's responsibility, and he should do what he thinks is best."

"I'll think he'll do just that."

"I have every reason to believe he will."

Donkers re-crossed his legs and was waiting for some indication of Trainer's immediate wishes, but as none came he asked, "How is Mrs. Hastings?"

"Not very well, they had to sedate her again the next day, and they have a nurse with her twenty-four hours a day. Beryl had gone to Wiesbaden to be with her, and so have other officers' wives."

"It must've been a great shock for her," Donkers intimated, not quite knowing what to say.

"Yes, it was a great shock." Trainer bit off the end of the cheroot and spat it out into the wastepaper basket. "You'd better stay with Ted until this goddamn business is over and, Dirk, I appreciate what you're doing."

"Thank you, sir." Donkers was on the point of departing when he too knitted his brow in sudden remembrance. "There's something I didn't put in the memo because it's of a different ilk."

Trainer looked nonplussed but expectant. "Well, what is it? I hope it's good news this time; don't we deserve some good news?"

"It isn't a death if that's what you mean."

"Let's be grateful for small favors then, one down and twenty to go."

"The news came this morning by teletype from Army. We've been assigned a new chaplain."

"What!" Trainer exclaimed in genuine stupefaction. "At the best of times a unit gets to wait several months for a new chaplain and here we're getting one even before Bob's been properly laid to rest and all that! Incredible!"

"He's been assigned, sir, but he won't be here in person till a few weeks from now. He'll be shipping from the States."

"Who is he?" Trainer asked sharply.

"Captain Solomon Lieberman, waiting for overseas transport in Fort Bragg."

"Are you putting me on, college boy, are you putting me on?" Trainer was not really fuming although he gave every indication of doing just that.

"Not in the least, sir. I have the orders right here," and Donkers reached inside the folder.

"Never mind. Why do they send us a Jewish chaplain, we have no kikes in this outfit."

"We have some men of Jewish faith, but they wouldn't be caught dead attending religious services. There is only one I can think of who is practicing. Captain Hastings gave him a pass releasing him from duty, if at all possible, sundown Friday to sundown Saturday."

"Oh! And where does this kike chaplain hail from?"

Donkers glanced at the orders and chuckled.

"Well?"

"Captain Solomon David Lieberman was born and bred in Kansas City, Kansas. Would you like me to give you his date of birth and the name of his high school, sir?"

"I don't believe it, I don't believe it." Trainer grumbled. "It's Vickers all over again, the lowdown ol' cadger, he's after me."

"Vickers?"

"Yes, General . . . Lee Vickers. Don't you know, Group Clerk, that all religious and medical assignments within 7th Army are made in the office of the Deputy Commander, the shithead . . . Lee Vickers. Ryan has delegated this responsibility to his second in command."

"I remember now, I simply didn't make the connection."

"It warms my heart to see you're still on the ball." He stood up throwing his bulky arms backwards, loosening the shoulder blades, and twisting his back as if trying to get rid of the painful effects of a crick. Then he belched with all the power of his thorax. "You'd better rejoin Hurstwood," he said at last, "the good lieutenant might think you've left him for good."

Donkers smiled. "Try not to worry too much about all this, sir. I'd say in the end things will work themselves out just fine. Wait and see."

With Donkers out of the office, Trainer held up Captain Lieberman's orders with a mixture of aloofness and disdain and then let them drop on the desk with a slight, hardly noticeable movement of hand, as if he were doing a conjuring trick. He spoke in measured tones, articulating each word with care, like an actor reading a brand new script for the first time. "As for you, friend Solomon, why don't you get yourself on the first available broomstick and just fly away."

Chapter 17

It was raining cats and dogs when Honigklausen, a bundle of papers under his arm, knocked on Trainer's door right after lunch. He found the major in a placid mood.

"I guess you heard about the new chaplain," Trainer asked, expecting an affirmative answer.

"One of the cooks told me, sir, his girl works in Personnel at Army, and with the Major's permission I'd like to de . . . declare it may all turn out for the best." Honigklausen sounded carefree and sanguine.

"How so?"

"I've received a confidential report on Captain Lieberman, soon to be Major Lieberman 'cause his promotion was to be approved last Christmas like, but the papers got fouled up."

"Oh yes," Trainer evinced little interest in the topic.

"A very impressive man," Honigklausen was speaking slowly, letting each word count, "a fine sportsman, nearly made the Olympic swimming team and boasting a dis . . . distinguished record in Korea. He wasn't a chaplain then, just a lieutenant from Kansas National Guard, and he'd gone through most of the fighting, decorated and promoted to captain. A regular guy. After the Police Action he gone to become rabbi and chaplain . . ."

"Lieberman, Lieberman," Trainer was sucking his thumb.

"Tall muscular guy, 6'3" I reckon, bright, no nonsense fella . . ."

"Lieberman . . . KC Printing Press," Trainer began to tap the desk with his middle finger, the incipient recollection coming almost within his grasp.

"The same," Honigklausen put in with satisfaction, "the Lieberman family being like the sole owner of KC Printing Press, one of the largest outfits of this kind in Kansas—father semi-retired now, three sons, the eldest CEO of the outfit, the second an attorney in the city, and the third why," Honigklausen tossed his head back with happy flamboyance, "the third is our own boy."

"Those people are loaded, loaded . . ." Trainer was now beginning to remember. "You know, Lester, years ago, in '35 or was it '36, I tried to get a job there, not once but several times, but they were not hiring. This was the time when no one was hiring!"

"I know what you mean, sir."

"Well, you've got an excellent information service." Trainer laughed. "Nothing gets by you, that's for sure."

Honigklausen advanced a step. "I wish I could say something cheerful like about your promotion, Major Trainer, and you being named permanent Group Commander. I know that uncertainty is . . . is very painful."

Trainer threw his hands up in a gesture of unconcern as Honigklausen moved even closer to him.

"Sit down, sit down." Trainer motioned him to a chair. "For crying out loud you don't have to stand."

"Let me give the Major the scoop as I got it." Honigklausen was now in a sitting position and was appearing to be very comfortable. He began, "Everyone agrees this here matter is taking twice as long as it should; my information confirms that the message of thanks you sent to General Ryan did the Major a lot of good, and likewise his meetings with General Stebbins. All agree on this. The point is," Honigklausen leaned forward, "you have a powerful enemy, and all indications point to General Vickers. That's not all, there's something else . . ."

Trainer waited for a few seconds and then chuckled, "Do I have to sweat it out of you, Lester?"

"No need to, I was coming to it meself . . . but it's a delicate point."

"Well, let's have it, delicate or not." Trainer was at his best making a jest of it.

"General Ryan owes General Vickers one, and now General Vickers is cashing his chips."

Trainer was gazing at Honigklausen without uttering a word. Finally he leaned back in his armchair and pulled a cheroot out of a new pack.

"This is just about what I heard from Hurstwood . . . who tried to get to the bottom of it, and from Donkers. They both said Ryan was on the point of signing when something happened; as I have it, Vickers came to see him. An officer close to Ryan, who asked me not to disclose his name, you understand, Lester," Honigklausen nodded vigorously, "said the same. What you told me is just about what I heard from friends and well-wishers. It all makes sense. We have a situation."

"It's up to General Ryan now," Honigklausen commented guardedly.

"I guess so," Trainer said. "We have two uneven poker players, but there ain't no telling how uneven they truly are and how uneven they'd like the others to think they are."

Slowly and with difficulty Honigklausen rose to his feet. "I'll be in my office if the Major needs me."

Trainer nodded. "Thanks, Lester, thanks a lot."

The afternoon hours dragged on as the power went out twice, though only for a few minutes each time, and the torrential rains did not subside. Trainer and Honigklausen busied themselves with the daily routine. In addition, the latter went on explaining at length to Donkers' temporary replacement, a clerk from A Company, the arcana of the Group's administrative duties. It was only when 1700 hours had struck and Donkers' replacement had saluted twice, first in the direction of the brooding Group Sergeant and then vaguely at the door leading to Trainer's office, and had taken to his heels with undisguised alacrity, that Honigklausen had again the opportunity of exchanging words with Trainer.

"It'll be nice to have Donkers back," he said brusquely, mopping the sweat off his face with the back of his hand.

Trainer agreed in so many brief carefully chosen words. "I understand he's doing a top job for Hurstwood," he added as an afterthought.

"Absolutely, Lieutenant Hurstwood has given me a glowing report.

Another couple of days, and this Hastings business will be wrapped up for sure."

"Let's hope so." Trainer was making ready to go, but he again remembered something and turned to the sergeant. "When it's over see to it that Donkers gets a three-day pass, he deserves it, if he don't blow himself a good time he'll crack up. We've been driving the kid hard, very hard, and I'm the first to admit it."

"The Major may rest assured I'll attend to it."

"Good. Tell me, Lester, what does Donkers do for kicks?"

"With the Major's permission, he's very well behaved. I don't know if the Major is aware he does voluntary work at the local Lutheran church and helps all kinds of GIs with applying to colleges, choosing the right correspondence courses, and so on . . . and so forth."

"This ain't my idea of a good time. Got a schatzy in town?"

"Oh no, not Donkers!" Honigklausen took it almost as a personal affront. "Very well-behaved and very religious, his dad being a minister and all that and Donkers enjoying the full benefits of a religious upbringing, Protestant, as it should be, for we are a Protestant nation." Honigklausen thrust his chest and jaw forward.

"Yeah, yeah, yeah," Trainer began to yawn and picked up his overcoat.

"He is also a letter-writer," Honigklausen announced with pride.

"Good, every officer should encourage letter-writing in his unit. Often it keeps the men out of harm's way."

"But, Donkers' letters are . . . very, very special."

"Oh?"

"Addressed to a college pal."

"Nothing wrong with that."

"They have a very special content . . ."

"Not that we want to pry, but what the hell are they about?"

Honigklausen straightened himself up and appeared to be growing in height and girth, his countenance very grave.

"His letters are phi-lo-so-phi-cal."

"What the hell does it mean, Lester, speak English or better still speak Kansas so I can understand you."

Honigklausen remained standing at attention at his most majestic, and some twenty seconds elapsed before he spoke, "They have to do with the nature of the universe!"

"You don't say! That makes everything clear, clear as mud."

"I wish I could explain further to the Major . . ."

Trainer raised a hand. "Don't bother, I get the picture. As for the R and R for the kid, I want 'im to have a bundle of fun on his pass, lots of sex, lots of broads, booze coming out of his ears, gambling if he fancies it, and anything else his heart desires. This is just a precaution so he don't crack up, seen too many of them straight-and-narrow boys endin' up in mental wards."

"Yes, sir."

"When the kid has his pass in his pocket you put 'im on the train to Copenhagen, once there he'll have a good time, like it or not, and when he gets back he can line up with the rest of 'em for penicillin shots." Trainer's ensuing laughter was exhilarating, but Honigklausen did not join in it. He stood there, his head high up in the air, disgust painted all over his face.

"Good night, Lester."

"And good night to the Major."

Chapter 18

The rainy days and nights followed one another without intermission. Water dripped incessantly from the eaves and buzzed and gurgled down the gutters, and each morning the parade ground was covered with a thick whitish mist blown away in the early afternoon only to return later in its formless shifting garb. The puddles of water on the ground grew larger and ponchos were seen everywhere as riled up officers and men, their teeth clenched, were scurrying from building to building carrying out those tasks only which could not be postponed. Field exercises were canceled, and those who listened to weather reports were gloomy and dejected. But on this morning the mood in Sergeant Honigklausen's office was merry and carefree.

"When ye come to think of it," Trainer was saying, scratching his head and blowing out the inevitable clouds of smoke, "when ye come to think of it, maybe it was just the best memorial service some of us have ever seen."

Sergeant Honigklausen, Captain Spelling, Lieutenant Hurstwood, and Captain Fiorello, C.O. of A Company, a wiry man of regular height whose thick black hair had been reduced to a crew cut, murmured their assent. So did the two sergeants who had only just entered the office, but were kept fully abreast of the topic of conversation.

"I'm very happy Major Hastings was honored in this exemplary fashion," Spelling put in his shrill high-pitched voice.

"Right, hear, hear, absolutely," was heard from the others.

"And the turnout," Sergeant Honigklausen joined in, "one would perforce have to scratch one's memory long and hard to come up with a similar number of military personnel on a similar occasion."

"You're absolutely right," Lieutenant Hurstwood nodded and began to tick one group of mourners after the other off an invisible roster, officers and NCOs from the Group, chaplains from the 7th Army, and beyond, top brass, etc. etc.

"Not counting other military personnel who came to pay their respects and German politicians and dignitaries, German clergy . . ." added Captain Fiorello rounding off the list.

"Right, John," Hurstwood resumed, "and not forgetting the personal representative of the U.S. Ambassador to West Germany, gee whiz."

"Right, Ted. He looked so full of himself I at first mistook him for the Ambassador himself," Fiorello let out and the others laughed.

"General Ryan's address was, I thought, top-notch," Spelling was earnest and respectful.

"Yeah, very true, Lloyd's good with words."

Small talk followed. Soon the two sergeants who had come to collect various papers relating to their companies saluted and left, and Captain Fiorello stepped forward. "Please excuse me, Major, but pressing business awaits me in my company."

"You're excused, Captain, and keep up the good work." Trainer smiled and returned Fiorello's salute. He moved around the office and lay his hand on Honigklausen's back. "As I recall top brass paid more attention to you than to anybody else at the service, Sergeant Honigklausen."

The sergeant's eyes twinkled with satisfaction. "General Ryan was very kind," he said modestly.

"That's right, he sought you out in a crowd of busybodies and buttonholed you while the others were green with envy. You spoke for a long time, and if it isn't an intrusion of privacy what did you two talk about?"

"No intrusion of privacy, Major, none at all . . . we spoke of old times. We were both in Northern Italy in '44, in Velletri and other places, at one point our artillery was firing 180 degrees off base. We were dug in, but the Krauts could be on top of us any minute, so I sent a radio message, and when this did no good I gone to headquarters meself and came face to face with Brigadier Ryan. I told him what's what, and he listened. He changed the targets right away, as their intelligence reports were all fouled up. We talked of this and other things."

"And he remembered you going to see him?"

"Sure did, even told me what time of day it was."

Trainer looked away and then moved closer to Honigklausen. "That's good, Lester, that's very good."

Honigklausen was now handing some new equipment manuals to Hurstwood, who was inspecting them cursorily. "They're like the old ones," he laughed, "only the dates have been changed."

Honigklausen spread out his hands. "If you want the truth, Lieutenant, the dates on them yearly updates have as much validity like as a drunken man's solemn oath when his throat is dry and he tries to get the next bottle on tick."

"I get your point," and Hurstwood moved to the door. "I'll be in my office, if you need me."

"In point of fact, I will need you, Lieutenant, and I'll come by very soon."

"Please do, sir."

Now there were only three of them left in Honigklausen's office, Spelling sitting rigidly in front of the sergeant's desk, the sergeant himself sitting authoritatively behind his desk, his fingers floating idly from one stack of papers to the next, ill-concealed contempt lining his face, and Trainer leaning against the wall by the window, blowing out clouds of smoke.

"Such a turnout in such damnable weather," Trainer snorted, his mind going back to the memorial service, and positioning his head so close to the window that his nose was touching the windowpane. "Lots of folks must've thought it mighty important to be seen at that service for Bob." He was going to continue in this vein, but he noticed that Honigklausen was trying to catch his eye.

"Oh yes," he turned away from the window, "we have your emergency leave approved, Spelling, Group Sergeant has the paperwork."

"As you know this is a compassionate leave for seven days, Captain Spelling," Honigklausen went on, explaining slowly and meticulously, "granted to you because of family emergency, as you have indicated in your initial statement." He pushed towards Spelling several papers clipped together. "Your compassionate leave starts at midnight tonight and continues for seven days. All dates are in the orders. Is there anything that needs to be explained to you, sir?"

"No, nothing, thank you, Sergeant."

"I hope that family emergency of yours will have a happy ending," Trainer let the words drop off-handedly. "Anyway, best of luck. Flying stateside?"

"Yes, sir, but not immediately, one of my parents may be coming over here." Spelling was already by the door, forcing his leave orders into his briefcase. "I'll say good-bye, Major," and he saluted. Once the door was closed, Honigklausen hoisted himself up halfway, and his hands anchored in the desk for support, he shouted after the decamping captain, "Don't forget your golf balls, boy!"

Trainer put his hand to his mouth, trying hard to suppress laughter. "If you think something ain't right you can start an inquiry, and I'll back you up, you know that."

In turn Honigklausen began to shake his head very slowly, very deliberately accentuating his refusal. "Ain't worth it, Major, but what is worth its weight in gold we'll have this little shit-head off our rumps for at least seven days and maybe . . . maybe longer."

Trainer was still partly covering his mouth, and gazing at Honigklausen with something approaching admiration. "Carry on, Group Sergeant," he said at last. "I'll be back in a little while," and he left the office.

He found Hurstwood engrossed in the new equipment manuals, which indeed were like the old ones except for the publication dates, and he motioned to him not to get up. Then he looked up and down the corridor and shut the door tight.

"I want you to do something for me and this involves Donkers."

Hurstwood's face registered surprise.

"The night before last Donkers gone to that *gasthaus* down the road, I forget the name . . ."

"Die Krone," Hurstwood put in.

"That's right. Anyway, he apparently stayed there for a long time drinking heavily. It ain't really clear what happened after that, maybe someone said something to him, maybe he said something to someone else, we don't know, and maybe we'll never know, but the upshot was a scuffle, a small barroom brawl, you might say. Later Donkers left and started walking towards the camp. He must've been pretty loaded by then, and he probably slipped, that's what we think happened, and fell into a ditch. He passed out. The MPs on their rounds saw him lying there unconscious; for once the MPs did the right thing, they put him in the back of a jeep, took him to his quarters, and handed him over to his buddies who put him to bed. He's fine. End of story. The MPs filed no report, the *gasthaus* owner filed no complaint, nor did no living soul. Well, that little creep Spelling got wind of it and wants to know what really happened. I want you, Ted, to conduct a discreet one-man inquiry 'cause I wanna know what happened, and it's kinda important I know. Get the picture?"

"I do, sir."

Trainer swallowed hard. "Yesterday Donkers' early promotion came through, approved from top to bottom. He's now officially Specialist 4, and I don't want this *gasthaus* kick fouling up his record."

"Understood."

"Maybe just talking to Donkers will be enough. Don't see no reason why you should talk to the Krauts, or the Kraut cops or even to the MPs. But just in case, I wrote down all the relevant names." He handed Hurstwood a scrap of paper. "And, nothing in writing, when you're through you talk to me, word of mouth only, and you don't talk to no single livin' soul."

Hurstwood smiled. "I understand perfectly."

"Thank you, Ted." Trainer stood up, stepped towards the door, and put his hand on the knob. "Oh, in all this rehashing of the mighty memorial service for Bob, we plain forgot to bring to the public notice one very, very significant piece of intelligence . . ."

"What was that, sir?"

"That General Vickers was nowhere to be seen at the service, nor was his sidekick Major Simmons. I wonder why."

"I wonder too," Hurstwood said.

Chapter 19

At long last the rains had abated. There was a pungent freshness in the air, and the air was laden with moisture as if the moisture was trapped in it and could not escape no matter how hard it tried. Only long spells of warmth and sunshine could dry it and they were not expected. Pools and puddles were everywhere and working parties employing sucking machines were clearing stagnant water, rimming off paths with new pebbles, and drying the soggy decaying grass. Now and then a squall of wind was heard while the sun was barely visible behind the slow march of leaden clouds, and not a drop of rain fell.

When the telephone rang on his desk, Honigklausen let it ring three times before picking up the receiver, a resolution he had made the day before to let the world know that he was a busy man of importance, not just a gofer at anybody's beck and call. But as soon as he heard the voice at the other end he pressed the connecting button and answered with verve and respect, "Yes, sir, I am connecting you this very second, sir." Next he disentangled himself from his armchair and ran the few steps to the door leading to Trainer's office, pushed it open, and gasped out at the wide-eyed Trainer, "Colonel Anderson on your line, sir. General Ryan wants to speak to you." His commission carried out, he embarked on a sluggish return.

"Yes, General, Trainer speaking. Yes, I see, sir." Trainer was swinging his arms, beckoning towards Honigklausen and summoning Donkers.

"Yes, the three towns, Steinhof, Apfeldorf, Grotzheim on the river Elsenz." Trainer pointed a finger at Donkers and then pointed to the map on the wall.

"Yes, sir, we know where they are located . . ."

Donkers, ruler in hand, pinpointed the three towns and drew in the air a large three followed by a large zero and a large five.

"They are some thirty to thirty-five miles away from us."

Trainer was listening attentively again, his face taut and motioning to both Honigklausen and Donkers to stay where they were.

"Yes, sir, we can do it and we are ready . . . we can move out in thirty minutes . . . any casualties so far, and has the population been evacuated . . . ? I see, very good, General, and I consider it an honor that you chose 16th Engineer Group for this assignment. Yes, sir," he sounded off, and replaced the receiver.

"Bad floods up to northeast, the River Elsenz and those towns, the Krauts tried to stem it with sand bags and the rest, but the waters are rising; so far the actual dwellings have not been affected, but the flood is moving their way. It may be a matter of hours. General Ryan received calls for help from the mayors of these towns and the German Regional Government. He wants us to go and do the job." He paused. "Colonel Anderson will be calling us in exactly three minutes to give us further information, so keep the line open, Sergeant." He paused again, lit a cheroot, patted his bulging belly, and began shooting out orders: "Sound the siren Operation FLOOD, use loudspeakers, B Company to be ready to move out in thirty minutes, full gear, no weapons, officers to carry side arms, code BF, all leaves and passes are canceled. I want to see Mess Sergeant and Motor Pool Sergeant on the double; A and C Companies are on full alert and remain behind, in twenty-five minutes at 1511 hours I'll address B Company on the parade ground, trucks to line up both sides, and Honigklausen, when Anderson calls in squeeze all the info you can out of him, we'll need every bit of it . . ." He was interrupted by the deafening blare of the siren, followed by the disjointed bluster of the loudspeakers, and lifting his head he saw Hurstwood standing next to him. He grinned.

"Well, Ted, you can show the Army once more what you're made of."

"Sir!"

"I am appointing you my second in command. Captain Fiorello will be the acting Group Commander during my absence, and if that idiot Spelling shows up sooner than we expected he and John can fight it out."

"The companies have been notified and the men are getting ready."

"Good, now . . . I want you to choose one senior NCO who'll be directly under you, he'll be part of the command . . ."

"Sergeant Korovitz." Hurstwood uttered the name without hesitation.

Trainer grinned appreciatively. "Leroy's a good choice, ex-prize-fighter . . ."

"Ex-screw," Hurstwood added with a smile.

"And just about ex-everything, Leroy has managed to crowd a good many . . . occupations . . . into his short life. What do the men call him?"

"The song and whistle lad."

"Ah yes, I've heard . . . when he blows that log of a whistle the men run for cover."

"Something like that."

Trainer lay his hand on Hurstwood's shoulder. "Excuse me for a second," and he advanced towards Sergeants Sampler and Steiner, who were being briefed by Honigklausen.

"Everything clear?" he asked. The two sergeants assured him that it was.

"We'll be there for a couple of nights and maybe longer . . . probably not much longer though . . . but let's be ready," he thought for a moment, "and Larry take enough chow, K rations, and the rest in case we gotta share it with the civilian population."

"Right you are, sir."

"All vehicles in good working order, Carl?"

"Couldn't be better, Major."

"Take a few extras, just in case."

"Will do, sir."

Trainer nodded, "Thank you, Sergeants," and he moved away.

"Who's going with us, staff I mean," Hurstwood asked. "I just spoke to Sergeant Korovitz."

"You and me, and we'll have with us Donkers as driver, interpreter, and whatever else he can do, two communications men, and Leroy. Lieutenants Driscoll and Bohn from B Company and a couple of sergeants will be with the men. Honigklausen will stay here and hold the fort."

"I see Donkers is getting new frequencies so we can speak to Army at will?"

"He should be just about through with it. And once we get 'em the communications men will also activate a new phone line." Trainer looked at his watch. "Ted, we are pulling out in twelve minutes. Feeling okay?"

"Never better, sir."

Donkers was crossing the parade ground which now resembled the central layer of a beehive. By the Mess Hall he saw O'Leary and Tannenbaum already on the truck next to the pots, pans, stoves, hoses, and other kitchen equipment. The former was talking incessantly to anybody who would listen and the latter, tight-lipped and demure, was scanning the vibrant scene with a critical eye, the man who keeps his own counsel. Not far away he caught sight of Chuck Miller, now conscripted into a detail loading tents onto the trucks, who waved to him, his face twisted into that peculiar grin of his which signified, as it always did, *In whose aid is this goddamn show put on the road?* and *What the hell am I doing here?*

At 1516 hours, and not a minute past it, a long convoy of trucks carrying the equipment necessary in a BF operation together with what was needed for several days' stay in the field plodded out of the base on its way to the towns of Steinhof, Apfeldorf, and Grotzheim. Like a gigantic Stygian serpent white-plumed here and there the American serpent was also white-plumed at its fang and at its hind extremity, a white-hued MP jeep heading the column and another closing it. Two command jeeps trailed behind the MPs, the first with Donkers at the wheel and Trainer to his right already reminding Group Clerk of the hazards of the road. The back seats were occupied by Hurstwood and a specialist from Communications. In the second jeep another Communications specialist was in the driver's seat, and the redoubtable Sergeant Korovitz had all the room he wanted and more. An enormous black whistle attached to the top button of his fatigues dangled on his chest like an amulet, its powers indescribable. In close order, at a set speed, the convoy moved on.

Chapter 20

Two frantic days and nights lay ahead. B Company now divided into three platoons of equal size worked round the clock in three eight-hour shifts, and the men gave it all they had and more, much more. Already on the first day six huge reservoirs were blown out of the ground with dynamite in the wasteland six hundred yards behind the last line of buildings, and the overflowing water from the river rushed to them through mammoth pipes with the help of suction pumps. In the morning the river was much less unruly than before, and the American engineers moved to the second phase of the operation. Along the bank all the way from Steinhof to Grotzheim—Apfeldorf lying conveniently in the middle—they bored hundreds of dikes conducting the overflowing water far afield quarter of a mile past the last houses and barns to the meadows and open country where it emptied in trick-les into troughs, ditches, and under the spreading brush. Prudently at intervals of fifty yards along the same bank a levee was mounted, anoth-er line of defense against the threatening flood. The site was teeming with sweating bodies, digging, adjusting hundreds of instruments, oper-ating cranes, lifting the pipes from the ground, and depositing them on carriers or in designated areas along the riverbank and performing numerous other tasks essential to the operation. Here and there jokes were cracked, comments and observations bandied about, but in the main this was a quiet workforce.

On the third day the danger of the flood had been averted, and the water level of the Elsenz had fallen unexpectedly and reassuringly low. The mission of mercy had been carried out with complete success, and the specter of disaster no longer haunted the population. The inhabitants of Steinhof, Apfeldorf, and Grotzheim could go about their business as of old, and the children, their curiosity unquenchable, were gathering in threes and fours gaping at the American equipment and the marvels it had accomplished. The mood in the three towns was carefree, but the last details of the men of 16th U.S. Army Engineer Group were placing new rows of sandbags in close proximity to the streets and houses as insurance against the vagaries of the weather and recurring torrential rains. The Germans no longer saw the bulk of the Group breaking their backs saving their towns from a watery disaster but lounging and playing ball. Half a mile west from Apfeldorf and a safe distance from the Elsenz, the U.S. Army camp was stretched out in tiers of cub tents with the infinitely more prominent command and Mess Hall tents in the middle. Sentries were posted everywhere.

Standing outside the perimeter Donkers could see Major Trainer and Lieutenant Hurstwood talking by the embankment some four hundred yards away, and as he turned his head he noticed several German civilians advancing in a stiff and dignified manner towards them. The major also noticed the approaching party and made frantic gestures to Donkers to join him. Donkers began to run. A little girl, dressed in the traditional Swabian costume curtsied and presented Trainer with a bouquet red, yellow, and black, and he, like a wicked uncle, took her tiny hand in his own enormous one, shook it heartily, then picked her up and threw her high in the air, catching her just before she landed and kissing her affectionately on both cheeks.

"Thanks very much for the flowers, *danke sehr* much," he uttered with gusto as everyone in the German party beamed.

The tall, elderly silver-haired man in front, whom Donkers recognized as the Bürgermeister of Apfeldorf, took a step forward and began to speak in a markedly restrained tone, his eyes permanently focused on Trainer, as if he wanted to make his point as emphatically as possible without turning demonstrative or mawkish. Donkers translated.

"Once again, Major, the people of Apfeldorf, Steinhof, and

Grotzheim tender to you and to U.S. 16th Engineer Group, their heart-felt thanks. A disaster has been averted, you have tamed the waves, you have prevented what would have been certain damage to houses and property and very probable loss of human life. Some of us still remember the terrible flood nineteen years ago. It was terrible, and we were half resigned that this year something similar would occur as the signs of the approaching disaster were there for all to see; we thought our situation was hopeless . . ." At this point the speaker paused, made an effort to go on, but was unable to do so, as tears trickled down his cheeks. He began to sob, but soon regained control and fell silent.

Immediately the man behind him picked up the thread. "You have our undying gratitude. We shall never forget what you did for us." All the Germans began to clap, the little girl clapping merrily long after everyone else had stopped.

Major Trainer straightened himself up and glanced pointedly at Hurstwood. Hurstwood nodded slightly, and the Major began to speak while Donkers played the same irreplaceable role as before.

"I am profoundly touched by your words, and it is a privilege to be of help to you, however slight this help may be. Like you I am delight-ed that our Flood Operation was a success and, of course, we are proud of our successes. What I am going to do now is speak briefly—I am constitutionally unfit to make long speeches—about the reasons why 16th Engineer Group came to your rescue, why it may do so again, and why—we are confident—you will come to our rescue in the future, should the need arise.

"First of all, we are neighbors. A distance of mere fifty kilometers separates those three lovely towns Apfeldorf, Steinhof, and Grotzheim from the Headquarters of 16th Engineer Group in Kirchenberg, and as neighbors we have an obligation to help one another, because this is proper neighborly behavior. But we are not only your neighbors, we are also guests in your country, and while a great deal has been written in etiquette manuals about the responsibilities of the host towards his guests—much more than is really necessary—not enough has been said about the responsibilities of the guests towards their host, and this, I am sure you will agree, is equally important. Let's simply say that in coming here to confine the flood we were repaying you for the hospitality which you have so generously extended to us. Still, there is something else that looms over the horizon, namely that for some time now we have been allies; our countries, the German Federal Republic and the United States of America, formed an alliance, and it is therefore expected that as allies we should act in unison and come to each other's aid when danger threatens. Otherwise, what the dickens is the point of having allies, or being an ally?

"Well, I run the risk of talking more than is good for me, so let me gallop towards the end. Neighbors, guests, allies—these are very real, very significant bonds which keep us together, and we should never underrate their value. But, there is something even higher and more fundamental than these binding cords. All of us are human beings first, before we are soldiers or civilians, Americans or Germans, rich or poor, sharp as a razor's edge or a little more on the dull side, and this means that we are family, one big family whose members have a sacred obligation to care for one another. Why? Not because of treaties and covenants, but because it's plain natural and if we violate this natural trust and obligation we've lost even the pretense of calling ourselves human beings. That's all, and thank you very much."

When Donkers finished translating the last part, after the "Why?" the German party stood immobile as if their feet hand been glued to the ground, their faces expressionless. But this lasted only a few seconds. Then as if to make up for lost time the effect of Trainer's speech became all of a sudden electric. The Germans clapped their hands wildly, waved their arms in frantic jubilation, and they all wanted simultaneously to shake Trainer's hand. A stout big-boned woman in the back pushed her way to the front, forced the others out of the way, and bear-hugged Trainer. His face was now barely visible between her shoulder and the bulky arm looking in supplication to Hurstwood whose gaze was turned elsewhere and who too was smiling broadly and applauding. The rejoicing lasted a long time. Trainer answered questions about the Flood Operation, recounted various incidents from his childhood, told Kansas stories, and inquired solicitously about the town's business, the budget, the schools, the local politics. It was mid-afternoon when the party finally broke up after much handshaking, bowing, and the exchange of compliments. Donkers was praised for having carried out with distinction his duties as interpreter, nor was Hurstwood forgotten in the general leave-taking. As the German party was about to walk away, the Bürgermeister's voice rose above the chatter, "Don't forget, Major

Trainer, you and your officers are invited for dinner tonight at our town hall, 7:00 P.M. We are looking forward to seeing you there."

Later in the afternoon, as they were inspecting the equipment soon to be loaded on the trucks, Trainer said to Hurstwood, "I guess, Ted, one of these days you'll be asking me for some special leave so you can see your young lady."

Hurstwood froze. "No, sir. It's all over between Lucy and me, we won't be seeing each other again."

"Are you sure?"

"Absolutely, it's finished."

"Well, if you change your mind, Lieutenant . . ."

"I won't be changing my mind, sir," Hurstwood practically hissed the words out. "I won't," he added with heavy emphasis.

Trainer rubbed his nose and decided to drop the subject. "I hope that shindig tonight will go okay."

"It will, don't worry."

"Everything else under control, Lieutenant?"

"Yes, sir. As per your instructions, the men—except for the sentries and those on special assignments—will be allowed to go to the town, but they'll have to be back in their tents by 2200 hours. Platoon leaders will read a statement to the troops under your signature that proper behavior will be strictly enforced and any violations rigorously prosecuted. The MPs have been briefed."

Trainer cleared his throat. "We made such a hell of a good impression, it would be a pity to spoil it."

Hurstwood nodded. "In addition, I asked Sergeant Korovitz to have a private word with all the NCOs. Every man leaving camp will be personally instructed by a noncom, and the bottom line is 'if you want to raise Cain, son, wait till we get back to base'."

Trainer scratched his neck. "If Leroy is there at the tollgate, why, half the men will stay in camp," he murmured in a sly kind of way, smiling more to himself than to anyone else.

Hurstwood's face lightened. "With all due respect, a dry throat and a pounding libido are mighty persuaders."

Trainer pierced him with a quick sideways glance. "Now you're talking, boy, now you're talking."

They went inside the command tent, and Trainer cast a look of open disgust at his field desk jammed with papers.

"Earlier today a telephone message came for you from Army," he heard Hurstwood say matter-of-factly.

"What do they want now?" he countered pugnaciously.

"Actually the message was from Colonel Anderson's office."

"Oh, what can I do for Lloyd, my good ol' buddy?"

"It was advance notice, and you'll get detailed information when they are ready."

"Oh!"

"We are adopting the French Mobile-Bridge as standard equipment. It's official and the Pentagon gave its blessing."

"Son of a gun, I never thought they had brains enough to take such a step."

"Well, they did, maybe you were just a wee bit too harsh on them."

"Me too harsh, Ted? Never! But I'll tell ye what tramples me even today. We should've devised and built that Mobile-Bridge, not the Frenchies. The greatest country in the world and here we're told to play second fiddle to a bunch of . . . a bunch of . . ."

"Bunch of what?" Hurstwood asked laughing to his heart's content.

/ / /

Donkers was walking away from the river at a leisurely pace. He had been ordered to report to the command tent at 1830 hours, and now glancing at his wristwatch he realized it was barely five o'clock. He walked on through shrubbery and grass getting richer and higher with every step, and turning his gaze to the left he saw rows of small white houses marking the most northerly part of Apfeldorf, which reminded him of similar houses in a town in Minnesota where he had been born. He came to a halt, sniffed the air, tossed his head, kicked the dirt around his feet, and clenched his right fist. Seventeen days, seventeen days only before he would be reunited with Jonathan! Seventeen days only before he could live again as a human being, seventeen days only before he could love again! Closing his eyes he could see Jonathan's face and body very close to him, his long flaxen hair coming down all the way to his shoulders and obscuring parts of the cheeks, and then he saw him taking off his glasses and laughing triumphantly. Seventeen more days only and after that less than four months of bondage; in what was to follow he'd be saluting for the last time, spitting over his left shoulder for good luck, and heading back to civilian life and the University.

His eyelids open again, he reflected sadly that what he had seen in his mind's eye would have to wait a little longer before it became reality. Besides, reality was making new demands. A U.S. Army jeep had pulled up on a country road skirting the meadow. The driver remained behind the wheel, but on the passenger's side a tall lank figure wearing crumpled fatigues climbed out and was making his way across in the direction of Apfeldorf. Donkers advanced to cut the distance between them, and when they were getting closer to each other he noticed that the stranger was a one-star general. He stood at attention and saluted. The gaunt bird-like figure halted and saluted back.

"Who's in charge of this Flood Operation?" he asked matter-of-factly.

"Major Trainer, Major E. E. Trainer, sir."

"And your name, Specialist?"

"Dirk Donkers, sir, Group Clerk 16th Engineer Group."

"Ah yes," the general's head bobbed up and down. "Colonel Anderson was telling me about you." He drew closer to Donkers.

"I am General Stebbins, and I want you men at the 16th to know that you have a first-rate commanding officer." Then he continued in the same matter-of-fact manner. "As for me, I am an observer, and I've been here for three days, keeping out of the way most of the time and doing my observing in a fashion that wouldn't attract attention." He gave out a quick self-assured laugh. "My presence here is not a military secret, Donkers . . . far from it . . . but I would appreciate it if it were not trumpeted all over camp. Do you understand?"

"Loud and clear, sir."

"Good, well, I'd better get on with what I've been sent to do."

"General, I'd like to ask you something."

Donkers became acutely aware of the pair of charcoal-like eyes rising out of the bony face and burning deep into his thoughts.

"I don't think I can answer your question, Donkers," the general paused, "but I can tell you this, the matter you would like to ask me about is in good hands, in very good hands."

And as Donkers was saluting again he thought he could detect in the general's face a ghost of a smile.

"I hope they'll feed you well tonight, son," the general called to him as he was beckoning to his driver to follow him in the jeep.

/ / /

Major Trainer was sitting astride a chair on the visitors' side of his camp desk, shuffling papers. He leaned sideways toward Hurstwood and said, "Ted, the one thing I don't want to do no more is memorizing speeches . . . you get it?"

"That was probably the last one."

"You said it after we seen the Frenchies at the lake and now you say it again. How can I believe you?"

Hurstwood laughed and turned his head. "It paid off, though. It paid off."

Half-rising from the chair, Trainer muttered, "I wanna get some sleep tonight, and that's a fact."

"You will, sir," Hurstwood assured him. Trainer was now standing in the middle of the tent, his own ebullient self.

"So we are all cranked up to leave 0900 hours tomorrow."

"As you ordered."

"Good!" Trainer cast another glance at the papers on his desk. "There's just a wee bit of time before the officers and Donkers show up, so I'll get meself an inspection tour quick-like."

He left the command tent and walked over to where the smaller pieces of flood equipment were stored. Hydraulic power shovels, sucking pipes, converters, boxes of dynamite, huge coils of electric cord, fans, and other gadgetry were neatly arranged, ready to go home. At head level, disassembled and spotlessly clean parts of enormous blade cutters were hanging from short thick nails, shipshape and to be crated within the hour. Trainer smiled and touched one of them. "These babies can cut through thick and thin," he sounded off appreciatively, letting his hand roam over the slick surfaces, when a voice called from behind. "Careful, Major, we just hung 'em up, and they're steady only if you don't touch 'em."

"Right you are," Trainer called back, but it was too late. An arm-long cutter, its edge jagged, fell down from a fastener, chipping Trainer's right shoulder. His uniform was torn a couple of inches each way and blood was pearling up. Applying a handkerchief to the bleeding spot, Trainer left the equipment tent, baffled more than anything else. Outside he saw Sergeant Korovitz blow at his enormous whistle, three short sharp notes like the letter "S" in the International Morse Code, then hollering at the top of his lungs, "Medics over here," and two medics carrying a stretcher came running.

"Lie down, Major, we'll patch you up in no time," said the elder.

"Balls," Trainer retorted. "Stretchers are for pregnant WACs, Westpointers, and other unassorted assholes, not for E. E. Trainer, no sir! I SHALL REMAIN STANDIN'."

"Please yourself, Major, but you are also getting a shot," the same medic put in firmly, and the two medics went about their business. The news of the accident spread like wildfire, and as it traveled the length and width of the camp it was occasionally embellished and dramatized; so much so that at the outermost post to the northeast, well beyond Grotzheim, where two privates armed with a telephone and field glasses mounted guard, twelve hours on- twelve hours off, a message directed to one of them provoked the same private to shake his sleeping buddy with the words, "Wake up, don't you want to know what's going on? Major Trainer's been mortally wounded, he's breathing his last . . ." to which the other private, bleary-eyed and only half-conscious countered, "And you woke me up for this, asshole?!" and immediately went back to sleep.

Outside the storage tent Major Trainer, finally released from the ministrations of the medics, continued his inspection tour as if nothing had happened. But it was more than an inspection tour. He wanted to compliment the men, and the NCOs and the officers too, on a job well done. He moved easily from tent to tent from one group to another, and something in his demeanor made them listen to him and show respect. Most of them thought they knew him better now than before, that he had led them through a crisis and had measured up; that he had had a clear sense of what should be done every minute in those three frantic days and had directed their efforts in such a manner as to bring out the best in them. They had given him their best not because he had ordered them to do it, but because he had made them feel that the success of the mission was crucial not only for the native population but equally so for the 16th Engineer Group, for the entire U.S. Army, for the Red, White, and Blue. Above all, they trusted him, and they could feel it in their bones their trust would not be betrayed. He knew most of their names and he called each enlisted man, an NCO, or an officer by his first or last name telling him and all the others that he was proud of them and would be honored to lead them into battle any day. Here and there he would pose a question or two relating to what was the hardest part of the operation for the individual he was addressing, and he listened patiently to his answer. As he was winding up his tour and was turning in the direction of the command tent, a huge crowd sprang up from nowhere, the men, the NCOs, and the officers making it up, instantly falling into a military formation. "You speak first, Billy," several voices cried out, and PFC Billy Cadogan, a slender lad, voice of the people and frequent spokesman for the rank and file, a collier's son from West Virginia, himself no stranger to the pits, nimble with his hands as few others and glib with his tongue as no other, took two steps forward, stood to attention and saluted.

"Congratulations to Major Trainer on a job well done," he sounded off at the top of his voice and at once threw his right arm up.

The boom of voices rising from the formation was deafening.

"Congratulations to Major Trainer on a job well done," and they roared again and again.

Trainer saluted and his tone was uncharacteristically subdued.

"Thank you all," and he repeated in the same subdued manner, "Thank you all," as he stood at attention and saluted again. Brimming with vitality they returned the salute to a man, and Trainer hastened on his way to the command tent. He had tears in his eyes.

Book
Two

Chapter 1

News travels fast at 16th Engineer Group. They had, of course, known for weeks about Sergeant Honigklausen's imminent departure, his ceremonious last day on post and the attendant parade, but rank and file seldom listens to the hollering of platoon leaders or C.O.s' crisp announcements; if they listen at all, it is with one ear only. But then the solemn day was upon them, and they could not believe their eyes. On this tepid Saturday morning, many exchanged knowing glances and when someone dropped the remark "the no-good, fat slob is leaving us at last" or something of like ilk, it had all the force of a rock-like magnet falling down from the sky and inexorably pulling everyone towards the center. In C Company Quarters an unseasoned private sitting disconsolately on his bunk muttered to himself, but with every intention of being overheard, "So the mountain of lard is moving away / who can tell what will happen, who will now hold the sway?" Several of the men belched and two others spat on the floor in close proximity to the reciting private whose literary ambitions were well known.

"Eh, Fred," an irate voice gored the air, "you ain't goin' to do this poetic bit again, are ye?"

Fred ignored the question and was relieved when an enormous hulk of a man, square-faced and practically without a neck, laughed hoarsely and blurted out, "I'll tell you this, guys, I'll be there when the hour strikes 'cause I wanna be sure he gets his ass out of here and stays out."

"Which is one hour from now," Fred joined in.

"Right!" the square-faced man agreed.

"You had a run-in with the mighty Group Sergeant, Vince?" someone else asked of the square-faced man, "didn't you?"

"You might say that," and Vince let his head sway right and left, the muscles on his face tightening. "You might say that, but it's all done with." He gave a distinct appearance of wanting the subject to be laid to rest.

"When he put his mind to it, Honigklausen sure could be one son-of-a-bitch, make no mistake about it, specially when officers were around." The words came from the same PFC who took exception to Fred's worship of the Muse.

"That's for sure," several voices promptly assented.

"If you want my opinion . . ." Fred was now standing in the middle of the floor nonchalantly lighting up a cigarette, "if you want my opinion," he repeated, the self-congratulatory note drowning all else in his voice . . .

"Who the hell wants your opinion, college boy?" The detractor of the Muse sounded off again.

"Well . . ." Fred's quick eye now went roving from one man to the next, scrutinizing their faces and safeguarding against possible attack, "I'd say basically Sergeant Lester Honigklausen is very insecure, and therein lies the rub."

"Hell, this don't mean nothin' to me, in-se-cure, what the hell is in-se-cure?" Fred's castigator was now standing next to him, his temper close to the boiling point.

"Eh, you guys take it easy," Vince spoke firmly, his face betraying little emotion. "Are we going to fight over that ton of lard?"

Spasmodic laughter was heard followed by assenting and dissenting cries. Now everybody was in the fray.

From the far back a voice shot out, "Fred, explain to us peasants what the hell you mean by 'insecure.'" And Vince, visibly pleased by the question, advanced to the middle of the floor.

"Zack," he addressed the detractor of the Muse, "don't you want to know what makes Honigklausen tick?"

"I can live without it."

"Well now, here's a man who shows no curiosity at all . . . Simple Simon who'd rather be lying with them pigs and other beasts than watching the stars," the voice from the far back was at it again.

"Hell, boy," several men went on, each adding his own particular flavor to the request, "Explain yourself, spill it." "That's right, go for it," others were urging Fred, some patting him on the back. But they did not reckon with the zeal and determination of Zack's discontent.

He strolled over to the window, taking care to be as slow about it as possible, his hands buried in his pockets, doing his best to show to all and sundry he was fully in command and even though Vince was the C Company Barracks Chief, he, Zack, was a force to be reckoned with, and the others had better take heed. He stood there without uttering a single word, tapping the windowpane with a forefinger and studiously avoiding eye contact with anyone at all. And then he turned on them just as suspense was reaching a peak and would soon run riot.

"What the hell is this, Army barracks or a shrink's consulting room in the fashionable part of Manhattan? What is all this crap about insecurity?" As the speaker progressed, his speech became more and more grammatically correct, and indeed more and more flowery as he painted for his attentive audience the pitfalls of pseudo-scientific jargon and of the fragile tenets that shored it up. As he was winding down, he pointed a skinny finger at Fred and practically hissed out, "College boy, why the hell don't you go back to college and leave the real world to us!"

"Fine, if you can fix it with Uncle Sam I'll be on a plane for stateside tomorrow morning." Vince broke into a booming laughter, and just about everyone followed suit.

"Why so set against college boys?" The same resonating voice from the far back, which had already made its mark, flung the question at Zack.

"Who the hell are you?" Zack was peering intently behind the rows of familiar faces.

"Hal, Hal Shelton's the name. On temporary assignment from Army Medical Corps."

"Medic?"

"That's right, your bouts of influenza and such necessitated temporary transfers."

"Well, well, well, now that Army's offered a helping hand, not to forget a spare teat, all disease will vanish from the face of the earth." Zack was weighing his words carefully.

"Don't forget the ensuing peace and the universal good will on earth."

"That's right, right on the nose!" several of the men exclaimed, and small talk punctuated by belches and laughter rose from all corners.

"I want to go back to my original question," Hal scrambled to his feet, "remember it?"

"Eh, buddy, looking for a fight?" Zack transfixed Hal with a frigid prosecutorial gaze.

"Take it easy. What the hell is the matter with you!" Vince stepped forward and was now standing between Hal and Zack, ready to pour his meager supply of oil onto the troubled waters.

"Eh, guys," he went on, his eyes flashing from Hal to Zack, and from Zack to Hal, "grow up, for cryin' out loud."

But his words were not heeded. Almost immediately two camps were formed, and the adherents of each began to raise their voices all at once proffering advice and encouragement to their own favorite, Fred being momentarily erased from their consciousness as if he had never existed.

"Go on, tell him about the stinking college boys, Zack, speak up, give it to 'im, Zack, kick the medic in the ass," rose from one camp; and "You got it right Hal, who the hell does he think he is, teach 'im a lesson, boy, we are all equal here, kick his teeth out, Hal," rose from the other. A scrawny figure wearing nothing but underpants made his way to where the two antagonists were flexing their muscles and sputtered out, backslapping Zack: "You don't have to say nothin', I know it for a fact, Zack, 'cause the judge said so when I was before him on that case of sad misunderstanding between I and the state troopers . . . they can't force you to speak no matter what, that's in the Constitution."

Around Hal well-wishers were also solicitous, and he was given a wide range of excellent counsel. As the buzz continued, Zack decided to stake everything on a single card. He straightened himself up and raised a hand. In the ensuing silence he spoke distinctly and with feeling.

"Okay, I don't like college boys, and I'll tell you why. College boys conned my dad out of a princely sum of money. They were lawyers who were supposed to help Dad, but they turned out to be shysters and they took him to the cleaners. Ain't it a good enough reason?"

"Are you sure they were college boys?" someone asked.

"Sure thing," Zack answered with heavy emphasis.

But now there was something new in the air. The two militant camps that only a few minutes before had sworn death and destruction to each other were now disintegrating like sacred oaths taken in haste on a rainy night. An unidentified voice made itself heard, and it was eagerly listened to.

"To my way of thinkin', all this crap about what some folks call college boys and them others who, I guess, ain't college boys is kinda hard to take. It don't make no sense, you can't divide people that way 'cause it's plain false." The speaker uttered these words not solely on his own behalf. Almost at once other voices vibrated in the air, and a chorus of approval filled the area.

"That's right, it don't make no sense, hell, all of us is different in some way, and if you talk about being taken to the cleaners, hell, just about anybody can do it, and you don't need no college education to make a score!"

"That's right, that's right!" the others cried.

Hal Shelton was grinning smugly as the comments mounted, and he raised a hand.

"I'm with you, but I want to go back to what is already on the table. I want to know—"

He was vigorously interrupted from all sides and told what was on the table or under the table or in the vicinity of the table was no one's business. "You shut up or else!" Wisely, he chose the former.

"I'd like a beer," someone said. "Beer tastes kinda good before midday chow."

"Now you're talking," someone else said, and several voices gave him strong support.

"Let's get away from all this longhaired crap," the beer-lover went on, and many joined his side.

All this time Zack was silently observing what was going on. A barely perceptible grimace was taking root on his countenance, and his lips were pressed together. He took a few steps forward and reached the window where he came to a halt, his eyes now taking the measure of the events happening on the parade ground.

He had dissociated himself from the others, he had opted not to remain a card-holding member of the group, and his bearing combined aloofness, self-assertiveness, and undying contempt.

"Eh, guys, does anyone have any beer?" Vince asked jovially, all the problems of the world promptly vanishing under the impress of his words.

"Are you kidding?" several of the men countered, and Olie, the scrawny little fellow sporting only his underpants, threw his arms high up in the air and drawled out, "After last week's unscheduled inspection, you crazy or something? Korovitz and his gang confiscated my two bottles of bourbon I'd put in a corner of my locker behind a family album, and they didn't even say thank you. The beer and booze they'd found in other lockers could've been wheeled away in a barrow."

"Yeah," Vince began to scratch his nose, "we gotta find some place safe to keep the stuff."

"Now you're talking, Vince, now you're talking." The collective response was friendly and auguring well for the future. As the relaxed mood was returning, some of the men jumped to their feet and began to dress, others lay prone and serene on their bunks, and others still busied themselves with daily chores.

The sudden sound of Fred's voice did not startle them, and they took it in their stride.

"Does anybody want to know why I think Honigklausen is insecure?"

They demonstrated little, if any, curiosity, but they were hardly resentful. And Vince, gauging the mood of the crowd, called out to Fred, "Sure, why not, but keep it brief and simple, okay!"

"Right you are," Fred was beaming, and he positioned himself by the outer wall, close to the entrance, facing most of the crowd—a well-chosen spot for a public speaker. He began his presentation, and words came easily to him, as they usually did. But it was beyond his powers to be brief, and as he went on matching a sharp point to a weighty generalization and vice versa, he noticed with alarm that there were fewer and fewer faces in his line of vision and more and more backs and buttocks. As for keeping it simple, it had been inculcated into him already in high school and later with infinitely more emphasis in college that the world was extraordinarily complex, and engraved indelibly upon his memory was the figure of one of his favorite professors, a man with the penchant for the dramatic who, whenever an occasion presented itself, would toss to the side his excessively long cape which he wore in all seasons, thrust his arms forward in an incantatory gesture and bellow out: "Be on your guard against the greatest temptation and vice of the modern age—OVERSIMPLIFICATION!"

Though his audience had dwindled and then disappeared, and he was soon standing alone confronting bare walls and empty bunks, Fred consoled himself with the thought that he had not given in to oversimplification. Not that he was in the least tempted.

/ / /

It was a tepid Saturday morning, and the large, well-protected clock on the side of the chapel installed more than two years before at the behest of Chaplain Hastings to ensure a greater punctuality on the part of churchgoers displayed 10:45 in large luminous hands. It was a tepid Saturday morning very much like the other Saturday mornings in the month of March, the year 1958 boasting of a mild winter now drawing to a close, the harbingers of spring being not far behind it. But in every other respect this Saturday morning on the parade ground was very special; not on a grand scale, of course, as there were no helicopters squatting on the grass, their crews ready to fly the visiting dignitaries out at a moment's notice back to their seats of power in Frankfurt, Bonn, or Brussels. Nor was there a bevy of MP cars and squads of MPs to be seen, their radio transmitters glittering in the sun, set on crucial official business investigating a felony or getting ready for a deadly chase. No, this tepid Saturday morning was devoid of the hallmarks of national pomp or fireworks of high crimes. Yet it was a very special morning. All over the parade ground scores of men have positioned themselves in small or larger groups, and here and there a solitary figure stood out like a secret agent determined to keep a watchful eye on the imminent events of the day. Acute curiosity and boundless suspense could be sensed everywhere.

/ / /

By the reviewing stand a bevy of officers and senior NCOs kept one another amused with the latest gossip, reminiscences, and predictions of what might very well happen before the next full moon. In the middle of this illustrious company stood Sergeant Lester Honigklausen, flanked by Colonel Trainer, the Group Commander, and Major Fiorello, the Group Executive Officer. Captain Hurstwood, the Group Adjutant fulfilling also the duties of the Supply and the Morale Officer, and Captain Lieberman, the Group Chaplain, were chatting a few feet away.

Far to the left, where the chapel marked the edge of the field, the men of the Second Platoon of C Company in their dress uniforms pressed to perfection, their boots spit-shining as never before, and the locks of their M1 rifles sparkling in the morning air were forming a column with Captain Bohn at the head and two sergeants right behind him. "Forward, slow march!" Bohn commanded and the platoon began to move, each row of four in perfect alignment, the distances between those in front and in the back meticulously identical, the ends of slanted rifles one thin, vertical line, and another sideways.

By the reviewing stand Colonel Trainer glanced at his watch.

"Right on time," he let out appreciatively, "Jessup trained 'em boys good."

Not more than ten feet away Captain Lieberman leaned forward towards Captain Hurstwood.

"Quite a send-off for Honigklausen, Ted, honor guard and the rest. I've never seen or heard of anything like it in aid of a Master Sergeant."

"They've been kind of close, Ed and Lester."

"Oh," Lieberman laughed. "Now you're really giving me the inside poop."

Far to the right, Group Sergeant Korovitz spoke in an undertone to a staff sergeant.

"I'll tell you one thing, Swen, Lester can sure put it away . . . Well, you saw it with your own eyes, you were there."

"It must be the lard," the staff sergeant answered with alacrity, his eyes sparkling.

"An ordinary guy would've been under the table long before they put the bottles away, but not Lester, not him . . . it's the lard," he repeated with conviction, "booze just soaks through and evaporates in the fat."

"That's one way of putting it, Swen," Korovitz went on in a fatherly manner, "but it don't do no credit to Lester."

"How do you mean, Leroy?"

"Lester's no ordinary guy, and I don't mean his weight. No, sir, inside all them tons of fat there lives an extraordinary guy, a great man you might say, out-ruling all master sergeants in the U.S. Army, and a bit of a mystery to the whole world."

"If you say so."

"But I do say so, Swen, and it might be in your best interest to take it to heart lest you miss a beat in all this cranking and creaking as our wagon rolls on, uphill or downhill, no matter which, and we wouldn't want that, would we now?"

"No, Sarge, we sure wouldn't want that," and the staff sergeant moved away.

"Is Lester flying stateside from Frankfurt later today?" Major Fiorello inquired of Colonel Trainer as they watched the Second Platoon turn the corner and advance in the same highly disciplined and precise manner with one more perpendicular turn awaiting it before it would be in line with the reviewing stand.

"Hell, no," and Trainer bristled up. "The NCOs at Army are throwing a party for him tonight, and this afternoon he's reporting to General Ryan to receive the Distinguished NCO Award and yet another cross."

"Good for him, and good for the Group." Fiorello nodded, smiling reticently. "Will he be up to yet another bust after last night and the night before, I wonder?"

Trainer's countenance brightened. "Let me tell you this, John, and I kid you not. Years ago, it must've been '43 or '44, a fellow sergeant intiintimated to me, when I raised a similar question, that Lester Honigklausen can drink any amount, yes, any amount of liquor any time any place, and not look the worse for it the next day or in the days to follow. Well, at first I thought to myself my buddy was having some quiet fun at my expense, which they say is good for the soul, until . . . until I found it to be gospel truth."

"Son of a gun!" Fiorello barely managed to articulate between the guffaws. "Son of a gun!"

"And an inspiration to all of us," Trainer added, grinning from ear to ear.

The platoon was now no more than thirty yards away from the reviewing stand, and Trainer broke through the crowd, slapped Honigklausen on the back and sounded off, "You're on, Lester." The departing Group Sergeant stepped forth and took his place on the reviewing stand, in the exact spot where generals and colonels were wont to stand reviewing ceremonial parades. The officers and NCOs who had previously surrounded Honigklausen now retreated several steps and formed a single line before the reviewing stand with Trainer at the extreme right, officers in order of rank extending leftward, and finally the NCOs arranged in the same hierarchical order. "Attention," Trainer commanded, and everyone in the single line snapped to attention.

While they stood immobile but full of barely disguised combativeness, the honor platoon came to a halt in front of Honigklausen. Captain Bohn made an about-face and marched towards the Group Sergeant while the two sergeants who had marched behind the captain shouted orders to the platoon: "Left face, spread, preeeseent arms."

Bohn was still approaching Honigklausen when the latter sprang to attention and saluted. Bohn returned the salute and reported, "Group Sergeant Honigklausen, the Second Platoon is ready for inspection."

Within a wide semicircle adjoining the actors of this unique ceremony the curious and the respectful sprang forward to get a better view, and from the living quarters a swarm of bodies advanced, loath to miss the show and the excitement. Within seconds, it looked as if at least half of the base was there, wearing civvies or fatigues, or a combination of both, and they were dead set on taking in what was happening. Upon hearing Bohn's words, Honigklausen walked to the extreme right of the first row of the platoon and commenced the inspection. Stepping forth slowly and deliberately with Bohn following two paces behind him and to the left and the sergeants on the captain's heels, he pierced each man with a stern unflinching eye, gazed critically at their uniforms, shoes, and the effect of their latest haircuts, here and there fired a question about where the man was from, and twice evinced what could well have been the prelude to a surreptitious smile when he heard that the man was from Pennsylvania. With obvious pleasure and gusto he wrenched the M1 from the guarding hands of several troopers, flipped it, held it high, and peered through the barrel before thrusting it back into the trooper's hands. It appeared that the inspection was going well, and no gigs were to be given. When he had finished his task, Honigklausen moved at a swifter pace to the front, turned round, and stood at attention before Captain Bohn.

"Second Platoon has passed inspection with flying colors, Captain Bohn. I thank you, sir."

"Thank you, Group Sergeant," and Bohn signaled to his sergeants. They gave new orders, and presently the platoon was on its way marching back to the assembly area.

For a very brief moment, so brief that it would not even find its place in a most detailed scenario of the ceremony, Honigklausen stood alone, to all appearances lost in thought or perhaps revving himself up for the next event. Then abruptly he hurled his arms backward, threw his enormous chest forward, and marched off to where Trainer was heading the single file of bemedalled warriors. Facing the Group Commander in the most punctilious posture consistent with the military code of courtesy and saluting with a flourish, he spouted out: "Group Sergeant Lester Honigklausen reporting to Group Commander before shipping out to Fort Dix, subject retirement from U.S. Army."

Trainer made every attempt to look stoical, but emotions got the better of him and his eyes were misty.

"Look after yourself, Group Sergeant, we'll miss you." He tried to say more but was unable to, and breathing heavily he gave a long smart salute, his fingers touching the visor for an inordinately long time. Next Honigklausen was going down the line, saluting, shaking hands, exchanging a word or two, saluting again and again. When he reached Sergeant Carl Steiner, the Motor Pool Sergeant, his earnestness of manner gave way to deep concern which was painted all over his face.

"How is Larry?" he asked.

"Not good, Lester, not good."

"Saw him last week and they said . . ." The unspoken words hung in the air like explosives, their fuses unlit for the duration, but not a second longer.

"I know what they said, but it's no good, and Larry knows it. Trainer is appointing young O'Leary as temporary Mess Hall Sergeant . . . I can tell you this, it's breaking Larry's heart he can't be here today."

Honigklausen nodded, and the two men saluted and shook hands.

"You'll be hearing from me."

"I know I will, Lester, and all the best to you."

As Honigklausen was drawing to the end of the file, a staff car, brand new and shining from bumper to bumper, drove silently to the reviewing stand, and as if it was on a secret mission of national importance, positioned itself opposite Trainer and the officers closest to him.

Out of it scrambled the driver, a corporal in a dress uniform and looking every inch like a recruiting poster. He adjusted his hat and tie and
stood expectantly by the back door on the side of the reviewing stand.

As Honigklausen had finished shaking hands with the last sergeant
in the file, he threw his head up and began to walk diagonally to the
waiting car. Once he reached it, he made a smart about-face, drew himself up, and saluted in the direction of Trainer. "Attentioooon!" Trainer
roared as he and everyone in the file returned the salute. The driver held
out the door for Honigklausen who climbed in slowly and self-con-
sciously; the staff car rolled away and was soon past the main gate and
out of sight. But the file headed by Trainer continued the salute, and it
was only after a fitting interval of time that Trainer first and then the
others lowered their hands.

To the back of the reviewing stand and further to the left and right,
the all-absorbing interest in Sergeant Honigklausen's leave-taking never
flagged. They had stood there—the late arrivals adding to the crowd-
edness of the place—eager to partake of and digest every detail and
nuance of what was happening. They stood there watching for many
different reasons: some had felt the Group Sergeant's heavy foot on
their posteriors and would never forget the occasion, his present leave-
taking, no matter how glorious, serving as a kind of vicarious revenge;
others had simply heard on the bush telegraph that the big fat slob was
leaving for good, and they wanted to make absolutely sure that this
promise would not be broken. Many were lured by what was promising to be an extravaganza, pomp and circumstance rarely seen on a military base and ranking high in the histrionics of military life. The better
informed were privy to the secrets surrounding the unbreakable bond
tying Colonel Trainer and the Group Sergeant, bond which was vari-
ously explicated, a common version being the two had been bosom
buddies since day one and had chased broads together on the wide
plains of their native Kansas; though another pungent version soon
began to compete with it, namely that Trainer and Honigklausen had
met in the olden days as inmates at a state penitentiary, the length of
incarceration, the nature of the offenses perpetrated by them, and the
name of the state which housed them being anybody's guess or anybody's certainty. But for a sizeable part of those present, the ceremony
helped to relieve the tedium of regimented life, if only for a few hours,
while for others confined to the base or sentenced to light punishment,

it was a treasured moment of independence, an all too brief escape into freedom.

Colonel Trainer had always been an eminently popular Group Commander, one of the reasons for it being that he never cared one hoot in hell whether the men liked him or not. Master Sergeant Honigklausen had always been an eminently unpopular Group Sergeant, one of the reasons being that he made every effort to be well liked by the men, and went to great lengths to advertise what he considered to be his joviality and benevolence. But Army lingo, when it comes to praise and blame, can be bewilderingly deceptive, and the enlisted men's verdict on an officer or senior NCO, be it one or the other, may deceive the uninitiated containing as it does the same foul turns of phrase and the same obscenities. What determines praise or blame in this situation is something indefinable, unamenable to quantitative analysis as it is unamenable to carefully formulated criteria, linguistic paradigms, or any scientific test. Some things are destined to remain secrets, borne endlessly on the crest of one wave or another and never reaching shore.

The ceremony concluded; idle groups of men and the solitary watchers began to disperse. Few regretted being witness to the extraordinary events, and some felt Trainer had performed a noble deed, though whether Honigklausen was deserving of it was another matter. From a shifting, scattering crowd two figures detached themselves and began to bear towards the Mess Hall. The one in the rear was catching up with the other.

"Jimmie, could ye lend us a fiver or somethin' like it, it's for the game tonight?" The man in front reeled on his heel, his face impassive.

"Do you see those stripes on my sleeve, Private Gillespie, and if you do, what do they signify?"

"I thought we was buddies, Jimmie, I thought we was buddies," Private Gillespie remonstrated.

"Let me make it clear to you for the last time, Private, in the Army you address your superiors by their rank and you show respect at all times."

"Sure, sure, Jimmie." Words were sticking in Gillespie's throat.

"And this being so, the proper form of address in this situation, to be employed by you at all times and without fail, is Sergeant O'Leary."

"Christ Almighty!"

"I gotta strong feeling, Gillespie, the Savior is not in your corner."

"Sergeant O'Leary, how about that small loan. What's a fiver for a sarge?"

"Denied! And I just happen to recall an outstanding debt of ten dollars, regarding which said debt no attempt has ever been made to clear it."

"It'll be paid. It'll be paid." Gillespie was speaking from the heart. "I give you my word . . . Sarge."

"It'd better be paid," O'Leary practically hissed the words out, and casting another vitriolic glance at Gillespie, he walked smugly away.

"Forgive me for breathing, Your Magnificence," Gillespie muttered under his breath as he watched the decamping sergeant with unmitigated contempt. Then someone lay a hand on his shoulder, and he turned around.

"Did you get the dough from your Irish sergeant friend? It's for the crap game tonight, didn't forget, did ye?" a nervous voice asked.

Gillespie was more assertive now, and the disappointment and the gall had given way to a combative frame of mind.

"O'Leary may be a sergeant, maybe or maybe not, but never, never call him my friend, and never, never call 'im an Irishman. I have a buddy in G2 at Army who says North Koreans drop 'em infiltrators into our base, guys whom they'd sent up to language schools in North Korea to learn our lingo and have their faces cut up to make them look like us. Well, I wouldn't be . . . at all surprised if O'Leary was one of them gooks, slimy infiltrators and spies . . ."

"O'Leary a gook!"

"That's right, friend . . . 'cause nowadays you can't trust nobody, take my word for it, and most important of all you can't trust O'Leary, and that's a fact!"

"I'll be damned!"

"And don't you ever call O'Leary an Irishman because he ain't one. He don't have the heart of an Irishman."

Chapter 2

Group Sergeant Korovitz, his fatigues neatly pressed and the enormous whistle hanging from the top button of his tunic, was bending and unbending over his desk in a leisurely rhythmic movement, sliding forward and back in his seat and peering at this, that, or other set of papers.

"Good exercise, Sarge," Jesús Vallejo, Group Clerk, sounded off from the other side of the office, "good for the spine."

"Well, I am trying to kill two birds with one stone, Vallejo, finding out what those damned papers say and follow Doc's orders."

"If I were you, Sarge, I'd forget about the papers and just take care of your body. One thing at a time, as my dad keeps on saying."

"My compliments to your dad, but Leroy G. Korovitz can and will do more than one thing at a time, it's the family tradition."

"Right you are, Sarge," and Vallejo was on the point of launching into yet another speech on the appropriate therapeutic practices recommended for back injuries, when the door to the Group Commander's offices swung open and Colonel Trainer stepped in.

"How is the old back, Leroy?" he hollered from the threshold.

"Coming along very nicely, thank you, sir. Doc says nothing was broken or dislocated—just strain and a ligament or two pulled. It'll take maybe a week and no more."

"Good, excellent," and Trainer lit a cheroot and began to emit thick clouds of smoke in all directions. "I wanna talk to you about them three Articles 15 and the summary."

He began to ask questions, listened to Korovitz's comments without interrupting, made some observations, listened again, asked more questions, and finally yawned ostentatiously to signal that the subject was closed.

"Those men have been warned, they asked for it." Korovitz volunteered the last word.

Trainer puffed again at the cheroot and nodded gravely. Then all of a sudden, as if a new dawn was breaking, his face brightened.

"Saturday was something," he enunciated with infinite care, "it's a day to remember," and as he spoke, his gaze fell on both Korovitz and Vallejo in close succession, seeking eye contact again and again.

"Everything's gone without a hitch." Korovitz was now grinning and looking straight at Trainer, who grinned back, delighted.

"I'll swear again by all the manure in Kansas, that was somethin'!"

Presently Vallejo hoisted his head and shot an inquiring glance at Trainer.

"Go on, Jesús . . . gotta somethin' to say?" Trainer roared.

"Two points," Vallejo began in a level tone of voice, sounding like a C.P.A. addressing a pair of difficult clients whose fulminations had finally come to an end. "I don't know if you realize, sir, that the turnout was unexpectedly high. A conservative estimate put it at eighty-five to ninety percent. In other words, just about everybody who was on base was there on the parade ground, watching . . ."

"Feelin' like giving every man a three-day pass," Trainer roared again, "but it stands to reason I won't."

"I wouldn't, sir," Korovitz joined in jovially, "considering we have men confined to base."

"Shucks, you guys take the joy out of life."

"My second point being the Second Platoon did an outstanding job. They were like the Pentagon honor guard . . . someone said . . . anyway, the enlisted men's verdict is they were damned good."

"Captain Bohn took them on a pretty rough hike." Korovitz sounded well informed and appreciative. "It paid off."

"Right, Jessup is to be commended." Trainer uttered the words pensively and walked over to the window.

"Group Sergeant, please carry on, and you too, Vallejo. I'll just linger here for awhile."

He remained standing by the window, the cheroot planted firmly between his lips, looking vaguely beyond the office and displaying hardly any interest in the flower beds laid out symbolically between the Motor Pool and the Communal Building, the open area further down coated by thin, yellowish grass and an odd tree here and there. His thoughts focused on the two occupants of the Office of the 16th Engineer Group, Master Sergeant Leroy Korovitz and Specialist IV Jesús Vallejo.

As he had expected, Leroy had worked out well. Just about everyone he had asked before appointing him had only praise for this wiry ex-prize fighter, ex-screw, and ex—he had forgotten by now, if he had ever known with even a modicum of certainty, in how many different careers Leroy had engaged before he became Regular Army. But he had worked out well. The Group Sergeant's office ran smoothly like a well-oiled machine; directives were followed and fully implemented, the information from the individual companies duly noted and acted upon, all the papers filed in an orderly manner and easily retrievable, and the rings of authority and coordination fanning out from the Command Building encompassed the whole base with no exceptions. Yes, there's little doubt—Trainer meditated—that Leroy is one efficient son of a gun, and a godsend to the Group. He, Trainer, would take his hat off to him any hour of the day. Still, he missed Lester Honigklausen, who in the last three months merely oversaw the replacement at work. There had existed between the two a bond and a working relationship which could not be duplicated, and he no longer had in the office next to his a devoted friend and steward. He also missed all the fuss Honigklausen had daily made over him, his obsequious ways, which once comical were now remembered by him nostalgically as tributes of true devotion and fidelity.

"Would the Major care to consider this or another option, what does the Major propose to do about this ticklish matter, I am sure the Major has given every consideration to this very strange request from Army"—these may have been instances of fawnish attentiveness, but now they were cherished by him as very reassuring ways of doing business. He had gotten so used to Honigklausen's soft and genuflecting manner—it was like having his entire body wrapped up in warm blankets day in, day out with no disturbances allowed—that Korovitz's straightforward and unembellished approach was a shock in itself, a shock of recognition that the past was dead, dead as mutton, and the present nothing that he would fall in love with. Leroy never addressed him in the third person; he would have found it outlandish and preposterous. Trainer vaguely remembered that some European king in days past insisted upon being addressed in the third person, or was it that he, the king, referred to himself in the third person—Trainer could not remember which—but now a powerful sentiment filled every particle of his mind, a conviction impossible to dismiss, that he genuinely liked being addressed in the third person, king or no king, and that the sad disappearance of this custom was yet another sign of things going to the dogs.

As for Jesús Vallejo, well, this was a different proposition. Ever since Dirk Donkers had assumed the duties of Group Clerk almost four years before and during his entire term of enlistment, which ended two years later, Trainer considered him irreplaceable. Not only did Donkers help the acting Group Commander in getting promoted to colonel and becoming permanent Group Commander, he was also a minesweeper, defusing explosive clumps in his superior's path. Trainer ticked off on memory's fingers the salient instances: the goddamn morass of dealing with the French, Major General Vickers and the pot of trouble he brought with him, the niceties of dealing with General Ryan in a way calculated to win approval, the French again, and the bosom-baring encounters with the Germans. The list was endless, and Donkers was always there to advise and help make the right decision. In addition, his day-to-day tasks were carried out flawlessly. When Donkers had finally departed, Trainer felt that an enormous vacuum had descended upon 16th Engineer Group, rendering most men helpless and sealing off all exits. But then Vallejo reported for duty, and things got off to a good start. Vallejo had been selected and strongly recommended by Honigklausen and Trainer, scratching his neck to spark off flames of memory as he stood quietly by the window, recollected very distinctly that what his Group Sergeant valued most about the unlikely candidate was his being "respectful."

Clearly—and Trainer went on scratching his neck—Vallejo proved to be more, much more, than a toady and bootlicker to the fat Anglo slob. The "Mexican kid" as Honigklausen had originally dubbed him had other talents, and these have been standing out in bold relief for the last year and a half. In essence, and without the advantages Donkers enjoyed, Vallejo had established himself as being indispensable to the Command Building on the strength of his clerical and administrative talents, his thoroughness, intelligence, and good judgments. He could also be as smooth as silk and a bit of a diplomat. Donkers—Trainer went on recollecting—could be cheeky at times and needed a kick in the ass, which Trainer administered now and then "for the good of the service." Vallejo had never been cheeky and when overruled would simply sit there impassively without uttering a single word, only his large expressive charcoal eyes telling the story of how the wrong orders would certainly do harm, and this being so let someone else take the blame. More often than not he was right! Trainer shivered and tossed his head this way and that. Yes, the kid was usually in the right, and those who outranked him were often in the wrong! Trainer shivered again. What a hell of a situation! And then there was the vocabulary Vallejo used. Where did he learn all them big words, half of which he, Trainer, did not understand and had never heard before? According to Honigklausen, Vallejo was just a dumb Mexican kid from Taos, his principal qualification for the job being "respectful" toward those in authority. Well, Lester sure got this one wrong! Trainer concluded the chain of recollections and reached for another cheroot.

"You guys keep up the good work," he called out merrily and abruptly left the Group Sergeant's office. In the corridor he stood pluckily for a few moments, ready to take on anybody and arguing with himself.

/ / /

"Just a couple of things, Ed," Major John Fiorello, Executive Officer of 16th Engineer Group, was saying facing Colonel Trainer comfortably ensconced behind his desk. "Just a couple of things," he repeated as if he wanted to minimize the topics. But Trainer knew better. The sun had shifted all the way to the west; it was knock-off time for the personnel in the Command Building, and here was John, honest, hard-working John, dropping in ostensibly for a chat, but in reality bearer of important tidings, to him at least, calling for multiple decisions. Maybe this was the trouble—thoughts flashed and flashed again through his mind—that he was surrounded by highly efficient, dedicated men, who somehow became veritable experts in the art of paper bureaucracy and ringleaders of paper chases. This—he contemptuously reminded himself—was peacetime army, which meant it was no army at all until it was tested and bloodied in battle. What did it matter whether Group's reports arrived late at Army, whether some goddamn questionnaires were filled out or not filled out, whether memos and directives from the Commanding General's office were read or unread, answered or unanswered, properly filed or improperly filed, or for that matter not filed at all. It was all a game, and it had as much to do with soldiering as a church social had with going after convicts who had escaped from a maximum-security prison. His thoughts wandered back to the hills of Korea six years before, to Anzio and Cassino, to the Ardennes and Bastogne years earlier. That was soldiering, and in it there was absolutely no room for paper chases and bureaucratic pyrotechnics. But all of a sudden he heard someone cough softly, and lowering his head he saw John Fiorello sitting opposite him gazing absentmindedly at the floor.

"John, sorry, got away on my own, you might say . . ."

"That's okay, Ed." Fiorello was smiling uninhibitedly.

"Your couple of things?"

"Right," Fiorello shifted in his seat, "Sol Lieberman has been with us for more than a year, and it's time for a report on him from you as C.O . . . This will go to the Office of Chaplains in D.C. and a copy to Ryan."

Trainer squinted as if a flood of dazzling light invaded his eyeballs. "Right, we'll do, and what has Sol been peddling this season?"

"He's doing very well, he's the most popular chaplain I've ever known, the men flood to see him . . ."

"Oh!"

In his praise and factual manner Fiorello delineated the chaplain's discharge of his duties, the projects he had instituted, the interfaith meetings and clubs he had organized. Totally absorbed, Trainer listened with both ears.

"Sol has the common touch, and he can reach the men as few chaplains can," Fiorello went on, "and, of course, he's into various sports. You know he was a quarterback at Brandeis, nearly made the

Olympic swimming team, and what he knows about football and base-ball could go into volumes."

"Yeah, I heard about it."

"There's something else," and here Fiorello paused and smiled more to himself than at Trainer. "For Sol, religion is mostly a matter of con-duct, of the here and now; sure he performs all the required rituals, he marries people who sure expect to be happy, circumcises screaming babies, buries the dead according to the proper rite, etc. etc. But . . . all of this is somehow secondary to Sol. He pays little attention to life after death, to Heaven and Hell, and even to God Almighty, the Lord our God."

"I'll be damned."

"For Sol the essence of Jewish religion and of any true religion, I would venture to say, is contained in the maxim 'Do unto others as you would others do unto you.' That's it. There's little else, and his congre-gation is growing by leaps and bounds."

"Son of a gun," Trainer muttered under his breath.

"I wouldn't put any of this in your report on Sol, no need to con-fuse the powers that be . . ."

"Sure, I understand," Trainer interrupted him.

"But I'd say Sol Lieberman has been a first-rate chaplain, and I wish U.S. Army had more like him."

"Agreed," Trainer uttered with verve, and Fiorello passed onto other matters. When he had finished dealing not with a couple of things but with a score at least, he stood up and made ready to go.

"If you're leaving the building, John, I'll walk with you to the park-ing lot."

"I'll get my coat and meet you by the main entrance."

"Roger!" Unmistakably, Trainer was slipping back into the old ways.

Outside, their coats buttoned up against the frosty wind, Trainer said, "Didn't want to talk about it in the office, but it's kind of weigh-ing me down."

"Go on, Ed, get it off your chest."

"Today's Monday, well, several days ago, it must've been Wednesday or Thursday, Wednesday I think, I got my final divorce decree. I'm now a legally divorced man, and all my attempts to get Beryl back, after she'd left me, came to naught."

"I heard about it. I am deeply sorry."

"It's my own fault, not Beryl's . . ." Trainer stopped and thrust his head and shoulders forward. "I don't mean to keep you after hours."

"It's Eunice's bridge night, and we have a babysitter. You know those women's bridge sessions, they start early and end very late."

"In that case let's stroll down to the creek."

Fiorello nodded, and almost immediately Trainer began to unburden himself.

"I haven't told many people about it here on base. Lester knew and Ted knows, Ted Hurstwood, I mean. When I got my promotion somethin' gone haywire inside me. I don't know what it was. I started picking up broads and screwing them, mostly one-night stands, on the back seat as a rule, now and then in hotels. I guess this was my way of celebrating, showing the world I made it. Beryl probably latched on, and she begged me to be careful. Well, one night I brought a girl with me to the Village, and we was both drunk as hell. I ordered Beryl out of our bed and told her to go sleep on the couch in the living room so I could screw the girl in the bedroom."

"That wasn't very smart," Fiorello broke in.

"No, it wasn't. It wasn't. Anyway, the next day Beryl hardly spoke a word about it, and I thought the whole thing had blown over. Well, the day after that she was all packed, and she said she was leaving me and wanted a divorce, and I would hear from her attorney. I begged her to stay so we could talk things over, but she wouldn't have any of it, she just pushed me aside and a woman friend drove her to Frankfurt where she got a flight to New York and from there to Kansas City."

"You tried to get in touch with her, make her change her mind, I'm sure you did, didn't you?"

"You can say it again. I wrote her I don't know how many times. There must be a thick bundle of letters lying about somewhere in Kansas, but she never answered. I tried to call her God knows how many times, and once got her on the line, but she wouldn't talk to me and just said her attorney was handling everything, and after a time when she heard my voice, she'd just hang up."

Fiorello's eyes were sadly fixed on Trainer, and his lips moved for a brief moment as if he were about to say something, but he didn't. Trainer went on, "Well, where the letters and the telephone did no good, I said to myself, hell, what I gotta do is see her in person, so I hopped on a commercial flight in Frankfurt for New York and then to KC, and gone to see her in that insurance office in KC where she worked. That was April of last year. I'd got her address from her folks, and they were hoping things could be patched up. When she finished work we went to some café and talked for several hours, and she listened and I listened, but she wouldn't budge, not an inch. She said it was all over between us, and by this time I'd received several letters from her attorney, which I gave to my attorney, and the pot was startin' to boil. I went to all lengths to delay matters, still hoping we could get back together and be re . . . reconciled, and my shyster was filling out reams of paper with ap-ap-apologies and pro-proposals and sending them to Beryl's shyster who was filling out reams of paper with replies and ex-explanations, and the two boys had their hands full and a steady income while it lasted."

"And then?"

"Beryl wouldn't budge an inch, and the funny thing is she didn't even want my money. We had to practically force her to accept alimony, and in the end she cut it down, wouldn't take what I wanted her to have." Trainer paused and his grim, furrowed face was also dull and drained.

"I would give anything, anything in the world to get her back, John. But I know it's impossible. Beryl will never come back to me." He paused again. "Sam is telling me I should get married again."

"Sam?"

"Sam Stebbins, General Stebbins."

"Oh, maybe he's right."

"Maybe, but right now I don't have the in-inclination."

"I'm glad you took me into your confidence, Ed, and I don't mean to be mouthing meaningless platitudes, but time is the best healer and, who knows, time may be on your side."

"And how is that?"

"After a year or two if Beryl hasn't formed a lasting relationship, she may be willing to change her mind. In the meantime keep writing to her. It doesn't matter if she doesn't answer at first. What matters is she'll be reading your letters."

Trainer smiled warmly. "I couldn't ask for better advice, but I'd better tell you, Beryl is Kansas just like me, and I know how she ticks.

Once she makes up her mind, and there's no new evidence as my shyster would say, it's for keeps."

He was keenly conscious of Fiorello's earnest understanding, of the almost compassionate gaze focused on him, and of his silence more telling than a thousand daring words.

"Let's get back to the parking lot," Trainer said in a dispassionate voice.

"Let's."

Once they reached the steel and granite of the base, they saw a tall figure advancing towards them.

"Hi, Ted," Fiorello called out.

When Captain Hurstwood drew nearer to them he rapped out, "Ed, John," a self-protective smile lighting up his face.

"Has the day been set?" Trainer inquired zealously.

"No, not yet, but it's in the works."

"Ted, you don't want to get hitched here on base," Fiorello broke in, rolling his eyeballs, "you could have an honor guard and a thousand dry throats."

"I regret to inform you, gentlemen, it's the bride to be or rather her family that is making all the arrangements."

"So, what city are we talking about?" Trainer sounded persistent and combative.

"Philadelphia."

"Oh," Trainer was feigning surprise and concern, "city of brotherly love where they mug you as soon as you get off the bus."

"Something like that," Hurstwood concurred.

"Make sure, Ted, the two families and their guests don't arrive to the wedding by bus." It took Fiorello some time to squash his laughter.

"I'll put it at the top of the list, and I can't thank you enough," Hurstwood answered, and the three men began to walk towards their cars.

/ / /

The next morning the Group Sergeant's office was a veritable beehive. As soon as the doors opened, three special messengers from Army saluted in quick succession, bringing confidential papers marked *For Group Commander's Eyes Only*. Sergeant Korovitz took a good twenty minutes reading them, one being an urgent request to Colonel Trainer from General Ryan's office to call the general at once, which Trainer dutifully did on four different occasions, being informed each time that the general was in conference and could not be disturbed. On the heels of this, two more special messengers arrived with confidential papers and renewed requests to Trainer to call the general without delay. When Trainer finally reached Ryan, he was given scanty information. It appeared that the vital intelligence, which had to do with the imminent NATO maneuvers, was accumulating in a random fashion in the general's office during the morning hours but could only be deciphered in small segments without an overview or a general summary. Each segment by itself meant very little and would have to be joined to a future one which could be delayed for hours, or perhaps days. Trainer did not let the telephone out of his sight and waited.

Concurrently, the MPs brought in a private and a corporal accused of roughing up two German nationals during the night, a handcuffed PFC accompanied by two German policemen, and a young German woman who was accusing said PFC of attempted rape. There were also frantic calls from the Mess Hall to the effect that the bi-weekly provisions of meat, fish, and vegetables had not arrived on time, and should this delay continue the Master Menu conceived and embossed in Washington D.C. which controlled the daily distribution of rations to U.S. Army personnel irrespective of what corner of the planet they might be gracing with their presence might have to be deviated from, no laughing matter, since such deviations usually called for lengthy explanations and a possible Board of Inquiry. As if these tribulations were not enough, the officer's restroom in the Mess Hall had sprung a leak, sewage pipes in the living quarters of A Company were blocked, and a fire had mysteriously started in D Company's office, which was soon extinguished with no loss or harm to human life, but not before it consumed piles of official documents. By late morning the situation had stabilized itself, but a pall of gloom hung over the Group Sergeant's office and when Private Michael Gillespie from C Company entered it, Korovitz eyed him with callous and undisguised suspicion.

"What now, Gillespie? Don't tell me—I can figure this one out myself, earthquake has razed your building to the ground, and the men are dropping off like flies on account of the plague."

"You have a vivid imagination, Sarge."

Korovitz shrugged his shoulders. "What's up, son?"

"Captain Bohn sent me to collect those manuals you said you'd saved for him."

"Oh, yes." Korovitz's face brightened. He reached into a drawer and pulled out several manuals of varying size and thickness held together by rubber bands. "Here you are, son, and give it to the good captain with my compliments."

As Gillespie was leaving unhurriedly and awkwardly, Korovitz caught his eye.

"Are you keeping your nose clean, Gillespie?"

"Tryin', Sergeant, but not always succeedin'."

"My, my, that's a well-thought-out answer. Listen to me, how long do you have?"

"Nine months."

"You were busted twice already. Why don't you do yourself a favor and stick it out peaceful-like, your folks would appreciate it. Keep your nose clean till you get your discharge papers. We don't want to bust you again! I'm telling you we don't!"

"Like you say, Sarge, and thank you for your good wishes."

Gillespie leaned forward and waved at Vallejo.

"Hi, there, Jesús."

"Hi, Mike."

"Thanks for your help, buddy, and I'll be seeing ye real soon."

"You're welcome, and real soon it'll be."

As Gillespie was now really leaving, cross his heart, he turned towards Korovitz.

"Thank you for your fine counsel, sir. I'll do my darnest to live up to it." He placed a hand on the doorknob and was gone.

"You buddy-buddy with him, Vallejo?" Korovitz asked, looking jovial and sanguine.

"Yeah, a decent dude, a little wild at times."

"This is not what I hear from the NCOs in C Company. They say he's muddle-headed and can't take orders."

"There might be something in that, but a qualification must be added."

"You talk like a shyster, Vallejo."

"Let me put it this way, Sarge: it would've been far better for the Army if Michael Gillespie and others like him had never been drafted. Some men just can't endure being regimented, and Mike is one of them. For him and his friends in misery there should be some other branch of national service, something on the order of building bridges and dams, construction work, farm work, something which isn't Army."

"Pure poppycock!"

"Why?"

"Because in times of need, young man, it is the duty of every American to serve his country in the military, and this is the time of need. The military is what made this country great, and this goes for every swinging dick, no exceptions!"

"There are always exceptions, Sarge."

Korovitz pooh-poohed the comment and stretched out his long arms, swiveling his head and neck.

"When the Civil War came, all of us in the South went to the colors. There were no exceptions because this is what the country expected of us. I don't know what they did in Yankee-land, I guess up there in conformance with Yankee customs you could get a substitute for so many pieces of silver but not in the Confederacy, because as Americans we knew full well where our duty lay."

"You should go into politics, Group Sergeant Korovitz, and there is no mistake about it."

"Pooh!"

"When I suggested a non-military service for some I was thinking of what would be most efficient and productive. The government wants to get its money's worth from us, fine, but let's do it efficiently."

"So if a guy says he can't take orders and has an unholy fear of regimentation we take him by the hand and conduct him gentle-like to see a shrink who, after proper examination and re-examination, signs a paper releasing said guy from military service."

"You make it sound too easy."

"Do I now? Maybe there should be two shrinks and four examinations. Would that satisfy you?"

Vallejo smiled and let his hand run leisurely through his hair, a gesture allowing for reflection.

"We won't settle this matter now," he spoke softly and amiably, "if ever."

"Damn right, we won't!"

"As regards Mike," Vallejo went on, "the sad thing is he'll probably get into trouble again and again, nothing serious but enough to block promotion, have him restricted to base . . . maybe keep him in the stockade for a while."

Korovitz had finished his arms–head–and neck exercise and sat there grim and brooding. "We know how to handle habitual offenders. If a man can't be broken in he only has himself to blame. This is the Army, not a church social, Vallejo."

"So it is, Sarge, so it is. You know, some weeks ago at a beer bust Mike and I talked for a long time, and he told me a lot about himself. I had the feeling he wanted to tell me all kinds of private things about himself and his family . . . as if his life depended on it. He was dead set on it. I won't bore you with the details . . ."

"I thank you from the bottom of my heart."

But Korovitz's thanks accomplished little.

"Did you know," Vallejo resumed, "his two elder brothers are very successful? One is in the laundry business, and the other in liquor, and they despise him. They tell him again and again what a bum he is and how he'll never amount to anything . . ."

"I'm sorry to hear it."

"His parents came to America from County Mayo in 1928. They were very young, and settled in New Jersey where the children were born . . ."

"Aha."

"Mike's grandfather was hanged by the British in 1916 during the Easter Rebellion, he'd fought alongside Michael Collins and other Irish leaders, and Mike is very proud of his grandfather, in fact he idolizes him . . ."

"Why was the grandfather hanged?"

"Well the Irish rose against the British, who were in the middle of a war and were promised aid from Germany, but it never materialized. They managed to occupy several public buildings in Dublin, but without outside help the rebellion was quickly quelled."

"Where do you get all this knowledge from, Vallejo?" Korovitz practically howled. "You're supposed to be . . . never mind what you're supposed to be."

"A dumb Mex?"

"I didn't say anything of the kind."

"I know you didn't, and you would never say anything of the kind,"

Vallejo announced lightheartedly, transfixing the sergeant with an icy, sardonic glance.

"So the limeys hanged a few Paddies. Did the Paddies hang a few limeys in return?"

"How could they? They were crushed!"

"That's right, you said that much. And the cause of all this was . . ."

"Rebellion, the Irish wanted to throw off the English yoke."

"Right, you said that too. Where the hell do you get all that book learnin' from, kid?"

"I was the valedictorian of my graduating class in high school."

Upon hearing Vallejo say this, Korovitz fell into a deep silence, as if he wanted to sever all ties with the outside world and commune only with himself. At long last he broke the stillness that now enveloped the office.

"To tell you the truth I can understand those feuds between the English and the Irish better than most. They remind me of our own Civil War when bluebellies tried to destroy the great American nation and trample on the rights and liberties of a free people."

Vallejo pulled a Kleenex out of a box and blew his nose, making hardly any noise. And Korovitz, as if liberated now and standing on his own turf, was holding forth about the exploits of the gallant Confederate troops which against great odds still managed to defeat the bluebellies again and again. "Do you know, Vallejo, not far from the town in Kentucky where I was born there is a little village a mile or two south of which a handful of Confederates poorly armed, just country boys mind you, inflicted grievous losses on a Yankee force ten times their size and saved the day. That was summer of '62."

"Remarkable," Vallejo muttered, "truly remarkable. What is the name of that little village in Kentucky where the boys in gray gave the boys in blue a lickin' in the year of our Lord 1862?"

"What?"

Vallejo repeated the question, and Korovitz scratched his chin.

"The trouble with you, Group Clerk, is that you ask too many questions."

"I'm a bit of the Civil War buff, thought of adding this Kentucky skirmish to my collection."

Korovitz raised his head and was looking unflinchingly at the ceiling, his lips beginning to move. There was little doubt he was on the point of saying something, but before he had the chance the door leading to the corridor was swung open, and Captain Hurstwood stepped in.

"Good morning, Sergeant, and good morning Vallejo," Hurstwood sounded cheerful and carefree.

"Good morning, sir," the two men answered in unison.

Hurstwood walked over to the mailboxes and pulled out from his box pieces of internal correspondence, which he inspected cursorily. Behind him Korovitz scrambled to his feet and was stroking his moustache.

"Huh," he cleared his throat, "my heartfelt congratulations, Captain, on the occasion of your forthcoming marriage."

"News travels fast . . . I hear the men are running a book on the date of my wedding."

"It's amazing what the men can come up with when they put their minds to it." As soon as the words were out of his mouth Korovitz regretted having said them, but Hurstwood burst out laughing and lay a hand on Korovitz's shoulder.

"I feel honored, don't give it another thought, Group Sergeant."

From the other end of the office Vallejo, like a teacher's pet who always asks the most pertinent questions, raised his voice. "Captain Hurstwood, will it be a church or civil wedding? I am just curious."

"The event will certainly take place inside a church."

"And what church might that be?"

"The Episcopal Cathedral in Philadelphia, and the date will be set very shortly . . . not later than the end of the week."

"I'd like to offer my best wishes, sir."

"Thank you, Vallejo."

"Actually," Korovitz broke in, "the whole base is abuzz with it . . . running books on it is one thing, but lots of men suspect you'll be away for some time or else you may not be coming back. The plain truth is they don't want to meet your replacement."

Hurstwood laughed again. "I take it as a compliment, and tell the men I'll be coming back." But as Korovitz's demeanor was curiously cagey, and not in keeping with his everyday clamorous ways, he paused and looked the sergeant straight in the eye: "What is it? Let's have it."

Korovitz hesitated but only for a moment, and then the old self-possession and the old training were again at the helm.

"I heard it from different quarters, A, B, C, D Companies and others heard it too, that you, Captain, won't be coming back . . ."

Vallejo, who was now standing behind his desk, caught Korovitz's eye.

"Yes, Vallejo, go on."

"I heard it too, sir… When one asks them how they came by it, they say they heard it through the grapevine, just about everybody knows it and most believe it."

"There's something uncanny about it," Korovitz let out.

"Just a rumor," Hurstwood brushed it off, "just a rumor."

"But a very persistent one."

The three men fell silent, and then Vallejo broached a new subject.

"If the wedding is to take place in an Episcopal church there's bound to be a good deal of ceremony, sparkling vestments, a lot of coming and going, and glitter all around . . ."

"How come you know so much about Episcopal services . . . trying to come on board or what?" Korovitz was more than half serious.

"No, no, Sergeant, no coming on board and no expectation of it, but when I was still in high school in Taos one of our teachers was getting married in the Episcopal church. She was a nice lady so just about everybody turned up, the whole school you might say, and the clerics inside nearly died of a collective stroke . . ."

"So they didn't kick the bucket . . . or did they?" Hurstwood interrupted.

"Recovered on the last minute . . ."

"Robbing those assembled of their fondest expectations . . . how very inconsiderate can some people be."

"Anyway," Vallejo continued unabashed, "the service was all ceremony and glitter and coming and going, that's what prompted me to pose my question, sir."

"You're right on the button, Vallejo, about what is being planned."

"After the wedding we gave the teach a twenty-one-gun salute, the cops let us use an old shotgun with blanks, and I can tell you, it made one hell of a lot of noise . . ." Hurstwood and Korovitz, who listened with undisguised interest to Vallejo's accounts, saw before them a young man, happy as a lark, caught in the confluence of joyful memories, whose only real company was himself and positively no one else.

"Well, I am glad I dropped in," Hurstwood said as he was heading for the door . . ."I learned a great deal this morning, I want to thank both of you, and take good care of the store."

"We will, sir," Sergeant Korovitz sounded off.

"Yes, sir," Specialist Vallejo followed suit.

As Korovitz was settling himself behind his desk in his wide and ornate armchair throwing one leg up and sliding forward, he turned a brisk eye upon his clerk now totally absorbed in the daily paper routine.

"I guess you'd like me to give you the name of that village in Kentucky where . . ." he stopped abruptly while a thought ran through his mind that this was a perfectly adequate identification and no more data was needed.

"Forget it, Sarge." He heard the words with surprise as Vallejo's face flickered in his direction and then returned to its original position.

Chapter 3

Captain Solomon Lieberman III, the Jewish chaplain of 16th U.S. Army Engineer Group, was standing insouciantly by the window of the Group Commander's office, his tall wiry frame filling its immediate surroundings with the expectation of athletic buzz and sporting accomplishments, and dwarfing the commander's flabby and bulging figure idly reclining behind his desk. If only Lieberman held a towel or a stopwatch in his hand the image would be complete, but instead he held an odd assortment of papers by his fingertips, carelessly and disdainfully letting the world know that dropping them on the floor and letting them wither there was ultimately the only rational course of action.

"The Chief Chaplain's office has got a feather up its ass, Ed, and there's no remedy in sight . . ."

Absentmindedly Trainer nodded, re-crossing his legs while his eyes scoured the ceiling.

"Retreats have gotten to be for those guys the one and only panacea, ship the men out on a retreat twice a year, and they'll sing like a band of angels . . . whereas what matters is how they comport themselves on a daily basis, day in day out."

Trainer nodded again, yawning openly.

"I'll certainly carry out my orders and make the information available through usual channels, but I won't put any pressure on the men. Enrollment for retreats last year was lamentably low, and from what I hear it promises to be even lower this year. I can see very clearly why, and we who are in this business have more important things to do."

Trainer's gaze now rested on the chaplain, and he pulled himself up in his chair so that he was no longer reclining but awkwardly sitting in it and about to say something perfunctory.

"Do what ye think is right, Sol, and I'll back you up," he began, but was at once interrupted by a ferocious pounding on the door and Korovitz's voice roaring, "Colonel, Colonel!"

"Come in," he roared back, jumping to his feet.

Korovitz was beside himself, the state he was seldom in.

"We just got a call from the German Highway Patrol, there's been an accident"—he spoke rapidly and catching his breath—"Captain Hurstwood went over the fence at the Lunenberg Overpass and crashed all the way down, the captain's dead, the car smashed."

"When did this happen?" Trainer snapped.

"About thirty five minutes ago, the German police and an ambulance are already on the scene."

"Send our MPs there, Sergeant Korovitz," Trainer snapped again, "and get me a staff car in front of the Command Building in five minutes; Captain Lieberman and I will be on our way . . ."

"Yes, sir."

Trainer, his old boisterous self-reasserting itself, crossed into Group Sergeant's office.

"Vallejo, get on the horn to the local Kraut police station, and get me the name of the investigating officer . . . it'll be a lieutenant or captain, and gather as much info about him as you can . . . use your charm!"

"Yes, sir, right away, but I didn't know I had any charm."

Trainer gave him a long suggestive stare and turned to Lieberman. "Are you free to come with me?"

"Of course."

It took Trainer but a short minute to brief Korovitz. "Hold the fort, Leroy, and if anything happens serve it on a silver platter to Major Fiorello," he ended by saying, "he's in charge during my absence."

"Righto, sir, and Lunenberg Overpass is about nine miles away, turn right when you leave the base, then left when you come to state road 57. From there it's straight like an arrow."

"Thank you, Leroy." Trainer picked up his overcoat and hat. "Better take a leak before ven-venturing out," he added as an afterthought, his eyes flickering devilishly, and hurried to the men's room.

As they scrambled into the staff car, they caught sight of Vallejo running toward them, a scrap of paper in his hand, waving vigorously.

"Here's the information you asked for, Colonel. Actually the Germans opened up like overcooked tamales."

Trainer was scrutinizing the scrap of paper, smacking his lips. "Well done, Vallejo! And don't let no one tell ye ye got no charm, Jesús. Why you got as much charm as the piss-pot that got no leaks." Lieberman put his foot on the accelerator and they were off. "How is your German today?" Trainer asked, his voice ringing with anticipation.

"Non-existent, I took French in high school and college, and I am proud to say I am reasonably fluent in French. Would you like me to give you French lessons? *Mademoiselle, voulez vous?* How about it?"

"That's great," Trainer muttered, "just great. You're the guy one pines for when one's in trouble. Wake me up when we hit Kansas City."

This morning the Lunenberg Overpass was nothing less than the center of attraction for the whole county. On State Route 57 by the summit where remnants of a wire fence lay in sad disarray, two German police cars were parked close to each other as per regulations. Some distance away an empty American MP jeep stood desolately by, serving no earthly purpose, to all appearances abandoned and irreclaimable. Lieberman slowed down and drove to the exit on the right, a steep mounting and then sliding lane, which in an expansive semicircular fashion took one to the bottom of the overpass where State Route 17 intersected State Route 57 two hundred meters below. Here two ambulances were stationed, one German and one American, and several German police cars were scattered around the scene of the accident while an MP sedan stood on the grass by the row of tall bushes stretching all the way to the adjoining field. When Lieberman stopped the car, an MP sergeant jumped out of the sedan and walked briskly towards Trainer.

"Bad business that"—he reported—"the body is partly burned. When the car went over the fence up there on the summit and hit the ground down here"—he pointed to the wreckage on the field close by partly shielded by the bushes—"the gas tank exploded. The Krauts were here first and they extinguished the fire. We got the name of the driver from registration, Captain Theodore H. Hurstwood, 16th Engineer Group, is . . . or rather appears to be the name. The body will have to be identified officially, of course." The sergeant paused and looked questioningly at Trainer. "We have no jurisdiction here, an American national killed on a German highway is subject to German laws; they investigate, conclude, write the reports, we are mere observers, but," the sergeant tossed his head to the side and let the palm of his right hand rise slowly in a scooping gesture, "the Krauts are usually very cooperative."

Trainer nodded, "Thank you, Sergeant, we'll take it from here." Surveying the scene, Lieberman and Trainer saw several German paramedics talking idly among themselves, two MPs jesting raucously with a very attractive young German woman equipped with tape recorders and ultramodern shining Zeiss camera slouched over her shoulder, a tall stooping man in dark clothes carrying a black bag, presumably the M.D., and a German police officer with captain's insignia surrounded by a cluster of subordinates. To the right and left the curious crowd had grown immensely ever since Captain Hurstwood dived to his death, and two German policemen, one on each side, kept it at bay, giving laconic answers to questions or ignoring them. Cars were stopping continually, and anxious voices in German or English demanded to know what was going on, and then, offended by the cloak of secrecy, drove on.

Colonel Trainer cleared his throat and turned to Captain Lieberman. "Let's go see that Kraut police captain, he's the top dog."

"Right."

As they drew near, the German beckoned to the others to withdraw and stood there on post, his boyish face lit up by an official self-satisfied smile.

"Captain Gerhard Bessner," Trainer called out, holding out his hand.

"It is very considerate of you to remember my name, Colonel." Bessner, speaking fluent English, appeared to be pleasantly surprised.

"Well, you've been to 16th Engineer Group, and we always remember our friends and want them to know damn well we hold them near and dear."

"Thank you very much, Colonel Trainer."

"This is Chaplain Solomon Lieberman, the Group Chaplain," Trainer went on in the same jovial, folksy manner as if he did not have a care in the world.

"Ah, the Jewish chaplain who knows more about baseball and football than anyone else in the U.S. Army."

"This is the compliment I shall always cherish," Lieberman gave out a broad resonating laugh.

"You seem to be very well informed, Captain," Trainer put in sounding exceedingly impressed.

"We too have our spies," Bessner replied with dignified pride.

"Fifth column, eh?"

"Something like that, Colonel, something like that." In turn, Bessner introduced the doctor and his own assistant, a rigid lieutenant, his demeanor tense, his protuberant eyes inquisitive and full of suspicion.

"I imagine you gentlemen would like to see the remains," Bessner asked. "Terrible business." The Americans nodded, and he led them into the field, beyond the row of bushes where by a knot of irregular roots lay the smashed, horribly bent and twisted chassis of the Buick 1958, its inside partly burned and torn to pieces, the windshield and left windows smashed into the finest particles. Hurstwood's body lay on a tarpaulin and was covered by a blanket. Trainer and Lieberman went on inspecting the wreckage, making mental notes, then stood by the body, lifted the blanket, and saluted. Hurstwood's legs and the lower part of his torso were badly burned, the black smudges pointing in all directions and a thick, sooty mass made of skin and flesh covering the protruding bones. In contrast, the chest partly covered by articles of clothing was in a far better condition, but the head was crushed, the cranium gaping open and only one side of the face recognizable.

"The doctor tells me," Bessner broke the silence gently and almost apologetically, "that death was instantaneous. You see the car went over the top," Bessner moved his forearm down at a curve to simulate the path of Hurstwood's car, "smashing into those rocks. The driver was hurled through the windshield head first and hit them with great force." He paused, expecting a question or two, but none were forthcoming. "Are you ready, Colonel and Captain, to identify the body? The law requires that it be done by two individuals who knew the victim."

"We are ready, terrible accident," Trainer said.

When the identification was concluded and the requisite form filled out, Bessner cast a very serious glance at Trainer.

"Actually, sir, we are not at all certain this was an accident."

"What on earth are you talking about?"

Bessner spoke in German to his lieutenant and was handed a folder.

"We took pictures of the lanes on the summit going west as soon as we arrived, and please note there are no skid marks. This means in all probability, Captain Hurstwood was in the left lane going west, and as he was approaching the summit he at first swerved gently to the right lane and then turned sharply right, hit the wire fence and plunged downward. We calculated the angles before the car went over the top, it was an even drive, no sudden attempts to turn left, and the fence was hit at practically a ninety degree angle, the front bumper practically aligned with it."

"Are you trying to tell me Hurstwood plunged to his death on purpose, and this was suicide?"

"It looks like it."

"Have you taken leave of your senses, Bessner?" Trainer lit a cheroot and emitted shapeless clouds of smoke. "Captain Hurstwood was to be married in a few weeks, he was a happy man full of good humor and," Trainer was now eyeing Bessner with that overwhelming confidence that comes solely from knowing the inside story, "one of the best liked officers within the U.S. 7th Army. Why should he want to kill himself?"

"This is not for me to say, but facts are facts, and as policemen in the state of Baden-Württemberg we have to rely on facts, on physical evidence, and draw proper conclusions. You saw the pictures of the highway, sir, let's now take a look at the highway itself."

"Very good idea, Captain, and we are in your debt for conducting this very thorough investigation." Trainer was trying to make amends for his outburst. "We'll take our car and meet you at the summit."

"As you wish, Colonel," and Bessner motioned to his lieutenant, the doctor, and a uniformed highway patrolman to get into the car.

As they were driving up, Lieberman said, "I was afraid of that."

"Me too," Trainer cried, "but hell, we gotta stand fast."

Two hundred meters above Route 17 at the summit the air was pungent, the mild winds from the southeast touching lightly the tops of trees and shrubs and then sluggishly disappearing into the nearby woods before another temperate wave took over. The view in all directions was majestic: to the north and west for countless miles ahead two rivers meandered merrily encircling villages, rock formations, craggy hills, and patches of gorgeous green—meadows sloping gently into limitless hollows and farms.

Far to the east, brimming a variegated landscape, stood a chain of forbidding mountains licked here and there by a shifting mist, like the final station for daredevils embarked on a glorious adventure against impossible odds; and to the south, a succession of lakes bordering a web of highways and roads, of gardens, orchards, and large country houses, of small and large settlements and soccer fields, all kept in proportion, all kept in check. Here the hand of man made its indelible mark, but it did so discretely and wisely, destroying nothing and building for the benefit of many.

"It is here,"—Bessner was explaining patiently—"that the driver began changing lanes." They had stopped some sixty yards from the summit, had left their cars behind, and now were retracing on foot the last leg of Hurstwood's journey. "We had calculated it, the impact on the fence, the careening of the car and it falling down," Bessner went on explaining, "and here the driver is getting himself into position to go over the top." They were now some twenty yards from the summit and the wrecked fence. "Please note, Colonel, there are no skid marks anywhere, the driver was not slipping, sliding, skidding, he appears to have been in full control. It all points to a deliberate act." They were now standing ten yards from the summit, and Bessner consulted his notes. "At this point, the driver made a sharp turn to the right and went over the top. We estimate the speed of the car at this moment to have been around fifty miles per hour. A minute or so earlier, when the car was changing lanes, its speed was close to seventy miles per hour. The inescapable conclusion is that Captain Hurstwood willingly and deliberately jumped to his death."

Lieberman shook his head. "Captain Hurstwood may have become temporarily distracted, he may have blanked out, confusing the fence with the next exit; he may have passed out. Your conclusion is erroneous and not supported by facts, Captain Bessner."

"I retraced for you the movements of the car, Chaplain, what else do you want from me?"

"This you did, but how do you know what went on inside Hurstwood's head?"

"The physical evidence is overwhelming."

"It does not go to motive. Did you find a suicide note on him?"

"No, but many individuals who commit suicide do not advertise it beforehand. I shall have to report my findings." Bessner drew himself up and even though his demeanor was studiously artless, the inevitable pall of pomposity was beginning to wrap itself around him.

"You have absolutely no evidence that Captain Hurstwood was planning to kill himself," Lieberman picked up the thread firmly and obstinately, "whereas his commanding officer Colonel Trainer is prepared to testify under oath that the captain was in an excellent frame of mind for weeks before the accident, that he was to be married very shortly, was looking forward to married bliss, and that in every respect he was a happy man."

"I know where my duty lies, gentlemen." For the first time during the present encounter, Bessner was exhibiting signs of frustration. "We are the West German Highway Patrol, the best in the world, and we conduct our business . . . by the book, to borrow a phrase from you."

Some twenty feet behind Bessner, the two Americans noticed the young lieutenant, rigid and watchful, his eyes protuberant as before and fixed on them with venom and suspicion and the doctor, stooped and flaccid, his black case propped up against his shin.

"I shall follow regulations, the physical evidence is overpowering," Bessner shouted, "*Mein Gott, was wünschen Sie doch,*" and made ready to go, but Trainer got hold of a button on his uniform and held him fast.

"Your name came up in a conversation I had very recently with General Lukas von Metzler, your police commissioner."

"*Was?* You know General von Metzler?"

"And the general thinks very highly of you because of your thoroughness and dedication to duty, yes, I know the general well, have known him for a long time, and in the course of our very recent conversation he asked me what I thought of you. I gave him a glowing account . . . you've been to 16th Engineer Group on many occasions as our guest and also in your professional capacity, it has always been a pleasure to do business with you, we trust you and we respect you."

Signs of tension and frustration were fast disappearing from Bessner's countenance, and he stood there a little lost and slightly baffled.

"You have a brilliant career ahead of you, and there are lots of us, Germans and Americans, who are rooting for you . . . it would be a pity to disappoint them . . . and yourself." Trainer was still holding the German by a button.

"Yes, I understand fully, but . . ."

"The general has his eye on you"—Trainer interrupted—"and the time for promotion may be sooner than you think, assuming, of course, that you want to rise on the totem pole."

"That goes without saying, Colonel."

"As your allies we do things for you, and you as our allies do things for us; it's a two-way street, we help each other, if you catch my meanin'."

"Perfectly, sir."

"The whole matter of German-American relations is crucial in the Cold War and nothing must be done to upset it . . . unless of course, you want the Russkies to overrun the state of Baden-Württemberg . . ."

"Heaven forbid!"

"The team comes first, Bessner, this is what General Lukas von Metzler believes, this is what General Ryan believes, this is what your government and my government believe. Don't disappoint them."

"And my report?"

"You should certainly mention the physical evidence but briefly, not making too much of it. In fact, the best and truest report would be that the driver lost control of the vehicle at the Lunenberg summit, and the vehicle crashed down two hundred meters onto a field causing instantaneous death. Accidental death. End of story."

Trainer let go of Bessner's button, and Bessner in total silence moved his head this way and that, as if ascertaining that he still had full use of his limbs and was a free man.

"16th Engineer Group will be issuing a statement this afternoon, and so will 7th Army Headquarters in Weiningen. Copies will be sent to *The Stars and Stripes,* and a telegram to next of kin bearing the sad news that Captain Theodore Herbert Hurstwood was killed in an auto accident on a West German highway. And it will be my sad duty to write to Ted's parents and describe the circumstances of his death. Furthermore, as a matter of courtesy, since he wants to be kept abreast of the quality of performance of his highway officers, I shall personally telephone General von Metzler this afternoon and tell him how immensely cooperative you have been, and how well you have carried out your duties, stressing that you and I are in complete agreement about what happened."

"Yes, Colonel," Bessner enunciated feebly. Trainer reached into his coat pocket for a handkerchief and wiped his face.

"If you have finished with the vehicle and the body, may we take them away, Captain Bessner?" Trainer sounded official and respectful.

"Yes, we have finished, Colonel, you may take them away."

"Our ambulance will now take the body to 7th Army Hospital, where they have a morgue, and I'll be sending a wrecker very shortly for Captain Hurstwood's car. We'll be taking apart what's left of it in our shop at the 16th."

"Yes, Colonel."

Trainer reeled on his heel, catching one final glimpse of the surrounding woods, fences, hills, and stretches of the highway as though he did not want any of it to be erased from his memory because he might need it again, when and for what purpose he could not tell. He again faced Bessner.

"No one can deny we did a good day's work, and I thank you for your loyalty and cooperation, Captain. They will not be forgotten." He saluted and held out his hand. Bessner saluted and shook Trainer's hand, bowing slightly. Next Trainer saluted with gusto in the direction of the two other figures waiting nearby and called out, "Good-bye, Lieutenant, good-bye, Doctor."

They both returned the salute and called back in strident official voices, and Trainer, followed by Lieberman, began to walk toward their car.

"When we get down, Captain, tell those goddamn medics what they are supposed to do, and tell the MPs to radio our Motor Pool for a wrecker."

"Yes, sir."

On the way back to base each man was at first shut up in himself, wholly uncommunicative. Then Lieberman broke the silence. "You were on thin ice with that Metzler story, Ed. Suppose Bessner calls your bluff and speaks to the general."

"He won't, he knows the general wouldn't stoop to answering his questions, the matter is too . . . delicate. Besides, I know Metzler, spoke to him one hell of a lot of times, though not recently."

"So there is at least a grain of truth in what you regaled Bessner with." A very peculiar smirk broke out all over Lieberman's face and, Trainer was convinced, would remain plastered to it for eternity.

"Don't be so goddamn stingy, Sol, a grain of truth, my, my, my, get your ears examined, Mr. High Priest, and make it a bushel!"

"I wonder."

"Besides, that Kraut captain needed a kick in the ass. Re-gu-la-tions, re-gu-la-tions, that's what the Krauts live by. Take away their precious re-gu-la-tions and there's nothing left. Might just as well cut their own throats. One of 'em days re-gu-la-tions will be their downfall."

"Will it stick?"

"It will, don't worry about it."

With one eye Lieberman was looking vaguely through the half-open window at the receding landscape, and Trainer was lighting another cheroot, which in a matter of seconds filled the car with thick, cough-raising smoke.

"What I witnessed this morning, Ed, was the most effective, but also the most devious and ruthless instance of rank-pulling in my memory."

"Warms my heart you said effective, or did ye figure it was better to be stuck with a suicide verdict?"

"No, definitely not."

"Well then." Trainer shifted in his seat, slid more to the side, and appeared contented in a quiet, unobtrusive way. "Let me tell you somethin', Sol, I haven't told many folks about," he began in a reminiscent mood. "When I joined the Army I was pure as the driven snow. Sure, I previously had some brushes with the law, juvenile offender you might call me, but what youngster didn't? I got drunk now and then and got to be plain disorderly, tell me who hasn't, and I was chasing girls like I had a spindle up my ass, with various success. One girl I took to like a coyote to raw meat just couldn't stand the sight of me, and as my passes got closer and closer to her alluring flesh she called the cops telling them to keep that filthy bum, meanin' me, away from her. But I also had my modest share of successes. Anyway, putting them minor incidents to the side, I was pure and innocent. I never lied; lying to the cops ain't lying but a painful necessity, so I can honestly say I never lied, and I never did no backbiting, intriguing, exploiting others, and cheating my fellow man and my fellow woman of what was rightfully his or hers, no sir, and I treated everyone, except them cops, fair and square. When we got hold of somethin' one way or another, be it food or cigarettes or booze we always divided it equal-like, all for one and one for all. And I respected Pa and Ma, and never talked back to them because parents are to be respected, and tried to follow their advice to work hard, to make something of myself, except there was no work to be had."

"Go on," Lieberman said, employing both hands and the entire force of his powerful lungs to blow the smoke away through the windows now open to capacity.

"When I joined the Army it all changed," Trainer continued, rolling up the windows. "I soon found out I had to fend for myself 'cause no one else would fend for me. And I had my first taste of politicking and everything that goes with: half-truths, or no truths at all, pretense, hy-hypocrisy, asking for more than was my due, lies every hour of the day, pleasing the right people and ganging up on the losers, flattery when it pays, and keeping my mouth shut and that pays double, friend."

Lieberman slowed down, and they could see the base, the Motor Pool laden with shining trucks and jeeps, the flagpole, and the grim buildings encircling the parade ground.

"When I was an enlisted man, why I had to fight off the NCOs and the junior officers—I'd known some pretty mean NCOs and some dumb bastards glorified with a bar or two—and when I in turn became an NCO, why I had to look after the men and never take my eye off my superiors. More politicking! You know the old adage, Sol, if you can't beat 'em, join 'em, so after being a politicking sergeant, I became a politicking lieutenant, and then a politicking captain, and a politicking major. And now I am a politicking colonel. How do you like them apples!"

Lieberman drove slowly on the driveway and parked the staff car in front of the Command Building.

"One more thing," Trainer droned out, giving no indication of being ready to scramble out. "I don't believe all that crap about the original sin, us losing spunk 'cause that dude in Paradise took a munch too many, that's a lot of hooey if you ask me." Then he straightened himself in his seat and kept gazing at Lieberman with uncommon earnestness. "Listen carefully, and mark my word, Sol."

"I would hate myself for doing the reverse, Ed."

"Man is born innocent and pure as the driven snow. But he is corrupted, forever corrupted, and there ain't no 'remedy.'"

"Corrupted by what, by whom? That's a fair question."

"You leave me no choice but use them big words which I have no stomach to use."

"Go on."

"Corrupted by ci-vi-li-zation, Sol, and that means everything we as adults set in motion, government, banking system, every kind of employment high and low, law courts and what the half-wits call the administration of justice, and so on and so forth. Everything of that ilk corrupts, and it's corrupted you and me."

"Challenging insights into the human condition, Colonel. I may use some of it in my sermons."

"Have your laugh, Sol, but all of us was once innocent and pure as the driven snow and free, there ain't no denyin'."

"Is there no remedy?"

"There is," and Trainer thrust his head defiantly forward. "We gotta save that state of innocence from the clutches of the grim reaper and make it live forever."

"How?"

"Kicking ci-vi-li-zation with both feet without respite till it turns to dust."

/   /   /

Next day, Group Sergeant Korovitz was reporting to Group Commander on the latest developments surrounding Captain Hurstwood's tragic accidental death.

"The telegrams from Army had gone off this morning, sir, in point of fact Army sent two telegrams, the first to Mr. and Mrs. Everett and Priscilla Hurstwood in Connecticut, the captain's parents, and the second to Mr. Nathan Hurstwood, his brother, at a private address in New Haven, the reason for it being the captain had designated his brother as his next of kin and beneficiary. Also there were calls from the MP Headquarters and from the German Highway Patrol to the effect the captain's death was ruled an accident . . ."

Trainer nodded. "It was a terrible accident, what else could they say?"

"That's right, sir, but now that we have an official ruling the matter will be easier to handle here on home stretch."

"Sure, sure," Trainer agreed, gazing vacantly around the office. Then he snapped into alertness. "Sit down, Leroy, please sit down," and he motioned the sergeant to a chair.

"Thank you, sir," Korovitz went on, carefully and respectfully sitting down. "I meant to add Kraut highway patrol will be sending us their report . . . This will take three or four days, but their sergeant read to me the key paragraph on the phone. It reads something like this in English translation, which the sergeant obligingly provided," and Korovitz pulled out from his pocket a crumpled piece of notepaper: "'It is most likely that Captain Hurstwood momentarily lost control of the vehicle which swerved sharply to the right and went over the top before he was able to regain control and redirect it.'"

"This sums it up pretty good, the Krauts have helluva experience in them matters, when one remembers what lousy drivers they are."

"I couldn't agree more," Korovitz joined in smiling indignantly.

"Was death instantaneous or was the captain lying there, poor soul, in much pain before he was whisked away?" he asked with concern.

Trainer shook his head listlessly. "Instantaneous, on impact, he was hurled out of the car through the windshield and smashed his head against a rock."

"At least thank God for that."

"I called his parents yesterday afternoon," Trainer continued in the same melancholy mood. "I can tell you, Leroy, I would've gladly given one hell of a lot not to have to make that call, it wasn't easy, but then serious stuff seldom is. Actually I'd met them last Christmas, they flew here to look up their son and visit friends at Army. As I recall they spent Christmas in Stuttgart. Fine people."

"He was a fine guy, the men respected him . . ."

"Liked him too, I know it for a fact . . . and he was a friend, a friend I could always depend on, come hell or high water."

Korovitz was brooding, and Trainer picked up some papers from his desk and absentmindedly jammed them into a wastepaper basket.

"Death never sleeps, not even in peace time." He looked inquiringly at Korovitz. "Did you know Hastings, Captain Hastings?"

"I was transferred to the 16th a week after he died, but I heard the whole story and the details."

"His was unnecessary death," suddenly Trainer hoisted himself up and exploded, "there was no cause, there was . . . absolutely no cause!"

"He sacrificed himself."

Trainer pulled a face and threw his hands up. "Call it what you will, and Ted's was another kind of unnecessary death ... carelessness or what have you, he should've known better."

A long minute passed before Trainer spoke again. "We'd better get back to what we are paid to do, Leroy, another buck, another day ..."

"Yes, sir," and Korovitz stood up energetically. "The chaplain took charge of Captain Hurstwood's personal effects which are being sent stateside. They will be flown to Frankfurt and delivered to Mr. Nathan Hurstwood in New Haven. The chaplain has a couple of men bundling everything up. They are in his quarters now, and his office will be emptied next."

"Thank you, Group Sergeant."

"And word is being sent to all the companies with respect to the guard formation on the parade ground tomorrow at 1715 hours when you will address the troops about the captain's sad demise."

"The men have the right to know."

"Righto, sir," and Sergeant Korovitz marched out of the colonel's office.

Left by himself, Trainer crossed and re-crossed his cramped official quarters, stood by the window long enough to notice the intermittent rays of the sun brightening the rapidly bending shrubs and tree branches escaping the gusty winds, collected a master key from a desk drawer, and swung the door to the corridor wide open. Walking toward Hurstwood's office, he ran into Fiorello. At first the two men stood face to face, each communicating his sadness to the other mutely, and finally Fiorello asked very quietly, "Do you have everything under control, Ed?" Trainer smiled bleakly and let the words out quietly, "Thank you, John, everything's under control," and moved on.

In Hurstwood's office his eyes scoured the bookshelves, the top of the desk and of the filing cabinet. They rested for a brief sentimental moment on the collection of family photos and the West Point mementoes before he opened the cabinet, took out each folder individually, went through it, and replaced it. They all contained official documents and correspondence, minutes of courts-martial, Hurstwood's own notes and evaluations of the different types of military equipment, letters about class reunions—nothing, Trainer thought, that could not be shipped to his parents and brother or handed over to the Army without creating even a ripple of embarrassment. He lifted the few books off the desk, the prominently displayed *Uniform Code of Military Justice*, several Army manuals, several technical handbooks, a thick hard-bound history of the United States, paperback histories of Germany and of Russia, and a paperback English–German dictionary. Next, sitting down behind Hurstwood's desk he went methodically through the drawers, beginning with the bottom one on the left and working his way up, and then crossing over to the right, working downward, keeping the front drawer until the very last. In the side drawers he discovered nothing of personal nature, not even an address book. He opened the front drawer and concealed by the pell-mell, paperclips, Scotch tape, writing paper, and other paraphernalia, he noticed the tiny corner of a rose envelope jutting out. It was addressed to Hurstwood in a prim feminine hand at his quarters. It was sent from Philadelphia, and it bore no sender's name or address. Trainer remained crouched over the desk for what he thought was a very long time, but he really could not tell. At last he drew out several sheets of expensive rose writing paper from the envelope, which had previously been cut open with a paper knife. The date neatly inserted in the right upper corner was that of two months before. For a few seconds he held the sheets in his hands without looking at them, and then he began to read:

Dear Ted,

First of all let me give you the latest news and gossip from Philadelphia; it will provoke you to hooting laughter as it provoked me, and when the spasm was over I chuckled endlessly. Mother—you know Mother—has been telling everybody in town that her eldest daughter will be married before Xmas and that this is the way things are, so the long-awaited day may be approaching. Actually, I think it should be well before Xmas, at the beginning of the summer, May, June possibly. The last time we spoke on the phone you were for an early wedding so we are surely on the same page. Your parents came to dinner last week, and Mother, who'd made all the arrangements already, was giving them the benefit of her organizational talents: the bridesmaids have been chosen, my wedding dress is hanging impatiently in the closet, a hundred other details about the service and the reception and so forth have been finalized, and what's his name the Groton chaplain will officiate. I believe he's a tame old codger—I never met him—but Father is doing it for sentimental reasons, unless of course you prefer somebody from Choate, which could be easily arranged. As we were finishing the dessert, Mother said with great aplomb, "If Lucy doesn't marry Ted, which Heaven forbid, she's going to marry young Winslow." There was a moment of heavy silence, and then everyone burst out laughing, everybody except mother who was apparently quite serious. Your father said, "Lucille, you would make a magnificent CEO in time of crisis or a general, you have a contingency plan for everything!"

"I am only exercising common prudence, Everett," Mother answered, transfixing him with a long searching look. More laughter from everybody! Then we ladies departed, leaving the men to their brandy and cigars. Anyway, it's all set, and you and I can talk transatlantically putting the final touches. I wonder, though, how young Winslow is taking it, being "in the reserves" so to speak, which really provokes one to uncontrollable laughter. Actually young Winslow is very sweet, like a teddy bear you'd want to put on a pillow next to you. Father told me Mother apparently spoke to his parents about matrimonial matters in very general terms, but tangibly enough to establish a frame of reference should there be a need for it. In any event, Mother wants me to be married before Xmas, and here once more I am going into convulsions because she wants a wedding at all cost and is much less concerned who the bridegroom will be. I think Mother is terribly annoyed because of all the dawdling, which went on for so long and for which both you and I must take the blame. She makes a point of reminding me now and then that my two younger sisters have been married for some time, and—these are my words, not hers—they regularly give birth to little monsters. So, my darling, let's do it sooner rather than later, soon, very soon, not to please our parents—and your parents are getting as restive as mine—but for us, for you and me and to hell with the rest of the world. I imagine you want Nathan to be your best man; he's the only one on whom the two families really dote! Let's do it soon, very soon, my darling.

And now let me turn to other matters: I know, Ted, that you want to be independent, that you want to stand on your own two feet, and you abhor, yes abhor, outside help when it comes to your military career. This is the way you are, and I don't want to change you, but I wish you could understand what I feel, because I want the best for you, and the best for the two of us. We are not going to change the world, and you know very well that in this world of ours whom you know is very often infinitely more important than what you know. This is the way things are, and let's *take advantage of it for our own sakes. Last week I called Uncle Wesley, after all until a few months ago he was Undersecretary of the Army, and I told him I wanted to speak to him about you. He knows your family, and he's very sweet as well as being a rock of common sense. Anyway, he invited me to lunch at his club, and on the last minute he realized his club doesn't admit women, not even as luncheon guests. At this point I am going to digress, but this is on behalf of a cause which is absolutely vital and which brooks no delay. How long will those outdated, medieval, and criminal practices be allowed to linger? How long will more than half the population of the United States be barred from entering certain holies of holies where the male ego holds eternal sway? How long I ask. We smugly pat ourselves on the back and call ourselves a civilized people, which is ridiculous, because discrimination against women is a hallmark of barbarity, and no time should be wasted in ending it by whatever means presents itself as the most effective. I too have my causes!!! Anyway, Uncle Wesley took me to a very chic French restaurant instead, and I told him about you and where you stand in the Army. He said that promotion to major would be very easy to arrange; he knows everybody at the Pentagon, and he knows top brass at 7th Army Headquarters in West Germany. But he also said something else which may be a godsend for you: the Army is looking for liaisons with Congress. The brigadier general who was the chief liaison is retiring, and the colonel who was working with him is seriously ill and will be going on a prolonged sick leave followed by retirement. Uncle Wesley said that you would be a strong candidate if you are properly recommended, and he would be happy to recommend you and be in charge of the whole operation. Good old Uncle Wesley! I felt like kissing him endlessly on both cheeks, but I restrained myself! He said the rank of major would be appropriate for this post—and promotion would be speedy—and he added what the insiders are saying, namely that they want someone younger this time. And then he went on describing the particular qualifications and talents required for this job—good at dealing with people, possessing what he called the common touch as you will have to deal with all kinds of people in Congress, some of them very common and uncouth, patience, and being trusted by the military establishment, a small group of generals and civilians who really run things. Here your name and your background would give you an immense advantage. When I heard Uncle Wesley paint this picture in words, I said to myself this is the job that is tailor-made for Ted. You would really shine in it; you would be ideal. We could live in Virginia, and we would be right at the center of things. You would still be in the Army, which is where you want to be, but you would be doing something infinitely more important than being a foot soldier. Let others crawl in the mud and sleep in leaky pup tents, let others do it, but not you, Ted. You deserve something infinitely better; you are different from the others, better than the others, and this entitles you to a different lifestyle. I am sure we are on the same page. Hence I am calling Uncle Wesley and setting the operation in motion. For your part, you should speak to your C.O. because his recommendation will carry some weight, and you should make yourself available for interviews. Uncle Wesley says they are going to fly you to D.C., and you may be there for several days. Ample opportunity for us to see each other!!! It's been such a long time!!! And so my major-husband-to-be, Army's liaison with the U.S. Congress, things are looking up, as well they should! Take care and we'll be talking by phone at the usual hour.*

Fondly,
Lucy

Trainer put the sheets of the writing paper on the desk and sat in Hurstwood's chair in silence, brooding. Several minutes had elapsed, but he was still there, not having moved an inch, the rosy sheets before him, and brooding as before. Finally he stretched out his leg and kicked the wastebasket towards him, mechanically and for no other reason than to exhibit movement, no matter how pointless and insignificant but cutting clean across the strange impassiveness that possessed him.

Then his eyes fell on the wastebasket and the layers of ash visible under scraps of paper. He scooped up a handful and noticed at once that the ash was of different colors; some of it was gray and soft to the hand, but some was bluish and hard with tiny particles of carton and leather not fully consumed embedded in it. He tossed the ash back into the wastebasket and resumed his impassive posture. This is what one could expect from the thorough and efficient Hurstwood. He had burned or otherwise disposed of private papers and of anything else that could cause embarrassment to others or invite questions. Some of it now lay in the wastepaper basket, five inches high of mixed ash, five inches of privacy, burnt for eternity. He had left Lucy's letter in the center drawer knowing that he, Trainer, would find it there, and should someone else find it first, Hurstwood knew that the letter would eventually be handed to his commanding officer. "Thanks, for trusting me, old buddy," he whispered, "thanks, Ted, and all the best."

Now at last he was struck by intuitive certainty that Lieberman and his men would not find anything of a private, intimate, or compromising nature in Hurstwood's quarters. Ted had taken care of it before he deliberately set out on his last journey, and what remained was an open book. Trainer flicked on his cigarette lighter, and holding each page of Lucy's letter over a wide ashtray fashioned fancifully out of beaten copper, let it be consumed, stirring the ash after each page. He waited for a few moments to allow the ash to cool, emptied the contents into the wastepaper basket, and turned towards the door.

Chapter 4

Ensconced enduringly behind his desk, Trainer recognized immediately who was knocking on his door. It was Vallejo, and his knock was
distinctive and unmistakable, two quick taps followed, after an interval
of three or four seconds, by a single one, louder and seemingly longer.
Vallejo's knock was something like *ta-ta-taaa*, and Trainer associated it
vaguely with the bars of music he had heard, or thought he had heard.
In contrast, Korovitz's knock was just a knock, two powerful raps on the
door without any frills. He had been congratulating himself on having
broken the code so to speak and on being able to identify each member of his immediate staff requesting admission. "By the knocks ye shall
know them," he had been in the habit of reciting, "by their knocks,"
regretting at the same time that Korovitz's raps had no identifiable
musical association. And now as soon as he heard ta-ta-taaa, he called
out with spirit, "Come in, kid."

"There's a lady to see you, sir," Vallejo was saying, "a German lady,"
and he handed the colonel a business card. Surprised and sensing pitfalls ahead, Trainer read: *Fräulein Doktor Inge von Treschkow, Director,
Section of Higher Education, Ministry of Education, State of Baden-
Württemberg, Stuttgart, West Germany*. A cord was struck very feebly in his
mind, but he could not connect it to a place or circumstance.

"Give me a minute, Vallejo, and then show her in," he rasped zealously, adjusting his tie, buttoning his uniform, straightening the papers on his desk.

"Fräulein Doktor von Treschkow," Vallejo announced proudly, and a tall young woman dressed in expensive, rather official clothes—a darkish skirt, an off-white blouse, and a darkish jacket—entered the office.

Trainer, by now trim and all buttoned up, stepped forward and extended his hand.

"How do you do, ma'am, I am Colonel Trainer."

She laughed a silvery self-assured laugh as she took his hand.

"I am Inge von Treshkow, Colonel, and we met before, at a reception at 7th Army Headquarters last year. I was with Captain Hurstwood."

Now the place and the circumstance were finally establishing a connection.

"Of course, ma'am, I remember, and Ted introduced me to you."

She nodded, and he, feeling suddenly a little awkward and a little lost, pointed to a chair. But he quickly regained his self-control, and looking her straight in the eye he spoke in an official tone, noticing that she too looked him straight in the eye, both of them making it plain that flinching was never an option.

"Terrible business, one of my best officers mowed down in the prime of life . . . Ted was usually a careful driver but this time the slippery surface maybe wet in places . . . or whatever the reason . . . was responsible for this tragic accident. We can at least be thankful," he went on doggedly, "we can at least be thankful," he repeated, but she interrupted him.

"Colonel Trainer, you were his commanding officer, and I understand the two of you were also staunch friends . . ."

"It was my privilege."

"I was very close to Ted, perhaps closer than any other woman," she continued in her flawless English, "and therefore we shall be frank with each other; we owe it to Ted, so long as what is being said here today goes no further."

He blinked several times, taken aback, and then nodded vigorously in total agreement.

"Ted killed himself, it was suicide, and I don't think it was done on the spur of the moment. Ted was too thoughtful, too sensible and reasonable not to think such a step through and through. The reasons for his suicide were personal, they had nothing to do with the Army or politics." She watched him searchingly and added: "I imagine what I am saying doesn't come to you as a surprise, Colonel."

"No, it doesn't, I have reached the same conclusion, Miss Tre-sch-kow." He took great pains to pronounce her name correctly.

"Let's take first things first," she spoke with force and conviction. "Officially it was a tragic accident, and it should remain so on the books." She smiled warmly and he finally recognized what it was that was dashing inchoately through his brain, half thought, half-felt, but now at last shaping itself into coherence, namely how very attractive she was in a Teutonic way, tall and statuesque, her compact, darkish-blond hair swept back and curling around the ears, the features perfectly regular, the eyes immensely large and sparkling, the whole face drawn out, but not excessively so, thrown into relief by slender but very pronounced lips. The executive apparel Inge von Treschkow was wearing, destined for boardrooms and public meetings, could not damper, let alone eradicate, her femininity however hard it tried. Her lushness and sexuality shone through.

"This is one of the reasons I came to see you, to find out if I could be of any help in dealing with the German authorities, even though the official report puts it down as an accident . . ."

"So you heard about it already?"

"General von Metzler's secretary telephoned me, the general who now serves as Commissioner of Police is an old family friend, and he was also my brother's commanding officer on the Eastern Front."

"I see, I thank you for your concern."

She made a quick gesture of dismissal.

"Colonel, I come from an old military family, both my father and my grandfather were officers in the German army, my great grandfather was a general in the Prussian army. You have to protect the reputation of the officers under your command, this is understandable . . . at least I understand it perfectly."

It was not that he was lost for words, but he was being deliberately cagey, not wishing, at least for the moment, to share the unofficial and clandestine information with her and the part he played in obtaining it. He kept silent, watching her closely. But he realized very soon that she understood the reasons for his caginess, that perhaps she understood them better than he himself.

"We have an expression in German, 'a pious lie,' 'fromme Lüge,' and it is highly appropriate in this situation."

He nodded but kept silent.

"I want to ask you whether you are convinced the official version of what happened as it was reported by the German Highway Patrol and underwritten by your Army will stick. We have to make certain."

Something in her voice, the persistence and the tension, and her unexpected openness impelled him to greater candor. He was taking a risk, he knew, but his gut feeling was telling him the odds were good.

"Captain Gerhard Bessner saw it as an accident."

"And your MPs?"

"Likewise."

"Did you have to convince Bessner?"

He hesitated.

"Colonel, let me assure you I am on your side."

"Yes, it took a little doing."

"How did you do it?"

"I pulled rank, did a lot of mouthing about German-American relations, threw in the Cold War for good measure, raised a specter of the Russkies occupying Stuttgart and hacking people down, and boasted of being a bosom buddy of your general."

She burst out laughing. "Full deck!"

"You might say that."

"Bessner is thorough and usually dependable. He's also very ambitious."

"That's right, even a blind man would've noticed it."

She laughed again. "He made his own decision, but he checked with the general's office, and the general, through one of his assistants, gave him a go-ahead."

"But not before you spoke to the general and asked him to do . . . what he did."

It was her turn to keep silent but not for long.

"Yes," she almost whispered, then tossed her head back, shifted in her seat and re-crossed her legs.

Trainer was crouching over his desk, his hands gripping the sides, his boots anchored in the floor, as if he were fighting for his life and only a superhuman effort could save him. From this grotesquely hero-ic and heroically grotesque position, his face beetroot-red and his hair ruffled, he addressed Inge von Treschkow.

"Fräulein Doktor," he began, gradually unflexing himself into a more orthodox carriage of a man sitting behind his desk, "why are you trying to help me, and why are you taking interest in this matter?"

"It should be obvious."

"Indulge me, please."

"I am doing it for Ted and his family. I loved Ted, and I don't want him to be disgraced and his family humiliated. Suicide is often a cow-ard's way out, but not in this case. Perhaps Ted had no real choice." She pulled out a monogrammed handkerchief, and with a rapid sweep of hand wiped off a tear.

"I don't mean to pry, but since we are in the same camp, may I ask you about . . . about your and Ted's friendship, if you want to talk about it, that is. Ted was much more to me than a junior officer under my command."

"I know, he often spoke of you and he considered you to be an excellent officer, a role model for others. He also said you were a war-time soldier more or less wasted in peacetime."

"He was right."

She regained her composure and went on in a level voice, "I met Ted almost two years ago, and before long I fell in love with him. At one time I thought he loved me, but there was that other woman in America, Lucy. We had often talked of marriage, and I thought Ted would ask me to marry him, especially after he introduced me to his family"—she gave out a quick muted laugh—"or rather after his par-ents and his brother came to Stuttgart and introduced themselves to me. We all spent last Christmas together at my mother's house—my moth-er, Everett and Pricilla, Nathan, my brother Wolfgang, Ted, and me. We had a wonderful, old-fashioned Christmas, the kind of Christmas I remember from my childhood days when we all lived in East Prussia before the war. It was wonderful! My mother still owns a large house in what has remained unexpectedly a rather exclusive residential district in Stuttgart. I wonder how long it will remain so. Anyway, the Hurstwoods were our houseguests for more than two weeks, and I became very fond of them. As for Nathan, well, at least half of the young ladies in our neighborhood had fallen head over heels in love with Nathan, and when I talked to the daughter of one of our neighbors, she simply said that falling in love with Nathan was the easiest and yet the most serious thing in the world, and absolutely effortless. Imagine that!"

"I am sorry," Trainer muttered, looking momentarily at the ceiling, "you and Ted would've made one hell of a couple."

She smiled sadly and went on: "I was given to understand Ted and Lucy broke up more than two years ago, and everything pointed to this being so, but then about a year ago they were apparently reconciled and resumed their relationship. This is the time when Ted was away in the States on a month's leave. Ted was always very honest with me and I was honest with him, and we could be as happy as a pair of larks for weeks on end before Lucy made an appearance, a letter, a phone call, at one time she flew in to Stuttgart. The last three months were very tense and unhappy for me, I knew Ted was profoundly troubled, and I wanted him to be absolutely frank with me, but he kept saying, 'I need time, I need time to sort things out, and everything will be fine, fine, d'you hear me, stop worrying, trust me.' Perhaps I should've been more insistent, but I admired Ted so much and I loved him so much that I had complete confidence in what he said he was doing to set everything right for the two of us. As weeks dragged on I waited and waited and cried a good deal, but I never gave up hope that my Ted would see us through."

"I am very sorry, believe me, very, very sorry."

She smiled again, sadly and understandingly, and cast a glance in his direction of sympathy and good will.

"I spoke to Ted on the phone the evening before the day he died. He was going to come to my apartment the next day when he finished his duties here." She paused, and Trainer made every effort to look as warmhearted as he could.

"Tell me about Ted's last few days; he'd said several days before he would be very busy, work was piling on his desk, there were lots of things to do . . ."

"That's very true," Trainer was trying hard not to sound sententious, "it's the end of the month, peacetime army lives on paper which takes the place of rifles and guns, yes, work was piling on his desk."

"And otherwise?"

"If you mean the personal side, he was the same good ol' Ted, we noticed no difference." As he uttered those words he became convinced she expected a much fuller account of her lover's final days, but he also felt she would not be pressing the point.

"One of the most difficult things I had to do in my entire life was to give the news to Everett and Pricilla. I called them as soon as I got the word from the general . . . I hated doing it, but it had to be done."

"I felt the same way, and I am writing to them." He nodded. "Ted was very frank and open, but he also had the tendency to keep things bottled up inside him . . . I may never know everything there is to know, what really drove him to suicide, how I could have stopped him, if indeed I could have."

Trainer spread out his hands. "Same here, same here, and I'll never know. But maybe it's better to let sleeping dogs lie."

"Maybe," she consented almost mechanically, but her face was drawn now, puckered and lined, and she went on asking questions off-handedly about personal items that may have been left behind in Hurstwood's office or quarters, as if she did not really care to know the answers.

"Ted took care of everything personal, we didn't find anything that might cause embarrassment to his family, if you know what I mean, and we are shipping everything to his parents in Connecticut—clothes, books, and private papers."

"There is nothing compromising in my apartment in Stuttgart either, a few shirts, a suit, some shoes; churches in the city are begging for clothes for the needy. I'll donate Ted's things to them, this is what I think Ted would like me to do."

"I'm sure you're right."

She rose and took a few steps around the office. "Ted was the great love of my life; I have a gnawing notion such love comes but once in a lifetime. I'm sure in the weeks to come my friends will be telling me that I am still young and that time is the best healer. They will be right, of course. But I doubt if I shall ever love a man again as I loved Ted, let alone if I shall ever love a man again." Trainer was standing too now on the side of his desk, keeping silent and gazing vaguely into space.

"It is ironic, when you come to think about it, that Ted loved Lucy but didn't want to marry her, and that he probably didn't love me but might have wanted to marry me. It is truly ironic." She was on the point of saying good-bye, and Trainer stepped forward with aplomb and stood very close to her, their shoulders almost touching.

"I don't mean to be mouthing imbecilities, but you have a career . . . I mean you have something to fall on."

"True, I am a professional woman, and very early in life I came to occupy a high and responsible position at the Ministry. There are considerably fewer professional women in West Germany than in your country, per capita that is. We are at the end of the queue, but we are working at it."

"This is what I had in mind."

"To be sure, but let me tell you that right now my career and my professional status are no consolation at all."

"It's been a privilege to see you again, ma'am, and I deeply regret the circumstances," Trainer put in gravely, grasping her hand and shaking it with feeling. "Let's stay in touch."

"Let's."

"If I can be of any help . . ."

"And if I can be of any help to you, Colonel."

He held the door to the corridor open for her, and as she was passing through he reminded her in a fatherly sort of way, "Please drive carefully." She halted and her face was at least a tad happier than before.

"I am trying to think what Ted would've said were he standing here now, I think I've got it," and she called out joyfully, "STOP HARASSING THE TROOPS!"

"Oh! I couldn't promise that, hell, I couldn't promise that, not on your life," he yelled and returned her wave as she was fast disappearing down the hall.

In the Group Sergeant's office, Vallejo, his arms akimbo, was leaning against the window, a zesty, resolute smirk contorting his face.

"You look like the cat who ate the canary. What's the occasion?"

"That was one sexy dame," Vallejo drawled out appreciatively, adding passion and emphasis.

"You noticed?"

"Of course, I noticed! There is nothing wrong with my eyesight, there is nothing wrong with my senses, there is nothing wrong with my libido."

"Your what?"

"Libido, sexual drive!!!"

"Oh! Good for you!" And the Group Commander's well-trained eye took in the Group Clerk, every inch of him, and summed him up.

"At ease, soldier, you've been standing at attention too long, gotta slack off now and then, it's an order!"

/ / /

Everyone at 16th Engineer Group knew that Colonel Trainer, given to unexpected bouts of folksiness though he might be, was also a stickler for discipline and protocol. At the appointed hour the four companies were already smartly lined up before the reviewing stand, which the colonel was now ascending. Far back a few stragglers were making spirited attempts to join the ranks without being noticed by squad and platoon leaders, a vain effort at best since their names were duly and sternly noted. And now they stood there, full strength of the Group, some privy to the reasons for their being there, but many others ignorant of them and wishing with the rest that the occasion might be brief, exceedingly brief, thus contributing substantially to the common good.

"ATTENTIOOOON!" Sergeant Korovitz's roaring command rose above the parade ground and then fell down like the imprecation of an angry god, whacking each man's eardrums. They knew well this voice that refused to avail itself of a loudspeaker, and many found it irksome, its high volume positively indecent, and doubly so because Korovitz looked happiest when he was in the middle of a roar. In certain well-informed enlisted quarters of the Group all kinds of merry tales were spun about Korovitz's obsession with roaring, which many thought exceeded his military duty and the need of the hour. According to one of them eagerly told and lovingly embellished, Korovitz's bellowings were a trigger to sexual gratification, and the louder his commands and anger the more semen would wet the inside of his pants. At least half a dozen men, including a disgruntled corporal, had taken credit for this discovery, but it was tacitly agreed to that it was Olie, recently not favored by Fortune in hiding firewater from the inquisitive Group Sergeant, who had been its true originator, and Fred, the college boy, its devoted elaborator and amplifier.

"At ease." Colonel Trainer's voice sounded positively gentle in comparison with the Group Sergeant's as he reached for the microphone. "Many of you may have heard of the grievous loss 16th Engineer Group suffered the day before yesterday when Captain Theodore Herbert Hurstwood was killed in a car accident on Lunenberg Overpass several miles away from our base. Captain

Hurstwood was the Supply and Morale Officer, and during the three years he has been with us, he earned unflinching respect of the enlisted men and of the officer corps alike. He was highly efficient without being meddlesome, far-seeing without being arrogant, and he was always ready to help others, asking for nothing in return."

"He could also walk on water or failing this on puddles of his own piss," Zack muttered under his breath.

"A native of Connecticut," Trainer resumed, "and a graduate of the West Point Academy where he graduated third in his class, Captain Hurstwood served with distinction in other engineer units before he was assigned to 16th Engineer Group. As many of you had occasion to find out, his knowledge of equipment was extensive and detailed, and our Group's high rating in manning and putting to multiple use a wide array of equipment was very largely due to his efforts. He was also a morale officer, and here again he distinguished himself by reaching out to all and sundry, listening particularly to complaints, identifying causes of discontent, and dealing with them promptly and always fairly."

"For once I agree with Trainer, Hurstwood was a regular guy," Olie whispered to his buddy on the left.

"Aha!" the buddy shot back also in a whisper. "Getting soft in your old age or what?"

"In many respects," Trainer continued, "Ted Hurstwood was a model officer and," he paused and stole a quick look round, "I simply can't find words to tell ye how much he will be missed." His voice was quivering now, but he went on: "We are a unit, a family if you will, and the loss of one is the loss for all." He paused again, and his voice regained its control. "Captain Hurstwood's body is being flown back to Connecticut for burial. He is survived by his parents and a younger brother." His commanding presence restored, his gaze shot out right and left, piercing the ranks and establishing eye contact with as many individuals as he could, taking them all into his confidence, telling them all that he was standing next to them a brother-in-arms and they were standing next to him, his brothers-in-arms.

"We shall now observe a minute of silence in honor of a fellow soldier whom we lost. At the completion of this minute of silence Group Sergeant will dismiss the troops."

"ATTENTIOOOON AND SALUUUUTE!" Korovitz roared again, and the four companies arranged into so many rows snapped to attention better than what they thought they could do, keeping the line each man rendering a hand salute. The officers assembled by the reviewing stand did the same. "DISMISSED!" The familiar voice was whacking the eardrums once more, and there was no way of getting away from it and from the collateral damage it may have produced.

Trainer hopped down from the reviewing stand and returned Korovitz's salute who was about to march off to his office. Then the officers clustered round the colonel, complementing him on his address, and he went on smiling, thanking them, and nodding. But he looked downcast, and after everyone else had gone he turned to Sol Lieberman and touched him lightly on the shoulder. "Thanks for helping me with them words, Sol."

"You're welcome, anytime."

But as Lieberman was still timidly rooted to the ground he asked, "Is there anything?"

"In point of fact there is, and it concerns Ted. I just want to round off the case and get something off my chest."

"Come to my house tonight, and we can talk; seven, seven-thirty?"

"Could we make it around eight?" and Trainer nodded. "Rachel and I have to have a serious talk with Sol, Jr." Lieberman was adding as an afterthought. "He picked up a phrase, from one of his friends no doubt, which he tries on every adult he sees . . ."

"What kind of phrase?" Trainer was grinning, visibly intrigued.

"Drop dead!"

"Oh!" and Trainer burst into raucous laughter. "Why the little fella is right after my own heart, how old is he?"

"Six, and going into first grade in the fall. The kindergarten teacher sounded very upset when she called Rachel, and now Rachel is upset. Apparently . . . apparently," Lieberman went on as if trying to exorcise the household demons, "Sol, Jr. told two teachers to drop dead and then tried it on the principal who paid an unexpected visit to see how the kindergarten darlings were doing."

"A well-planned operation, leavin' nothin' to chance."

"Maybe so, but something like the hour of reckoning is approaching for Sol, Jr. And that principal guy, whatever his name, nearly had a fit."

"How I wish I could follow Sol, Jr.'s example when I go to Army to talk to the generals," Trainer was letting out musingly, "how I wish."

"You'd better wait till you get your first star, Ed."

"But I am not a waiting man. You know that." Then he slapped his knee hard, very hard, bellowing "What the hell," and faced Lieberman grave and business-like.

"By the way, my men didn't find anything of personal nature in Ted's quarters. It looks as if he burned lots of papers in the fireplace only a few days ago and then stirred the ashes. Good and proper. Not a personal scrap or sausage."

"This don't surprise me in the least," Trainer muttered, walking away.

/   /   /

The so-called General Lounge in the building housing C Company was filled to capacity. The dearth of chairs had forced many a GI to sit on the floor, but a clear passage extended from the main portal all the way past a few derelict bookshelves to the spacious inside wall at the back. Against it stood a medium-sized Army desk with a soft-seat chair right behind it, its back propped up against the wall. From the right and left and from the areas by the elongated windows letting through the bleak remains of daylight, a murmur of impatience was rising and was soon punctuated by anger and invective.

"Where the fuck is he? Broken a leg or somethin'?" asked several voices, and others followed in the same vein. As several more minutes elapsed, the mounting discontent became so acrid that the General Lounge stood on the brink of rage and violence. Tempers would fly and much else with it! But then all of a sudden the main portal was swung open, and all the heads turned eagerly in its direction. On the threshold stood Zack, confident and nonchalant as ever, a sardonic smile shimmering round his mouth, an expensive looking crocodile briefcase in hand. He was flanked on each side by a bulky football player-type, his countenance mutely watchful but otherwise expressionless.

"Hi, guys, sorry to be late," he sounded off amiably as if he had no care in the world. "This was a knockout!"

The three of them sauntered the length of the Lounge, and Zack pushed the chair down and sat in it, hurling the briefcase onto the desk while the football player-types took their position immediately to the right and left of him.

"This was a knockout," he repeated, "but then this is life."

"Do we get our money . . ." Mike Gillespie began, but before he could finish the question his words were drowned in the general din of excited voices. Zack was observing the crowd with the same sardonic smile as before and finally raised his arms, his hands making a succession of quick downward movements requesting silence.

"We must have order . . . one guy at a time."

"We all have the same question," Olie spoke up, "who wins and who loses."

"That's right, that's it, what the hell is going on?" and for a few seconds the din was deafening again. Zack cast a suggestive glance at each bodyguard and stood up, his right hand resting on the briefcase.

"Okay," he shouted across the welter of discordant voices, "okay, let me speak." The noise subsided, but he went on shouting, not taking any chances.

"There are no winners and no losers. Hurstwood never got his ass stateside, there was no fancy wedding, and he neither stayed there nor came back. He kicked the bucket right here in Krautland, and hence all bets are off."

A leaden silence fell upon the General Lounge, but they wanted to know more, much more, and their faces were glowing with expectation and desperate hope.

"He came back," someone cried.

"No, he didn't, because he never went away." With a commanding gesture, Zack silenced the muttering and the grumbling, and went on: "This is what we call an unforeseen event or an act of God. Therefore"—he again raised his hand—"therefore everyone gets his money back minus the twenty percent commission."

"What commission?" Mike had moved to the front and stood there defiantly, seething with anger.

"Look at the bottom of the betting slips, buddy, it's all there in black and white and stamped. We didn't expect Hurstwood to be hurled down two hundred meters in his fancy Buick, but there it is and betting rules are betting rules and have to be obeyed. I'm truly sorry, guys, some of you didn't make a small bundle, but don't blame me." His eyes sought out Vince in the crowd, and he added in a comforting conciliatory way, "Tell them Vince, let 'em hear from you that everything's on the up and up."

"That's right, guys, it's like Zack says, and the commission is right too." Vince spoke with reluctance, but he was believed and the mood of the Lounge grew a little more affable.

"What were the odds at the starting line?" Hal Shelton asked, stepping forward.

"Nine to one for no return."

"Good odds!"

"That's right, and as I said some of you were on the way to making a small bundle, but the gallant captain took us by surprise."

Most of those who had betted were now reconciled to fate taking a strange and unexpected turn, and when Zack announced it was time to present their betting slips and collect their money less a twenty percent commission, they began to form a line, quietly, resignedly. When it was all over, Zack zipped up the briefcase and looked significantly at each bodyguard. "Another buck, another day! Let's go, guys," and turning toward the ever-dwindling crowd he called, "if you want to place a bet, you know where to find me. Take care, guys." He made ready to go but Olie, already half-undressed, blocked his passage, frowning.

"I still don't see that commission jazz."

"Listen, buddy"—Zack sounded like a forgiving friend, his patience and charity limitless—"listen, Olie, my old man was a bookie, his old man was a bookie before him, I'll be a bookie to the day I die though courtesy of Uncle Sam it's small potatoes right now, still, I want you to know you're getting the best from me."

"Maybe."

"It's a fact, friend," and Zack, his bodyguards very close to him and not taking their eyes off the others, strolled confidently to the main portal and disappeared behind it.

There was only a handful of them left now, among them Vince, looking strangely out of sorts, Olie sulking by the window, Fred laughing to himself and shrugging his shoulders, and Hal resting on a chair leafing idly through a magazine, and soon only those four remained. Before long Olie broke the uneasy silence.

"My old man always said if you have to choose between rubbing out a dog collar and a bookie, well, put your money on the dog collar, reason being they'll come at you with baseball bats, pipes, iron bars, and anything else that's hard and deadly, but in all likelihood this won't happen before you pass over to a better world so you'll have a bit of time left; but if you rub out a bookie, why they'll come at you with baseball bats, pipes, iron bars, and anything else that's hard and deadly, and they won't wait for the next world to come round in all its blessed majesty; no sir, they'll clubber and beat your brains out here and now 'cause them guys swears by a swift and undelayed justice."

"All you have to do now is find a dog collar," Fred said.

"That's right."

Hal tossed the magazine to the side and glanced inquiringly at Vince.

"What's eating you?"

Vince averted his head. "Nothin'," he said in his heavy, colorless voice.

"Come on, we're all buddies here, now that the bookmaker has taken French leave, you can speak your mind."

Vince kept looking away, then turned his head and faced Hal.

"D'you think I like his games and tricks? No, I don't, but most of the time they're above board. He's crooked like a three-dollar bill, okay, but he still gotta be found out. He turns my insides out, but I reckon I can do nothin', nothin' for the present."

"Besides, you get a cut."

"You watch it," Vince blurted out. "Zack pays me a few bucks now and then for somethin' that's got nothin' to do with his operations."

"Still, you are on his payroll," Hal persisted.

"You watch it, Johnny Reb," and Vince strode menacingly forward.

"Eh, guys, what the hell is going on?" The scrawny figure of Olie hardly reaching to Hal and Vince's neck interposed itself between the two giants with assurance and gutsiness that temporarily put both of them off guard.

"Fred, get your ass over here, I need reinforcements," and Fred, without a moment's delay, jumped forward and joined the group.

"I won't call you any particular name, because any name would be too great an honor."

"You call me anything you want, and I'll floor you."

"We'll see who is going to floor whom. Come on, shithead, just lay a hand on me."

Even before the words were out of Hal's mouth, Olie, standing ferociously in the middle, pushed each of them away, stamped his foot, and placed his hands on his hips.

"I want you guys to cool down, because there ain't no point in your fighting, and your energies can be put to better use."

"I am with Olie, there's no god-given reason for all this muscle-flexing," Fred drawled out, "and you, Vince, as the barrack's chief should know better."

"Insults were flung in my face."

"Facts of the matter were duly brought to light."

"And now both will be thrown to the winds," Fred adjudicated.

"And the two con . . . contestants will shake hands," Olie yelled with the full power of his lungs, crouching around them like an umpire in a boxing ring.

"Shaking hands with that . . ." Hal began, but before he could finish, Olie yelled again: "My old man always says after . . . after a thing like this the con . . . contestants are to shake hands, 'cause if they don't the thing ain't finished, and the worst is still to come." He stopped. "Besides, this is the way things are done." He went on exuding an air of authority.

"Makes sense," Fred announced with gusto. "You will do as Olie says, and if you don't Olie and I will fight you, and I took boxing in college in my sophomore year."

Prolonged silence ensued, and at last Vince, strangely quiescent, stared Hal in the eye. "I guess we got no choice."

"None whatsoever, we're against the wall."

"And against a superior force."

"I'm sorry if I . . ."

But Hal cut him short, "Forget it," and held out his hand. While the handshaking was in progress Olie and Fred beamed, the two figures whose unexpectedly meritorious conduct would be long remembered.

As they were putting away the chairs, straightening the rugs, and shutting the windows, Vince said, "Eh, guys, I got some beer in my room, anyone want a taste?"

They all replied without a moment's hesitation, individually and collectively, that indeed they wanted a taste, and Vince led them to his living quarters.

"This is good stuff," Olie muttered, leaning backwards and taking another swig.

"Quality Kraut beer, not like the piss they serve you in the Enlisted

Men's Club." Vince was smiling contentedly. The others wholehearted-
ly agreed and very soon he was pulling new bottles out of his locker.

"That was a bad accident, real bad . . . with Hurstwood I mean. Was
anyone at fault?" Olie asked.

Fred raised a new bottle to his lips and very nearly emptied it at one
go.

"Well, I heard this was no accident but a straight case of suicide, and
Hurstwood planned it well ahead."

Hal rubbed his nose. "Oddly enough I heard the same as Fred, a suicide, women being involved."

"May one ask where you heard it?" There was vibrant curiosity in
Vince's voice.

"Sure. I heard it from my fiancée who is a nurse, a German nurse;
she heard it from some doctors at her hospital. According to her the
Germans consider it suicide, even though our official position is that it
was a terrible accident, Hurstwood being careless and not watching the
road for a moment or two."

"I heard it from our doctors at the Infirmary," Fred volunteered,
"when Sarge sent me there to bring back some papers. One of the docs
is from my hometown, and he put his arm around me and said, 'Isn't it
a shame, Fred, that someone like Ted, born with a silver spoon in his
mouth, has to resort to this, jumping two hundred meters down the
overpass to his death.' The other doc nodded sadly, and then all of a sudden the first doc, the one from my hometown, rushes me to the side
and cries out, 'Fred, do me a favor and forget what I said. Officially it's
an accident and will remain so. And no matter what you do never let
out you heard it from me. Can I count on you, Fred?' 'Yes, sir, you can,'
says I, and off I go. And I am not naming any names, guys, because I
don't want that doc from my hometown to get into trouble."

"Fair enough," Olie reassured him.

"No, we don't want your friend to get into trouble. That's understood," Hal put in making a deliberate point.

"I never knew the guy," Vince was laboriously searching his memory, "except once, he came here and we exchanged a few words."

"What was the occasion?" Hal asked.

"This was a year or so ago, when we first started having this lounge.
Hurstwood had to approve it, and he came to have a look." Through
swiftly changing expressions Vince's fleshy face registered the successive

stages of the partial and half-remembered and finally of what promised to be remembrance proper.

"I got it," he exclaimed. "Hurstwood was standing right here. We'd already gotten several couches, but we was short on chairs, and he questioned me. 'If this is going to be a lounge, you'll need some chairs, won't you, Quinn?' says he.

"'Yes, sir,' says I, 'we put in several requisitions already, but them supply guys ain't biting.'

"He laughs and says, 'Well, we'll have to see about it, won't we, unless you'd rather have hammocks instead of chairs. You could go up and down in the merry go-round.'

"At this point in time, I look at him very intense-like 'cause I have a good idea he's losing it. But he laughs and says, 'Carry on, soldier,' and takes off. Well, this was my one and only eye-to-eye with the noble captain, and it very nearly slipped my mind, until now . . . Except that three days later a truck pulls up, and three GI apes jump out waving a form to be signed and unload a dozen chairs for the General Lounge, C Company, 16th U.S. Army Engineer Group. How do you like 'em apples!"

"This sounds like Hurstwood . . . he could be very, very efficient when he put his mind to it. But he also had another side," Hal managed to report between gulps.

"What other side?" Fred was all suspicion.

"When I was on duty at the Infirmary he would drop in now and then and talk to the men on the sick list, spending time with them, and asking them if there was anything he could do for them, write letters, get them books, etc., etc."

"For crying out loud, he was the m . . . moral officer, it was his goddamn duty," Olie shouted, red-faced and breathing heavily.

Vince eyed him critically. "Drink it slow, kid, this is strong stuff, we don't want to have to carry you out, and Hurstwood was the morale officer," and he spelled it letter by letter m-o-r-a-l-e.

"Whatever, and don't you worry about me, fella, I can hold my liquor."

"He was well-liked, he was very well-liked . . . Where I come from we call a guy like that a real gent." There was a reminiscing glint in Hal's eye, and segments of the past were forcing their way out of obscurity.

"What about the broads, you talked about the broads?" Olie asked again.

"So long as what we talk about goes no further," and as they all nodded assent, he went on, "there were apparently two women, an American of his class whom he was going to marry and a German lady, very attractive, very bright, and also of his class who was head over heels in love with him, but he apparently wasn't head over heels in love with her. This was the dilemma."

"If what you say is true," Vince spoke softly, "then I feel for him. It's a hell of a jam to be in. I wish he'd somehow gotten around it."

"There are times when women spin their spider webs around men and keep them in bondage. The man is powerless, and the woman is callous and cruel. There are times when it is the woman's fault entirely, and there is a host of such examples in literature. Hurstwood could've been trapped by two overly possessive and unrelenting women." Fred shifted his body nervously and hoisted the bottle, admiring its markings.

Vince gave him a hard, distasteful look and belched to his heart's content.

"Yeah, yeah, yeah," Olie picked up the thread, "me too feels for Hurstwood and the jam he's gotten himself into. Love your neighbor and all that! Sure. But there's no denying the son of a bitch robbed me of close to a hundred bucks 'cause I was headin' for a winner." He paused. "Not that I want to make a mockery of things, but Ted Hurstwood could've considered postponing his mad dive till after the here and now betting ran its course."

"That's one way of looking at it," Hal laughed, and Fred and Vince followed suit.

"Well, this is a real party, and there's more beer to come," Vince's demeanor was full of the good host's bonhomie, "but could you guys chip in, this stuff don't come free."

"Of course," and Fred was promptly reaching into his pocket while Hal had his billfold out and was opening it.

"I have no cash on me, Vince, it's hidden in my civvies, but tomorrow I promise, I give you my solemn promise before witnesses, you'll get every cent of it."

"There's one in every crowd," Vince almost whispered and busied himself with the assortment of full and empty bottles.

/ / /

"Well, you keep your house shipshape"—Lieberman was saying spread out carelessly in an armchair and looking idly around—"Beryl would be proud of you."

"I don't wanna hear her name, it brings damned awful memories," Trainer said with feeling standing at the buffet and pouring out bourbon. "As I see it, the great advantage of drinkin' at home is you can add ice, in the office it gotta be straight."

"A very intelligent observation."

"Well now, Sol,"—Trainer handed his guest a large bourbon on the rocks—"what is it you wanna tell me about Ted?"

"The matter has been settled and listed as an accident, and this is all for the good, but there's something troubling me, and in fact I blame myself."

"So ye'll be telling me about yourself, not about Ted."

"About both of us."

"Okay," and Trainer sat down on the couch opposite Lieberman and took a swig.

"Some ten days ago, Ted unexpectedly paid us a visit shortly after 6:00 P.M. as the four of us were sitting down to dinner. Rachel invited him to join us, but he refused and apologizing to her he said he had to speak to me on an urgent matter which simply couldn't wait. I beckoned to him to follow me into the study, but he said he would rather talk in the car. We spent a few more minutes in the house while Ted was talking to the boys—by the way they adore . . . they adored him, especially after getting those wonderful presents for Hanukkah—anyway we got into his car and the boys were shouting, 'Come back soon, Uncle Ted,' and we drove off."

"Where did you go?"

"Well that's the point, we didn't go anywhere. We just drove in circles. Every few minutes Ted would say he needs my advice on a personal matter which is terribly important to him, and he would be on the point of saying something but finally didn't. This happened a number of times, and it didn't sound like Ted."

"Sure didn't."

"Now and again I'd say, 'Take your time, Ted, take your time,' and he would nod and get himself into the act and then stop short and not utter a single syllable. We stopped once for ten or fifteen minutes, and he smoked one cigarette after another and finally said, 'Please listen very carefully to what I have to say,' and that was it. Then he shut up like a clam! I didn't want to press him and thought I'd wait till he spoke of his own free will, but he never did. After about an hour of futile driving around the Village he dropped me by my house and said, 'I'm very sorry I put you to all this trouble, Sol, I truly am.'

"'Perhaps another time,' I said. 'Call me when you're ready. I'll be waiting.'

"'Perhaps,' he said, and he drove off. Well, needless to say I didn't hear from him, and when we ran into each other on base we just exchanged the usual greetings. Ted behaved in a perfectly normal way, and neither of us alluded to the futile meeting."

"Yeah, it's strange, and it don't sound like the Ted we knew," Trainer articulated, peering pensively into his glass.

"There must've been some personal problem that was simply tearing him apart."

Trainer nodded and continued to peer into his glass.

"Are you any closer to finding out what this problem was?"

Trainer shook his head. "No, I am not, and besides I don't want to know. Ted was killed in an auto accident, this is official, and it is the end of the story."

"I fully agree, Ed."

"Well, what else is there? There's nothin' else."

Lieberman scrambled to his feet and leaned towards Trainer.

"Can I get you another drink?"

"So long as you get one for yeself."

"Done," and he walked over to the buffet and refilled the two glasses. He gulped down his own, refilled it again, let ice cubes drop into both of them, and handed Trainer his glass. Then he remained standing, leaning against the fireplace. When at last he spoke it was with deliberation, choosing his words with utmost care.

"I could've helped Ted if I were more insistent, if I put my foot down, if only I could have convinced him that baring his heart was in his own best interest. I failed to do so, and I am therefore partly responsible for his death."

"That's a pile of horse manure."

"No, it isn't. I failed Ted both as a friend and as a rabbi. When a friend is in trouble, in great trouble, one has an obligation to use all means at one's disposal, to offer help, real help. That's what friends are for. And a friend should do what is best. I didn't do my best, what I did was half-hearted, and it is hardly a surprise it turned out to be totally ineffective. Maybe I didn't lack courage as such, but I certainly lacked understanding, judgment, and above all determination. And as for being a rabbi, well . . ."

"He wasn't even of your faith, Sol . . ." Trainer interrupted running to the buffet, frantically refilling his glass, gulping it down, and immediately refilling it again. "For cryin' out loud, Sol, you're a Jewish reverend, and Ted was from a different stall. You done enough, you listened, what else could ye have done?"

"I am a rabbi, and as a rabbi my obligation is to the entire human race, not only to men and women of Jewish faith . . ."

"Sure, sure, Sol."

"I was ineffective, and I could've saved a life. I didn't, and I am afraid the memory of it will haunt me for the rest of my life. That's all I wanted to say."

"If you want to feel guilty and wear a hair shirt . . . you know I can't stop you. But it don't add up."

Lieberman was fiddling with his glass and looking into space. Then he placed the glass on the side table and began drumming his fingers against the side of the armchair.

"Your address to the troops was timely, Colonel. Any reaction from them?"

"Korovitz assures me a great many of the enlisted men took it to heart. He was known to all of them, and he was popular. Korovitz says in all four companies there was heated talk about making the part of the highway by the overpass safer. It's a very steep climb and then a steep descent."

"It's good to know the men took it that way."

"There will be a memorial service for Ted at Army . . . oh in ten days' time or so, and Korovitz is already notifying the company commanders. Any enlisted man who wants to attend will be given transportation and time off. All the officers will be there, of course, and I expect most of the NCOs."

"It's cheery news the men were so touched." Lieberman was still shut up in a cocoon of his own making but was beginning to come out of it, a cryptic, self-protecting smile the measure of his thoughts.

Trainer strutted up to his guest and slapped him hard on the knee.

"That jazz about me keeping the house shipshape, well, it ain't exactly true."

"Oh!"

"I mess everythin' up, dirty everythin' and so on, but my cleaning lady she comes three times a week and makes every little thing spotless and sparklin'!"

"So I gave credit where no credit is due."

"Something like that, but I can live with it. And now that we took care of official business you might say, relax, Sol, be sociable, put your feet up, have a drink."

Chapter 5

It was now the beginning of April, and day-by-day the interplay of highs and lows resembled a checkerboard. On certain days it was unseasonably warm only to be counteracted by rainy and cooler days when the temperature dropped appreciably to rise unexpectedly and drop again. Two brief snowstorms stenciled the buildings and the parade ground white, but snow melted overnight, the sun burnt more forcibly than before, and the temperature returned to its inconstant, unpredictable pattern. Those who had been stationed at 16th U.S. Army Engineer Group for several years or longer said they could not remember anything like it, and what it augured for the rest of the year was anybody's guess. It was the craziest of Aprils.

Over midday chow Fred leaned forward towards Vince and asked: "Is it true about those two guys from A Company who were roughed up during the night?"

"Yeah, it's true, Coleman and Janitsky."

"Why, what happened?"

"Let's talk about it outside, better still let's go to our quarters. Mess Hall walls and empty spaces have ears too."

Fred gave every indication of being nervous, and keeping silent at first went on looking beseechingly at Vince. "I must know," he drawled out.

"I'm meeting up with Hal and Olie in Hal's room. Want to come?" Looking more nervous with each passing minute, Fred nevertheless managed to give an energetic nod. They found Hal and Olie sitting on the bed glum and uncommunicative.

"Is this other info true?" Vince asked.

After a while Hal half-rose from the bed. "Yes, and it's worse than we thought. He also conned two guys from B Company, I've got their names somewhere."

Olie turned his gaze on Fred. "What is he doing here? Is he with us?"

Vince ignored the question and began to speak to no one in particular.

"Zack has a new racket, and this one is real dirty. He invests money for others stateside, but on the last minute something goes wrong and the money is never returned. I know he took Bud Coleman for close to five hundred bucks, and Steve Janitsky for close to three hundred. The guys from B lost close to a grand between them."

"Can't it be reported to proper authorities?" Fred asked. "It looks like an open-and-shut case."

"No, it isn't." Hal was now fully alert and moving nimbly around the room. "I saw one of those agreement forms Zack churns out, and I showed it to the legal clerk at Army. It's so vague and imprecise that Zack can't be held to account. Any two-bit shyster would demolish the prosecution's case in no time. Those guys were suckers, and there will be plenty more. Zack preys on the careless and the greedy, and oftentimes he holds another card up his sleeve: he's got something on the guys he goes after; petty theft, AWOL which never discovered, smuggling girls into the base, that kind of thing, and he turns on the pressure."

"And Coleman and Janitsky?"

"Well, Fred, they got kind of pissed off upon finding out their money has vanished straight down Zack's pocket, and they threatened to see the Colonel."

"What happened next?"

Hal began to laugh raucously. "What happened next can be gleaned from the daily papers as the saying goes, and by the way those guys from

B got it worse than the guys from A; broken bones, half of the teeth gone, all attributable for the purpose of official documentation, to slipping on cakes of soap or falling out of windows. I'd say"—Hal continued—"Zack had the real goods on those guys."

"Does the Group know what happened, do they have any idea . . . ?"

"None, Fred, and this was just a warning."

"How come Zack returned our betting money?"

"He had no choice, Olie, there were too many witnesses, too many of us had bet, he couldn't have made his case." Vince glanced at his wristwatch. "I gotta go."

"We gotta do something about it, guys!" Olie yelled defiantly. "You with us, Fred?"

"I am," Fred said very quietly, moving sheepishly towards the door.

"We'll talk tonight, same place, right after chow," and Hal started buttoning his fatigues.

"Meeting adjourned," Vince called lightheartedly, one foot outside the door.

/ / /

"The first thing we gotta do," Olie was saying, "is sign a pact in blood, 'cause this is the way things are done, that's what Tom Sawyer would do," and he pulled out from his pockets a long needle, a quill, and a folded parchment. "I'll prick my arm, and you can dip the quill in the blood and sign. Though we gotta have the pact written up first. Any volunteers?"

The others watched him in stony silence.

"Gee whiz, guys," Fred called out, "I don't know what I am doing here, what pact, and what the hell is going on?"

"Haven't you been told?" Olie's impatience was mounting.

"I've been told zilch, does this satisfy you?"

Vince held up a hand. "Simmer down, guys, and don't let's start fighting among ourselves," and seeing Olie and Fred still at loggerheads, he shouted with all the power of his lungs, "Simmer down," and pounded the table with his fist.

"We have a slight problem," Hal put in, "and prompt action is advisable."

"I spoke to one of Zack's snitches, he owes me one," Vince resumed in a loud voice. "Zack wants to teach us a lesson, he thinks in the future we may be a thorn in his side, he also knows Hal and I are buddy-buddy with Coleman and Janitsky, and he's got no use for you, Fred."

"That leaves me," Olie said with pride. "What does the shithead say about me?"

"You questioned his business practices and his judgment, and Mr. Zachary Apfeldorf is very, very touchy when it comes to them. My snitch-friend told me his employer considers you, Olie, and the rest of us dangerous characters who are likely to undermine one of his future operations. The four of us are to be taught a lesson."

"I haven't done anything to the guy," Fred was pleading between sighs. "Why is he after me?"

"It's the nature of the game, as things stand we have to protect ourselves." Hal straightened himself up and fixed his eyes on the three faces. "We have to strike first, everybody agree?"

"We ought to go and see Korovitz or Fiorello first, lay everything before them, expose the crimes," Fred was working himself up to a tizzy, "after all, this is not Chicago in the twenties."

"Anybody who's not with us can leave," Hal said looking pointedly at Fred.

"I just want to explore all the legal avenues before we start hitting one another over the head, the law first, not the alley."

"It may interest you to know several months ago a fresh recruit in C Company did just that. He borrowed some money from Zack at high interest, and when he tried to pay it back Zack doubled the interest. Our friend went to see Major Fiorello who started an investigation, but nothing could be proved. Two weeks later as our friend was pulling KP a boiler exploded, and he was badly burnt in the chest and legs. Another investigation and one big zilch. Our friend spent two months in a hospital, and when they released him he was transferred to another unit. Complaining to the brass will accomplish nothing. We have to strike first. This is the only way."

"I am with Hal," Vince's voice was ringing with decisiveness, while Olie, misty-eyed and looking abstractedly at the ceiling, was swaying at the hips. Then he cut in quickly, "A preemptive strike," and he repeated the words with exhilaration, "a preemptive strike, this is what MacArthur did in Korea and George Washington when he crossed the Delaware."

"Zack has eight gorillas who do his dirty work, they are action boys because he does all the thinking and planning himself." Vince was speaking very slowly, allowing the words to sink into unreceptive skulls. "This means we gotta hit all nine of them roughly at the same time."

"I'd say at precisely the same time," Hal cut in, "so no benchwarmer can go after us out of undying loyalty or for pocket change."

"Right," Vince agreed. "What I have in mind is we knock them down from behind, tie 'em up with duct tape, leave a piece of paper with some immortal thoughts engraved on it in each mouth, and let them lie there till they are discovered in the morning."

"So this is going to be a clandestine night operation, somethin' like the Rangers scouring the Italian Alps under the cloak of darkness in search of German machine gun nests?" Olie asked excitedly.

Hal nodded. "Maybe," he said cautiously. "But there's still a lot of planning to do. Personally I'd prefer straight wire and chloroform."

"This promises to be rough," Fred was very candid, "and you fellows have to understand I've never been involved in anything rough . . ."

"You'll learn quick enough or else Zack's men will kick your teeth out," and Hal suppressed a yawn.

"Is there no other way?"

"None! This is a rough world, sonny, and if you don't want others to be rough with you, you gotta be rough with 'em." Vince paused for a brief moment. "Do you want out, Fred? The door is open, and no one will blame you."

"Hell no," Fred shouted frantically. "I don't want out, and I'll show you what Fred Bonsuer is made of. I'm in, d'you understand, in, and I'll do what is expected of me."

"Never thought you had it in you, pretty boy," Olie lisped the words out, assuming a combative air.

"You go to hell, boy, d'you hear, you goddamned piece of under-sized crap, take a hike, or else I'll wipe the floor with you."

"Whaaattt?" and Olie, panther-like, sprang forward only to be intercepted by Vince and Hal.

"Eh, guys, take it easy," Vince advised calmly. "There'll be fighting enough before the week is out."

"Did you hear what the creep said to me?"

"Yeah, I did. But you kinda asked for it, Olie."

"I can't stand the sight of that scumbag, he ain't one of us."

"Judging by his outburst"—Hal joined in—"he's very much one of us, and he's specially like you, Olie, with one slight difference . . ."

"Oh, and what might that be?"

"His mind is even dirtier than yours," Hal concluded, while Fred, grim and on the alert, would not take his eyes off them.

"There's a lot to finalize tomorrow night, a lot," Vince was frowning and scribbling on a pad. "I have access to all supply buildings, and I'll pick up some planks, boards, poles what have you, you can kill with a baseball bat, and we want something lighter, to knock 'em down, maybe break a bone or two, without kicking their asses into the next world. Wire and chloroform would be handy."

"The Infirmary has both, leave it to me," Hal said. "We have a particular kind of wire, soft and pliable that doesn't break."

"The little mementos we want to leave with Zack and his cohorts, maybe something to print on their mugs?"

Fred lifted a finger. "I work in the print shop, and there's equipment galore for cutting stencil and hand presses that print on all kinds of substances; printing on cheeks or foreheads is no problem, and it takes one hell of an effort to take it off."

"We also need a lot of adhesive tape 'cause we are going to mouth-tape those creeps and maybe hoods so they don't see what's going on. Also, who knows, we may have to use masks."

"That's my department," Olie exclaimed, "you can have all three and no sweat."

"Good so far," Vince continued. "Now as all of you realize, we won't be meeting those guys face to face; there are more of them, and we wouldn't stand a chance. Deception, trick, dirty-dirty is what we have to rely on. Best of all would be luring them two or three at a time, to the supply depot, or some other building that few troopers set foot in and dealing with them there. And the time of the operation got to be carefully planned. Is it to be in the dead of night, or just before dawn, or late in the evening, or what? Want you guys to think about what I've said and come up with constructive suggestions tomorrow, our final organizational meeting."

"What about the pact and signing it in blood? This is the way things are done," Olie asked eagerly.

"You're right, Olie," Vince replied with much patience, "but as this is a very special case we need a bit more time. You understand? I'm sure Tom Sawyer will forgive us."

"Don't worry, Olie, I know Tom personally," Hal added in a reassuring tone of voice. "I'll have a quiet word."

/ / /

Zack was powerfully shaken by the shoulder, and he entered that peculiar state when dream and wakefulness intertwine, when what is dreamt is subtly overlaid by reality and what is consciously experienced is embellished by visions and reveries, till one of them, dream or wakefulness, wins the final contest and drowns out the other. Another powerful shake of the shoulder made Zack turn on his side and peer into semi-darkness.

"Zack, it's Charlie," a voice whispered.

"Yeah, yes, Charlie, what's up?"

"You won't believe it, them two creeps Shelton and Quinn are in the Supply Annex more or less gassed up. They've been there for some time, and they've begun shooting their mouths about teaching you a lesson, and I overheard them . . ."

"Go on."

"Well, you said way back you wanted to kick their asses 'cause they might be trouble, and now is as good time as any . . ."

"Good thinking, Charlie."

"Do you want to come yourself with two or three guys?"

"No, I'll tell you what . . . what's the time?"

"4:30 on the dot."

"Wake up Cutts, Derlinger, and Simms; you know where they sleep?"

"Sure do."

"And tell them to go to Supply Annex and rough up those two; usual treatment, no broken bones, and if there's any booze left pour it down their throats. We want each of them to be as drunk as a skunk."

"Right, Zack."

"And when the job is done, report back."

"You got it."

Soon three tall, bulky figures, each holding a baseball bat under his heavy winter overcoat, stole out from A Company Sleeping Quarters, made a dash for the reviewing stand where they hit the prone waiting for the sentries to turn back and then ran, as fast as their legs would carry them, all the way to the side door of the Annex. The lock on the door was broken, and when they noiselessly pushed the door they could see in the distance by the far wall a small lamp shedding meager light, some blankets tossed about, and empty bottles piling up on the right and left. Tiptoeing, they entered the Annex and advanced several steps.

The three heavy boards came down quick as lightning in splendid unison on the three heads, and Cutts, Derlinger, and Simms fell down unconscious. The four masked men, one appreciably shorter than the other three, set about their business, no word being spoken. Zack's friends' hands were tied behind their backs with soft pliable wire and their feet similarly attended to. Their mouths were covered with thick packaging tape, and with the help of clippers their hair was cut so short that only a stubble remained. Next came the hand press: on each forehead, chest, the upper portion of the back close to the neck, and soft underbelly, just above the groin, an identical message was imprinted in large black letters: A SOLDIER WHO CHEATS ANOTHER SOLDIER AND STEALS FROM HIM DESERVES TO BE KICKED LONG AND HARD. The three bodies were turned over and now lay on their bellies. The masked men quickly tore the clothing off their backs, and a moment of silence ensued. One of them pulled a whip out of a bag and nodded to the others. The whipping began, and as the three prisoners were regaining consciousness groans reaching through the gagging tape could be heard. Each prisoner received twenty lashes, and from each back over bruised and torn-off skin, blood was trickling down. This accomplished, the prisoners were hauled to the far wall and then to the left behind where dozens of tarpaulins were hanging from the lines creating an opaque screen. Heavy objects were placed on their backs and legs and on their eagle-spread arms, and the masked men took up their position by the side door.

A few minutes later Zack was again awakened out of his bucolic dreams, and Charlie's grinning face stared into his.

"Everything's hunky-dory, Boss, and we got two very unhappy s.o.b.'s pissed and begging for mercy."

"What else did they say?"

"Several others will be joining them very soon for a pow-wow against you."

"How many?"

"Three or four at the most, and tomorrow they'll be making an appointment to see the colonel."

"I see, and this morning . . . ?"

"They should be entering the Annex in fifteen or twenty minutes."

"You have the list, Charlie, rouse up three more guys, this will make it six on our side; do you reckon that's enough?"

"Plenty, and the sooner they get there the better."

"Okay, give the order, but I want Lenke and Jones to stand by. They're my personal guards."

"You got it, Zack," and Charlie disappeared into the night.

When the three newly activated defenders of Zack's monetary interests crossed the threshold of the Annex, the earlier procedure was duplicated almost to a tee, the only difference being that one of them, possessed of a singularly hard skull, had to be walloped twice before he passed out. When Charlie reported to his boss again, he found him half-awake and brooding.

"You're the winner, and would it be asking too much that you go in person and inspect what's been done? Dawn will be breaking soon."

"You're right," Zack exclaimed, jumping off his bunk and reaching for his fatigues. "Tell Lenke and Jones to meet me outside in five minutes."

"You got it," Charlie sounded off and once again blended in with the night. Hardly more than several minutes had elapsed when three tall figures, two of them bulky and broad-shouldered, adroitly evaded the sentries and made their way by the side door into the Supply Building Annex; and a good half-hour passed, when those visiting the latrine in the early hours of the morning and casting an idle eye through the window onto the parade ground, no longer pitch black but grayish and infused with patches of light, could distinguish four figures, one of them much shorter than the others, carrying several well-filled duffel bags and striding with aplomb across the parade ground straight into the building housing C Company. Had one been within earshot, but no one stood that close, one would have heard them whistling with verve, not to the world, no sir, but just to themselves.

/   /   /

On this particular morning, Sergeant Korovitz was late in reporting to his office, and Vallejo was handling routine business promptly and most of the time mechanically. When he stepped in at last shortly before 10 o'clock, the sergeant looked grim and troubled.

"Have you heard about that thing in the Supply Annex?" he asked, his eyes bathed in anger and suspicion.

"Something . . . as I was having breakfast."

"News travels fast," Korovitz snorted. "Any idea who did it?"

"None if you want names, etc., Sarge, but let me blab one or two generalities."

"Be my guest, Vallejo."

"The good guys did it to the bad guys because the good guys saw no other way of redress."

"That's crap, goddamn crap, Vallejo, and you know it." Unexpectedly and showing passionately that side of his character which had habitually remained in the background, Korovitz became excited and crisscrossed the office at a frenzied pace as though he felt that rapid movement and anger galore could exorcise the demons.

"Anybody who has been unfairly treated, cheated, molested, set upon can see his First Sergeant, or the Company Commander, or me, or the Exec Officer, or the Group Commander. The door is always open, and it behooves you and those who think like you to remember this is the United States Army and not one of them decadent cities up North where the crazies ranting in strange tongues take potshots at one another in the middle of the Sabbath."

"With all due respect, Sergeant . . ."

"That's a joke if I ever heard one," and Korovitz, his face red with anger, went on mimicking Vallejo's words, inflating his sense of respect and then mocking it out of existence.

"You have respect for nobody, let's face it," and he drawled out, "nobody, nobody at all."

Vallejo remained sitting at his desk shuffling papers and saying absolutely nothing, but Korovitz had not yet relinquished the field, cocksure and propped up against the window, his eyes sweeping inquisitively the floor, he launched again into the topic of the day.

"The Army has a mechanism for everything, because the Army is the most efficient and best run of all government agencies. In the last year we've had several complaints of abuse and brutality, and the Army investigated, as it always does, thoroughly and impartially. We are firm but fair. In some cases we couldn't gather enough evidence, and Army regulations are very specific about what we can and what we can't do." He was going to say more, but he saw Vallejo stand up resolutely and head for the door.

"Please excuse me, Sergeant, but I gotta go to the men's room," he barked out, closing the door. Korovitz mopped the sweat off his face and sat behind his desk calm and resigned. When Vallejo returned he hummed and caught his eye.

"Did you see those nine troopers?"

"No," Vallejo replied shrugging his shoulders.

"Tied up like wild beasts, heads shaven, tattooed on their faces and other parts of the body, clubbered over the head, and whipped, yes, whipped till blood ran down their backs. That MP sergeant told me he hadn't seen anything like it ever. The MPs found them on their rounds just before reveille. What a sight!" Korovitz paused and did not notice that Trainer had entered the office and was now standing next to him.

"Sir," he muttered scrambling to his feet.

The colonel beckoned to him to sit down. "There will be an investigation," he answered curtly, "and the guilty will be punished. It's one hell of a coincidence though, Army sending us that memo about hooliganism in the ranks and what to do about it. And two days later nine guys are tied up, beaten up, and gagged in the Supply Annex."

"Maybe it wasn't a coincidence, sir," Vallejo observed quietly.

"How do you mean?"

"It is just possible that throughout the Command the men are beginning to take the law into their own hands because regular channels don't work."

"Bullshit!" Trainer shouted. "Regular channels do work. Besides the men are not judges or executioners. Their job is to carry out orders. Nothing more."

"That's right, sir."

"Answer my question, Vallejo. I expect a frank answer."

"Is it an order? And what is the question?"

"Yes, goddamn it, it's a direct order, and stop playing for time."

"I'd like to say something, Colonel." Trainer nodded, but studiously avoided looking at Vallejo. "Maybe right now the law is in nobody's hands, maybe it's just been kicked off the playfield, and good guys want it back on the playfield."

Now Trainer was transfixing Vallejo with a merciless, prosecutorial stare and shaking his head.

"You got some strange notions, mister. Why, every officer and every NCO in this Command can testify we investigate every gripe, we take no sides, we break our backs to get to the bottom of each case."

"Maybe the bottom is too deep and kind of muddy, and it takes lots of brains to get to it."

"You watch it! Getting too big for your breeches, that's the trouble with you."

"You ordered me to be frank, sir."

"So I did, so I did, frank but not insulting."

"Sir, what is it you want from me?"

"Do you think we, the Command, allowed all kinds of shenanigans and worse, much worse, to take place right under our noses and did no goddamn thing about it?"

Vallejo was silent looking dully into space.

"I expect an answer, Specialist."

"I am not qualified to give an answer, sir."

"You're dodging again."

"Whatever you say, sir."

Trainer was gazing frantically at Vallejo, head to foot, and took a few steps forward, almost colliding with Korovitz. His lips were moving, and he was on the point of saying something, but he restrained himself. Korovitz, who was now sitting behind his desk, leaned forward deferentially and asked grinning broadly, "Is there anything we can do for you, Colonel, on this fine April morning?"

"No, thank you, Sergeant. I got work to do. Carry on." And he walked out quick time, slamming the door behind him.

Korovitz turned to Vallejo. "Me too think you have red raspberries growing inside your head, still you stood up to the Kansas Maelstrom well, and I am proud of you, son!"

Immediately after lunch Trainer summoned Vallejo to his office. "Sit down, Jesús," he called out jovially, "sit down. I want to ask you a question or two, and I want you to be as frank as you can be. This is just between us."

"This morning when I spoke frankly you very nearly sent me to Fort Leavenworth for twenty years."

"Well," Trainer was fiddling with his pen and blotter, "that was in the mornin' like, another time another place, but this here is serious, and you can help the Group."

And as Vallejo just sat there mute and stony-faced, Trainer added in an undertone: "This is just between you and me, and I give you my word your name will not be named outside this office. Give you my word . . . and Jesús, I need your help."

Vallejo looked calmly around betraying no emotion.

"What is it you want to ask me, sir?"

"Falls into two parts if you catch my meanin', first why what happened happened and how we're going to deal with it, and second what can we do in the future so that what happened don't happen again. You read me, son?"

"I read you."

Trainer waved a folder. "This is the preliminary medical report on . . . on the nine victims. No serious injuries, just a bump on the head followed by rough handling. Anyway, they'll live."

"Unfortunately they will, sir. I can hardly restrain my grief."

Trainer frowned and then began gesturing frantically to convey his understanding of Group Clerk's attitude, his surprise at Group Clerk's attitude, his own helplessness, his astonishment that such events were allowed to take place, more of his own understanding of the event, and finally his undying conviction that Vallejo was just the right party to make inquiries of.

"I understand that Apfeldorf fellow's been fleecing our boys for ever and a day," he began pompously.

"That's right, sir, he had his finger in every dirty pie."

"Please describe for me the range of his crooked activities, and omit nothing. I want the truth, the whole truth, and nothing but the truth."

Vallejo did what he was asked to do, taking one operation at a time, sparing no details, but revealing no names of those who had been cheated in one way or another, or subjected to extortion and violence. When he had finished, Trainer looked embarrassed and sad.

"And this has been going on for how long?"

"Ever since Apfeldorf was assigned to 16th Engineer Group. A year, I'd guess, give or take a few weeks."

"There have been official complaints?"

"Several, but they got nowhere. Either there was insufficient evidence or on the last minute the witnesses refused to testify, and the matter was quickly forgotten."

"I understand Major Fiorello conducted one or two of these investigations."

"He did, sir, and he tried to leave no stone unturned. But he was hamstrung and going by the book, he could do nothing. When complainants are intimidated, threatened, beaten up you need a different kind of investigation, and this never happened." Vallejo laughed contemptuously.

"And Captain Hurstwood?"

"I know it for a fact several guys spoke to him privately about Zack, and he was very sympathetic and promised to do something about it."

"And?"

Vallejo was keeping silent, looking extremely uneasy.

"For heaven's sake, Jesús, let's get on with it. I am bound by an oath of secrecy. You do believe me, don't you?"

"I liked Captain Hurstwood, I guess everyone did, and that's why I find it difficult to talk about him."

"Will you try?"

"In the last few months the captain was . . . well he wasn't quite there. I had the impression his mind was far away. He carried out his duties, but he wasn't . . . the same man. Now it probably doesn't matter, and anyway let him rest in peace."

They were both silent now, their heads bowed, responding to a call which was neither loud nor clear, if it was a call at all, and not an illusionist's trick.

Trainer was the first to rally, and he did not mince words.

"If you were in my place, Vallejo, how would you handle this . . . this underhanded attack on nine enlisted men?"

"You should conduct an investigation, by all means, and send the order through usual channels to all company commanders. The men should know about it, but don't expect too much from this investigation. Remember that for ninety-nine percent of the guys, some NCOs, and many officers happily joining in, this at last was justice. They couldn't ask for anything better. At long last, listening to the imprecations of the tribe and taking them to heart Pallas Athena descended upon 16th U.S. Army Engineer Group and brought with her wisdom and justice."

"Who's the dame?"

"Sprung from the forehead of Zeus, virgin goddess, and goddess of wisdom."

"Aha," and Trainer pulled a knowing face. "Anything else?"

"As for those nine bozos, rightfully clubbered, kicked, branded, and tied up, the simplest thing would be to ship them out to other units and as far away from us as possible."

"Are they likely to prefer charges?"

"I'll give you a hundred to one they won't, sir."

"They were Apfeldorf's foot soldiers?"

"That's right, his foot soldiers and bodyguards, and as luck would have it an unexpected slot for a company clerk has just surfaced at the 122nd."

"But they got their new company clerk last week, that's what John, Major Fiorello I mean, told me."

"You are absolutely right, and so is the Major. 122nd drew a new company clerk last week."

"Well then?"

"After a day or so they found out he couldn't read and write. There was some sort of foul-up at Army, two men with the same last name or whatever. Anyway, this morning one of their first sergeants called, and as Sergeant Korovitz was out of the office, the first sergeant spoke to me . . . at length, he wasn't leaving anything to chance."

"So that slot is still open?"

"Right you are, sir."

"D'you think Zack Apfeldorf might be the answer?"

"I can't think of a better one," and Vallejo added with emphasis, "He can read and write."

"And the rest of his buddies?"

"I'd send each one to a different unit. After all, criminals shouldn't fraternize with other criminals."

"Got a point. We have multiple commands within 7th Army, but we also have bases in southern Italy."

"No, sir, this should be off limits."

"Why, Vallejo?"

"Because the climate between Rome and Sicily is too salubrious, the land too beautiful, and the people too engaging for those eight bastards. Do we have bases near the North Pole?"

"Not for U.S. Army as such, but the C.I.A keeps sending us classified information about U.S. trained battalions that can become operational at the drop of a hat somewhere in the middle of Siberia."

Vallejo frowned and scratched his nose. "It's a long shot."

"I agree, still there is always Iceland."

All of a sudden Vallejo's face was one beatific smile, the smile of men of good will, the smile of saints.

"It's a bull's eye, Colonel," he exclaimed. "You're a sharpshooter, and there's no denyin'."

"I'm glad we've settled this small matter," Trainer said modestly and helped himself to a cheroot. "Now, what do we do in the future, but first another question. Do you know who these avenging angels were who," he mustered all the sarcasm that was in him welling up, "meted out justice? The MPs tell me there were four of them."

"No, I don't," Vallejo answered without hesitation, and Trainer waived a hand. "You should call a general formation soon, preferably on the day those nine shitheads have been reassigned and shipped out."

"What do I say to the troops?"

"You have to level with them. Say all kinds of abuses and villainous acts have been perpetrated by a small group of criminal GIs on many innocent GIs, and unfortunately I as Group Commander have not been able to do much about it. I deeply regret it and you have my apologies."

"Apologies?" Trainer cried out in wrathful disbelief. "D'you want me to give 'em my left testicle as well? This is what's you're after, isn't it, Vallejo, to hu . . . humiliate me, to kick my body and my soul into the gutter. Well, forget it."

"If you don't take at least part of the blame, the men won't believe a word of what you'll be telling them. Maybe they won't start a revolution just yet, but they'll burn you in effigy as sure as God created the great state of New Mexico, and your picture drawn by most uncomplimentary artists will be on every dartboard right here on base under your very nose . . . sir!"

"Go on," Trainer commanded, blowing out clouds of impenetrable smoke.

Vallejo began to speak in a loud and dispassionate tone, went on for some time, and Trainer listened intently and took notes.

"That's good," he said when Vallejo had finished. "Real good."

"It's bare bones, the speech has to be lengthened, filled in, fired up."

"Can you do it, Vallejo?"

"If you would like me to."

"Yes, goddamn, I would!"

They put their heads together expanding and revising the text, Trainer scribbling feverishly in a bold, crude hand and hollering now and then from behind a veil of smoke, "Not so fast, kid, can you repeat what you just said, I am no stenographer, take pity on an old man, slow down!"

When Vallejo at last entered the Group Sergeant's office, Korovitz looked at him with a mixture of pity and concern.

"He really must've picked your brain this time; putting final touches on something that'll make our lives richer than ever before, what?"

"Something like that, Sarge. And I have to tell you I'm bushed."

A carefree smile flickered around Korovitz's mouth and then dilated far and wide. He crossed and re-crossed his legs, his manner becoming more and more convivial.

"We still have a quarter of an hour or so before knocking-off, and I wonder if I ever told you the story of how a handful of Confederates beat the stuffing out of several battalions of Yankee cavalry in northern Kentucky, not far from the town where I was born, in the year of our Lord 1862. It's an inspiring story."

"No, Sarge, you never did, and I am dying to hear it."

"Take a pew then. Dusk was falling, and our scouts reported that a superior force of bluebellies was heading our way, being apparently uncertain of their bearings. A council of war was held at once, and it was decided that . . ." Korovitz's dramatic mode was at its most impressive, and he was totally absorbed in what he was saying. The story had its twists and cliff-hangers, its richly descriptive portions and sudden calls to action, and it unfolded jerkily here and slowly and majestically there, like a gigantic sea serpent that knows without fail where his friends and foes are. Vallejo listened spellbound.

/   /   /

Late in the evening of the same day Fred, Vince, Olie, and Hal met in Hal's quarters.

"That was nifty, Olie, us wearing masks, I mean," Hal said. "Another precaution and it paid off."

"So were the surgical gloves, Hal," Olie said, "and as for the masks,

I well remember Zorro always wore one, and he knew what he was doin', didn't he? Just follow the masters."

"All you guys did great, and the hand press was the final touch." Vince glanced approvingly at Fred. "Hope that unbreakable wire didn't create any lasting damage on the delicate wrists and ankles of the gentlemen in question," and Vince turned to Hal.

"The boards were of just the right weight, Vince," Fred commented. "One blow was enough to knock them out, it would take several to waste them."

Vince nodded and grinned. "All in the line of duty."

"And us being mute, I liked that, carrying out the operation in complete silence, that was great. I read somewhere in a detective story how one gang wasted a rival gang in a single night using silencers and not uttering a single sound." Olie's excitement was unmistakably on the rise.

"What happens now?" Fred asked.

"Nothin', they've got nothin'. Nothin' can be traced." Vince was a rock of conviction.

"There'll be an investigation, to be sure, but it will lead nowhere. I am told even Trainer is skeptical of any results." Hal was relaxed and sanguine.

Fred stretched his arms energetically backward. "I feel good, I feel very good, but I can't put it into words, and besides I don't want to."

"Holy smoke. The tales I'll be telling my buddies back home once I get out of this goddamn gutter. Holy smoke! They might not even believe me at first and say I dreamed it all up. That's right, they might, but I know better." And Olie slapped both of his knees in exhilaration.

"I think maybe we did something that is okay." Hal spoke very slowly and very hesitantly.

"I don't know if this was okay or not okay," Vince cut in. "But we did right by Coleman and Janitsky."

Chapter 6

Chaplain Lieberman was leaning carelessly against the window surveying with a kindly eye the throng swelling up in the lounge-auditorium right behind the chapel. "It's better than last month," he ventured as an unfamiliar face greeted him and then promptly retreated out of sight. He waited a few more minutes, occasionally smiling and waving a hand at those he knew by name and allowing everyone, or nearly everyone, to find a seat and settle in it. Some of the men preferred to sit on the floor, and he had a joke for them, which he varied from month to month, but which invariably included the same adage that the stability of the floor was vastly more reliable than the stability of chairs, armchairs, stools, etc., etc. This usually gave rise to some laughter and helped break the ice. Scouring the vast interior he saw only a handful of empty seats and a trickle of latecomers inching sheepishly on through the two side doors at the back.

"Right," he articulated briskly, glancing at his wristwatch. "Let's get cracking." He advanced a step and began in a firm, direct manner, "I'd like to welcome all of you to the fourth Inter-Faith Gathering this year where, as the name of our meetings indicates, we look at the teaching of various churches and religions and try to extract from it rules of conduct which can help us in leading a decent daily life and behaving towards others in a neighborly fashion. Our first gathering in January of this year was modestly successful, and the one in February saw us grow in numbers and in the scope of our discussions. We have been growing ever since head over heels, and so much so that one of you said to me the other day that our gatherings begin to resemble those strange creatures brought from outer space in science fiction movies and caged in labs only to astonish the dudes in their spotless white smocks that overnight the creature has grown tenfold, and the cage can be draped around its big toe while the entire building now in shambles serves as its footrest."

Laughter and applause.

"I hope this chapel here will remain standing—there are all kinds of regulations prohibiting destruction of government property—but should it prove too cramped for us, well, we'll have to find another pad."

More laughter and applause.

The speaker paused for a moment, cocked his head, and continued.

"Before I pass on to our theme for today, I would like to thank once again those of you who made those fascinating presentations at our March meeting, presentations drawn from your own personal experiences which allowed us to share with you the multiple ways of nurturing good habits, common decency, and respect for our neighbors. We thank Private First Class Malcolm McGrath," Lieberman thrust his arm forward, and with a smack of the lips let the fingers dart up in a brief commanding gesture, "for telling us how his father, stern and inflexible though he often was, nevertheless taught his sons to be always civil towards others, and even if they crossed the line, not to fight back right away but let tempers cool down and look for a peaceful solution."

McGrath, bullnecked, his torso shaped into an oversize square, was standing now grinning from ear to ear.

"Dad was okay, 'cept when he got to preachin' theology to us youngsters, Presbyterian Calvinistic theology, and what I remember about it now, 'cause I was scared out of my wits most of the time, was we was evil, evil, and would most likely end up in hell."

Modest laughter and applause.

"Many thanks to Sergeant Gabriel Medina—will you please stand up, Sergeant, and be recognized once more?—for telling us about your experiences as an altar boy under the auspices of a very enlightened priest."

"That's right, sir"—the sergeant was standing more or less at attention—"Father Tomasso taught us that good works are just as important as faith and contrition and prayer, and we were all impressed into the service, as the saying goes, trying to better the life of those less fortunate than ourselves in the city of Modesto, in the great state of California."

Much hooting and muffled applause.

"You were very fortunate to be associated with Father Tomasso, Sergeant," Lieberman's voice rose above the sluggishly diminishing hubbub. "Very fortunate."

The sergeant was once again in a standing position. "Yes, sir, and he called us God's crack battalions."

Feeble and sporadic applause.

"I can't think of a more appropriate name." Lieberman paused for a reflective moment and continued, "Our special thanks go to Private Donald Yen-Li who in March told us so much about Zen Buddhism and was so informative and convincing that—I have it on good authority—many of us are either contemplating conversion to Zen Buddhist faith or are one foot in it already. Rise, Private, so that we can have the pleasure of seeing you again."

A mixed reaction of wows, applause, belching, and catcalls.

A tall slim figure stood up without haste, as if standing up for him was a ritual in itself, imbued with timeless and ineffaceable significance, his delicate features resting in impassive relief to his well-shaped head, only his eyes intensely live with an eerie, super-terrestrial glow.

"Thank you, sir," he said in the flat accents of the Midwest, bowing his head slightly.

"Your presentation was truly an eye-opener, Donald, and I am happy that you spoke not only about self-denial and nirvana, but also about everyday human interactions, about kindness and tolerance, about the ways of strengthening the bonds of friendship, and about the sacred rule of not harming any living creature. You gave all of us a great deal to think about."

"The closer we get to the Buddha, the more mature we become. We cease to be unruly children and take on the character of thoughtful, understanding adults."

Prolonged silence came on the heels of these words, but it was silence charged with unquenchable latent force, and when the response burst out at last it was a storm of applause lasting well over a minute, uniform in its pounding and debased by no contrary calls.

Lieberman's face lit up dramatically in well earned satisfaction, and Yen-Li, looking a little disconcerted, a small boy lost, was sitting down quietly in his seat smiling bleakly, his head turning occasionally this way and that to catch a glimpse of a friendly face.

"Finally our heartfelt thanks go to Specialist Fourth Class Melvin Davies who addressed us last time on the subject of Methodist church-es, the work they carry out in their communities, their sense of social cohesion, and above all their sense of Christian fellowship."

"Thank you, Chaplain," and Davies rose to his feet and stood there glum and speechless.

"Eh, Melvin," a voice shot out, "me heard you Methodist fellows are kinda happy-go-lucky lot, but ye might sign on fer an undertaker."

"Get lost," Davies shot back. "I got two more months in this hole, and you wanna see me with a smirk on me face, see me then."

Tumultuous applause.

"The picture you drew for us, Melvin, was most inspiring, and again you didn't speak only of repentance, but also of the social responsibili-ty which members of your parish assumed to help one another, to understand one another, to be civil to one another, and to be one fam-ily. When you go back to civilian life, will you be keeping in touch with your church?"

"I guess I will, our church is doing good work and everyone is the winner, but I have no stomach for all them highfaluting notions, like God's grace, and original sin, Heaven and Hell, and such like."

"Thank you, Melvin, and again thanks to all of you who made pre-sentations at our March gathering."

A round of applause, polite and unenthusiastic, but showing that now and again one can rise to the occasion.

Lieberman cleared his throat, cast an all-enveloping gaze around the lounge, and went on:

"Our theme for today is the great religions of the world and every-day ethics. All of you are aware of the exalted standards of conduct that are part and parcel of these religions.

"When I meet with you, Jewish boys, for regular services and workshops I speak about the Law, and I try to interpret it and help you understand it. Psalm 1 says that the happy man finds delight in the law of the Lord, 'and in His law doth he meditate day and night.' Every great religion preaches a high and exalted moral code, and this code is at the center of every religion. In the Torah, the five books of Moses which is the heart of the Jewish religion, we read 'love thy neighbor as thyself' and 'ye shall be holy, ye shall love the stranger as thyself,' and in the Christian teaching, Jesus Christ, who prized the company of the miserable and the oppressed above all other company, teaches in the Sermon on the Mount, the cornerstone of Christianity, 'ye resist no evil, turn the other cheek, love your enemies, and forgive men their trespasses.' Jesus establishes magnificently high and splendidly exalted ethical standards, but so do the founders and prophets of other great religions. The Buddha teaches that men should return good for evil and calls for boundless unselfish love directed at all creation. His message is that of transcending spiritual love and limitless compassion. And when he turns to personal relations between men, he says: 'If a man foolishly does me wrong, I will return to him the perfection of my ungrudging love.' No less sublime are the lessons of the Koran, whose ideas of heaven and hell are similar to those of Judaism and Christianity and which urge men to reach beyond the daily practicalities to high spirituality and altruism. 'Allah loves the beneficent and the loving.'"

Lieberman came to a halt and stole a quick look around. Their faces were tinged with sympathy, and he half-believed they were ready and willing to listen to him no matter what the topic might be. But this wasn't the point; this wasn't the point at all. He ground his teeth and dismissed the thought as one dismisses a momentary reprehensible temptation, alluring and plausible one second and flawed the next, its prospects of success vanishing into thin air. No, what he was after was the vital importance of the modest yet wholly honorable everyday ethics that could accomplish more, infinitely more, than the unapproachable peaks of excellence and perfection. He tossed his head and grinned conspiratorially.

"These examples of extraordinary altruism and compassion," he went on, "should always be firmly entrenched in our minds for they are the beacons of what lies deep in our psyches and what a small band of unique individuals tried to put into practice. But how many of us can join hands with his gallant band? Not many! And at times the saintliness and perfection of these men, whom we admire from afar, makes us forget our daily obligations of treating everyone with civility and respect. Ethics is for all seasons and for each of the seven days of the week. It can boast of no showy holidays and festivals, no vacations when the clock stops ticking and our responsibilities as human beings are put on the shelf to gather dust until the old dispensation kicks in again. No, siree! This ain't the way things are meant to happen."

Faint laughter and mild applause.

He was grinning now, taking a leisurely, uninquisitive look all around, and he could see at once they had followed him to the letter and were ready for the kill.

"For most of us the everyday ethics of civility and respect should be infinitely more important than all-embracing love and compassion, and this everyday ethics is infinitely more beneficial for mankind as a whole than the self-immolating heights of religious ecstasy. Ethics is for every hour of every day, day in, day out; religion, as it is interpreted for us by the high priests, the chiefs, and the mighty clerics is for special occasions. And I say unto you"—his voice rose to a roar—"every minute of the hour and every second of the minute is a special occasion. If you have to choose one of the two, choose ethics, because ethics draws from religion as it draws from a hundred other sources, customs, mores, habits, ideas tested by time, the natural law, the depths of human psychology, consanguinity, the unwritten laws of the tribe, and many others. Ethics is what binds us together and what prompts us to bind up the wounds of others. Ethics, everyday ethics, is our passport to every country where common decency still lives, it is the fare for every ship where the crew and the passengers treat one another with consideration and esteem."

The speaker paused and ambled briefly around the lectern, shooting wild exhilarating glances at the audience, and many in it responded in like fashion, comrades of the chaplain all crouching in the same boat and heading into the open sea, damning the approaching storm and hundreds like it.

"Maybe some of you can love your enemies, but I tell you I can't," Lieberman let out with passionate candor. "We can't either, we can't neither, not me, not us, no, we don't love our enemies," the disjointed chorus of deafening voices rose like a gigantic breaker.

"Maybe some of you can return good for evil, and I take my hat off to those of you who can, but for crying out loud, don't ask me to do it, because if you do you'll be sorely disappointed."

Again they bellowed back, some already on their feet and others glued to their seats, scores of shrill and bass voices bawling out their unqualified support with varying words but united in their passion and conviction.

"If you can love the stranger as thyself, I have only praise for you, but how many of us are capable of it?"

Once more they registered their consent in a tumultuous manner, no-holds-barred, and giving their all.

Lieberman observed them searchingly for a few long seconds, and then a happy, reassuring smile broke out all over his face.

"Let's look at a way of life which aims at less ambitious goals and may benefit mankind as a whole and more concretely than any other way of life. The key word here is common decency and respect for the individual. Every man, woman, or child has the right to be treated decently, and we have the obligation to treat others decently, unless they turn against us. We members of the human race are one big family, at times happy and at times less than happy, and we are kept together by a powerful bond, a bond of decency, which could also be called a bond of humanity. No one is excluded from the magic circle, and if one wants out, one does it at his or her own risk. Think of an enormously long electric cord, thousands of miles long, tying all of us together, through which flows a mild electric current; all of us touch the cord and all of us feel the current racing through our bodies. This is our bond and all of us can cry out with infinite pride: we are members of the human race, the most advanced species on the face of this earth, and we know how to behave towards one another in the spirit of decency and humanity. We shall not willfully harm others, we shall treat others with consideration, and we shall come to the aid of others if need be, but it ain't written we oughta sacrifice ourselves for others or bless the bastards who want to knife us front or back, or love every son of a gun who comes our way. No, siree, this ain't written. Sure, help change a tire, or buy a guy who's flat on his back a beer, and keep a civil tongue. But look after yourself, because there's only one of you, and there'll never be another, and you got kinda vested interest in him. Put your best foot forward too, keep smiling yet be on the lookout and steer clear of them saintly heroics unless you're really in the saintly-heroic business."

A storm of applause interspersed with a few catcalls interrupted him as he was nearing the end, and he smiled again broadly and confidingly to let them know he was on their side and could be trusted no matter what.

"One more thing, guys, before you are released from this here bondage and are free to return to things that really matter . . ."

Energetic laughter.

. . . He resumed, jerking his head this way and that and shifting his weight from one foot onto the other. "Much of organized religion is based on fear, fear of hell, fear of what awaits us in afterlife, fear of divine punishment. We are told to behave, or else, and that else carries with it bloodcurdling images of us being fried and roasted in an inferno from which there is no escape. But if we behave we are promised the glories of Heaven. In either case, future life, life beyond the grave, carries a great deal of weight, and is seen as the final consummation of our life on earth which, according to some religions, is a mere preparation for the eternal life after death. Well, you can tinker with the notions of heaven and hell to your heart's content, and you're free to believe whatever you please but, says I, we human beings shouldn't be governed by fear, because there are nobler emotions than fear, and we ain't a bunch of savages wetting our pants 'cause The Big Chief is coming. No, siree, we ought to lead a good and decent life because in this way we bring out the best in us.

"Two more things, guys," Lieberman tossed his head in a magnificent gesture of defiance, snatching a glance round the lounge and being buoyed up by the ardor in their faces, "our concern should be first and foremost with the life this side of the grave, the life here and now, because this is the only life we know of. The final thing about religion, true religion, means conduct everyday and nothing more!"

The speaker took a step backwards, and threw his hands high in the air. "Give what is best in you to this life, to the here and now, and don't you ever forget every day is as important as any other day, every minute important as any other minute, every second as important as any other second, and every day a glorious high holiday!"

They were clapping wildly and rushing towards him as he stood off the podium erect and beaming, and they drew broken little circles around him, each man shouting his own overpowering question in his face. Adroitly he would answer several of them at once briskly with the help of cheerful grimaces and bold body language, and when the topic merited a longer explanation he would draw others into it, urge them to speak, and solicit an infinitely broader exchange of views. Soon the area adjoining the podium was filled with multiple clusters of men engaged in animated palaver, and the chaplain hopped from one of them to the next, encouraging, elucidating, and now and then calling for calm and composure. Several points were raised which required him to speak at length, and he did so unobtrusively, gaining new converts. The question-and-discussion part of the gathering had been in progress for well over an hour when an array of figures indistinct and lingering in the shadowy rear of the lounge came to life and advanced slowly towards the podium. From within the disputatious clusters heads swiveled to take the measure of the intruders who kept advancing steadily in stony silence.

"What the hell you guys want?" asked a fully participating member of the Inter-Faith Gathering. "The Enlisted Men's Club is the other way," and he made quick jabbing movements with his little finger.

"We too got questions for the chaplain," the square-faced and square-shouldered PFC in front said politely enough, his face lined deep with contempt and his manner forbidding.

"Join the group," the fully participating member advised with steel in his voice, "but this ain't your beat, buddy."

"How would you know?" the PFC retorted, moving his foot forward and touching the fully participating member with his chest. "How would you know?" he repeated ominously.

Out of the blue a change came over the other speaker.

"You're Vince!" and scratching his jaw the fully participating member cried again delightedly, "Vince Quinn! Did I get it right?"

"You did."

"Vince, you and your buddies did a hell of a job on those creeps who disgraced the uniform. Why, everyone is mouthing about it. You wait till *Stars and Stripes* gets wind of it, you guys will be on page one."

"I hope not."

"Yeah, well, is this supposed to be a secret?"

"Hell, yes, can't you tell?"

"Sorry, Vince, no offense intended, I just got carried away. Anyway what do you guys want with the chaplain? You were not at the Gathering."

"Well, slipped in late, any objections?"

"Not from me. I'm here 'cause before I shipped out from stateside I met that very cute Jewish girl. I'm not Jewish, but her family didn't seem to mind. Now we write to each other regularly, and I wanted some info from the captain about interfaith marriages. And you?"

"We just want to exchange a few words with the esteemed chaplain."

"We wanna speak to Lieberman about real things, about what goddamn matters," the words were hollered out by a short, skinny private standing next to Vince who was immediately recognized as Olie Hartmann.

"I should've known," the suitor of the young Jewish lady let out making buzzing noises. "Don't you ever talk in a normal way, Hartmann, what the hell's the matter with you? I'll tell you what the matter is"—he continued smugly—"you're so short people just don't notice you, and when you holler like a lunatic they notice you even less."

"You watch it, boy, you watch it," Olie hollered twice as loudly as before. Not more than ten yards away Lieberman, in the midst of elucidating the doctrine of mitzvah to thickheaded infidels, turned in Olie's direction. "What's up, fellows?" he asked flatly.

"We'd like to ask you a few questions, sir," Vince began.

"Is this Inter-Faith business?"

"Hell no! I mean sorry, sir, it's about football." Olie was hollering away with no intention of stopping.

"Sure, but you'll have to wait till we finish here."

"Right you are, Chaplain," and Vince nodded to the silent, expectant bodies to his rear. "Have your questions ready, men."

Soon the old business of Inter-Faith and the new business of NFL became enmeshed, and Lieberman grappled with numerous questions, subtly combining the old and the new. But as minutes ticked away, football began to hold the upper hand, and the partisans of ethics and religion either changed camps or simply departed.

"We need another McElhenny," shouted several voices. "Maybe so," a disjoined chorus rasped back, "but it wasn't them 49ers who made good at Kezar Stadium, it was the Detroit Lions."

"Watch for the Baltimore Colts this year," Lieberman confided in them. "Watch for Don Joyce, Gino Marchetti, and half a dozen others. The Colts have reserves, a wildcard, if you ask me. The Giants may have a tough nut to crack."

Training and new faces, halfbacks, quarterbacks and coaches, offense and defense, famous passes and touchdowns of former years, but above all predictions and prognostications for 1958 were all tossed into the cauldron of an elated free-for-all which captured everyone's attention. It was for the most part an orderly meeting where just about everybody showed some consideration and a modicum of courtesy for another, and their faces shone with the conviction that what they bandied from one end of the lounge to the other was their common property and their common trust. It would have been unpardonable to defile them by manifestly rowdy behavior.

/ / /

It was yet another April Saturday, and the leaden clouds stood firm in a long, stationary lump, not a chink in it. With alacrity Colonel Trainer jumped onto the reviewing stand and let his eyes roam over 16th Engineer Group marshaled into a general formation.

"At ease, men," he roared into the loudspeaker. "I'll come straight to the point. In the last twelve months all kinds of abuses and heinous acts have been perpetrated by a small group of criminal GIs on many innocent and law-abiding GIs, and unfortunately I as Group Commander have been unable until now to do much about it. These involved fraud, trickery, deception, intimidation, extortion, and violence, and our attempts at putting an end to them, using conventional Army means, came to naught. I know that some of you still bear the scars of those scandalous and criminal acts, and you have my deepest sympathy. But I also want to apologize to all of you for our ineffectiveness in the past in dealing with those abominable crimes." He stopped, and what he could discern all about him was aggressive, all-consuming silence. He made a point of looking squarely into as many individual faces as he could and went on:

"As many of you know, the guilty have been punished and shipped out to other units." He barely had time to finish the statement when the ranks exploded. In the ever-mounting uproar no individual words or phrases could be distinguished, but the uproar demonstrated unmistakably the rank's jubilation. Trainer waited for several minutes until the volume of voices had somewhat abated, laughing inwardly at the platoon leaders' futile attempts to enforce silence. Then he thrust his arms forward in a commanding gesture and bellowed, "Hear me to the end, hear me to the end!" They made it clear they would, and he took a deep breath and started again:

"That was the past, and what happened in the past shall not happen again. As of this day any violence perpetrated by an enlisted man on another, or any violence perpetrated by a group of enlisted men on a group of enlisted men will be very severely punished, and this time we'll get to the bottom of each crime if we have to plod and dig till hell freezes over!"

WILD APPLAUSE AND INDIVIDUAL EXHORTATORY REMINDERS SUCH AS "GIVE IT TO 'EM, COLONEL, KICK THEIR ASSES, KICK 'EM HARD SO THE WHITE OF THEIR EYES FALLS OUT."

"And the same goes for cheating, deception, intimidation, extortion, and any goddamn kind of dishonesty. And what I say here will be enforced to the fullest extent of the law. To this purpose I am appointing an equity board which will be made up of two officers, three NCOs, and three enlisted men not higher in rank than Specialist IV whose bounden duty it will be to assist the Executive Officer's office and see to it that fairness and justice prevail. This board will be the watchdog, and I give you my word that nothin', and I say nothin', will get by it.

"Today 16th Engineer Group is beginning a new life. The enlisted men and the officers alike will exercise redoubled vigilance not only that we may be ready for combat at all times, but also and equally importantly that we may be inspired by the highest ideals of duty and honor which make all of us, no matter what our individual rank may be, brothers-in-arms."

He stopped and waited for a few seconds for their reaction, and when it came it was tepid and disjointed. He leaned forward, a reassuring smile fixed on his face, and blared, "Now I shall take individual questions from you, soldiers. Identify yourself before you speak."

Questions came in dribs and drabs, and most of them had to do with the alleged new life that was to be pumped into 16th Engineer Group like fresh blood into a horse on his last legs already. Would the future be really different from the past, some asked. Why did it take the Command twelve long months to find out what was really going on? Wasn't it only the brave act of a handful of men who took the law into their own hands that woke the Command up to the disgraceful mess they had on their hands? How impartial and justice-oriented would the equity board be? Just another gimmick, or more than a gimmick? Trainer did not flinch. He answered each question as candidly as he could, steering clear both of flaunting his poorly executed responsibility and opting for a whitewash, but he knew he was not reaching the men, knew full well lack of confidence in him and the Command enfolded them like a thick, shiftless mist.

Something stirred in him, and he pushed the loudspeaker to the side and leaned forward smirking roguishly in full view of the men.

"This concludes the meeting"—he bawled at the top of his lungs— "and you men are dismissed. But I shall hang on, and I'd like to speak individually to as many of you as possible. So, unless you have a hot date this time of a Saturday morning, hang on so I can hear from you."

He jumped down from the stand and saw the officers and most of the NCOs decamping. He lit a cheroot and advanced towards the shapeless mass of men, some just standing and waiting, others ready to slink away, and others still bandying jokes about with their buddies.

"Light up, if you got 'em," he sounded off, and he saw around him several of the men smiling guardedly, hampered by doubt and uncertainty.

"How is the Army treating you, soldier?" he addressed a boy, freckles and all, presumably eighteen years of age but looking fourteen. The boy immediately stood at attention and managed to stammer out, "Fine, sir, no complaints."

"Where you're from, son, and what's your name?"

"Private Harrol Collins, sir, from Jefferson City, Missouri, sir."

Trainer nodded. "And how is the chow, Collins?"

"Well, sir, it fills you up, but I miss the little caramel cakes Mom makes and big sis Edith."

"That's understandable, your mom and big sis must be mighty good cooks."

"Oh they are, sir, there's no denyin'."

"Try to learn as much as you can while you're here, Collins, and I encourage you to take correspondence courses."

"Yes, sir, that's what First Sergeant keeps telling me."

"Will you?"

"Maybe, sir, but I miss home, never been away from home before."

"Good luck," and Trainer moved on.

In the next hour he spoke to scores of enlisted men, hoping he had touched base with at least some of them. He did his utmost to treat each one as an autonomous individual about whose goals, ambition, and problems he wanted to know more. In some instances he was convinced he had succeeded as the initial barrier of distrust began to melt away. He was saddled with relatively few complaints about Army life, the discipline, the regimentation, the curfews, and the reveilles, though some of the recruits who opened up to him made no bones about their anger at being forced to give up well-paid jobs and having two years torn out of their promising careers.

He was understanding and sympathetic not only because he was on a mission, but preeminently because only combat, real combat, could make soldiers out of these kids still tied umbilically to home and Mom. There was no combat in sight, however, and in the present geopolitical situation carefully crafted by the Pentagon, the American Watch in Western Europe was not to be quickened by frequent war games. Presently he began to repeat to himself what he had said so many times to others, friend and foe alike, that peacetime army is a contradiction in terms, the sickest notion to come out from an idiot's brain.

As for the RAs, well, they were Regular Army who had chosen the military as their profession as he had chosen it twenty years earlier, the professionals and the future cadre, the future senior NCOs and possibly officers, and now he saw them at the very outset of their career. He was far from being impressed but held his tongue. Overall he found in many of them a small-mindedness which, at best, was laughable. They were full of petty complaints: one man's bed was too short for him, another man was told by the dentist that the partial the Army was willing to fit into his mouth was the only kind available, and if he wanted another he ought to see a civilian at his own expense. He exercised iron self-control when a ruddy, athletic looking PFC told him petulantly that the bacon served at breakfast was usually overcooked, and his protestations carried to the Mess Hall staff brought him nothing but volleys of abuse.

"Well"—Trainer contorted his face into what he hoped was a mask of gentleness—"see the cook in person, speak to him man to man." He reflected that when he had enlisted in the Army he was happy to have a roof over his head and three meals a day, with bacon overcooked or undercooked, or with no bacon at all. Then there were complaints about annual leave which recruiting sergeants had apparently stretched out as a lure to those bent on making the Army their home. One indignant volunteer had been told by the recruiting sergeant that every GI is entitled to ninety days of leave each year, and not to thirty days as he subsequently discovered. As Trainer was winding up his tête-à-têtes with the young RAs he called to them, "Remember you men are the foundation of the Army, the seed that will grow into a mighty oak," and he could not help jeering at his own words as soon as he uttered them.

Before long the parade ground became almost deserted, and from a corner of his eye he could see a thin line being formed outside the Mess Hall for the midday chow. He sauntered in the direction of the Command Building, paying no attention to anything around him, deep in thought, shutting himself off from the world. His address to the troops and his individual chats with so many of the men were pounding in his mind with no detail missing, as though this were happening now again and again, a continuously unfolding reality, so stark and overwhelming that it could not be absorbed by memory. He adjudged his performance, as he was excruciatingly reliving it, nothing short of failure. Rank and file rose as one man in a storm of jubilation because the guilty had been punished. But by whom? Not by the Group Commander or on his orders. No! They had been punished by the vigilantes in contravention of Army Regulations! The men stood up and cheered, but whom precisely did they cheer? Not the chain of command, this was obvious, but the daring four GIs—this he recalled was the figure given him by the MPs—who had said enough is enough and had taken the law into their own hands. After he had described to the men the new measures taking effect immediately, at the center of which stood the awe-inspiring equity board, they pooh-poohed them, most likely putting their money on another gallant team of vigilantes. And when he tried to break the ice and meet them man-to-man, laying aside rank and protocol, the result was hardly encouraging.

Wearily Trainer moved on, and he came to a sudden realization as if a sharp point had pierced his flesh—that he heartily detested the gimmickry he had so readily executed in the last few days, gimmickry and with it the entire public relations business that had been foisted on him.

Sure, Vallejo and Sol had acted in good faith and something had to be done. He had taken their advice and had acted for the good of the 16th Engineer Group and for the good of the Service. This had been the paramount motive for his actions and he had been so engrossed in it that he had banished from his mind all other considerations, which like exigent and uninvited guests were pounding on the portals of his consciousness. "I ain't made for diplomacy," he shrieked, lifting his head high, and again, "I ain't made for diplomacy." Then he began to feel utterly drained, not caring about what had been happening in the last few days. He was breathing heavily, and he stopped in his tracks, laying a hand on his forehead, which he thought was inordinately hot. "Am I running a fever?" he asked in a loud, shrill voice, casting anxious glances all around to see whether he was being overheard.

After a while he resumed his walk, inhaling deeply, and without the slightest effort on his part memories of his combat days flashed and flickered in his brain like a long awaited draft of water; Italy, Holland, Germany in the World War and then Korea. In each instance on every battlefield he knew what to do and what to say to the men who were serving under him, first as sergeant and later as an officer. There were uncertainties and questions galore, but they were tangible and one could take the measure of them. The enemy was out there, and all the efforts had to be coordinated to capture or destroy him. A relief from the oppressive present surged in him, and the memories of those days stamped by clarity and unity of purpose buoyed him up. He felt invigorated, and his pace quickened. He was no more than twenty yards away from the Command Building when he saw the wiry figure of Jesús Vallejo in civvies dashing out through the main entrance. Vallejo caught sight of him and advanced briskly, saluting.

"What the hell are you doing, Vallejo? You're supposed to be resting on your days off, so come Monday morning you can give the Army all you've got."

"That's a very interesting proposition, sir, but I had some unfinished business, and besides I wanted to hear what you had to say to the troops."

Trainer knit his brow and frowned.

"We had a clear view of the formation from a second-story window. You did very well, sir, and mingling with the rank and file afterwards was just what the doctor ordered."

"How can you tell?"

"They haven't heard anything like it in the past, no one has. It'll take a little time before it all settles down in their entrails good and proper. But they'll remember."

"Meaning . . . ?"

"You gotta keep your word, sir, the Army gotta keep their word," and Vallejo took off like a man on the run.

/   /   /

Vincent Quinn was standing before Major Fiorello sitting behind his desk in the Exec Officer's office, his head bowed low, his fingers groping aimlessly between the blotter and the imitation Greek vase holding a variety of pens and pencils.

"This is terrible business," he let out at last, more to himself than to Quinn, his eyes still fixed on the blotter, and his fingers resting.

"Terrible business," he repeated, lifting his head energetically and transfixing the PFC with a look of anxiety. "I called you here, Quinn, because I'd like to learn more about what happened and . . . whether it could've been prevented. I have the MP and the medical reports . . . but really they tell me little. You were there at the time, and Private Michael Gillespie was your friend, wasn't he?"

"You might say that, sir, and I agree it's bad business. As for anyone being able to prevent it, well, I just don't know."

Fiorello nodded and tossed a pad in front of him pulling a fancy-looking pen out of the Greek vase.

"When did it all start?"

"Around 10:00 P.M. the day before yesterday."

"Did you know that Gillespie was perhaps ill or, that at any rate, he needed medical attention?"

"Not at first, sir, he was just babbling as he always does, but it got worse as time went on."

Fiorello was scribbling busily on the pad, then stopped and looked up. "Go on, please, and Quinn, this may take some time so pull up a chair, no need for you to stand."

"Thank you, sir," and Quinn promptly swung a chair propped up against the wall, moved it in front of the desk, and sat down heavily.

"What I mean is he began to sound delirious, but it happened gradually, and we thought this was temporary like and would pass."

"Was he under the influence, Quinn, I have to know?" A tense moment of silence intervened. "I appreciate your loyalty to your friend, I do, but it is imperative that I know. The MPs made it clear he was reeking of alcohol, and so did Doc when he examined the mangled body. For the life of me I don't understand why the Infirmary didn't take a blood test. It's routine procedure."

"Maybe they figured it didn't make no difference since Mike was already dead, run over by a truck."

"Maybe," Fiorello half-agreed, looking cagey and distrustful. "Or maybe they didn't want to add insult to injury."

Quinn laughed knowingly. "That would make sense, Major, but I guess we'll never know for sure." Then he shifted his enormous body in the chair which looked grotesquely diminutive and continued: "Mike was babbling on, but as I said, it made less and less sense, and his face was getting redder and more feverish all the time. One of us—I forget who it was—brought some cold water, and we went on wiping his face and giving him water to drink. But it didn't help a mite. One minute he was on the edge of a precipice, and he was going to jump no matter what, another minute he was somewhere in the middle of the ocean calling to a passing ship but they didn't hear him, or he was in the thickest of all forests and was hopelessly lost. Still, as he went on raving, he kept repeating one thing, and he did it to the very end. 'I shall not be held behind bars, I shall not be held behind bars,' he'd scream every minute or so, and I guess he was sinking deeper and deeper. He also began to foam at the mouth, and by this time Shelton, who'd just come in, said, 'Mike must be taken to the Infirmary right away.'"

"Is that Shelton, the medic, transferred to us from Army?" Fiorello interrupted, beckoning at the same time to the speaker to go on.

"The same, sir. He'd gone to the Orderly Room to call ahead of time and say we are bringing in an emergency case, so they'd be ready. Once he came back we'd drive Mike the short distance, or else carry him if need be." Quinn paused and drops of sweat glistened on his face and neck. "And then it happened," he said in a dull, muffled voice.

"Please continue; I have to have all the facts." Instantly Fiorello was on his feet urging Quinn to go an extra mile and not to omit anything, however painful.

"Well, there were four of us at this point bending over Mike, and he'd be a tad more quiet than before and muttering to us 'Eh, eh, guys, don't crowd me, gimme room to breathe,' so we kinda stepped back, and he jumped up like a Hell's angel, pushed two of us clear away, and quick as lightning ran out the door. We ran straight after him, but he was too damn quick for us, like the Devil himself gave him new lease on strength. And as he ran he cried, 'I shall not be held behind bars, I shall not be held behind bars.' The MPs spotted him at the gate as he flashed by them, and gone after him in hot pursuit. But he was quick as lightning. Right across the heath he ran, between the trees to the little playground where Kraut kiddies play, and onto the highway. We was maybe twenty yards behind, us hollering like mad all the time for him to stop, but he never looked back. The MP car cut very close to him just before he hit the highway, but he paid no heed. He paid no heed at all. Right away and without as much as casting a glance to the right or left he was on the highway, and the Kraut truck coming from the left had no time to slow down much, though we found out later the driver did what he could."

"You saw the body," Fiorello spoke very quietly, half-inquiring and half-stating a fact.

"We did, sir, he was all mangled and broken up something terrible, except for the face that had hardly a scratch on it; body torn up and twisted like you can't imagine, but the face . . . well intact here was a rosy cheek of a not so happy Irishman."

Fiorello nodded several times in sad agreement as though he were trying to give Quinn courage to go on.

"Colonel Trainer will be writing to Gillespie's parents, and he asked me to find out if there's anything positive he can say to them, something to his credit." He waved a folder high over his desk and tossed it down resignedly. "Gillespie's 201 is one disaster after another, as soon as he is promoted to PFC he's broken down to private three times in a row, that is two summary courts-martial, four Articles 15, I won't bore you with restrictions and other punishments. Is there anything on the credit side?"

"Well, Major," Quinn was tightening his facial muscles and shifting uncomfortably in his seat, "Mike was well liked, very well liked, you might say. He was a good friend and was always willing to offer a helping hand. Times like he'd forget to return the money he'd borrowed, but when he had it he could be generous. He didn't count his pennies, he kinda lived from day to day, if you know what I mean."

"I think I do; anything else you can tell me?"

"Yeah, there's something else, but that's touchy business as it cuts into Mike's family, and I don't know if you want to hear it."

"Go on, Quinn, it may help me to understand better what happened."

"My kid sister is getting married next month, in May that is, as soon as she graduates from high school, so I showed Mike the pictures she'd sent me of herself and Lionel, that's the guy she's getting hitched up to, the boyfriend, the bridegroom to be . . ."

"The fiancé," Fiorello added, making every attempt not to sound unduly formal.

"That's right, sir, the fiancé, that's a good word for the nonce. Anyway, I also showed Mike some of Brenda's letters chattering away about the big day, and what a gift from Heaven Lionel is to the human race, and how deeply he loves her, and how deeply she loves him, and the rest of the mushy stuff. Well, Mike was much taken with it and told me he didn't have much of a family life, and then a few days later he showed me the letters he'd gotten from home, from his Ma and Pa, his Ma writing them and signing for both. Well, sir, I couldn't believe my eyes! That anyone could be getting such letters from flesh and blood like meanin' from parents. His Ma was writing they didn't want him back at home, and his room was given to one of his Pa's buddies, so he can use it whenever he's in town; and further that Mike had better stay in the Army, if the Army would have him, because he's no good for anything else and he'll have a very hard time finding a job, any kind of a job, 'cause he's no good and as dumb as a sack of hair." Quinn paused and shook his head in muted despair. "And here comes the clincher: if you come back to New Jersey, you'll be allowed to come to the house to collect whatever personal items belonging to you are still on the premises, but after that we don't want you here so you'd better make other arrangements, and we don't want you to keep in touch."

"You remember it all so well," Fiorello let out, observing Quinn searchingly.

"That's right, sir, I remember every word in those letters from the loving parents, because I'd never seen anything like it."

"It's sad, very sad." Fiorello was still taking notes, but presently he finished and began to revolve his shoulders, inhaling and exhaling deeply. Then holding up Gillespie's folder he let fall, "Gillespie has, excuse me, had two older brothers."

"Oh, yes," Quinn joined in at once, "they figure in the letters, and besides Mike told me about them," a scornful smile forking his mouth. "Very successful businessmen, one in the laundry business and the other . . . in . . ."

"Liquor," Fiorello finished for him.

Quinn smiled indulgently. "Well, we know what kind of company you gotta keep to be successful in the laundry business and in liquor in Jersey . . ." and his smile broadened. "But them brothers kept Mike at arm's length. In truth they told him to get lost."

"So the entire family was against him, no one to turn to, not a very enviable position," and then Fiorello straightened himself up in his seat, unexpectedly changed the subject, and said with verve, "I know what you mean about the laundry business and liquor better than most men. You see, Quinn, I hail from upstate New York, and my brother is a federal prosecutor in the City. I know how hard it is to make any headway when you're up against you know what."

"Unless you take the law into your own hands."

"This mustn't be tolerated. In the long run it's not the answer."

"Like you say, sir, not the answer."

Fiorello was silent for what seemed to Quinn an eternity. He was fiddling with the pens, the erasers, the paper clips, and the typewriter ribbons arranged neatly against the Army manual at the far end of the desk.

Finally he confronted Quinn utterly serious, streaks of anxiety breaking through his voice, and very soon it was anxiety that stood out above all else. And Quinn, looking more and more suspicious with each passing second, was goggling at the major, refusing to take his eyes off him.

"Just a few more questions, and we'll be through."

"Whatever you say, sir."

"I understand Gillespie often acted in a forgetful, irresponsible way. Did he have blackouts?"

"You might say that." Quinn hesitated at first, and then answered the question with reluctance, pursing his lips and staring pointedly at the ceiling.

"To the best of your knowledge was he on medication, did he receive any kind of medical treatment?"

"Don't know, sir. Couldn't tell."

"So when these blackouts came, was there anybody who took care of him?"

"In the manner of speaking we all did. And them blackouts usually came in the evenings. We let Mike lie on his bunk and brought him food from the Mess Hall if he needed any. Now and then he'd say he didn't know who or where he was, or he'd just sit there, staring into space, not saying a word, lost to the world."

Fiorello was on the point of asking another question, but Quinn preempted him.

"We were telling Mike to see the Doc, but this was a sore point with him. When we did he'd start swearing, telling us to go to hell, calling us names, and I have to tell you, sir,"—a ray of a smile touched off Quinn's grim countenance—"Mike knew every swear word under the sun, and he was proud to use each and every one of them."

"I'm sure he did," Fiorello concurred laughing, "I'm sure he did."

"To put it in plain language, we had our minds set on sending Mike to the Infirmary, and none was more for it than Shelton who spoke to him bluntly more than once, but maybe our minds were not fixed on it strong enough."

Fiorello leaned back pensively in his seat and let his eyes wander over the walls.

"Do you know whether Gillespie ever underwent a psychiatric examination, in the Service or before he was drafted?"

"Before he was inducted I couldn't rightly say. But I know for a fact some two months ago the chaplain told Mike he ought to see a shrink."

"How do you know that?"

"I walked right on it, you might say. One afternoon two months ago or so, the chaplain was talking to Mike private-like in the lounge right behind the chapel, and I walked in through the back door; at first they didn't see me."

"Go on."

"Well, it went something like this: Chaplain Sol saying I urge you again, Mike, to see the Medical Officer and tell him about your blackouts, periodic losses of memory, and other things that bother you. You will be referred to an Army psychiatrist, and you'll undergo a thorough examination. You should want to know why these things happen to you, and so would we. Help may be round the corner, and if you want I'll be happy to go with you to see the Doc, Mike, and the sooner the better."

"Well?"

"And Mike yelling like he wanted to raise not one ghost but a hundred, 'I'm not crazy, I'm not crazy,' and 'I don't want no truck with the shrink.' He got so heated up I thought he'd get in trouble with the chaplain, hollering and all that, but Captain Sol took it very patient-like, and at the end he just said, 'Well, Mike, it's your decision, and not a very good one; come and see me when you change your mind.'"

"And?"

"That's about it, sir." Quinn fell silent, but his countenance was lively, betraying extreme concentration. He was pulling at his nose and fixing his gaze on the floor, scooping up an elusive memory.

"I don't rightly remember, but Captain Sol may have told Mike he would see the Medical Officer anyway," he began and then stopped. "I couldn't rightly say whether he did or not, unless Mike talked him out of it." Then he shook his head repeatedly and angrily. "I don't rightly remember."

"There's no record that he did," Fiorello commented, "though I wish he had seen the Medical Officer. Anyway it's all in the past. Anything else, Quinn?"

"No, sir, that's it, and we know the rest."

Fiorello rose to his feet and came out from behind his desk. He stood in the middle of the office holding a folder, not far from Quinn who also stood up.

"You will be glad to know your friend will be getting an honorable discharge, and this may be a matter of pride, if not to his immediate family then surely to his friends."

"I am happy to hear this, Major, real happy."

"This also means that Gillespie's beneficiaries will be getting his Army insurance, $10,000," Fiorello continued.

"Not those two scumbags, I beg the Major's pardon," and Quinn added with perverse and vociferous emphasis, "not his biological old man and his biological mom."

"That's all right, Private First Class, you were speaking from the heart." And peering into the folder he exclaimed, "Your friend changed his beneficiaries only a month ago. His parents are out, a couple living in Maine is in."

"Their name wouldn't by chance be Shaunnessy?"

"It would, it's all here in black and white, a Maine address."

"Good for him," Quinn cried out, his voice vibrating with delight, "that's the couple that befriended him when he was on a construction crew in Maine. He liked them a lot and talked about them. Mike knew what he was doing, and maybe he wasn't crazy after all."

Fiorello spread out his hands. "We shall never know, but let's be thankful for small favors." Then assuming a military mien he addressed Quinn, "I want to thank you for everything you have told me. You have been of great help."

Private First Class Vincent Quinn stood to attention and saluted Major John Fiorello, and Major John Fiorello took a step back and returned it, one of the smartest salutes of his entire life. One would have thought he was saluting the Chairman of the Joint Chiefs of Staff and not a lowly PFC. But there is no record of it in any Army file.

/   /   /

Later on the same day Sergeant Korovitz heard a knock on his office door, a gentle, muted, almost hesitant knock as if the knocker were of two minds.

"Come in," he bellowed, and out of the shadows of the corridor stepped in slowly and sheepishly Sergeant James O'Leary, recently promoted to Acting Mess Hall Sergeant.

"How goes it, Jimmie?" Korovitz bellowed again, and O'Leary stood at attention and saluted.

"Okay, I guess, Group Sergeant, and I thank ye for asking."

"So." Korovitz, in one majestic sweep of the eye, encircled the length, width, and height of his office, walls, furniture, and all, and the lonely figure of Jesús Vallejo at the other end of the military planet, giving the impression of being frantically preoccupied, his head buried in piles of papers.

"What can we do for you, Jimmie?" Korovitz's voice was in a much lower key, now wholly appropriate to indoor conversations.

"A truly terrible end visited on that poor boy Michael Gillespie, truly terrible, Group Sergeant, but the ways of the Lord are mysterious

. . .." O'Leary spread out his hands in a resigned gesture of humility and acceptance.

"Right, right," Korivitz spluttered out like a rusty tape recorder, "but this is the U.S. Army, Jimmie, not a Bible class. Come to the point."

"Lots of guys've taken Mike's tragic death to heart, and all of us want to do something to honor his memory. We thought of sending a wreath to the funeral, with an inscription 'To Mike, from his buddies at 16th U.S. Army Engineer Group, place and date.' Something like it."

"Very commendable, Jimmie, very commendable."

"And we thought anyone who wants to contribute something to the wreath should know where to turn. The guys elected me to be the treasurer, and we aim at the widest possible participation. So I thought an announcement could be read by company commanders or platoon leaders at the morning formation, let's say the day after tomorrow and then repeated. For this I need authorization from the Group Commander."

"You have it, Jimmie," Korovitz imparted sententiously to the young sergeant. "This lies within my power, I'll just inform the Colonel."

"Thank you, Group Sergeant," O'Leary stammered out.

"That's okay, but you'll need to prepare a statement that can be read out and describe the purpose and occasion."

"I have it all prepared, sir," and O'Leary pulled out from his breast pocket a folded sheet of paper covered with neat lines of typing. "Here you are, sir."

Korovitz accepted it smiling benevolently.

"And you'll have someone contact an outfit stateside to deliver a wreath or whatever to the funeral?"

"It's all taken care of, and if we collect more than is needed for the wreath, the remainder will go towards a headstone."

"Well thought-out operation," Korovitz smacked his lips apprecia-tively. "The body will not be flown home till four or five days from now which gives you time to collect the dough and make necessary arrangements at the other end. It's New Jersey he's going back to?"

"Maine, I'd say, Sergeant, Maine it is; and we have the matter in hand," O'Leary put in proudly and with alacrity.

"You and that fella must've been bosom buddies, eh?"

"Not exactly, but his death made us think twice."

"He was crazy, mad as a March hare."

"Who isn't, Sarge?"

"Maybe, just maybe you've got something there. Anyway, Jimmie, your request is granted, and you can count your blessings."

"Thank you most kindly, Group Sergeant." O'Leary saluted, brandishing his arm high and low and beat a hasty retreat.

From the other end of the office like the menacing hissing of a slithering cobra rose the sinister snicker of the all-knowing Group Clerk.

"What now?" Korovitz snapped. "What makes you so goddamn happy?"

"If nothing else, it must be Sergeant James O'Leary's good deed for the day."

"Well, say what you will, Vallejo, but this is a neat thing to do. A wreath from his buddies, why it'll make just about any stiff sit up and smile."

"If you say so, Sarge. But many a guy knows there was no love lost between those two; in fact O'Leary loathed the ground Mike trod on and was always after him. And when Mike was on KP, O'Leary tried to make his life a living hell, I mean a living hell, and I am not given to hyperbole."

Korovitz pulled a long disbelieving face and gave a shrug. "Maybe his conscience was beginning to prick him, who knows, man is a damned complicated machine, and don't you believe those who tell you different, d'you hear me! And as Jimmie said, the Lord works in mysterious ways."

"I would keep the Lord out of it, if you don't mind, it isn't his beat."

"I couldn't rightly say if I mind or not. But I just might be getting into the frame of mind to mind, and to mind a lot."

"Please yourself, Sarge, but resist the temptation of looking always on the bright side."

"My, my, my!"

"I don't care for Jimmie O'Leary because he's a lowdown piece of trash. But he's smart enough to sense which way the wind is blowing. Mike may have been as mad as a March hare—your words, not mine—but lots of guys liked him, tried to help him, and knew he was often getting the wrong end of the stick, the principal culprit being one Jim

O'Leary who fancies having a victim or two on their knees licking his boots."

"So?"

"So, Mr. O'Leary is buying himself a little life insurance, so he may breathe a little longer, so his throat will not be cut in the dark alley just yet, not just yet, but only when the time is ripe."

"Tell me, Jesús, how does a young fella like you get to be so . . . so cyyynical?" Korovitz uttered the last word caressingly, elongating it, and taking immense pleasure in every vowel and consonant. "How?"

"You ask how, Group Sergeant. By gazing at the stars and watching grass grow."

Chapter 7

Colonel Trainer, only partly awake, became irritatingly conscious of a buzzing noise drilling into him, like that of an enormous bee circling menacingly around his ears, his puffed up flesh its prey. But as the buzz went on he began to realize that it was interrupted at even intervals—his impassive mind lamely recalled that he had heard it before, not once but many times—and he now recognized it as being disturbingly familiar. Seething with anger, he bounced heavily to the right so that he now lay very near the edge of the bed and groped in the dark for the switch on the night lamp. He found it at last, and leering at the immediate surroundings he concluded that it was the telephone that caused all the trouble. Hoisting himself up and rearranging the pillows he yelled into the receiver, "Trainer here, and it better be good or I'll have your scalp."

From the other end of the line a level voice came through. "It's Vallejo, Colonel."

"D'you know it's exactly 0330 hours, Vallejo, and what the hell are you doin' playing a night stalker!" Trainer's temper was unabated.

"Well, sir, we have what you might call a situation. The MPs discovered a dead German national in the Motor Pool, and Sergeant Korovitz, who is on the scene, told me to call you."

"Does anybody know that Kraut national?"

"Not much, except that Sergeant Steiner apparently knew him well. And, sir, the German police are also here. They'd acted on an anonymous tip."

"Okay, Vallejo, I'll be with you in fifteen minutes," Trainer growled, his composure returning, and he slammed the receiver down.

There were long faces all around in the Motor Pool as the MP sergeant reported to Trainer.

"We found this fellow, Dieter Hauch is his name, where he's lying now, sir. We didn't move him, and we didn't touch anything; waiting for the CID boys."

"Right," Trainer muttered under his breath, and then he broke out buoyantly, "hell of a place to leave a guy you've just clubbered to death; looks to me like he was left here, just outside the main entrance to the workshop, on purpose for all to see and so even a blind man couldn't miss him."

"Three heavy blows with a blunt instrument to the back of the head," the MP sergeant put in. "I'd say death was instantaneous."

Trainer nodded and saw Korovitz walking towards him.

"The Doc, Captain Fairchild that is, is on his way, and so is the CID team from Army," Korovitz announced gloomily.

"And Carl," Trainer's voice rose with passion, "where is he? He should be here, it's his Motor Pool, he's in charge."

"We didn't notify Sergeant Steiner, so far. We didn't think it was necessary," Korovitz spoke self-assuredly. "First things first."

Trainer pulled a face. "That's right, first things first, Leroy, so now get on the goddamn horn and tell Carl to get his ass over here on the double, it's his goddamn shop." And as Korovitz was hurrying away, Trainer spat out defiantly the sad remains of a cheroot and shook his head in disbelief. "My, my, my, first things first! Whoever dreamt up this one!"

Presently the MP sergeant was again by his side.

"Your Group Clerk, Colonel, is in the office standing by the phone, in case there are questions or messages . . ."

"Good!"

"And the German cops were saying that earlier in the evening, last evening I meant to say"—the sergeant corrected himself with pride—"Carl had a hell of a row with that German civilian who is now lying dead . . . Would you like to hear what the Krauts have to say, sir?"

"Good idea, Sergeant, will you take me to them?"

At the other end of the driveway two German police cars glistened in the phosphorescent light glaring out of rectangular fixtures mounted on poles that unfolded towards the top into three-pronged flattened rods giving support. Next to the cars four German patrolmen chatted idly apparently with nothing to do, yet giving a strong impression of waiting for something momentous.

"Good morning, gentlemen," Trainer began, "not a bad night for April in these parts . . ."

The Germans had straightened themselves up, and one of them, stocky and chubby-faced, addressed the colonel with some formality. "As you say, sir, not a bad night for April, but the winds still do much damage in the countryside . . . I shall speak for the four of us because I have seniority."

"Right you are," and Trainer smiled and shook hands with the four men, noticing when he had finished the handshaking a hardly disguised smirk of contempt on the three youthful faces flying out all the way to the self-appointed spokesman.

"I understand the German gentleman who is now dead," Trainer started off again carefully weighing each word, "had some sort of quarrel with a soldier under my command."

The patrolman with seniority was on the point of responding, and his lips were already beginning to move when another patrolman cut him short, barking his words out at a breathtaking speed.

"*Ja*, we got a tip, someone who wouldn't give his name, saying Dieter Hauch quarreled very loudly, *ja*, with one of your sergeants, Colonel, who answers to the description of Carl Steiner, your master sergeant in charge of the Motor Pool, around 2300 hours, and ja this quarrel lasted for a long time, right here outside the main building of the Motor Pool . . ."

"And we heard," another patrolman cut in, "that the two men very nearly came to blows, ja, like Fritz says it was a long and violent altercation . . ."

"And maybe we don't have to look for a murderer because it may be your Sergeant Steiner, at least everything points that way," the third patrolman set forth pretentiously.

Trainer gave out what he was hoping was a disarmingly jovial and carefree laugh.

"Well, don't let's jump to conclusions, boys, after all, the evidence has to be examined, facts sifted out . . . witnesses if any rounded up." He stopped abruptly and leaned forward towards the German contingent: "That man Dieter Hauch, Honch, Houch, or whatever, who was he, what did he do?"

At this very moment, the senior patrolman was faster than his peers.

"Our preliminary investigation reveals," he reported imperturbably, "that Dieter Hauch worked for a large electrical company in Stuttgart; he was an engineer, age forty-eight, a widower, and there are two grown up children. Later on today we shall find out more about him and whether he had a criminal record."

"I see," Trainer muttered pensively. "And you are now waiting for your superiors?" he asked amiably, looking from face to face.

"We are waiting for the police doctor," the barking patrolman put in before any of the others had the chance, "who will examine the corpse and try to establish the time of death. As death occurred on an American army base the body will stay with you for a time before it is returned to us. But we have the right to observe your procedures. This is the law."

"Of course you do, of course you do," Trainer eagerly agreed, and catching the eye of the MP sergeant he called: "Sergeant, please send one of your men to the Mess Hall and organize some coffee. All of us could do with a hot drink, but first and foremost I want our German friends to be served. We owe them a great deal."

"Yes, sir," the MP sergeant sounded off and beckoned to one of his men, and the German patrolman with seniority bowed slightly and addressed Trainer unctuously: "I thank you for your consideration and courtesy, sir, and I speak for the four of us." Determined to keep a poker face, Trainer made a supreme effort to hold his eye fixed on the speaker, and on the speaker alone, and he narrowly succeeded. Then reeling on his heel he peered expectantly into the semidarkness of the driveway and distinguished a tall silhouette hurrying towards him, recognizing after a few seconds an officer's overcoat and hat.

"It's about time, Dick," he called in a mock-rebuke, "why, if us wait much longer the dead man'll jump up and run away." He was delighted with his own joke, and one guffaw swiftly led to another and yet another as the tall silhouette now endowed with facial features, flesh, and bones saluted and gasped, "Captain Richard Fairchild, Medical

Officer reporting as ordered, sir," and then adding nervously and as gaspingly as before, "I came as soon as I could."

"Sure you did, Dick, sure you did. Look at the stiff, and what we want to know is the time of death and what kind of murder weapon was used. And report directly to me, not a word of it to the Krauts or to our own CID, d'you understand?"

"I think I do, sir," Fairchild agreed meekly, and Trainer beckoned to the MP sergeant to join them: "It's going to be light in an hour and, Sergeant, I want you to organize a search party for the murder weapon on the double. How many men d'you have with you?"

"Only three, sir."

"Then use some of ours. Tell Sergeant Korovitz that you speak for me, and he is to rouse the first platoon of B Company and place them under your command. They are on security duty this week. Captain Fairchild here will tell you what kind of weapon we're after and give you further instructions. Find the weapon that snuffed out the Kraut, Sergeant, we must have it," and Trainer rapped it out again, his fury rising, "we must have it, if you have to crawl underground to get it!"

"Yes, sir," the MP sergeant sounded off, a ferocious grin breaking out around his mouth, "we'll do."

Trainer nodded and gestured to Korovitz, now emerging from the outlying darkness into the brightly lit driveway, to join him. He was silent for a protracted moment breathing heavily, and when he spoke at last it was softly and confidentially.

"Leroy, when the Mess Hall opens I want all the Krauts to be treated to a royal American breakfast, and I mean all the Krauts, those four boys standing over there and others who may barge in official like, tell the cook, Leroy. And one more thing, I want all them Krauts to be treated with courtesy by everyone, without exception. We may need the bastards sooner than we expect." Trainer paused and began to tilt his head coquettishly this way and that, his countenance of pure saccharine ilk. Then he belched and continued with the air of exquisite refinement, "The kind of breakfast generals get at the Pentagon when . . . when they're . . . under pressure." And he belched again.

"I understand perfectly," and Korovitz gravely nodded his head several times. "I understand perfectly."

They were both startled by the screeching of unmarked four-door sedans bursting at high speed and at a sharp angle onto the driveway and instantly coming to a complete stop, their bumpers practically touching, under the glaring lights.

"Circus's come to town," Korovitz muttered under his breath.

The doors of the two sedans sprang open, and eight men in civvies jumped out, some sporting what might pass for American business suits, others favoring a European style attire, some wearing fedoras, others German regional hats and caps, and others still hatless no doubt for a definitive purpose, some in overcoats and others without them. They were a motley crowd, loudmouths, backslappers, and masters of small talk already comparing notes and quick to judgment, summing up the building, the driveway, and the people in it.

"The one with the beer belly and the Bavarian hat is Major Hottelet, he's married to General Ryan's niece, and the tall and skinny with a limp is Major Olson, his second in command, his brother's a congressman, and he's got a lot of leverage," Korovitz spoke softly, his mouth close to Trainer's ear and taking every precaution so that his voice did not carry.

"I see," Trainer replied and added, "what a crew!"

"The MPs at Army hate to work with these CID clowns, but there are times they have no choice."

Trainer lay a hand on Korovitz's shoulder. "Take charge, Group Sergeant, I'll be in my office. If there's any interference . . . any trouble, send a runner. And tell the MPs I want the murder weapon no matter what!"

As he turned the corner and was walking away from the parking lot, Trainer saw a car coming slowly towards him. He recognized the driver, and the driver recognized him and stopped when they were adjacent. Master Sergeant Carl Steiner clambered out sluggishly as if he were on sufferance and stood on the driver's side eyeing Trainer with a kind of desperate anxiety.

"I quarreled with that Kraut scumbag, but I didn't kill him. That's God's truth," he called.

"I believe you," Trainer called back, "I believe you," and he put all the vigor and buoyancy he could muster into his words. "You just hang on, fella! You just hang on, Carl, d'you hear me, you just hang on!"

/ / /

"We all expected he would be charged," Fiorello was saying, watching Trainer closely and devising ways of keeping his C.O.'s temper with-in limits, if not entirely down. Outbursts of fury against the injustices of the world and the imbecilities of military legal procedures would accomplish nothing. They would only shift the focus of their attention away from the principal goal and drain them emotionally. Fiorello had little use for the visceral flurries. They, the officers, had to keep a cool head.

"But Carl is innocent, I tell you. He's innocent," Trainer shouted from behind his desk, half-rising and scowling in all directions.

"Look at the evidence, Ed," Lieberman joined in. "Judge Advocate will have no choice but to indict."

"Evidence!" Trainer dismissed the notion with a snarl. "It was a goddamn frame-up, Carl was framed."

"Perhaps, but if so we have to prove it at the court-martial, just fuming over it will accomplish nothing."

Trainer nodded resignedly, and unrelieved sadness, not anger, was now imprinted over his face, while Fiorello went on in the same dis-passionate manner: "Let me follow on Sol's train of thought. Steiner admitted he had violently quarreled with that German Hauch, rough-ly between 2300 and 2330 hours, outside the main repair building at the Motor Pool, though he was very reticent about the reasons for the quarrel. In fact, he told the MPs and the CID it was a private matter and none of their business. The quarrel was overheard and partly wit-nessed by a German couple who will be testifying at the court-martial. Furthermore, the murder weapon, an ordinary iron bar, according to the best judgment of our medical officer and the German police doc-tor, is thickly covered with Steiner's fingerprints and, of course, it has blood on it, victim's blood. As if this wasn't enough, Steiner's bank account at U.S. Army Savings was mysteriously credited with $5,000.00 two days before the alleged murder."

"Doesn't Carl swear up and down he never made the deposit?" Trainer growled again.

"Oh yes," Fiorello smiled obligingly, "except that the signature on the deposit slip is unmistakably his own, and this has been attested to by writing experts at Army. Three other items will end this tale of woe: our CID has received anonymous calls and letters that Steiner had been selling Army auto equipment to the Germans, and some of these calls and letters acknowledge complicity in the black market operations, but assert that once murder had been committed the complicit parties felt it was their public duty to report the matter to the American authorities."

"Model citizens, eh?" Trainer's laughter was raucous and aggressively scornful, and when it had exhausted itself he asked in a lighter tone, "But we don't know who they are, those informers, I mean? Do they exist at all, and are they telling the truth?"

"No, we don't," and Fiorello turned towards Lieberman. "Will you carry on?"

"Sure. There is some talk in the Judge Advocate Office about giving these complicit informers immunity, so they can testify at the trial, but this is still up in the air." Lieberman paused and looked embarrassedly at Trainer. "There is a coda to that black market allegation . . ."

"Another nail in Carl Steiner's coffin, I bet."

"Several months ago Steiner reported a series of break-ins at the Motor Pool. The items taken correspond to what the anonymous snitches have listed."

"Christ," Trainer exclaimed. "Someone must've gone to a helluva lot of trouble."

"It's a possibility, but I wouldn't put my money on it," Fiorello interjected guardedly.

"Anyway those anonymous reports carry some weight with the military, and their fate is still being decided," Lieberman continued with more feeling in his voice than Fiorello had ever shown. "Now we come to the time of death: the two M.D.s agree to it being between 2330 and 0130 hours because of blows administered by an iron bar; three heavy blows to the back of the head, the first of which may have already caused death, the other two being by way of not taking any chances. That night Steiner did not return to his quarters till well after 0100 hours. His wife testified to it, and she said she was surprised he had stayed out so late. Upon entering his quarters Steiner went straight to the bathroom, took a shower, and put some of his clothes in the washing machine. Once again his wife was baffled."

"I know it don't look good for Carl, but I'm convinced he's innocent, and I'll tell you why, college boys, 'cause my friend Carl Steiner whom I've known for almost twenty years ain't no murderer, no sir, and I'll swear to it on a stack of Bibles."

"I am afraid the evidence is practically irrefutable," Fiorello put in very quietly.

With an expansive gesture of the arm Trainer relegated said evidence and with it all other evidence empirically and scientifically obtained to the outer regions where it could do little harm.

"I saw Molly Steiner again yesterday," Trainer went on, "she's one brave girl I tell ye, sticking by her husband and telling everyone high and low that the thought of Carl being guilty never even entered her mind."

"Yes," Lieberman echoed Trainer's words. "Eunice and Rachel," and he pointed obliquely and awkwardly at himself and Fiorello, "are with her today. She's getting a lot of moral support from everybody, including that Lutheran pastor and his wife, I forget the name . . ."

"Storm, Major Edward Storm," Fiorello helped him out, "otherwise known in the holy profession as the laughing Eddie."

Trainer's face lit up. "I like that."

"Eddie is apparently given to unexpected and uncontrollable fits of giggles, not that it ever interfered with the performance of his pastoral duties or did him any harm professionally."

"In my book a guy must have at least one redeeming feature." Trainer had a merry look about him, then he scrambled to his feet, began to scratch the back of his neck with passion, and in the twinkling of an eye was a man transformed, grim, serious, resolved.

"Guys, what do we do now, what is our next step?"

"Unless a miracle intervenes"—Fiorello spoke softly and quietly— "Sergeant Steiner will be formally charged in the next week or so, murder two almost certainly and possibly grand larceny or something of the sort if the Army can bring itself to grant immunity to those snitches, but who knows even without immunity."

"So he hasn't been charged yet?" Trainer asked eagerly.

"No, he hasn't. He was taken into custody three days ago as a material witness, and the Army is still conducting its investigation; but it's a forgone conclusion." Fiorello paused. "As you can imagine, Ed, investigations take time, particularly when we deal with murder."

"Even so, the Army is moving fast," Lieberman added. "It's barely a week since that German national was killed, and the Army is halfway there." Having said this he stood up and began to stretch out his arms rhythmically and energetically as if going through a daily athletic exercise. Then he looked gloomily at his brother-officers and said firmly, "It's time to find Carl a brainy shyster insolent enough to ask all kinds of questions and not afraid to look under the bed. I recommend Julian Harrington."

"I concur," Fiorello's words were treading on the heels of Lieberman's, "he might find mitigating circumstances, an intolerable provocation or whatever, might be able to reduce the sentence . . ."

"Who the hell is that Julian Harrington?" Trainer cried out, all red in the face.

"A black lawyer at Army, Captain Harrington, just about any man facing a general court-martial in this Command—"

"And beyond," Fiorello put in.

"And beyond," Lieberman agreed, "wants Harrington as his defense counsel."

"A black shyster," Trainer mumbled. "Is that the best we can do for Carl?"

Fiorello and Lieberman smiled indulgently, and the former picked up the thread.

"This is not the time to lecture you on the evils of racism, and you have to take our word: Harrington is the best!"

"He usually doesn't take open-and-shut cases though," Lieberman remarked. "He may have to be convinced."

"Which means you'll have to put your considerable persuasive skills to the test, Ed, and don't take no for an answer." In his own way Fiorello sounded most persuasive.

"How soon will the trial see the light of day?"

"Oh, the defense counsel will be given ample time to prepare his case," Lieberman answered reassuringly. "The main objective is to get Harrington."

"General court-martial!"

"Right! General court-martial with all the trimmings. My sources tell me Waldo Smithers may be the Law Officer."

"That's interesting, Sol, I heard similar rumors."

"It wouldn't be that old curmudgeon Colonel Smithers, patron saint of the high and mighty?"

"The same, there is only one in the entire Milky Way."

"Still, Waldo and Julian have one thing in common," Fiorello observed with gusto.

"What might that be?" Trainer was definitely showing signs of impatience.

"They are both Yalies!"

"What the hell does that mean?"

"It means they are impossible to live with." Lieberman decided to stack everything on one card.

Now Trainer was blinking his eyes repeatedly and obsessively rubbing them, his patience wearing thinner than the finest silk. "Okay, guys, I'll speak to Harrington if ye think he's our best bet. But I wanna tell you somethin'. You college boys are kinda stumped, you only see, hear, feel maybe half of what's out there or maybe less, and your thinkin' don't take you very far neither, so most of the time you're kinda dried out and half strangled, and there ain't nothin' you can do about it. As for me, I know what's what, and I tell you Carl's innocent, yes innocent, and I'll tell ye how I know it, 'cause I can feel it in me bones."

/   /   /

Captain Julian Harrington pushed the massive revolving door and stood in the foyer of the Officer's Club at 7th Army Headquarters. Dag, the obliging Estonian maitre d' for years now in the American employ, beamed at him and inquired whether he would be dining or would direct his steps to the lounges and the ballroom.

"Thank you, Dag, I think I'll just have a drink at the bar." Harrington smiled broadly while the maitre d' assumed a pose both dignified and conspiratorial and imparted to him in a stage whisper that the band was about to play Viennese waltzes. "And I know, Captain, you like Viennese waltzes to distraction." He made an emphatic point, scanning the captain's entire person.

Harrington gave out a quick jolly laugh. "The temptations you put in my path, Dag; it'll take all my resolution and more to resist them," and he moved on, but the friendly maitre d' had not yet quite finished.

"My heartfelt congratulations on the Donleavy case, sir, the young lieutenant's parents were in tears when the acquittal was announced, tears of joy to be sure. How precisely did you conclude that after all Lieutenant Donleavy was not a Soviet spy, but just an indiscreet, foolish young man?" Dag was pricking up his ears.

Harrington laughed again. "It's all part of a day's work, and thank you again."

In the ballroom he waved to several acquaintances and noticed General Stebbins and his wife sitting at a table on the very edge of the dance floor. He stood to attention and saluted.

"Good evening, General and Mrs. Stebbins."

Stebbins returned the salute and smiled affably. "Good evening, Captain, your defense of the poor Donleavy was of high order. You carried out your commission well."

"Thank you, sir."

"My husband tells me you are an incurable workaholic, Captain Harrington"—Mrs. Stebbins joined in—"I beg of you not to overdo it senselessly, and take good care of yourself. I speak as a former nurse and a mother of five."

"Thank you, ma'am, I'll be sure to take your advice to heart."

Advancing further through the ballroom to the bar situated at the far end, Harrington caught sight, shifting and twisting his head to see better between the waltzing couples, the rising and bowing raconteurs, and the irregular lines of mute onlookers, some empty counter stools. He was slowly making his way towards them when he heard his first name called out, and curving his head to the left he saw Colonel Waldo Smithers sitting at the very extremity of the bar in happy isolation, waving to him.

"Good evening, sir," he started off not quite knowing what to expect.

"Sit down and have a drink."

"Thank you, but not for long. Duty calls."

"Yours is scotch, I believe," and Smithers snapped the fingers of a raised hand and spoke briskly to the bartender, "Double scotch for the captain, and put it on my tab."

As they were sipping the liquor, Smithers held out his hand. "My congratulations to you on the Donleavy case. Your performance was nothing short of brilliant."

"Thank you, Colonel."

"Still, one thing bothers me."

"Yes?"

"Donleavy was acquitted of the charge of espionage, he's a free man, well and good, but he should've been found guilty of lesser charges, possibly negligence, if not criminal negligence, conduct unbecoming an officer, substandard discharge of his very sensitive duties, violation of specific G2 regulations, the list could be considerably lengthened."

"I fully agree."

"Well, is Prosecution solely responsible?"

"I am afraid it is. As defense counsel I expected numerous charges, culminating in espionage for the Soviets. But Heywood was so confident he could get a conviction on espionage that he dropped the lesser offenses. I understand he made a convincing point to General Ryan of wanting to get the big fish because the rest was relatively unimportant. He also may have been fearful that the lesser charges might somehow overshadow the capital charge, and he wanted to nail Donleavy on the capital charge."

"Overconfident?"

"It would seem so."

"You see, Julian, without pretending that my secret ambition is to be a hanging judge I still think that some sort of punishment should've been meted out to Chuck Donleavy for the mess he landed us in, and in fact I shudder at the thought he is still in the service."

"I agree in part, sir."

"Which part?"

"Let me put it this way: as the trial got into full swing I daily expected a call from Ross Heywood because his espionage case was crumbling, and when that woman Marilla, or whatever her name is, testified that Donleavy was simply the dupe and had no inkling whatsoever of what was going on the case collapsed."

"True, but what happened affects national security."

"And the role of the defense counsel in a court-martial. He should not be asked to help the prosecution, in fact such a notion is a travesty of everything we hold sacred in our legal system."

"Yes, yes, yes." Smithers was making uninhibited gestures of impatience with both his arms as if cardboard figures from a pageant were being dropped onto his sledge and habit as Father Christmas. "I am not going to debate the obvious," he blurted out.

"Look at it this way," Harrington raised the glass to his lips, "Donleavy will be reassigned because no G2 within the U.S. Army will give him a pad. In all likelihood he'll end up somewhere in supply counting bolts and bars that go to the making of field latrines . . ."

"He might secretly reroute them to the Soviets." Smithers smiled perversely.

"He might, and this is the risk we have to take," Harrington put in soothingly, "but if he has any sense he'll resign his commission, sooner rather than later."

"Perhaps, but I still feel uncomfortable," and he added in a lighter tone, "That girl Marilla?"

"Yes, that was her name."

"I never lay eyes on her, but I understand she was . . . extremely attractive?"

"Bewitching! That pallid complexion with shocks of jet-black hair falling all over"—Harrington leaned back and closed his eyes—"she was a Celtic princess rising from the sea, but on this medieval beauty was superimposed another beauty, that of a ferocious twentieth-century Amazon, wielding not lance and sword, but the latest automatic weapons, and ruse, yes, ruse that would confound both the hermit and the statesman."

"It is gratifying you were able to carry out your duties as Donleavy's attorney, considering you too were under the spell." Smithers' voice carried just the right proportion of irony and understanding.

"I think everybody in court was. And as for Donleavy, he was her slave, he'd do anything for her so long as they remained lovers. He admitted that much on the stand, he was utterly bewitched, was no longer a free agent."

"She was, I mean, she is Russian?"

But Harrington ignored the question. "We also have to bear in mind her figure; tall, magnificent large breasts, the narrowest waistline imaginable, and those divinely fashioned legs, long legs, and every inch of her filled with irresistible sex appeal. She wore a very short skirt in court and a low-cut blouse."

Smithers moved his head appreciatively. "She certainly was something."

"She was a knockout. If you believe that human life ought not to be a fluctuating line with modest up and down variations but a straight line that in rare moments shoots upward to the very limits of experience, then being Marilla's slave could be that rare moment." Harrington leaned forward and shifted on the stool.

"I'm sorry, you asked about her antecedents. No, she's not Russian;

she's an East German and a fanatical believer in the communist doctrine. At present she may be facing a stiff sentence in a West German court." And noticing that their glasses were empty he asked, "Will you allow me to buy you a drink, sir?"

"That's very kind. Mine's bourbon, on the sword side I am a Northerner, New England and all that, but on the distaff side I am a Reb, Virginia and further south, Alabama, Mississippi. For generations now my forefathers married southern ladies and brought them north to New England to roost. I bet you didn't know that."

"As a matter of fact, some of us have been aware for a long time that you are of mixed blood," and Harrington was busily ordering the drinks.

"Who are these 'some of us,' dear boy?"

"Junior officers endowed with a keen sense of what is what."

"'Mixed blood', very witty, but this is also verging, verging."

"I would hate to be accused of churliness."

"I am graduating glass of 1928, and you, pray?"

"1952, sir," and Harrington was paying for a double bourbon on the rocks and a double scotch as they were being placed before them.

"I imagine Yale of the 1920s was very different from what Yale is today, in the 1950s. You know, Julian, in those days you didn't speak to a professor unless the professor spoke to you first? Dress code was vigorously observed—we all wore suits and ties—and the country bumpkins among us who thought they were on the way to the fair were promptly put in their place. We thought of ourselves as a very special body, an elite if you like, the best of the best, and we eagerly accepted the rituals, the conventions, and the customs we have inherited as a necessary concomitance of our unique status. Above all there was respect for authority because it was widely believed that authority was usually right. There was also respect for silver hair because it was often assumed that age and wisdom strolled together. I have to confess I regret those well regulated times when most of us knew where we stood. There was order, but it was order that ultimately depended on merit though, I admit, the so-called wisdom of the ages had something to do with it. Yale has changed hasn't it?"

"Yes, Yale has changed, and the change is for the better. Most of the self-appointed mandarins are dead and gone, and in their place there is more thought, more examination of what in your days had been taken for granted. Frankly more things should be put in mothballs, and I, for one, found most of the bula-bula ridiculous. I would also let out to pasture numerous faculty who got to be senile rather prematurely."

Smithers was silent and Harrington went boldly on, "You wait, in twenty years professors will be begging students to let them finish their lectures." Then he raised his glass: "Here is to the wrinkled old maid!"

Smithers' face brightened. "To the wrinkled old maid!" and they clinked their glasses.

After a decent sentimental interval, Smithers said with a new touch of earnestness in his voice, "You've been very lucky, Captain, in the last year or so. Several acquittals, several successful appeals, many a reduced sentence have shown to the world you can pull rabbits out of a hat at a rate that makes Prosecution gnash their teeth. How long, do you think, will this streak of luck continue? After all there's such a thing as the law of averages."

"I wasn't aware that my performance at the bar at 7th Army Headquarters is being viewed as a matter of luck."

"Oh, come off it, Julian, you're a bit of a magician—we all know that—and magicians make their living amazing their audiences."

"In all modesty I thought the verdicts you refer to showed beyond the shadow of a doubt that justice prevailed, and that I was merely its humble instrument." Harrington was still soothing and conciliatory.

"Words like modesty and humility do not become you, Captain," Smithers put in with some irritation. "I have never known you to be modest or humble, just the reverse; I've known you to be cocky, arrogant, and at times damn impertinent."

"I am very sorry to hear that the Colonel has reached this extraordinary conclusion."

Smithers emptied his glass in a single gulp. "One of these days you'll meet your match, Captain Harrington, and multitudes of those who wear the same uniform as you do will cry for joy."

"I'll bear the Colonel's words in mind."

Smithers laughed sardonically. "I hear you'll be representing that lowdown sergeant who killed a German national. It's an open-and-shut case, Harrington, and you may come to regret it."

"Thank you for inviting me to join you, Colonel Smithers, it was an honor." Harrington jumped off the stool, stood at attention, and saluted smartly. Smithers was also standing, but he let the captain wait for the return salute while seconds were slipping away.

"Thank you for the drink, Captain," he snarled at last, "and one more thing, the Appointer tells me it may be my time to serve as the Law Officer at Steiner's general court-martial. I am looking forward to crossing rapiers with you for the first time on common turf."

/   /   /

"Are you well treated, Carl, are you well treated?" Trainer asked solicitously, his uneasiness rising while forcing himself into a sitting position on a narrow bench built into the concrete wall of a six by twelve cell. Sergeant Carl Steiner, sitting gloomily on the edge of the bed, did not respond at first, his head hanging low. But as Trainer repeated the question, with his lungs pressed into vigorous service, he looked up resignedly and nodded.

"No complaints so far, Colonel, they allow Molly to come every day, and I've had helluva visitors, just about every sarge in this Command." Trainer noticed at once that Steiner's eyes were dull, lifeless, and his voice harsh and muted. He was a changed man.

"My buddies believe I'm innocent," he went on listlessly, "but who else will? Maybe the hour has struck to pull stakes."

"No, no, no!" Trainer shouted frantically, propelling himself forward from the discomfort of the bench, gripping Steiner's biceps, and shaking his friend's body in a paroxysm of hope.

"Listen to me, we have helluva attorney, Harrington's his name, best there is, and we gonna fight till your name's cleared."

Steiner smiled warmly. "I know, the good captain came down here this morning and spent several hours with me. I told him all I know. Hauch sought me out at the Motor Pool to get my help for that goddamn association of his to build up again Kraut nationalism and maybe get ready for World War III. He wanted me to attend their meetings and be free with the dough. He also said his association considered me a German born outside Germany but still a German. I hollered in his face I was an American, and so was my dad and his dad before him, but the shithead kept pressing me. I told him to get lost, but he went on and on, and we argued for somethin' like half-hour. Finally I'd had enough of his crap so I told him to beat it and never come back, or I'll call the MPs. He left and shortly thereafter I did. He was kicking when he left, and that's just about the end of the story. When I took off for home I was so riled up I drove around for maybe an hour just to forget I ever saw the bastard. That covers it, and I got nothin' more to add."

"We'll do all we can, Carl, and we count kinda heavy on Harrington 'cause it'll be his show."

Steiner let his spiritless eyes roam all over the cell, from the low concrete ceiling to the white tiled floor, as if he were engaged in some infinitely trivial enterprise that no one gave two hoots about. Then he fixed the same spiritless eyes on Trainer and spoke without a tinge of emotion.

"Captain Harrington will see me again in a few days to discuss the plea. But he said today if there is no hard evidence blowing my way, it might be best to plead to"—he pulled a scrap of paper from his pocket— "I wrote it down, 'involuntary manslaughter, and citing extreme provocation and various extenuating circumstances.'" He kept staring at Trainer numb, deflated, devastated.

"We'll move heaven and hell, Carl, we'll move heaven and hell," Trainer hollered, "trust me," but his heart was sinking, and he felt utterly helpless. From the edge of the bed the same hollow, disembodied voice was heard again.

"Twenty-two years in the service, and now they call me a murderer."

Trainer's features hardened, but he was lost for words. He knew he must keep Steiner's hope alive, he must keep the fire burning, but how, how? He was on the point of crying out once again that no stone would be left unturned to prove his friend's innocence when the peephole on the door was slid open and a voice asked:

"Sergeant Steiner, your wife is here, shall I let her in?"

"Right, Greg, let her in," Steiner shouted less listless than before, "and thanks, Greg."

"Anytime, Sarge." Presently the heavy door was swung open, and Molly Steiner stepped in.

She was of middle height like her husband, blonde, light-complexioned, and slender, and she wore her hair short and turned upward in dainty little tufts which gave her a playful, coquettish air. *How young she looks,* Trainer thought at once. *One wouldn't guess they have two grown-up sons.* But her face was marked by darkish ridges and furrows, and her eyes were puffed up and red.

"Ed," she cried as soon as she saw him, and then she folded her hands and was eyeing him guardedly. "I should've said Colonel Trainer."

"It's Ed, Ed always, Molly," and he put his arms around her and kissed her on the cheek.

"I thank you for coming to see Carl, these days we need every friend we've got," and she advanced a step, her hand touching lightly Carl's mouth and chin. They were immediately locked in a passionate embrace, his lips breaking into hers, his hands caressing her body, while she whispered into his ear at brief intervals, her lips seeking his again and again, her hand stroking his back and buttocks.

As the embrace showed no sign of abatement, Trainer began to wonder what he should do. He had once read several pages in a book merrily entitled *Guide to Polite Behavior in All Situations,* and he remembered the advice given when the host and hostess engage in some outlandish conduct: it was to pretend that nothing strange was happening and count dots on the ceiling. Obediently Trainer's eyes strained upward only to discover there were absolutely no dots on the concrete and no dots on the walls or anywhere else either in this grim colorless cell. Nor was there a window and hence the only avenue of escape was the door, which unfortunately unlocked from the outside. For a brief moment he contemplated crawling under the bed but realized his bulk would almost certainly impede the act of love which, he reckoned, was due to begin on this very bed any second now. Coyly and determined not to make the slightest sound, Trainer stood facing the left wall, avoiding looking at the bed and wall opposite. It seemed to him he stood there forever and a day, enveloped in absolute stillness like a lone communicant tarrying in a deserted church. Then he heard Molly's matter-of-fact voice: "If the bastards find my husband guilty, we won't take it sitting down."

Trainer made an about-face and saw the two of them standing shoulder-to-shoulder holding hands, their faces radiating blissful devotion for each other.

"My honeybun, I'll fight for you alongside," she purred and kissed his neck again and again.

"I am innocent," he called proudly. "Those bastards had better take note." And he went on kissing her brow and neck.

"If the trial goes against us, Ed, meaning Colonel, sir, I'll go to see

General Ryan, and if this proves no good, why, I'll go and see General Eisenhower."

"Maybe there'll be no need for that," Carl whispered, holding her very close.

"Come to think about it, Ike himself decorated Carl in that town up there in Belgium or Holland or wherever that was hopelessly surrounded, our boys relieving it against all odds in the end, winter '44," Molly resumed, reverting to her matter-of-fact tone.

"Bastogne," Carl put in. "That's right, Ike decorated several of us there."

"And next to Staff Sergeant Carl Steiner there stood another staff sergeant," Molly went on, transfixing Trainer with a knowing glance, "who like Carl received a high decoration for bravery, and his name was . . ."

"Edward E. Trainer." Trainer finished it for her. "Both of us received high decorations from Ike, and you're right, Molly, we stood next to each other, shoulder to shoulder."

"Since that time," Molly continued with despondent fury barely held in check, "that other staff sergeant leapt higher and higher, and finally made such a bound he vanished and was seen no more."

"But he is right here and racking his brains to help that other staff sergeant," Trainer burst out.

Molly watched him in silence. "Maybe so, Colonel. But if powers that be don't do right by my Carl, expect the worst."

"Take it easy, honey," Carl whispered, squeezing her arm.

"Like I said, Colonel, expect the worst. I'll kick ass, Ryan's ass and Ike's ass even though he's the President, and if that do no good, why Wesley, Tony, and me'll make one hell of a posse, and we'll break into whatever jail it takes and free Dad. And to hell with the U.S. Army."

/   /   /

"I am so sorry, Rachel." Trainer was speaking into the receiver, doing his best to appear gentle and concerned. "So sorry." And she laughed it off and said briskly, "Here's Sol."

"I'm sorry to be calling you so late, Sol," Trainer began again like a mendicant reciting the same preamble to a new and valued would-be patron.

"That's all right, Ed, we were catching up on our reading." He sounded matter-of-fact and not in the least put out.

"I invited Harrington to come and see us and outline his defense of Carl. Furthermore he may have questions for all of us. He's a busy man, so he'll come tomorrow night sometime between 1900 and 1930 hours, and he and I will have dinner in the Officer's Mess; I'm counting on O'Leary to serve us somethin' that ain't lethal. After dinner we'll drive to my duplex in the Village, and could you join us there shortly after 2000 hours? I'm also asking John and Sergeant Korovitz who may have some insights from the NCO side of the fence. It's my goddamn hope that fella Harrington is as good as they paint 'im. And by the way, I'm putting the genius up for the night, so we'll have time galore."

"Good night, Ed, and I'll be there."

"Thank you, Sol, and good night."

"Good night, Colonel."

Over dinner, Harrington told Trainer of his meetings with Steiner, and at the colonel's invitation offered a brief account of his army legal career.

"I invited the Exec Officer, the Chaplain, and the Group Sergeant to come and meet you; thought they might be able to clear a point or two," Trainer said gloomily, as they were driving to the Village.

"This may be very helpful, sir."

Trainer nodded and the rest of the journey passed in utter silence.

At his duplex house kept spotless by his trusty German housekeeper, the guests arrived so punctually and at such short intervals from one another that the host suspected a solemn compact had been signed by the three of them to present themselves in the best possible light and impress him greatly. He at once busied himself with introductions and then threw his massive arm forward in the direction of the side bar on which cunningly deployed arrays, two large crystal trays supporting scotch and bourbon bottles, flanked irregularly by glasses, water containers, and ice buckets—advancing battalions with artillery pieces enclosed on two sides by light horse and infantry: "Please, gentlemen," he intoned cordially, "help yourselves to the drinks." And taking note of Harrington and Korovitz's rapt expression at the sight of these resourceful military groupings, he remarked casually, "It was my housekeeper who arranged 'em this way, in her spare time she's a keen student of the great battles on the two continents."

Korovitz pulled at his mustache. "The early hours of the battle of Antietam, the bluebellies called it a victory, but we carried the day."

And Harrington, totally engrossed in what he was now observing, exclaimed with delight: "The first day of the first Battle of the Marne, the French spearhead, a highly successful defensive maneuver, 1015 hours."

"Maybe it's both," Fiorello commented with a shred of interest, helping himself to a large scotch and soda.

After they had settled down with their drinks, and the exchange of pleasantries had run its normal circuitous course, Trainer went straight to the point.

"Captain Harrington, what are Sergeant Steiner's chances of acquittal?"

"Right now not very good, sir," and Harrington looked conceitedly from face to face.

"But he is innocent," and Trainer motioned to Korovitz.

"Sir, I have here a list of names of officers and NCOs in this Command who would be happy to appear before the court as Sergeant Steiner's character witnesses," and he handed the defense counsel two sheets of paper covered with names and stapled together.

"Thank you, Sergeant, this clearly establishes the loyalty that members of this Command feel towards the accused." Harrington patted his knee several times and lit a cigarette. "It's a noble sentiment. But I have to be frank with you and with everyone else in this room. If I were to parade a hundred character witnesses swearing to Steiner's honesty, probity, and all the other virtues under the sun, it wouldn't make the slightest difference," and he ticked off the principal charges against the sergeant with which everyone in the room was familiar. "What I need is hard evidence, and I regret to say Prosecution is in possession of this hard evidence." His gaze touched the very limits of intensity, but it was not directed at anyone in particular. "We, on the other hand, have very little. Give me something to work with, and I'll put it to good use. If not, I can probably make a convincing case for manslaughter making the best of Hauch's criminal attacks on Steiner's patriotism, his insulting comments about our sergeant being a German and not an American, provocation of one kind or another, threats, and so on. There are very real mitigating circumstances." Pensively he raised the glass to his lips and emptied it to the dregs.

"How does Steiner want to plead?" Lieberman asked, fiddling with his glass.

"He maintains he is innocent and doesn't want to change his plea. It goes without saying I'll do my best to persuade him."

"I still say he's innocent of all the charges," Trainer broke in. "It's a frame-up."

"Anything is possible, but give me some proof," Harrington countered, looking stern and determined.

"Who is the trial counsel?" Fiorello stood up energetically and walked over to the sideboard.

"Regie Senko, Major Reginald Senko. He's very methodical, very well organized."

"So there will be several charges?" Fiorello inquired again, his hands busily reaching this way and that.

"Oh yes, without a doubt, based on what you know already with murder being a sort of pièce de résistance. Regie won't leave anything to chance," and Harrington laughed contentedly.

"If Carl is really innocent then a horrendous miscarriage of justice will take place." Korovitz made it sound as if this terrible miscarriage of justice had already taken place and he, Leroy Korovitz, had been cast in the role of the Leveler to mete out justice again after years of misrule. He poured himself another drink and sauntered back to his plush armchair.

"Gentlemen, we have a responsibility," he called out, and words were sticking in his throat. They all cheered him, except Harrington who was eyeing him quizzically.

"Gentlemen, we have a responsibility before God and man to see that justice is done," Korovitz ranted again, holding his head high, his features frozen into a magisterial, messianic mask. The others fell silent, and Lieberman poured ice and water into a glass and handed it to the sergeant. "Drink this, it'll quench your inside." Korovitz held the glass absentmindedly and kept gazing into space, immobile, lost to the world. Then the corners of his mouth began to twitch, and in a jiffy he was back with the troops, on the battlefield exercising command.

"It's our duty, men, you know what I mean, and this is no time or place for palaver." His clear, powerful voice resonated like the ultimate order, dwarfing everything in its wake, to be carried out at all costs.

At the other end of the living room Trainer propped up his hands on the sides of the armchair and was hoisting himself up, his brow full of apprehension. He was very nearly up on his feet when the shrill twang of the telephone startled everybody. Trainer, now fully mobile, made a beeline for the side table and spoke into the receiver with some irritation and then listened attentively to what seemed to the others an unusually protracted time. At last he said firmly, "No, you'd better come right now, time is running short, and besides Captain Harrington, defense counsel, is with me. Come as soon as you can, Vallejo . . . no, no . . . you did the right thing."

"Specialist Jesús Vallejo, my Group Clerk, tells me he's got some information that can be helpful to Sergeant Steiner," he told his astonished guests. "He'll be here in twenty minutes."

Upon entering the house Vallejo saluted smartly, and when he stepped into the living room he again stood at attention and saluted— his salute being promptly returned by the three officers and Group Sergeant. He was dressed in German-style civilian clothes, his scarf was reddish-black, his soft, wide rimmed, darkish hat stylish and a replica of what German fashion magazines recommended for outdoor lovers. Nothing in his appearance suggested the military, especially the American military viewed by most Germans as the foreign and unsavory world of GIs, Coca Cola, and chewing gum.

"Sit down, Jesús," Trainer called to him jovially, "and, Sol, give the kid a drink, it may loosen his tongue."

"His tongue doesn't need loosening, Colonel." Korovitz had blithely snapped back into the here and now, leaving his former transcendental state far behind. "His tongue needs tying up so he can't chitter-chatter as the day is long."

"Scotch or bourbon, Vallejo?" Lieberman was already in position by the sideboard.

"Scotch, sir, and a little branch water. Thank you, sir."

"When I come to think about it, I've never seen you in civvies." Fiorello was demonstrably taken by Vallejo's attire. "Quite an outfit, I see a woman's touch."

"One tries," Vallejo mumbled softly effacingly, "one tries."

Grinning from ear to ear as he was watching the scene, Trainer gulped down the bourbon, refilled the glass, and after much shifting and a display of mild pyrotechnics, settled down in his armchair. He leaned in the direction of Vallejo.

"The gentleman sitting to your far right whom you may not have seen before is Captain Julian Harrington from Judge Advocate Office. He will be defense counsel in Sergeant Carl Steiner's general court-martial. You say you have information that may be helpful to the accused. Are you comfortable, Specialist?"

"Very comfortable, sir, thank you."

"Then tell us in your own words what this information is. Take your time, and be as thorough as you can. As you go on, some of us may wish to stop you and ask questions. But that's understandable."

"Quite understandable, sir."

Trainer grinned again and caught Lieberman's eye, pointing obliquely to Vallejo's glass.

"You have a captive audience, son."

In a level voice, succinctly and with quiet precision, Vallejo told of his relationship with Steiner and his wife, of being invited by them to Christmas dinner two years in a row, and of the kindness they had shown him.

"One day when I was in their home, Molly said that fellow Hauch had been bothering them for some time, always wanting to speak to Carl privately and making a mystery of it. 'It's the shades of the Bund, isn't it Carl?' she asked. I said I didn't know what the Bund was, and Molly said: 'Tell him, Carl, Jesús is a friend, he ought to know, it's better that way.'

"Carl hemmed and hawed at first and finally spilled it all out, namely that his dad had briefly belonged to the Bund, the American pro-Nazi organization back in the thirties when he, Carl, was still in short pants.

"'Dad didn't have a clue what they were after, they promised us a good deal, a practically free vacation in Germany for the whole family,' he bridled up, 'and when he found out they were plain Nazi thugs, he told them to go to hell.'

"'But they didn't take no for an answer, did they?' Molly joined in.

"'No, they kept pestering Dad for years, reminding him of what they called 'his German duty', and he reported all of it to the F.B.I. who told him they had the outfit under surveillance but couldn't stop it from contacting Dad.'

"'And now they keep pestering his son,' Molly said, 'the bastards!'"

"I wonder what relevance this really has to Sergeant Steiner's predicament," Harrington remarked. "The Bund thrived twenty, twenty-five years ago on another continent thousands of miles away. This could be the reason why Steiner never brought it to my attention."

"I can speak to this," Vallejo said avidly.

"Go on."

"Deep down Sergeant Steiner is ashamed his father was duped. He tries to forget the whole damned business; being a member of the Bund is not the kind of thing you brag about. In fact, even today it's a stigma."

"Perhaps." Harrington sounded mildly interested.

"There is a new Bund, Captain, right here in West Germany, and its strength lies in that part of the country which was formerly the American Zone of Occupation."

"How d'you know that?" Trainer was restless in his seat, rotating his empty glass.

"It's general knowledge . . . sir."

"No one ever told me about it." Trainer was a tad annoyed.

"Now that you mention it," Fiorello was biting into that large reservoir of half-forgotten, semi-abandoned recollections where nothing is stored in proper order, "now that you mention it, the subject came up at a G2 or IGA briefing several months back."

"What is IGA?" Lieberman inquired curtly.

"Internal German Affairs, all Adjutants were familiarized with various aspects of the West German state and society, political parties and trends, the economy, attitudes towards us, and so on."

"Well, what did the goddamn gurus have to say about that Bund stuff?"

Fiorello was trying his very best, but the odds were hopelessly against him.

"I'm sorry, Ed, all I remember is the name."

"Actually the new Bund is very different from the old Bund with which Sergeant Steiner's father had had a passing acquaintance, and it has a brand new name," Vallejo picked up the thread.

"Go on, give us the works, kid, it ain't decent to keep folks on tenterhooks."

"Sir, would it be possible for me to have another drink?"

Confronted by such a question Trainer usually exhibited the most amiable side of his personality, the sound of the magic word not only bringing forth every single drop of his priceless kindness, but directing each drop to the proper organs of the mind and body where it could do the most good. On this occasion he scrambled to his feet, leapt to where Vallejo was sitting, swept up his glass, leapt again, filled it with scotch not forgetting a dash of icy water, and thrust it into Vallejo's waiting hand.

"There you are!" he cried buoyantly. "There you are!"

"Bund 45 is a super-nationalistic organization employing former Nazis and neo-Nazis, and one of its principal aims is to undermine and discredit American military presence in West Germany. A typical example of how Bund 45 operates would be to get an American enlisted man or officer drunk by overt or covert means, drug him if necessary, adding a very strong laxative, and leave him in a public place so that in the morning he would be seen by crowds of people on their way to work; or to plant criminal evidence in an American home and tip off the German cops; or to accuse Americans of criminal misconduct and hire bogus witnesses to testify against them; or else deposit sums of money into American bank accounts and connect their holders with phony charges of criminal acts." Vallejo was warming to the subject.

"You seem to understand it so well, Vallejo," Fiorello said very quietly, inspecting the tips of his shoes. "I take it this information comes from reliable sources?"

"One hundred percent reliable."

Harrington rose to his feet and threw his arms backward again and again. His mien was earnest, but a flash of anger broke out round his mouth, and then shot upward to his cheeks and nostrils.

"Aren't our own people aware of what's going on? I heard no more than whispers. If what Vallejo says is true, this is scandalous." And he stood there, towering over them exasperated and defiant.

"Another small point," Vallejo broke in. "The complete records of the German-American Bund from the 1930s were kept in Berlin, but towards the end of the war sometime in 1944 they were moved to Stuttgart because of the unrelenting bombing of the German capital."

"Did they survive the war?"

Vallejo laughed, skeptically, cynically.

"Officially they were destroyed three or four weeks before the German surrender so they wouldn't fall into American hands, but there's reason to believe they were spirited into a safe place by those who were already planning post-war Nazi hegemony."

"So Bund 45, as you call it, has these records," Fiorello doggedly returned to the subject. "And the Steiner name in them makes quite a reading. Traitor to the *Vaterland,* German-American softy who lacked the courage!"

Vallejo nodded emphatically.

"To come back to our muttons, Jesús . . ." Lieberman began thoughtfully, sipping scotch, "you believe Carl to be innocent of all the charges, am I right?"

"Carl Steiner is the victim of a colossal and very cleverly devised frame-up, engineered by Bund 45. They really surpassed themselves this time."

"But you have no proof, only a gut feeling," and Harrington pierced him with all the callousness of a prosecutorial stare.

"Proof is out there and can be obtained."

Lieberman coughed and waved a hand in the air, apparently for no purpose.

"Knowing you," he resumed, "I'd say you have a plan."

"And we want to hear it," Trainer at once shouted across the room. "We want to hear it."

But first they all had to stand up, flex their muscles, shake a leg, unwind, refill their glasses. A short carefree break was what they all wanted; they marched off one by one to the bathrooms, and then lounged about, engrossed in voluble small talk, drawing strength from fleeting idleness. When in due course they took their old seats, their mood was grave and resolute.

"My plan, gentlemen, comes in two parts." Vallejo was sitting up very straight, his chin thrust forward.

"First of all we need more information about Bund 45, its organization, who goes up who goes down, their agenda for the near future, personnel, manner of recruitment, their headquarters and branch offices, and above all the activity within Stuttgart cells, because it's almost guaranteed the Steiner operation was planned and implemented in Stuttgart. I obtained some information through German friends of my buddies, but there's still a great deal to know. I don't think there is much to find out through official channels at Army, one important reason being the Bund, in addition to being ferociously anti-American, is also ferociously anti-communist, anti-Soviet, and this presents a problem."

"How so?" Fiorello asked gloomily.

"I have a pal at Army who tells me orders are coming from above to soft-pedal investigations of German outfits that are militantly anti-Soviet."

"Even if they harm our boys." Lieberman was only partly incredulous.

"Cold War, as I understand it, has literally hundreds of sides to it," Korovitz sounded off to everybody's surprise. "It's like a huge jigsaw puzzle, and one piece's as good as another. You gotta play a hundred games, and if you don't, you're a goner."

"Yes, yes." Trainer made a gesture of casual agreement. "You're right, Leroy, but . . ."

"Further investigation in this regard is absolutely necessary for the success of the second part of the plan," Vallejo resumed. "Colonel Trainer and Major Fiorello, sirs, you may know people in the German political world, or the world of their high governmental administration—those people would be well-informed about Bund 45, as would be the German police which at times is very reluctant to share information with us."

"Information that we at times would be very reluctant to use," Lieberman interjected.

Trainer began to rub his chin with passion. "I think I can help out. I know whom to contact, and if she can't give me the lowdown nobody can. John?"

"I'll leave it to you, Ed."

Trainer's eye was now fixed on Lieberman.

"You got a cow you can milk forever and a day."

"Me?"

"That's right, Pastor Günthers, the Lutheran pastor here in town."

"Oh yes, for months I've been meaning to pay a courtesy call on him, but never got round to it."

"Now is your chance. He's very well-informed."

"All right."

"And our esteemed Group Sergeant?" Trainer turned in another direction. "Any contacts with the Krauts that might help the defense?"

"Nothing to speak of with the Krauts, but," and here Korovitz paused with well-rehearsed dignity, "my fiancée serving at Army, she's in the military, in fact she's a sergeant . . ."

"I had no clue you had a fiancée, Leroy."

"Well, this being a private business and all that."

"Right, I got the message, can she help?"

"I'll check with her, Colonel, she's in Personnel, in charge of confidential records."

"This sounds promising," and Trainer immediately refocused his eyes on Vallejo. "We'll try to give you as much info as we can, Group Clerk, and now what kind of beast is the second part of your plan?"

"We need someone to infiltrate the Stuttgart Headquarters of Bund 45. This is the only way to obtain proof they were responsible for the Steiner operation . . ."

"Do you have anyone in mind?" Harrington hurled the question at him.

"Yes, Captain, myself."

"How do you propose to go about it, Specialist?"

"I shall pose as a discontented Mexican-American GI who is poorly treated by his Anglo superiors, laughed at, humiliated. He can no longer tolerate the constant prejudice and discrimination, and he just wants to get back at his oppressors. He'll do just about anything."

Fiorello smiled at Harrington and made an expansive gesture of hand. "Just a point of information, Captain. What is the time frame with respect to this case?"

"Sergeant Steiner will be formally charged this Friday, that is in two days, and defense will be given adequate time to prepare its case. The Convening Authority is usually quite liberal about it." Harrington coughed and wiped his brow. "A month or thereabout would be the usual time given to the defense in a case like this, unless circumstances warrant a longer period."

"That means if you were to do it, Vallejo, you'd have roughly a month."

"That might be enough, sir, if things click."

"And if they don't?" Fiorello pressed the point.

"In that case I'll ask for a continuance, and I'd be very surprised if I didn't get one," Harrington broke in.

"That act you're planning to put on, Jesús." Trainer rose from his comfortable armchair and crossed the living room, positioning himself by the window covered tightly by the colorful drapes. "Will it fool the opponent?" He spoke in a kindly, fatherly tone.

"It may, sir; I am a good actor. I was a leading man in several high school productions, including *Dracula*."

"In that case, son, your success is already a matter of record," and Korovitz took a large swig of bourbon.

Trainer remained kindly and fatherly and asked again: "Why do you want to do it at all? You know your caper could be dangerous."

"I am a soldier, I am Regular Army. Besides, Sergeant Steiner is innocent and needs someone who can clear his name."

"Even so," Trainer articulated very gently, very slowly, "even so."

"There's something else, sir."

"Oh!"

"If I am successful in my mission and Carl is acquitted, I'll request promotion to sergeant."

"You request what!!!" Trainer was beside himself. "This is the U.S. Army, Vallejo, not Taos, Mexico, where you swap a stolen sheep for a gallon of moonshine."

"With all due respect, sir, it's Taos, New Mexico, and a stolen sheep up there is worth at least three gallons of moonshine."

"Watch your tongue if you value your life!"

"Yes, sir, but in that case the deal is off."

"What deal!" Trainer shouted again. "This is the Army, you don't cut deals, you take orders, boy!"

Unexpectedly Harrington stepped forward and intervened.

"Colonel Trainer, Vallejo is right. He cannot be ordered to undertake that assignment as part of his regular duties. He's a clerk, this is his designation, and not a secret agent. If he were to do it, it could only be on the basis of some arrangement, private or semi-official, between you as Group Commander and him as Group Clerk and your subordinate."

"So I can't even piss in my own home."

"This is peacetime, Colonel. Enlisted personnel can be employed in a variety of ways and be given a wide variety of tasks, but in this instance your hands are tied."

Before Trainer had time to retort, Fiorello was on his feet facing Vallejo.

"Could you please leave us for a few minutes, Specialist? Can he wait in the kitchen?" Trainer nodded.

As soon as Vallejo was out of the room, stony-faced Fiorello approached Trainer.

"Ed, your temper tantrums lead us nowhere. Vallejo is the only one who can help get Steiner acquitted. You should understand that!"

Trainer was studiously looking away, at the walls and ceiling, bristling and not uttering a word, and Fiorello cracked his fingers several times, and for a while he too did not utter a word.

Then he exploded: the others watched with uneasy readiness that spelled out no imminent course of action. Presently Fiorello drew even closer to Trainer, so that their chins practically touched, and snarled: "You pride yourself on being independent, regulations being no more, you say, than trash penpushers at Headquarters dream up, or else they'd be on the dole since no sane institution would take them on. But you're the biggest penpusher of them all, a jumped-up little Draco who doesn't know nothin' from nothin'! Where's the logic of it?" Trainer reeled back open-mouthed, not infuriated and feeling wronged, just dumbfounded.

Then he turned sluggishly to the others, his countenance stony and expressionless. "I'd like each of you to give me your honest opinion if Vallejo should be recommended for sergeant if he makes it. Sol?"

"Yes, Ed, and without reservations. He may be facing real danger, and it'll take both guts and brains."

"Thank you. Captain Harrington?"

"If what Vallejo said is true, and it appears to be true, this is the only way of meting out justice to Sergeant Steiner. My answer is an emphatic yes."

"Thank you, Captain. Sergeant Korovitz, how say you?"

"This is the only way of saving Carl's bacon. And volunteering to be an undercover agent takes helluva lot of daring. It's above and beyond the call of duty! Yes, sir, I'm with the others."

Trainer nodded. "Thank you, Sergeant," and turning towards Fiorello he said with a lump in his throat, "I think I know where you stand, Major; would you come with me, we'll bring Vallejo back." And straightening himself up, the colonel marched off with the major immediately following.

"I've always known John to be a cool cat," Lieberman whispered with a chuckle. "So this is what broke the camel's back."

"If you want to know the truth, Chaplain, it's been brewing for months," Korovitz whispered back with all the conviction of one in the know.

When the three of them returned to the living room, Trainer asked Vallejo to sit down. Words did not come easily to him, but he spoke out each of them, holding nothing back.

"I am sorry about my outburst, Specialist. I apologize for it."

"That's all right, sir." Vallejo shrugged his shoulders, and his tone was friendly, understanding. "For you it comes with the territory, as Group Commander you are the top watchdog seeing to it that regulations are followed. U.S. Army runs on regulations—notwithstanding Napoleon's statements to the contrary—and violation of regulations, however trivial it may be, is tantamount to high treason."

"Have you finished?"

"Well, yes, sir, I have finished."

"In that case I want to inform you that with the total support of the other officers in this Command, and of the Group Sergeant, I approve your plan of acting as an undercover agent to infiltrate Bund 45 and obtain evidence clearing Sergeant Carl Steiner of the criminal charges leveled at him."

"Yes, sir, very good, sir, I'm glad you came to this decision."

"Vallejo, I must caution you again your mission may be dangerous."

"I know it, sir, I believe I've already said I accept the challenge."

"And you are acting . . ."

". . . of my own free will and without the slightest pressure from you or anybody else," Vallejo finished for him. "But if successful I expect to receive my sergeant stripes . . . without delay."

"If you are successful, I will recommend you for promotion right away, and I shall use the authority of my rank and office to implement matters on the double."

"Thank you, sir."

Trainer, whose moods came and went with the speed of light, if not faster, was at ease and affable once more, and the others imitated his example.

"How do you propose to go about it, the logistics of it I mean?" he posed the question.

"First I'll go and sniff around. I have the name of a place where the Bund 45 crowd apparently congregates. It's Restaurant Dolores, and it's right in the middle of the red light district, red light district for the

Germans, not the GIs, in the southwestern part of the city. I'll be in uniform but unshaven, unwashed, sloppy in every respect and full of venom against the Anglo domination of Mexican-American population in the States and against the tyrannical treatment we are subjected to in the Army . . . When the time is right, I shall intimate I can be bought and I am ready to join in the fight against the American oppressors of my race."

"You might also taper your language. Most of the time you sound fluent, literary, and your vocabulary is goddamn extensive," Lieberman advised. "If you present yourself as a bum, you should speak like a bum."

"I thought about it too, Chaplain. I'll murder the English language and intersperse it with lowdown Spanish. I'll be an illiterate and by golly ready for anything."

"How will this affect your regular duties, Vallejo?" There was more than a tinge of anxiety in Korovitz's voice.

"Not much, Sarge. I'll be straining to make contact with that mob mostly on weekends, and if need be I'll spend a night or two in a fleabag where German vagrants stay. Later, I may need some three-day passes. And one more thing, sir," Vallejo cast an inquiring glace at Trainer, "I don't want to be picked up by the MPs because of my sloppy appearance; I know the German cops will leave me alone."

"We can fix that," Trainer assured him. "Don't worry."

"Will you be assisted by someone else, Specialist," Fiorello wanted to know, "or is this strictly a one-man operation?"

"One-man for the most part, Major, but I have a buddy who'll be kept informed of my every step, and who may be a cutout between the Army and me."

"And who might that be?"

"Hal Shelton, Specialist Shelton, sir."

At these words Korovitz bellowed with happy laughter. "Shelton, the medic?"

"The same, Sarge."

"Excellent choice," Korovitz roared, "a fellow Reb into the bargain."

"Is this supposed to be a recommendation?" Trainer inquired, not expecting an answer.

"Hal's German fiancée has an apartment in Stuttgart, and he spends lots of time there. Both are great people, and there's a big wedding set for July in Alexandria. Both families want to hoop it up."

Korovitz was heeding Vallejo's words, but the waves of sentiment and history began to engulf him, and memories welled up in his breast like the breathtaking creatures of the deep, seductive and irresistible.

"Colonel Trainer," he spoke up with feeling, "have you heard the famous tale of a handful of Confederates, country boys and some of them under age, who whipped the stuffing out of a vastly superior force of bluebellies in northern Kentucky in the fall of 1862? Have you, sir?"

Something was happening to Trainer, though it was difficult to put one's finger on it. He leaned vigorously forward, apoplectically red and belching, and hollered at the cheerful and dreamy Korovitz: "Group Sergeant, I give you a direct order to stop mouthing about what happened in northern Kentucky in the fall of 1862, or in another part of Kentucky in the spring, summer, fall, or winter of the same year or any other year. Do you hear me, I'm giving you a direct order, and if you disobey I'll throw the book at you."

"Well if you put it this way." Muttering, Korovitz moved away, but in this very instance Harrington stepped forward trim and cool as a cucumber, blowing the cobwebs away.

"Please remember, Vallejo, the most useful to the defense will be documentary evidence and names of those who consent to being interviewed or put on the stand."

"I understand, sir."

Harrington retreated to the back and plunked himself down into an armchair, while Lieberman came to where Vallejo was standing and lay a hand on his shoulder. "May God go with you." Then he turned abruptly to face Trainer. "I think it would be best if Vallejo reported directly to the defense counsel. Julian needs the information more than we do. Don't you agree?"

Trainer nodded. "Did you hear that, Captain?"

"Yes, and I am in complete agreement."

"One more question for you, Jesús," Lieberman continued. "Does Steiner know what's in the offing, has he been told?"

Vallejo smiled indulgently as though he were expecting the question and was now proven right.

"I'd gone to see Carl yesterday. At first he wouldn't hear of it and threatened to kick me right out of the cell. Then Molly came and heard what I had to say. She persuaded Carl."

Korovitz was pricking up his ears and again bellowed with laughter. "Quite a girl our Molly, tough as leather, and woe unto him that's out to harm her precious Carl."

"Yeah," Vallejo let fall dreamily, "she's something, she's like Mom." And he went on more to himself than to Lieberman, "I wish someone would tell me more about the Bund back in the thirties, it must've hit some people pretty hard . . . Carl holding it back even though he's facing a murder charge . . . I wish someone would tell me more."

From the other end of the living room Trainer's commanding voice came loud and clear.

"I think we're done. Anything else you want to bring up, John, Sol, Leroy, Vallejo, and you, Captain Harrington?" The first four made it clear there was nothing else, but Harrington uttered no sound, and Trainer came over to the armchair in which defense counsel was reclining and stood over him. There was calculated kindness in his voice. "Asleep he looks so harmless. Can you guys give me a hand in hauling him to the guest room?"

Lieberman and Korovitz got hold of the honored guest from Army, stood him up, and, offering firm support from both sides, carried him to his bed.

"We took off his coat and shoes and covered him with blankets," Lieberman said.

"A very heavy sleeper, if you ask me. Didn't budge at all." Korovitz made his own diagnosis.

"Yeah!" Trainer gave the impression of gargling. "Thank you, gentlemen, and thank you for coming. We did a good day's work."

"Ed," Fiorello caught the Group Commander off guard, "I am sorry about my outburst, I acted out of school."

"That's okay, John. No harm done, and you got it off your chest."

As his guests were crowding by the front door, he shouted, "Drive carefully, d'you hear me, drive carefully," and then he added in a more confidential tone yet still perfectly audible to the others, "A guy needs his sleep, sure, but if he takes off into the unknown in the middle of the trial, this won't look so good, I mean, in the middle of the day, with all the brass watching his every move. No sir, this won't look so good."

Chapter 8

Vallejo parked his car on a street inside the Hohenzollern Garten conveniently close to the ravishing Isabella Lake, with its bevy of rowboats admired the year round by droves of tourists and the narrow, partly unlocked gate on the left, quick entry for impatient lovers. Glancing at his wristwatch he set out on foot, cutting diagonally across the southern tip of the park to yet another entrance where the aggressive imperial buildings of the business district within a stone's throw of where he was now sagged abruptly into sooty and irregular tenement houses inside which large families struggled in cramped quarters and amid revolting hygienic conditions with the washing hanging every which way on crisscrossing lines and being daily buffeted by clouds of dust, smoke, and gravel. Here one stepped into a different Stuttgart, irredeemably removed from the splendor of Königstrasse and Schiller Platz which was to disappear shortly after 1945 when politicians of the two major parties outbid one another in glittering promises to clear the slums and embark on urban renewal unprecedented in the annals of man—a *meisterstück* of German ingenuity handily surpassing the TV tower which was to amaze the world some years later. But the promises remained unfulfilled. As political speeches multiplied and the rhetoric grew more and more inflammable, new priorities were put on the drawing boards, new coalitions formed, new party realignments cemented. The controversy, the dialogue, and the initial planning did not abate, but it was progressively more and more difficult to tell who stood for what and what precisely was being done. In the mid 1950s the epoch-making project was abandoned in favor of lesser ones, which, it was bruited, would be easier to fund and implement. But in the main, things stayed as they had been and little progress was made.

Vallejo boarded a streetcar and settled firmly down on the hard wooden bench. It was almost 1:30 P.M. on a Saturday afternoon, and the car was more than half-full with blue-collar workers on their way home after the Saturday half-shift, other nondescript workers, and mothers holding their small children snugly to their breasts. Vallejo realized at once he was viewed with ill-willed curiosity and suspicion. The inhabitants of this part of the city were not wont to see many GIs on their home streets—the allurements and temptations to which their new allies so easily fell victim were situated closer to the hub of the town, though they saw them often enough speeding in their bulky automobiles, cocky and dangerous; or if they ventured of an evening outside their working class frontiers, they had no difficulty in spotting the phalanxes of the Amis attired in strangely informal or jarring garments, or in uniform, usually neat and well-groomed. But when they took the measure of this young, dark-haired, olive-complexioned man, unshaven and demonstrably no friend to soap and water, now sitting in their midst, their minds boggled. He wore an Ami uniform, soiled and frayed at the cuffs, too short even for his moderate height so that the bottom of the trousers showed the tears and the careless patching, the collar of his shirt was dirty and crumpled, and the necktie so narrow and squeezed together that it looked like an overgrown shoelace.

He was apparently an Ami soldier—a GI, they inferred—but he was no American, no Yank, and their stereotypical conceptions of what an American looks like left no room for doubt. An air of poverty and underprivilege enveloped him, but this did not endear him to them, even though many of them were poor and their social status low, just like his, they reckoned. Perhaps he was a proletarian, victim of American capitalism that subjugated his race. Perhaps! But he was also a foreigner, an intruder in their midst, and willy-nilly they associated him with the Gehenna that had been visited upon the German nation, the humiliation of defeat, the lawlessness of the occupation, the destruction of the German state as they and their fathers and grandfathers remembered it. No, there would be little sympathy for him! Besides, he was filthy and squalid; he needed a bucket of cold water by the well, a slob, and little more, and the Germanic Virtue of cleanliness drowned militantly all the other voices in their minds.

Vallejo was counting stops. The eighth would be Herbertstrasse, where he would get off and walk three blocks to the left, to Number 77, Restaurant Dolores. He had been told even though this was the red light district it was also Bohemia and that a number of lesser known painters and writers lived on Herbertstrasse and on the adjoining streets. Walking leisurely towards the restaurant he observed keenly the dilapidated houses, the paint peeling off doors and windows, the uncollected garbage, and throngs of youngish and heavily made-up women at street corners.

"Want a quickie, Joe?" one of them asked in English, but the others squeaked and squealed in German, interrupting and trying to elbow one another out. Vallejo made a self-depreciating gesture, spread out his hands, and assumed an amicable posture. "Maybe later . . . *später* . . . *später*," he rejoiced in his use of German, hard put to break through a palisade of resisting bodies.

As soon as he set foot inside Restaurant Dolores he was impressed by its size and layout. In front stood a spacious foyer with a winding bar at the back and a few tables and chairs scattered around. You could either sit at the bar or sit at a table, but most of the patrons just stood, a beer glass in hand. To the right, the dining room was fully visible through a wide sliding door, dozens of small wooden tables stretching from wall to wall, covered with simple silverware and no tablecloth. Turning to the left you entered a roomy lounge far bigger than the foyer or the dining room filled with smaller and larger tables placed at some distance from one another so that a conversation could indeed be held in private. Vallejo suspected if the conspiracy to punish Carl Steiner for the crimes he had not committed was hatched and planned in Restaurant Dolores, it was probably here, in this lounge, round one of its functional, innocent-looking tables. In each part of the establishment glaring light flooded in all directions from a huge globe suspended from the ceiling, and its abundance made it easy to distinguish and separate each detail of the decoration on the walls, signed paintings and drawings of local artists and a profusion of patriotic Wagneriana, fearless reproductions and motifs drawn from Germanic mythology, its gods, heroes, and heroines.

The clientele was mixed, including mostly men but also some women of different social backgrounds. Streetwalkers rubbed elbows with men in business suits who may have dropped in for a quick drink if for nothing else. Working class parents with children in tow were hurrying to take their places in the dining room for the midday meal, and several well-bred women in quietly expensive clothes were keenly inspecting, with the help of a magnifying glass, the visual accomplishments of the local artists spread out on the already overcrowded walls. Here and there in the foyer and the lounge an extravert silver-haired man regaled the company with tales and insights into recent history, the indomitable spirit of the Wehrmacht, German heroism on the Russian front, the vagaries of war, mistakes made. In places other patrons could be seen: men in unorthodox habits, which had seen much wear, unshaven and unwashed, sporting berets, smoking incessantly and enclosed hermetically in their own world, and the women tense of face in trousers, their capes trailing behind them, and their thick armor-like sweaters flaunting the outdated notion of feminine attire for women. These were the keepers of the artistic flame, the toilers in the artists' colony, most of whom turned their back on traditional middle class German mores and were basking in a new sun. Conversation in the restaurant was loud and universal, and the spirit of tolerance and *Gemütlichkeit* was about. You could either remain locked in a private, intimate conversation with your companion or join others in fun and games, *chacun à son goût*. It is worth mentioning that a cub reporter from one of the Stuttgart dailies referred to Restaurant Dolores in print as the microcosm of West German society and was immediately on the carpet before his editor, whose telephone did not stop ringing with complaints from private citizens and civic groups. But this happened months ago and was promptly forgotten.

Vallejo walked up to the bar and asked for rum. "I'm Mexican," he held forth partly in English and partly in German, "rum is our national drink, demon rum, rum is for the Latinos, and it's better than whiskey ..."

"But you are serving in the American army," the bartender countered with a smile, "you're Ami."

"What matters is what's under the uniform." Vallejo went on, the grip on his emotions loosening by fits and starts. "Texas, New Mexico, Arizona were once the proud provinces of Mexico. The GIs took them away from us by force . . . animals!"

"Do you want a refill?" The bartender had his eye on the empty glass.

"Sí, why not, and pour one for yourself."

"It's too early for me," the bartender said in German, "and I have to know what I am doing. But I punched it on the cash register, and I'll have a cognac later." Then he leaned forward and said in English, "Did you understand all that?"

"Sure."

"Are you interested in female company?"

"Absolutely."

"Go to the lounge and sit down. I'll send a girl. She's not a regular, she does it on the side now and then."

Vallejo followed his advice, ordered another rum from the waitress, and waited. Soon a tall ungainly blonde stopped at his table and unceremoniously sat down.

"Jasper says you want company." Her German was so fast that Vallejo did not understand a single word.

"*Könnten Sie english sprechen?*" he began haltingly.

"Of course," and she repeated in English what she had previously uttered in German.

"Yeah, the right company, and what will you drink?"

The girl beckoned to the waitress, "*Ein cognac*," and turned again facing Vallejo. "So what are you?"

"Mexican, serving like a slave in the American army."

"You look as if you took no bath in the last ten years. And your clothes are rags."

"Supply sergeant won't issue me a new coat and uniform, he treats me like dirt."

Still holding the half-full glass of cognac stylishly at arm's length, the girl subjected him to a prolonged scrutiny, saying nothing, with only her light blue eyes drilling into him in search of secrets. There was no hostility or sympathy in those eyes, only a determination to get to the bottom of what he might be hiding, and no premature judgments for or against him.

He matched her stony looks with stony looks of his own, eye for

eye, stillness for stillness, and was struck how hard her face was, not tense
or deliberately frozen, but just plain hard with not even a ghost of
humor or coquettishness. At long last she put the glass on the table and
lit another cigarette.

"I understand your dislike of the Americans, the American soldiers
killed my father after he surrendered to them at the end of the war. He
was a sergeant in the Waffen SS, and they kicked him to death, yes
kicked and kicked him again, the whole platoon of them, till there was
no more life in him. *Die Schweine!*"

"I am very sorry," Vallejo muttered, "yes, yes, *die Schweine.*"

"I'll be busy for the next few hours," the girl let it be known in a
strict business-like fashion, "but if you're still here after six or so, we'll
go to my place. My name's Helga, it's twenty marks for a quickie, fifty
for an hour. What's your name, Mexican?"

"Jesús," Vallejo intimated in a low voice. "Jesús Vallejo."

"Jesús," she repeated, and a sudden ray of amusement shot across her
face.

"Well, ciao!"

"Ciao."

Vallejo decided to mingle. He had a beer at the bar and introduced
himself to those standing by, shaking hands and sounding again and
again his pat repertoire of the ill-used Mexican in the clutches of the
evil Yanks. Several patrons struck up a conversation with him, expressed
sympathy, asked how he took to being stationed in Germany, and in the
spirit of conviviality he bought drinks for them, listened patiently to
their kindly meant mixture of German, English, and Spanish, and asked
tourist-like questions that would embarrass nobody. He was enjoying
himself. After a while he reentered the lounge, and as there were now
hardly any unoccupied tables he sauntered across and stopped by a boy
and a girl sitting snugly together, the smallest procurable beer glasses in
front of them. He asked if he could join them, and they nodded with
alacrity, laughing, kissing, and then laughing again. *How very young they
look,* he thought, and he fully expected a parent or both parents to barge
out of the restrooms to watch again over their precious offspring. But
his belief that the boy and the girl were siblings, perhaps twins, had to
be qualified as the affection they so passionately showered on each
other was of a distinctly un-brotherly and un-sisterly kind, even though
what caught the eye was a remarkable family likeness, or in its absence

a chance likeness as remarkable as that which in ninety-nine cases out of a hundred consanguinity, and only consanguinity, creates.

Slight of build, their blond hair was of the same hue and texture, their delicate features very nearly replicating each other, their heads shaped from the same mold, the high forehead infusing composure, their baby blues prominent and identical. Even more arresting on each face was the absolute frankness of expression, kindness, innocence, a smiling satisfaction, indestructible inner bliss. Soon the three of them were engrossed in conversation—their names were Frida and Stephan, they were both seventeen, deeply in love, and incapable of living away from each other. But her parents did not approve, and they were on their own, making ends meet toiling as laborers in a nearby paper factory, and waiting until they were eighteen, the legal age to marry.

"I hope I won't get pregnant," Frida was saying. "We don't want a child yet."

And Stephan, caressing her hands and arms, kept reassuring her, "We take all the precautions, *mein Schatz*, all the precautions."

"Even so, it can happen," Frida persisted. "I am afraid, afraid."

Vallejo did his best to chase her dark thoughts away, and then he said: "How about getting something to eat? I could eat a horse."

Stephan looked at him embarrassedly from the corner of his eye. "We don't get paid till next Friday. You go ahead, Jesús."

"We'll all go," and dismissing their mild protestations, Vallejo led the way to the dining room.

Over meatloaf, pommes frites, and cooked vegetables, Vallejo told them more about himself, playing down his secret mission and voicing interest in seeing more of the German countryside and especially those marvels of Stuttgart and its environs which could never be erased from a thoughtful man's itinerary.

"You have to see the T.V. tower," both of them exclaimed, their eyes flashing. "It's tremendous, indescribable."

"Absolutely," Vallejo promised. "I'll tie a knot on my left sock."

And Frida, now in the role of a tourist guide, began to tell him about the Stuttgart Zoo, the Weissenburg Park, the sommerfest, and other wonderful places and events in the town itself and in its proximity that must be visited at all costs.

Soon the conversation shifted to movies. "Your Humphrey Bogart is one hell of an actor, and so is John Wayne, they're supermen," Stephan went on excitedly.

"Oh yes," Frida joined him, "they are like no one else, two peerless originals."

"Which of their movies did you like the most?"

But his dinner companions were in a quandary.

"We can't remember the titles." Stephan was scratching his chin.

"We saw several Bogart and Wayne movies . . ." Frida became pensive, knitting her brow and making a gallant effort.

"I don't know why, but we pay no attention to titles, only to the content," Stephan tried to explain lamely. "I don't know why this is so."

"I think I understand," Vallejo assured him. As the conversation continued, Vallejo cast an idle glance around the dining room. Several tables to the right he spotted two men, one middle-aged and the other in his late teens or early twenties, who were watching him intently while pretending to admire a set of new drawings on the wall. These were the same two men with whom he had clinked glasses by the bar and who were positioned in the lounge several tables away when he sat down with Stephan and Frida. Here they were again! Vallejo moved his chair a few inches to the right so that he could observe them from the corner of his eye while pretending to be looking the German couple in the face. He saw the older man's lips move on and on as if he were giving detailed instructions to his friend, but he could not catch a sound. The younger man nodded briskly several times, and his lips moved too but only for an abrupt moment. Vallejo was hypothesizing he was acknowledging or confirming. He apparently had no questions to ask and, at any rate, this was not a staff meeting. Vallejo took pains to engrave the two men, their facial expressions, gestures, and body movements on his memory so that he could recognize them again wearing different clothes and possibly a disguise.

Deep inside, something hammered at his gut that Bund 45 had taken note of him, no more, no less. Next he began to clear his plate, as he had been taught at home ever since his toddler days, and heard Frida's voice.

"Do you have brothers and sisters, Jesús, or are you the only child, apple of your parents' eye?"

"I have an older brother and a younger sister."

"Oh, what are their ages?"

"Miguel is twenty-three and a medical student, and Andrea sixteen; she hasn't got the faintest idea what she wants to do with her life apart from going dancing and listening to records."

"Give her time, don't be a bullying brother."

"I am not," he laughed. "And you, Frida?"

"I have two older sisters, but . . . we are not on good terms."

"And you, Stephan?" The young man looked furtively away and fetched up a bleak smile.

"I don't know if I have any brothers or sisters, I just don't."

"Stephan is a Berliner and proud of it, considering how much Berlin has been through . . . as for me I was born right here in Stuttgart, my family has lived here for generations, but I have no special attachment to it . . ." She paused, and her face lit up in an artless, celestial way as if she heard a whisper of extraordinarily good news in her ear that the birthday presents could at last be opened.

"My attachment is to Stephan and to Stephan alone," she said firmly, lovingly.

"And my attachment is to Frida and to no one and nothing else," and they began to kiss wildly, forgetting the world, forgetting the rest of the human race.

Vallejo kept them company for a little longer and at the appropriate time bid his adieus.

"We shall see you again, of course?" Stephan asked with a glint in his eye.

"Of course, next Friday or Saturday."

"You've been very kind to us, and we won't forget it."

"Thank you for the meal," Frida whispered. "You're like a good angel, come from Heaven."

"We are moving to a new place, and once in we'll want you to come and visit us. Frida will cook one of her specialties, she's a darn good cook."

"Of this I have no doubt."

After hearty handshaking Vallejo left them to digest their dessert, and as he was about to step into the foyer he noticed the two men who had taken such a keen interest in him were no longer sitting at their table.

He was brushing off his tattered overcoat and uniform when Jasper, the bartender, accosted him.

"Frau Schrämer would like a word with you, Jesús."

"Who's Frau Schrämer?"

"She's well-known in the community and a valued customer; she owns a grocery store down the road."

"And she wants to take me on as a checker?"

"Be serious, *Junge*, she's a very influential lady. When she speaks we click our heels."

"No shit!"

"Be on your best behavior and no foul language!"

"I swear on the graves of my Moravian ancestors."

Hardly were these words out of his mouth when a plumpish woman in her late forties or early fifties daringly dressed in a long, dark fur-coat underneath which the jarring colors of her blouse, skirt, and scarf fought for recognition against the overlying somberness, and sporting an extravagant hat stood before him. She could easily have been mistaken for a tribal matron from some exotic land flown to the Western world on the strength of a bureaucratic foul-up or worse, a political misjudgment of the first magnitude, now clinging desperately to her indigenous way of life under the thick veneer of a Western top-coat.

"*Ich bin* Frau Schrämer," she announced in a hoarse, low voice, holding out her hand, and Vallejo mumbled his name.

"*Also*, Jasper." Her fingers danced in the air in an unmistakable gesture. "*Sie werden übersetzen.*"

"*Jawohl*, Frau Schrämer," and Jasper reeled on his heel to have both of them in his line of vision.

"I have to compliment you, young man, on your kindness towards Frida and Stephan. I saw you extending hospitality to those two children of God lost in the callous adult world of egoism and chicanery. You did the right thing. I am being kept informed."

Jasper stopped. "And now I'll translate into German what you want to say."

"Thank you very much for your gracious words, ma'am. It was a pleasure to be of help, however insignificant my help may have been."

Jasper translated into German and reverted to his primary duty.

"I don't mind telling you, Mr. Vallejo, that in some respects our German mores are outdated and therefore useless. Frida's parents threw her out of their home because she refused to give up her lover.

Goodness me! The sooner we wake up to the fact that we no longer live under Kaiser Wilhelm, the better it will be for the country, and I speak as a patriotic German woman."

"Anything on the tip of your tongue?" Jasper asked scornfully.

"Nothing, let her rile on till the cows come home."

Jasper frowned and continued.

"We urgently need progressive thought in all areas of human endeavor, in all countries, and it can't be too soon."

"I agree one hundred percent."

"Good! I am glad you have a progressive mind," and she drew nearer to him. "I understand you are ill-treated by the American Command because you are not an American . . ."

"Mexican-American."

"Such subtleties elude me, but a situation like this could never have arisen in the German army. Take my word for it. Nevertheless, we mustn't dwell endlessly on what is depressing and macabre. There should always be a lighter side. You have shown yourself in your true colors and we applaud. Sometime soon I should like to invite you to my house for tea. We can spend a pleasant hour together. But you must dress better and for goodness' sake take a bath. I hope to see you again soon. Jasper will tell you how to reach me." She briefly stroked his arm and turned on her heel.

"*Auf wiedersehen,* Frau Schrämer," Jasper was exuding respect, and the wide-eyed Vallejo stood there helplessly tongue-tied until words formed themselves of their own volition in his throat and rang out:

"*Jawohl,* Frau Schrämer, *Jawohl,* Frau Schrämer."

"Do you fancy older women, Jesús?" The smirk glued to Jasper's face was slithering double-quick in all directions.

"Sure, preferably the age of my great-grandmothers and confined to a wheelchair twenty-four hours a day."

"Always the comedian."

"Is it true Frida's parents kicked her out?"

"It is, they are wealthy, an old Swabian family."

"And Stephan?"

"He's an orphan with no family, no education, no prospects. He'll never amount to anything."

"So all they have is their love."

"You could put it that way."

Vallejo moved towards the front door and halted. "Where the hell did you learn that super-fluent English of yours, Jasper?"

"Four years in POW Camp, two years in England, two years in the U.S. I was in the Afrika Corps, captured in 1942; in the U.S. our POW camp was in the state of Missouri, I liked Missouri, and I liked the people."

"Good, I'm glad."

"And now I think I'll have that cognac you kindly treated me to, Jesús. By the way, you made a highly favorable impression of the kind no other GI even came close to in this establishment. So we hope to see you again soon."

"Thanks, take care."

"You too."

Vallejo moved further towards the front door and halted again. At the very far end of the lounge, at a table adjoining the wall two men and a woman were bending towards one another, their heads almost touching, to all appearances consumed by an urgent topic. His two watchers and Helga!

"Maybe I planted enough seeds for today," Vallejo said to himself and pushed the front door wide open. He could see the sun, a ball of fire perched over the horizon sinking fast into oblivion, and felt the cool breeze of the approaching evening. At the first street corner he heard the familiar voice of the girl who had called to him in English when he was on his way to Restaurant Dolores. Something about her now caught his fancy, the upturned nose, the quick roving eye, the smooth cheek, and the folds of her body so infinitely alluring, which he saw clearly in his mind's eye. He stopped and was watching her, and she was watching him but for no more than a moment.

"*Also, Junge, komm, komm,*" she meowed, "I have a room round the corner, but first you have to wash."

And he, finding a new resolution within his breast and new words to hurl it with into the world, called out with spirit, "*Ich komme, ich komme,*" and eagerly surged forward.

/ / /

"They are evil men, a bad lot, Chaplain." Pastor Günthers handed Lieberman a glass of wine and was shaking his head in shivering repugnance. "*Ja, ja,* there had been incidents before," he went on haltingly, "but our police could not find . . . could not find . . ."

"Sufficient proof?" Lieberman supplied the words with a question mark.

"*Richtig, ja,* sufficient proof . . . the evidence was weak and circum . . ."

"Circumstantial, Dr. Günthers?"

"*Jawohl,* circumstantial, Chaplain."

Günthers' eyes traveled all the way to the far end of the living room where a massive clock fitted into an equally massive oak stand and embossed on all sides, a precious piece of furniture and a steadfast timekeeper, proclaimed in silent dignity the time. It was five minutes to three.

"*Aber, wo ist sie,* where is she!" Günthers exclaimed with some impatience.

"Who?"

"My niece Nina . . . she's fluent in English . . . to translate for us, I understand everything you say, but cannot find . . . the right words in a foreign tongue . . ."

"Oh yes, I remember your mentioning her."

Just then the door connecting the living room and the hall was hurriedly opened, and a very attractive, dark-haired girl in her early twenties stepped in smiling merrily. She walked up with aplomb to Günthers, kissed him on the cheek, and twittered in English.

"I am terribly sorry to be late, Uncle, but my mother and aunt are still hopping from one shop to the next, and I simply forgot all about the time."

"*Ja, ja, ja,* Nina, but time is time."

"Uncle Joachim"—she twittered again—"I apologize most abjectly for my tardiness and am the first to admit it is inexcusable and will forever tarnish my reputation as a member of the Günthers family."

The pastor spread out his hands. "Nina, *ich bitte dich,* this is not the place for rhetorical exercises."

She smiled enchantingly and turned towards the American visitor, but Günthers, now fully recovered after a moment of pique, assumed control.

"Chaplain Lieberman, this is my niece Nina Günthers, daughter of my younger brother Klemens, and Nina, this is Captain Solomon

Lieberman, chaplain at 16th U.S. Army Engineer Group which is stationed here in Kirchenberg." He was succinct and to the point.

"How do you do, Captain?" She bent her head slightly, again smiled enchantingly, and held out her hand.

"How do you do, Fräulein Günthers?"

"And how is your congregation?"

"My congregation." Taken unawares, Lieberman repeated these words as one repeats an expression wholly unfamiliar and perhaps incomprehensible in order to open a crack in the door of one's consciousness in search of scant understanding, if nothing else.

"Yes, you're right of course, 16th U.S. Army Engineer Group is my congregation. But Army chaplains are mostly in demand on certain painful occasions, compassionate leaves, deaths and births, non-legal arbitration, and such like. Most of the time no one listens to us."

"Pity," she said softly, and gradually she became composed, all sauciness spent. Then she began to watch him with piercing attentiveness, and he reciprocated with mounting interest, his tenderness held in check.

"You are a student, I understand," he asked gently.

"Third year architecture student at Tübingen," she replied, and now her gaze was directed far away from him, into limitless space, doggedly, abstractedly.

"I'd like to pay you a visit at Tübingen. I haven't seen the university."

"I would like that." And she was still shut up in herself, secluded from him and all else.

Günthers' rousing words broke the spell.

"I must tell the captain many things, we mustn't waste time, the captain is a busy man," he began intermingling the two languages, "and you will translate, *liebchen.*"

"*Selbst-verständlich, Onkel Joachim.*"

He motioned to her. "Nowadays people waste so much time. When I was young we always had our instructions, our schedules, from parents, teachers, our superiors, those in charge; we didn't waste time. But now everyone is in charge, everyone is a law unto himself or herself, this is anarchy."

Nina stopped as Günthers walked over to the side table to refill the wine glasses.

"Uncle Joachim is a sweet man," she said in an undertone, "but the world has turned over many times in the last fifty years, and he just refused to budge."

"Also," Günthers handed Lieberman the glass and again motioned to Nina.

"As I was saying, Bund 45 is a criminal lot, and its members are drawn mostly from the ranks of former Waffen SS, the Gestapo, soldiers of fortune, and neo-Nazis. All are fanatical and ruthless. In Stuttgart, two names are particularly relevant, Florian von Vogelsee, a former captain in the SS . . . oh, he would be in his early fifties now, and his trusty lieutenant Hans Ketterer, he's very young, far too young to have fought in the second World War, he's in his early twenties. Vogelsee is reputed to be the chief of the Stuttgart Chapter, and he is highly intelligent, resourceful, thorough."

"So you think the Steiner operation was mapped out in Stuttgart?"

"I should think so, local chapters are responsible for all the planning and execution of the planning, and the head office in Nüremberg seldom interferes."

"A German national was killed, and you think this was intentional?"

Günthers smiled the assured smile of the high priest who knows infinitely more than all the neophytes thrown together.

"After I'd received your call, Chaplain, I called my brother Klemens, Nina's father," he pointed to her with a flourishing gesture, "an eminent member of the legal profession," and Nina tossed her head back and beamed with the devoted histrionics of the family pride. "But Klemens could tell me little apart from the fact that our police knows more about Bund 45 than is willing to tell," he paused. "My brother is what you call a corporation lawyer, he represents very large corporations, not thieves and murderers." He paused again. "So I called a friend of mine on the police force in Stuttgart, and he told me Dieter Hauch, the man who was killed on your base, had been suspected for a long time of being an active member of the Bund. He also said something else, namely that Hauch had had difficulties with the Bund; I asked, of course, what kind of difficulties, but my friend said he couldn't tell me any more. His lips were sealed."

"And you think . . . ?"

"It is entirely possible Hauch was killed by Bund 45, for some infraction he'd committed, or maybe he was becoming an embarrassment."

"And the blame was laid on Carl Steiner, whom we always believed to be innocent?"

"That is right," and Günthers took a step back, like a well-trained rhetorician nimble on his feet who knows the audience expects him to stir this way and that to give credence to the analogy of an active mind in an active body. A stout smile now adorned his features, both cryptic and self-congratulatory, and he threw his hand high up signaling to Nina he would brave that devilishly tricky English language himself. Drawing himself up and transfixing Lieberman with a bold stare, he enunciated slowly and carefully:

"This was what you call killing two birds with one stone."

"If this is what happened, you're absolutely right."

And Nina, speaking for her uncle again, asserted, "I believe this is precisely what happened."

Günthers and Lieberman continued to review the subject for another half-hour, availing themselves of Nina's help, with only one interruption the pastor asking whether his niece knew when her mother and her aunt would be returning and receiving a prompt answer to the effect that with so many garage sales held on this Saturday afternoon the time of their return was anybody's guess.

"They are buying things for the church, drapes, etc., etc.," he grimly informed his guest.

Soon Lieberman rose to his feet.

"I am afraid I have to go now, and I want to thank you again for the valuable information."

"You are very welcome, Captain," and then a memory pricked his mind.

"Captain Lieberman, my wife and I are looking forward to meeting your wife and family. What are your sons' names again?"

"Matthew and Solomon, Jr."

"Quite so. The next time we would like to see the four of you in our humble abode."

"It will be our pleasure."

"We shall telephone and hope you will come soon."

"We shall, and thank you again for your help, Pastor."

When Lieberman shook hands with Nina, she looked him straight in the eye, bold yet on the defensive at the same time, wanting something desperately yet ready to go to any length to protect her independence and her entire being, as this being was constituted and as she knew it, rightly or wrongly, to be constituted.

"I shall see you in Tübingen," the words came out awkwardly, as if marred by gaucherie and a strangely unexpected irresoluteness, and she merely nodded her head.

When Günthers accompanied him to the front door, he caught sight of her again standing by the large French window in the living room, an erect immobile figure, her face frozen into implacable, unrelenting contemplation.

/   /   /

Hal Shelton put his foot on the brake and veered into Spruce Street. He had been given the number of Colonel Trainer's duplex by Vallejo, and now as the houses with their prominently displayed numbers and the equally prominent names of the occupants proudly recorded on the mailboxes stole by in silent review, he knew he was nearing his destination. A VW bug with German license plates appeared out of nowhere and shot by him, the driver a youngish woman of whom Shelton barely caught sight being apparently in a great hurry to leave the Village. He consulted his wristwatch—it was almost noon on a warm, blue-skied Sunday at the very beginning of May—and now Trainer's house was looming before him. He lifted the knocker, let it fall several times, and waited. Without delay the front door was thrust open, and Colonel Trainer, draped in an ornate Japanese-style robe, his hair ruffled and a half-consumed cheroot hanging roguishly from between his lips, stood before him.

"What d'you want, and who the hell are you?" he barked, his eyes narrowing in cold-blooded suspicion.

"Specialist Hal Shelton, 16th Engineer Group"—and he saluted—"request permission to speak to you now about the Steiner operation. It's urgent."

Trainer's hard features, thickly crisscrossed by wrinkles, widening furrows, black spots, and shaving cuts, broke into a half-smile.

"I didn't recognize you in civvies, young man," and he returned the salute. "Come in."

Seated on the living room couch, a cup of highly aromatic coffee in hand, Shelton came straight to the point.

"Jesús may have made contact with the Bund, and they know his name."

"Right."

"The first thing they'll probably do is check on him, and," Shelton hesitated for a very brief spell, "he may have overdone the duds. He'd gone to Restaurant Dolores dressed no better than a beggar."

"Doesn't it square with what he wants them to believe, that he's ill-used, discriminated against, treated like dirt on base by every officer and NCO?"

"Possibly, sir, but next time he'll have to be dressed like a regular GI."

Trainer was eyeing him with boredom.

"Fine, that's Vallejo's responsibility and yours too. But I agree he shouldn't be walking into the lion's den dressed like a bum. This will only arouse suspicions."

"Yes, sir, Vallejo and I have everything planned for the future, and anyway this is not why I came to see you at your home on a Sunday."

"What you really want to talk to me about is the Bund checking on him here on base."

"That's right, sir. By the process of elimination we concluded the most likely candidate for a Bund member working undercover on base is Frau Gruber, Natalie Gruber, the librarian in charge of our minuscule Group library."

Trainer's facial expression was sending rapid signals of unqualified astonishment.

"Frau Gruber, that very respectful elderly dame who practically clicks her heels when I enter her little kingdom; not that I visit it that often."

"I have a buddy at Army, strategically placed I might add, who did some checking for me. Natalie Gruber is fifty-eight, she was born in what was then East Prussia. She joined the National Socialist Party in 1924 and has been a dedicated Nazi ever since. After 1933 she was employed in the Ministry of Propaganda. Her husband, also an enthusiastic supporter of Adolf Hitler, was killed in an air raid in 1945. After the war Frau Gruber joined several right-wing organizations and worked for two of them. In 1955 she began to work for the American

Army as a librarian, and after a spell in Mannheim she came to us in 1956."

"Don't our people screen German nationals who apply to us for employment?" Trainer tossed out the question with bitterness.

"We did until early 1955. Beginning in the fall of that year we practically stopped all screening of German applicants, checking only with German authorities if there was a criminal record." Shelton spoke calmly and with assurance.

"So Gruber could've put down on her application she was a Party member . . ."

"Yes, Colonel, she could've and no one would've noticed or cared."

"Lousy hiring procedures, them jockers at 7th Army Headquarters don't know what the hell they are doing. Always said so," Trainer grumbled in the same bitter vein. "But are you reasonably certain she's the one?"

"Yes, reasonably certain, you've chosen your words well, sir. The other German nationals who have access to the base are workmen and salesmen, and they have little opportunity for observing or finding out what's going on. Also Gruber was seen on base on the night of the murder."

Trainer refilled the coffee cups and sat in utter silence, strenuously blowing out gigantic clouds of smoke. Then he hoisted himself up in his armchair, leaned towards Shelton, and with clumsiness peculiarly his own hardened by a newly-awakened mettle asked through his teeth: "What's your plan, son?"

"Vallejo lay on pretty thick he can't get a new uniform and overcoat from the Supply Sergeant who loathes him, and this should be borne in mind. Colonel, could you set up a bogus summary court-martial for Jesús charging him with extremely sloppy physical appearance, disrespect towards some NCOs and officers, and whatever else your heart desires? This might help convince the Bund our Mexican-American original was telling the truth, and it is essential, absolutely essential that they are convinced."

"I guess this could be fixed, but not too many charges, 'cause if we cross the line, then a special court-martial is called for, and we don't want that, do we now?"

"No, sir, we don't want that." Shelton sprang to his feet, took a few steps around the living room, and resumed his seat.

"If you can arrange the court-martial, I shall see to it that Frau Gruber is made aware of it. She is the Bund's operative on base."

Then he went on suggesting to Trainer the steps which ought to be taken to draw maximum attention to the bogus court-martial at 16th Engineer Group at 7th Army Headquarters at Weiningen; the advantages that would accrue to Jesús in the prosecution of his dangerous mission, and the very real possibility the Bund would again show its hand.

Trainer listened, summing Shelton up. Here was a young soldier planning and outlining what was beyond a doubt a delicate and dangerous operation, and he took it in his stride, cool as a cucumber, precise to the last detail. He showed no sign of nervousness or hesitancy, and though laboring under considerable pressure he neither flinched nor winced. Just the reverse, his speech grew slower and more deliberate, emphasizing certain aspects of the situation in a quiet, authoritative way, and his decisiveness and self-assurance were as firm as the hardest rock. *He would perform well under fire,* Trainer thought, *could be entrusted with any mission and would not break. He's the guy I'd like to have standing next to me when the chips are down,* the thought forced itself upon him.

"Thank you, Specialist, you have the matter in hand."

"Thank you, sir."

"And where's Vallejo today?"

"He's on the job, spent the night in Stuttgart."

"Oh! Anything else you want to bring up?"

"No, sir, except that we may be moving soon to phase two of the operation."

Trainer nodded. Lighting up another cheroot with gusto, he smiled pryingly at the now unobtrusive Shelton.

"You know, your name keeps bumping around in my head; did you have a brother or a close relative in the Service?"

"My two brothers, Bob and Jeff, were in Korea; they are both dead."

"Did you say Bob?"

"Yes, sir."

"Not Sergeant Bob Shelton of the Hungnan fame?"

"The same, if you put it this way."

"What was his full name?"

"Robert Lee Shelton."

"Right, we spent many an evening shooting the breeze," Trainer exclaimed enthusiastically, "a regular guy and a fine trooper. Anyway his record speaks for itself. He led his men to victory at Hutshon, and when the reinforcements didn't come, and why they didn't no one knows to this very day, he led his men back through that goddamn gorge, seeing that everyone was safe, and being the last to retreat. I only regret the Congressional Medal wasn't given to him in person and not posthumously. Your brother was a hero, son."

"He made all of us very proud."

"And your other brother, what was the full name?"

"Sergeant Jefferson Davis Shelton, sir, he was taken prisoner by the North Koreans. We didn't hear anything for a long time. Finally around Easter of 1955 we received a telegram from the State Department informing us North Korean authorities had advised them Jeff had been killed trying to escape from POW camp. Nothing since."

Trainer shook his head in mounting anger. "Those goddamn gooks, maybe MacArthur was right, maybe we should've gone the whole hog."

"We shall never know."

"I hope you're planning to make the Army your career, Shelton."

"No, sir, I am not," Trainer's visitor announced quietly. "My three-year enlistment ends this July, in less than three months, and my folks are planning a big wedding for us in Alexandria on July 28th."

"And your fiancée?" Trainer asked, warming to the subject.

"Brigitta, she's a German born and bred in Stuttgart. She's a nurse."

"And you're a medic!" Trainer called out, making it clear with a sweep of the hand he was contributing entirely novel elements to the conversation. "Have the two families met?"

"They have indeed, sir"—Shelton was making himself more comfortable on the couch—"early last year Brigitta's parents flew to Virginia and spent a week with my parents, and last Christmas my parents flew in to Stuttgart, and we were all together at my future in-laws."

"And they got along?"

"Like a house on fire, actually my dad and her dad are in the same line of business."

"And what's that?" By now Trainer was completely absorbed in Shelton's marital plans.

"Contracting," and Shelton chuckled, "except that Brigitta's dad owns his own business, and mine is the general manager for a contractor."

"Still close on the vine. Sure hope it don't create no problems."

Shelton chuckled again, "It hasn't so far, and besides it's Brigitta and me who matter, not the families, and she's one wonderful girl."

"I'm sure she is and my congratulations, but"—an inquisitive smirk affixed itself to Trainer's face—"are you positive you don't want to make the Army your home? We need men like you."

Shelton drained the last drop of the aromatic coffee from the cup and swiveled his eyes in all directions.

"You may not know it, sir, but in the South much more than in the North many of us enlist in one of the Services for three or four years, usually right after high school, or when we are still in our teens or early twenties. For some it is the honor of serving our country, others hope to learn a trade or become more proficient in it by being in the Service, and others still are finding themselves and deciding what to do with their lives. Or it may be a combination of all three, but irrespective of the reasons the Armed Forces of the United States are important to us in the South, all of us salute them, and many of us want to be associated with them. They are the backbone of the nation."

Trainer smiled. "I know it, I know it full well."

"When I enlisted for three years it was with the intention of working as a nurse and a lab technician, and the Army approved my request. During those three years I have greatly enhanced my skills and obtained higher diplomas in my profession. I am now much better qualified than I was before my enlistment. Maybe I got much more out of the Army than the Army got out of me. Maybe so, and right now I have no means of finding out. But I hope the gain, and whatever it may have entailed, is not entirely one-sided."

"I am sure the gain is not one-sided," Trainer said gravely. "Both you and the Army benefited, and this is the American way."

"Thank you, sir."

"So both you and your future wife will be employed in a medical capacity stateside?"

"Absolutely, in Virginia or as close to it as possible. We have our different specializations which hopefully will make us more marketable, and we have already been sending out inquiries and applications."

"You're certainly on the ball, Specialist," and Trainer accompanied these words with a pronouncedly foxy smile.

"So are you, sir."

"Thank you. I am very glad you came to see me, and I was happy to find out who you are. It was a pleasure. Furthermore, what you told me was important and urgent. Feel free to contact me at any time."

And as Shelton was slowly rising to his feet from the tempting softness of the couch, Trainer added in a commanding tone: "I shall speak to Major Fiorello tonight. We'll arrange for that bogus court-martial for Vallejo, and anything else to prove Carl's innocence. Keep me informed, and I thank you for what you're doing."

Shelton standing at attention was saluting, and Trainer in the process of standing up was bravely gathering to his bosom the multifarious folds and edges of that enormous Japanese-style robe in which he was still draped and saluting at the same time. He looked, if only for a second, like a figure of immense status and rank far exceeding the mere colonelcy in the United States Army.

"I want you to know it's an honor to have a Shelton in my outfit." But one more question hammered at his brain. "I have the full names of your two brothers, and what, pray, is your full name?"

"I am Hal Beauregard Shelton, sir," the young man answered, smiling gently and closing the front door behind him while Trainer muttered to himself, "Golly, I hit the jackpot, and there ain't no mistake."

He was going to pour himself a drink when the telephone rang. Mustering his sternest and most forbidding manner he rasped into the receiver, "Colonel Trainer here," and became at once affable and charming.

"I'm delighted to hear from you, Fräulein Doktor, absolutely delighted." He listened and then went on: "That's great . . . just great . . . I am sure the information you have about Bund 45 will be of great value to us." He paused and said, "I agree we shouldn't be talking about it on the phone." He paused again and said, "No it isn't a short notice at all, besides, the sooner I have this information the better. . . Would you give me the address of your mother's house?" He waited, wrote it down, and read it back slowly. "Thanks again, Fräulein Doktor, I'll see you around 5:00 P.M. this afternoon then," and he uttered the last two words with conspicuous relish, "*Auf wiedersehen.*"

/   /   /

It was Vallejo's third visit to Restaurant Dolores. The first and memorable one took place on the previous Saturday, the second on the following Thursday when once again he sowed the seeds of seething discontent and of vindictiveness against his military bosses. But on Thursday the attendance at the restaurant was thinner than on weekends, and there were fewer patrons to whom he could carry his mission. Still, he knew he was closely watched, and there was no dearth of eavesdroppers nearby. The two men who had taken such keen interest in him on Saturday, Florian von Vogelsee and Hans Ketterer he surmised, kept observing him from a distance, and Helga was faithfully in attendance, again offering her services. Already during the second visit Vallejo had presented himself in civilian clothes—"mufti of GI variety" as a perceptive Stuttgarter had once dubbed such incongruous parts of civilian attire—and nothing in his appearance had distinguished him from hundreds of other GIs roaming the streets of the city. He had also taken care to shower and shave before setting out on his mission. He knew that on Thursday he had made his presence better known to the motley crowd and had again asserted his availability to give a twisted turn to his venom. He would persevere and bide his time.

And now as he was thrusting back the front door of the restaurant on this clammy Saturday afternoon, one week after first crossing its threshold, he experienced an uncanny sensation that something would happen today that would bring him much closer to his goal. Adroitly carrying on several conversations at the same time with starkly dissimilar patrons, the trim Jasper stood at his usual place behind the bar and beckoned to him.

"I have a message for you from Frida and Stephan, they won't be here today, they are working overtime, that's good because they need the money, and they hope to see you next Saturday."

Vallejo thanked Jasper and exchanged a few idle words with him. Then he walked over to the lounge and sat down at a secluded table in the far left corner. He ordered rum and let his eyes wander over the smooching couples, the gaudy parties, an occasional lone wolf scattered hither and thither. Presently someone patted him on the shoulder. He turned round and saw a tall, bespectacled, middle-aged stranger, wearing a dark expensive-looking suit befitting members of the well-paid professions, beaming at him.

"Let me introduce myself"—the stranger spoke with a distinctly British accent—"I am Willy Gisevius, and I am a businessman here in Stuttgart."

"Hi, how do you do?" Vallejo was promptly reminding himself his English should not always be grammatical and his expression flawless. He pronounced his name slowly, and he added a few words in Spanish. After cordial handshaking Gisevius at Vallejo's invitation sat down and immediately launched into a preamble.

"I hear from Jasper and the others you are a Mexican serving in the American army, and some of us in the private sector, in business and in the press, are very interested in the views you and others like you hold with regards to the Western world and particularly with regard to the United States. We are more than willing to pay well for your opinions . . . and for any valuable information you'd care to supply." He paused and added with emphasis, "You can count on our absolute discretion."

"You don't have to pay me nothin'," Vallejo rasped, gulping the rum. "I'll give you the lowdown on how the Yanks treat us free of charge."

"The lowdown?" Gisevius questioned with a patronizing smile. "The inside story, you mean?"

"That's right, Mister, and you can have it any time."

Gisevius moved his chair closer to Vallejo. "You know, nowadays no place is an island and news travels fast. I understand that you, Mr. Vallejo, are facing a summary court-martial. I heard it from several American officers who are friends of mine."

"That's right, Herr Gisevius, I'll be court-martialed because the Army is out to get me. I speak freely about the exploitation of the Mexican people in New Mexico, and I make no bones about discrimination against minorities in the Service."

Gisevius ordered more drinks and asked invitingly: "Will you try some German Schnapps? I think you'll like it."

"Why not! And . . . thanks."

As they tasted the potent brew Gisevius began to speak in a confidential manner.

"It pains me and many of my friends that so much injustice is perpetuated under our very noses. I belong to various charitable organizations and our common goal is to help stamp out injustice everywhere. The Americans have absolutely no right to treat you and your compatriots in this contemptible way. For centuries Germany has been the haven of religious freedom, center of scientific research, and mainstay of civil rights. We empathize with you, we suffer with you, and we want to help." He paused and diligently probed those prominent Mexican eyes, the olive complexion, the spare regular features cast into immobility. Vallejo was thinking fast. This bout of national self-righteousness in presenting Germany as a liberal, democratic haven where everyone's civil rights had been protected for centuries and especially in the present century was staged, he concluded, for his benefit alone. But did the guy really think that he, Vallejo, had not heard of the German atrocities committed before and during the second World War, of the Nazi concentration camps, of the Holocaust? Could he seriously entertain such a notion? It was hard to believe that he could since he appeared to be well educated and a pillar of society. Or was this self-deluding palaver merely a trap to throw him off his guard? Vallejo wondered. Was Gisevius' first assumption—if it really was his assumption—that Vallejo's one and only enemy was the Anglo power structure that kept him and other Mexican-Americans down to be taken at face value? And was his second assumption—if it really was his assumption—that Vallejo would accept West Germany as his protector and ultimate liberator in his fight against the U.S. Army also to be taken at face value? Vallejo felt he was standing with one foot at least in the realm of fantasy because things did not add up. His instinct told him to be doubly vigilant at all times, and his sense of mission pressed him to play along because he might be on to something even though what he saw and heard was nothing short of fantastic.

"I can use all the help I can get," Vallejo cried. "I'm just one guy against the whole Army . . . the whole complex."

"We'll help, but you have to keep faith with us," Gisevius warned him.

"I will, I will, Herr Gisevius," Vallejo cried again with mounting fervor. "You got it!"

A cautious smile settled on the older man's countenance.

"If you're so stirred up, wouldn't you like to pay back those bastards for what they did to you?"

"It goes without saying, but how?"

"Maybe we can devise a way," but Gisevius made light of it and turned to another subject. "The American army has injured and ruined a great many Germans. It has also killed. Jasper tells me you are with the 16th Engineer Group in Kirchenberg . . ." Vallejo nodded emphatically. "In that case you know what your Sergeant Steiner did . . . He killed an innocent man, a hardworking German technician."

"He's going away for a long time," Vallejo allowed himself the luxury of being voluble, if only for a brief spell. "It's an open-and-shut case, and Steiner will pay dearly, very dearly. I guess just about everyone at Army has made up his mind he's guilty, and this includes the members of the court."

"Why do you think Steiner did it?"

"I understand Hauch and Steiner quarreled . . . about money . . . about a woman . . . who knows, and you gotta remember Steiner has one hell of a temper. He's struck those around him, threatened them."

"I see." The member of several charitable organizations and the defender of German justice throughout the ages nodded gravely and stood up. "You must excuse me, Mr. Vallejo, but I am expected elsewhere. Don't get up. An associate of mine will be here presently, and he'll want to speak with you." He peered down through gold-rimmed glasses, shook hands, and was gone.

Vallejo took another sip of the Schnapps and glancing to the left caught sight of a tall, blond, young man skillfully picking his way through the swelling crowd in the foyer and once in the lounge, making a beeline for his table. Vallejo recognized him at once. This was the man who had kept watch on the previous Thursday and Saturday, Hans Ketterer, lieutenant to Florian von Vogelsee, if his informants had been correct. Vallejo pretended not to notice him. But the man wasted no time, and his manner was brusque.

"I'm Hans Ketterer," he blurted out in heavily accented English, "and you're Vallejo, Jesús Vallejo?"

"Who wants to know?" Vallejo was making little drumming noises with his lips and then began to clear his throat in a most ostentatious way.

"Let's go for a ride," Ketterer blurted out again.

"Why?" and Vallejo belched to his heart's content, cognizant of the German's rising hostility.

"Because Herr Gisevius says so, *Idiot!*"

"Didn't catch the last word, dude, talking to yourself. If so, see a shrink!"

"I don't understand your *Quatsch*! On your feet, *Idiot!*"

They left the restaurant together and walked less than a block to a side street where a beige VW bus stood portentously parked, waiting for a designated driver.

"Get in," Ketterer growled, pushing Vallejo towards the front passenger seat. "Get in and no jokes! I have no use for cheap jokes and for com . . . comedians." A slight stutter was now marring his speech.

"Right you are," Vallejo uttered with sham consent and immediately began to recite, "There was a girl from Cape Cod / Who thought all babies came from God / But it wasn't the Almighty / Who crept on her nightly / It was . . ."

"Shut up, shut up," Ketterer shouted, taking his eyes temporarily off the road, his fists poised for action. "I . . . I . . . can't stand that low humor. Do, do you hear?"

"As you wish, Hans." Vallejo shrugged his shoulders keeping the driver under continual scrutiny.

They drove in silence for a long time, through the southern part of the city, unfamiliar and hardly enticing to Vallejo, and into the suburbs, with their wide thoroughfares and new residential buildings brand-new or propped up on this side and that by scaffolding with swarms of workmen on rooftops bending in all directions or kneeling at the base; past and past them into the country where there was little green about, no brooks or streams, trees or shrubberies, only open spaces, one next to the other, or clearly demarcated, ready to be sold or rented. Ketterer stopped the bus by a pile of broken bricks and little shapeless mounds of uncollected refuse.

"How much do you know about Colonel Trainer?" he asked out of the blue.

"Not much, he's the Group Commander, and I work in his office."

"We know that, *Idiot,* we know a great deal."

"Who are those 'we', Hans, what's your outfit?"

"For now we ask questions and you provide the answers, not the other way round. When I ask, you answer and that's all, and you keep your mouth shut. *Verstanden!*" Ketterer was working himself up into a tizzy.

"Well, what d'you want to know?" Vallejo appeared to be immune to Ketterer's anger.

"We understand he drinks."

"Sure does, drinks like a fish."

"And women, what about women?"

"Well, I could tell you he has a new Polynesian virgin flown to him every week so he can practice with her sixty-nine different positions of love-making, but I'd be short on proof."

"Don't blabber like this," Ketterer exploded, red in the face. "It's, it's, it's, filth, filth, d'you hear me, sexual positions and all; when the *Führer* was alive such talk was not tolerated. You, Jesús, are no better than an animal, and you must change your ways, reform, yes, reform. I will help you."

Undaunted, Vallejo stole a glance over the surrounding wasteland.

"How about stretching a leg, Hans, when all is said and done it's a warm day."

"All right, but I have specific questions for you, and you will answer them. Or else!"

"Okay."

They jumped out of the bus and at first stood idly about, but Ketterer's face soon registered signs of gravity, of relentless planning, of acute mental exertion. His mouth was half-opened, and he was going to speak. But Vallejo preempted him playfully.

"Listen to me, hotshot. You're good at talking, and that's just about the only thing you're good at. Talk, talk, talk, and talk, my friend, is cheap. You never broke a man's legs so he couldn't walk again, you never cut out a dame's tongue so she couldn't tell on you, you never sent a man six feet under. Maybe the old Nazis, the ones who blitzkrieged their way across Europe, had guts—I suspect they had and lots of it—but you and your cohorts are just wimps, dry shit near the sewage pipe, PR men at best who smile and tickle the buttons on the telephone exchange."

"You want trouble, *Schweinhund?*" and Ketterer advanced menacingly towards Vallejo.

Vallejo raised a hand. "I haven't finished yet, and it's important you listen to everything I tell you. Your chiefs require this information."

"All right, but no insults and no mouthing about filthy sex."

Vallejo's smirk had a vicious air about it. "I told you who you and your friends are, and now I'll tell you who I am."

Ketterer was standing fast and gaping, enraged but holding back.

"I spent four years with the Chomancheros, that's the biggest gang in the American Southwest; we rob, burn, kill, mutilate, rape, exact vengeance. We contract out, but most of the time we plan and execute our own operations. Do you know how many men I killed? Eight, and only one got away diving off a pier, but sharks got him in the end. Arson? Close to thirty successful missions. Robberies, including state banks, savings and loans, and houses of the rich and famous, in excess of fifty-five, mutilations, disfigurements, and rapes to order seventeen."

Vallejo advanced a step and turned the callous eye bulging out with derision on Ketterer's entire person.

"If you people want action against Trainer or someone else in the U.S. Army, fine, I'm your man. But if all you wanna do is pussyfoot and yap, good-bye, shitheads. I ain't interested."

"Wait, let's talk some more, and I want to know more about Colonel Trainer."

"Why?"

"This is still a secret, and I have to check with Captain Vogelsee. But Trainer could be our next target."

Upon hearing this Vallejo broke into clamorous, uncontrollable laughter.

"You want to tackle Trainer, wimp! He's hard as leather and tough as they come. He's a marksman and blackbelt in judo, and he don't play by the rules. He'll crush you and others like you as one crushes a swarm of creeping cockroaches." He paused. "You couldn't kill anybody, pretty boy, you wouldn't know how. How about rejoining the Salvation Army?"

Ketterer was at the end of his emotional tether. He looked wildly around, lunged forward, and the words which flew out of his throat were rasping and guttural. The stutter had all but disappeared. "You're asking for trouble." But before he had the time to lunge again Vallejo kicked him hard in the genitals. Ketterer reeled with pain and fell to the ground, the whites of his eyes widening and contracting as the stinging and burning rose, abated, and rose again.

"You . . . you bas . . . bastard," was all he could mutter, cupping his hands over his groin.

Vallejo took a step forward, gazing at the lying man with unfaltering contempt, and then kicked him in the jaw. As the head fell backwards and the lips parted spasmodically, he could see blood streaking down from between the sparkling teeth onto the prominent chin. Ketterer was breathing irregularly and heavily and tried to stand up, but the burning pain in the testicles and the tearing one in the jaw militated against it. He muttered something in German which Vallejo could not understand, and Vallejo kicked him again in the jaw. Ketterer was now lying on his side, one hand covering his groin and the other wiping the blood off his face and neck. He made no attempt to rise, and through the ill-omened stillness his wide blue eyes were flashing a message of indescribable hatred to his adversary who stood there calm, imperturbable.

"You're a softy, Hans," the American spoke at last. "You couldn't kill nobody. You're just a handful of crap. Get lost," and he waved a dismissing hand. The German hoisted himself up on his elbows and began to crawl. Blood trickled from his mouth, sweat pearled up on his forehead, and it was evident he was still in much pain. But presently he made another determined effort and stood up, wobbly, his legs far apart.

"You dumb Ami, *Idiot,*" he hissed, "dumb like all the other Americans, you don't understand anything, anything at all . . ."

Vallejo laughed contemptuously and spat down with gusto, the spittle landing on the top of Ketterer's shoe.

"We'll have to get someone to change your diapers"—he went on tauntingly—"the odds are ten to one you wet them already. You're just a little kid looking for his mommy."

Ketterer had rallied sufficiently to be able to stand firmly on his feet and endure the pain without exhibiting any sign of it.

"I am not a softy," he cried, "I am tough, and being a Nazi gives me extra toughness, *verstanden*, Ami? And as for killing, who d'you think killed Hauch?"

"Steiner, I guess."

"You guess wrong, Ami, Steiner's just another flabby Yank. He's worthless, he lives by all those idiotic American laws and regulations."

"Oh!"

"I killed Hauch, by myself, broke his skull with an iron bar Steiner had used during the day so his fingerprints would be on it."

"I don't believe a word of it, Hans, you're not man enough." With the speed of light his mind traveled to those precious days on the high school stage when, attired in the appropriately colorful costume, he would rise to his melodramatic optimum impersonating a jealous lover, chieftain of the band, or a haughty and overreaching magnate. "Maybe you were the look-out, but the actual killer no . . . no, impossible under any circumstances. You're too soft!"

"*Idiot*, I was the killer, and Moser was the lookout . . ."

"Oh, Johann Moser you mean . . . ?" Vallejo was hamming away, promptly inventing a name.

"No, no, dumb Yank, not Johann, his elder brother Felix."

"Of course, Hans, Felix Moser, how could I forget!"

"And now it's your turn to do something for us."

"So Trainer's your target?"

"Hush, Ami, you'll receive your orders when the time comes."

"I understand."

"And you must forget what I said. Promise?"

"Done."

Ketterer straightened himself up and let his arms rotate, rhythmically bending and unbending his body. He looked fitter now.

"You shouldn't have kicked me so hard, Ami, there was no need for it."

"Well, Hans, I had to find out what stuff you're made of, if we're going to work together I had to be sure my partner ain't no wimp."

"Okay, what happened is in the past, but it mustn't happen again, understand?" Ketterer's manner was calm, his voice level, and he gave every indication he bore no grudge.

Vallejo nodded, putting his heart and soul into it.

"Still, there's one thing I don't get," he began confidentially, "why did you kill Hauch? Was he dangerous?"

"You ask too many questions, and I already said too much. I'll answer this one and no more questions, Ami, no more."

"Scout's honor."

All at once Ketterer became agitated, and his puckered face bearing traces of blood here and there projected wild repugnance and malice. He was shouting at the top of his lungs.

"Hauch was weak, he had no character, no discipline, and he was always asking for more money, swine! And do you know how he spent his money?"

"Haven't got a clue."

"On whores, on expensive whores, on filthy sex! He was an animal, not a human being, and there's no place in the Bund for such scum!"

"He liked a good time, anything wrong with that?"

"*Jawohl,* plenty wrong! Sex is filthy, filthy, this is what animals do, and as human beings we have the res . . . resp . . . onsibility," Ketterer's stutter was returning fast, "to, to, to be bet . . . better than the animals. You watch your step, Ami, or you'll end up like . . . like Hauch." He went on raving less and less coherently with each new breath until only two words, sex and filth, were distinguishable, and they were pounded on continually with frenzy and savage disdain. It was a good while before Ketterer regained his composure.

"Shouldn't we be getting back?" Vallejo asked as naturally as he could, pretending that the German's outburst had never taken place.

"*Ja, ja,* it's time to go back. We are finished here."

Vallejo held out his hand. "We are partners and friends now, Hans. No hard feelings?"

"*Ja,* partners and friends," Ketterer repeated mechanically. "And you will report to Restaurant Dolores at noon tomorrow. It's an order."

"Right, do you want me to drive?"

"No, I am fine, get in."

"Drop me by the restaurant, I'm parked close by."

Ketterer nodded, and they drove in utter silence to their destination.

Chapter 9

"On a clear day," Nina Günthers was saying, pointing westward from the bank of the Neckar, "you can almost see the Rhine, but there's too much mist today."

Sol Lieberman leaned forward, adjusting a flat hand over his eyes and taking the business of inspecting the rolling landscape very seriously.

"I don't know how far is the Rhine, but even today one can see a helluva long way."

They had rambled through the arcades and cloisters of the university, had stood admiringly inside the Stiftskirche and the Rathaus, and had followed merrily the narrow, sloping streets crisscrossing the town. Nina delved with zestful humor into the arcana of student life in the olden days and now, supplemented the portentous official information with irreverent insights of her own, gave Sol an abridged history of Tübingen and of the state of Baden-Württemberg, and when she had finished she would gravely announce she had omitted a most significant detail and bid him again to pay strictest attention or else. He, of course, paid strictest possible attention, without wavering, and gazed at her with rapt respect ordinary folks show, or at least are expected to show, towards truly superior beings until she could play her part no more and burst out laughing, he at once joining, laughing as loudly as she did, if not louder.

When they had had their fill of the accomplishments of medieval and Renaissance masons and architects and of the dexterities of nineteenth century restorations, they took a stroll along the river and into the outskirts of the town, holding hands, bombarding each other with indelible impressions of people and things they could not help notice, interrupting each other, trying to shoot each other down, and then laughing uncontrollably and to their hearts' content. Sol set a quick pace, and Nina at once complained that her legs were not as long as his, to which he retorted that what she lacked in the length of her limbs must be compensated by the agility and swiftness of her entire body. She frowned at him between the guffaws, and he frowned at her between the guffaws. Their tempers flared up and words passed between them. But they promptly made up, quarreled again, made up, and continued their stroll, chatting, improvising, observing, agreeing, and disagreeing.

When they reached the end of the promenade, Sol said, "Would you like some lunch? I know I would."

"I am really not hungry," Nina said, "but I'll have something."

"Let's get away from the town. There must be restaurants out there."

"There are lots and some very nice ones."

In the car she was watching him with undisguised affection and lay a finger on his shoulder.

"Uncle Joachim says you are a highly decorated officer, that you showed exemplary bravery under fire in Korea."

Sol laughed. "It's nice of your uncle to say that."

"But it's true, isn't it?"

He laughed again. "I guess it's true."

"You're very modest, and modesty is the mark of a gentleman. I don't meet many modest people in Tübingen among the students or instructors or town people. Just about everyone is full of himself or herself, advertising oneself to the world, and trying to make an impression."

"I'd say it's the same in any country, anywhere."

"Maybe so, but this makes you special to me."

"You are also special, Nina."

"Special to whom?"

"To me in the first place. Because this is what really concerns me. Special, very special to me, but perhaps special to others."

She was silent for what seemed to him a very long time, and then he heard her giggle and saw an elongated finger pointing left.

"Take first left, it's a well-kept country road that will take us straight to that reddish building over there behind the line of plane trees."

"I take it you can vouch for the establishment."

"It's a very cozy *gasthaus*, catering to a discriminating clientele, and everything in it is in good taste. It's a little more expensive though than most."

"In the capitalistic world you pay for the quality more than for quantity." He let the words fall loudly and resolutely as if he were addressing a public meeting. She laughed, pretending to be shocked.

"Are you a socialist? Here in West Germany whenever someone uses expressions like capitalism, capitalistic system, or capitalistic economy we know where he or she stands."

"No, not a socialist."

And he laughed, pressing her hand and moving his head closer to hers so that he could look straight into her eyes and keep looking into them without interruption, just keep looking into them. Nothing else mattered.

"I am a liberal, I'd like to think of myself as a liberal, it's all I can say," he uttered haltingly, words not obeying his command but hiding in corners obstinate, recalcitrant.

As soon as they had ordered lunch, Nina said, "Tell me about the Korean War, what you did in it, tell me everything about yourself during those dreadful years, what were your duties, your feelings, your expectations. I want to know, because I want to know all about you. I must know. I want to be so very close to you."

He did her bidding and tried to reconstruct best he could his two-year tour of duty on the Korean Peninsula, the early victories, the initial optimism and euphoria in the ranks, and the subsequent setbacks after the Chinese entered the fray, the sinking morale, his own doubts after the initial enthusiasm, and the unwavering trust in the wisdom of the American political leadership. When she pressed him he told her about the food, the living conditions, the diseases, the casualties, the camaraderie, the officers and the men he was particularly close to. She was brimming with pride when he recounted somewhat reluctantly, finally giving in to her, the circumstances which led to his being decorated and then promoted to captain. She was reliving for herself and for him those moments of glory which were so precious to her, so absolutely necessary because without them and without being able to participate in his life, her own life seemed an utterly empty shell ready to be tossed back onto the refuse pile.

"You also wear foreign decorations," and her eyes sparkled exultantly. "I know all about it," she teased.

"Only a British one, my unit happened to be acting jointly with a British unit, and when it was all over the Brits gave me a trinket probably just to see the back of me the sooner the better."

"You are wonderful, Sol," she was very much in earnest now, and when the waiter brought the food she cried, "All of a sudden I feel terribly hungry, I could eat a horse."

"We need two horses," he put in, "and if you're not careful I'll steal the rump off yours."

"There's still so much to unearth about you, miles of labyrinths, miles of records."

He smiled. "Tell me about your studies, what you want to do, what your goals are. You're graduating in a few weeks?"

"Yes, but I still have my internship and apprenticeship to do in an architectural firm before I get my license and am a fully fledged architect."

"Would it be an imposition to ask you to talk about yourself? I, too, am very curious."

She had begun with bold strokes, overviews, generalities which marked her as a sophisticated conversationalist and a woman of the world, but very soon she got down to brass tacks and was answering Sol's questions with admirable precision.

"Yes, I want to be an architect, I've wanted it ever since I was eight or nine, and I've already got my preferences."

"Which are?"

"I want to design dwellings, structures where people live. That means I want to design and build homes, and I have absolutely no interest in official buildings, temples, churches, synagogues, city halls, seats of government."

"Why this interest in homes?" he asked, taken with the idea.

"I don't know, I really don't know, and I've asked myself this question a thousand times, trying to understand myself better, but without much success. Still, I'll give you a hint, and some of my friends say the two are closely connected. So does one of my professors at Tübingen who was kind enough to listen to my unending introspective monologues."

"I am all ears, Nina."

"I have to backtrack. I firmly believe that every moment of one's life is equally important. That means there is no such thing as preparation for something that will be the culminating point, no testing of the waves, no trial and error. We are continually at the summit, each passing moment being it, each passing moment being the most important, the crucial moment. We are part of the continuum, but in this continuum we are not tending towards something, we are not straining after anything, and we are not moving away from something which is insignificant or worthless. Each moment is the moment of truth, each moment is the moment of deepest revelation, and to put it in different terms each moment has its own rewards and punishments." She paused and a soft, delicate blush found its way to her cheeks.

Sol leaned back and was watching her closely.

"I understand everything you've said. I can't say I agree with all of it. For us Jews Sabbath has a special significance. And so has Sabbath for the Christians high holidays, Christmas, Easter—they are all occasions for celebration, for reflection."

She grimaced with comical contempt. "Celebration and reflection should be practiced every minute of the day, not just at set times, when everyone can relax and feel good." She paused and her face contracted in obdurate resolve. "For Uncle Joachim, Sunday service at our Lutheran church is the culmination of the week, but he is wrong. Every second in our lives rises in culmination. Tradition and ritual make a mockery of our obligations as human beings. It's a sad state of affairs."

He was silent, but what she had said was boring at his brain, and now he was listening with extraordinary pleasure to her light-hearted chatter about this, that, and the other.

When lunch was over, Nina asked, "When shall I see you again?"

His thoughts dashed and galloped. "Today is Sunday, I'll call you tomorrow."

"Could you make it in the afternoon? In the evening I am getting together with some friends. We're going to cram together for the finals."

He nodded. "Certainly."

They strolled for a while through the open field, holding hands, dodging thistles and cowpies, and being stared at by an odd unpastured and friendly cow. When he dropped her off at her apartment, he leaned out of the car window and said, "Till tomorrow, then."

"Till tomorrow," she said.

Lieberman drove again through Tübingen, and at the fork just outside the city limits bore to the right, then onto the highway leading back to Stuttgart. Several minutes later, spotting a rest stop, he made a sharp right turn, parked the car in the shade, and lit a cigarette. He knew precisely what he was doing and had no illusions that if he allowed his deepening attachment to Nina continue it would mean the end of his marriage. So be it, he reflected. Inhaling deeply he cast his mind back nine years to the time when Rachel and he had just gone through a traditional Jewish wedding and expected a harmonious and permanent union. It had been a satisfactory marriage built on trust and common interests fanned by their common background and antecedents, but he was painfully aware now as he had been on numerous occasions in the past that there was something lacking in this marriage, not exactly love as such, because there was much love in it of a certain kind fashioned out of trust, devotion, and congeniality—what was lacking was magic.

For several years now, and particularly after the birth of their second son, their marriage took on the character of a smoothly running study group, with as much sex thrown into it as they both desired; theirs was the glorification of companionship never allowing either of them to be lonely or disaffected because the other spouse was always there to counsel, exchange ideas, or simply make both of them laugh. For years Sol and Rachel had been reading a good deal—their interests happily coinciding—and they would devour a vast quantity of books in the field of modern and recent biography and autobiography, American and European history, and twentieth century art. Having read a book, they would talk about it, often for hours if not for days, and their minds would interact eagerly, scrupulously. They would spend a good deal of time with Matthew and Sol, Jr., though the boys' upbringing and education proper were Rachel's unquestioned responsibility which she exercised with unflinching devotion, Sol taking a stand in rare instances only when a disciplinary or other problem called for father's decision.

It had been a well-regulated existence, a family life which gave every appearance of harmony and where channels of communication between its four members were never blocked. *Yes,* Lieberman reflected again, *it's all very civilized, very much on the up and up and filled to the brim with trust and understanding.*

Nevertheless for some time now the admirable family arrangements had become for him a pall of unbearable monotony and boredom under which he angrily vegetated. *Everything is predictable and so thoroughly planned, there is no room even for a breath of fresh air,* he was bitterly saying to himself, his fingers reaching for another cigarette. Magic has vanished forever from my life. In its place there is ironclad routine and Rachel, the dear, well-meaning Rachel has become a highly sophisticated, a highly cultured robot. He was turning against his wife, but this lasted no more than a brief spell. Nina was the woman he wanted to spend the remainder of his life with, his decision had been taken, and in the meantime the matter of his marriage to Rachel and the termination thereof would have to be attended to in the most expeditious but also in the fairest possible way. When he thought of Nina and of the time they had spent together, he knew that he was not facing alternatives, that he was not balancing two existences, each of which had its own advantages and disadvantages. No! Being with Nina made him feel alive in the way he had not felt for years, gave him a taste of a new life, and of love which was infinitely stronger than the love he had ever felt for Rachel. He really had no choice. Either live, live to the full, or else sell your soul to habit and convention. Lieberman tossed away the cigarette butt and started the engine.

/   /   /

Sergeant Carl Steiner lay spread out on his bunk in a most relaxed position in his cell at 7th U.S. Army Detention Center, his belt loosened. He was digesting the sumptuous lunch he had consumed less than an hour before, and he reflected that in the last several days the meals brought to his cell from the Mess had been richer and larger than before. He had known, of course, most of the cooks at Army for years and could count on their sympathy and good wishes, but he knew from long experience that portions of Army chow were ladled out according to ironclad regulations, and he wondered why he had been singled out for this dubious honor. A thought struck him that perhaps they wanted to fatten him up before a speedy execution, and therefore the succession of better-and-larger-than-ordinary meals really stood for no more than the Last Supper duly distributed over several days through his superiors' kindness of heart or an administrative foul-up. *Perhaps the Army is going to shoot me first and then try me in abstentia,* he pondered. He sat up on the bunk and shrugged his shoulders. Such a development appeared to him at first illogical in the extreme, but Steiner had been in the Army for more than twenty years and never doubted that literally anything could happen in it. Moreover, when you had to deal with generals and colonels the bar of probability rose rapidly on a scale of ten to one.

Steiner shrugged again to let the world know that even though they were doing their goddamn worst, he didn't give a damn. Still, the incarceration was taking a heavy toll. It was his thirteenth day in the cell, and the court-martial was set for June 4th. He faced a little more than two weeks of waiting, and he was wondering how he would get through those irksome days. When he had first been brought in, he read a good deal and was happy to welcome visitors. But now he no longer cared for anyone's company except his wife's, who came to see him regularly twice every day, and he grew tired of reading. To the cautiously optimistic accounts and prognoses of his defense counsel he listened with undisguised skepticism, dismissing out of court what Harrington cozily termed possible "openings" and "silver linings." He had little confidence in Harrington's truthfulness and regarded him as a morale-booster more concerned about his client's mental health than about acquittal. In fact, he was slowly sliding into a state of depression brought about by a despondent realization that apart from himself no one save his wife and a handful of staunch friends believed in his innocence and that he was being thrown to the wolves by the institution he had served faithfully most of his adult life. The conclusion that this institution now acted ineptly or unjustly pressed itself into his mind, weighed heavily on it, but he was not yet prepared to turn against the Army anymore than he was prepared to doubt his own innocence. Steiner was neither bitter nor combative, and he was on the way to becoming listless and no longer caring. His mental activity had shrunk to the state of nervous impassivity, he was half-waiting for something he could neither understand nor define, though embedded in it was a vague apprehension that things were not as they should be and that he had been had. Of this much he was reasonably conscious, but the rest was a dark smother seeping into every nook and cranny by his sides, a mystery so impregnable he could not imagine a shell that would crack it. A knock on the door made him start, and he recognized the guard's features through the peephole.

"Sarge, you have a visitor."

"And who the hell is it?" Steiner ranted, glancing at his wristwatch, which showed precisely 1345 hours. Molly would not be back before 1800 hours. Who the hell was it?

"It's your attorney, Sarge, Captain Harrington."

Steiner belched with gusto. "Okay, Jeff, ask him to come down."

"And one more thing, Sarge, but that's between you and I and don't whisper a word of it to a third party, 'cause I'll get into trouble."

"I promise, Scout's honor, and now out with it."

"Well, I got buddies who have buddies who work in Judge Advocate."

"And?"

"One of them overheard a conversation between Colonel Smithers, who will be your Law Officer . . ."

"Oh, yes."

"And some other high ranking military attorneys."

"And?"

"They all praised Captain Harrington to the skies and swore he's one hell of a lawyer . . . and Colonel Smithers said if anyone could get Steiner off the hook, it's that arrogant son of a bitch, Julian Harrington. I thought I'd tell you what they said, Sarge."

"Thank you, Jeff," Steiner was casting a sharp eye on Jeff, being unable to take what he had just heard at face value and being less than willing to evaluate it. "Thank you," he repeated, "and you'd better call the main office and let the captain come through, or else he'll change his mind and run away."

"Right away, Sarge," and Jeff with alacrity picked the receiver off the wall.

Exuding self-confidence and self-possession Captain Julian Harrington entered Sergeant Steiner's cell with a swagger, grinning from ear to ear.

"I am sorry to be spoiling your Sunday with legal business, Sergeant," he began heartily, "but we may have something . . ."

"All in the line of duty," Steiner put in non-committally. "Please sit down, sir."

"Thank you. Last evening German police in Stuttgart took into custody two brothers Johann and Felix Moser as material witnesses in the murder of Dieter Hauch, and early this morning an arrest warrant was issued for one Hans Ketterer, also a German national. Please think hard, Sergeant, do these names mean anything to you? Johann Moser is twenty-four, of medium height, slim, dark-haired. His brother Felix is twenty-seven, also of medium height and dark-haired, but a little stouter than his brother. They are both from these parts so in informal conversation they would be using Swabian dialect. Does this strike a bell? Perhaps you saw two men answering to this description on base? Perhaps they came to us to repair something? They are both auto mechanics."

"No, I can't rightly say I do," Steiner answered with deliberation, rubbing his jaw, unsuccessfully delving and delving again into the very abyss of memories. "They sound like strangers, guys I never lay eyes on. And as for repair, Captain, in the Motor Pool we do our own repairs."

"They may have entered the base as part of a working force, rechecking furnaces, electrical gadgets, plumbing, sewage pipes, this kind of thing."

Steiner shook his head. "Our own people do most of these jobs. German workforce is only employed when we erect new buildings, and the last one was the chapel, some ten years ago."

"I see, but what about the third man, Hans Ketterer, age twenty-five, tall, very blond, athletic-looking."

"I'm sorry, sir, but he's as much of a stranger as the other two . . . By the way what is that Ketterer guy charged with?"

"Murder of Dieter Hauch, but he hasn't been apprehended yet."

Steiner hoisted his head so that he was practically sitting at attention, and his gaze directed at Harrington betrayed bafflement and disbelief. Then all of a sudden he began to laugh boisterously, laughter of a jolly bouncer after a good night's work, and he went on laughing while Harrington just sat there watching him in silence.

"You kinda played it down, Captain, didn't you? But that's one for the home team," he managed to holler between spasms of laughter, and he slapped the defense counsel hard on the knee.

Harrington winced, and Steiner was at once muttering apologies.

"That's okay . . . okay," Harrington cried, enthusiastically shaking Steiner's hand and rubbing his knee, "now the big issue is will the charges against those three stick. German police is convinced they are involved, but so far they haven't been able to ascertain who the actual killer was, and was it only one man. They need more time, and Ketterer will have to be apprehended."

"So what do we do now?"

"I am afraid all we can do is wait, but I am laying the new facts before Judge Advocate."

"Do I have to stay in this hole, or can I go home?" Steiner asked in desperation.

"For the time being you'll have to stay right here, but when the charges against the three German nationals are substantiated, or are on the way to being substantiated, I'll make an immediate application to have you released on your own recognizance."

"Meaning?"

"That you can go home to the Village."

"Suits me, and the sooner the better . . . sir."

Harrington rose to his feet and was standing by the bunk in a festive mood.

"You know, Sergeant, your court-martial, if there is going to be one, has generated much sympathy for you from many quarters, even among those who firmly believe you are guilty. Scores of enlisted men who had had contact with you spoke to me and are of the opinion you are either totally innocent or, if you are guilty of murder, then you had a jolly good reason to do what you did. Opinion among officers is also divided and is even more tilted in your favor. The only military segment which has already branded you as guilty has summarily dismissed any notion of extenuating circumstances, and has refused to show understanding or compassion, is your own kind, your immediate peers, the senior NCOs."

"I know," Steiner muttered, looking dully at the floor, "it's sad, but there it is. I could sense it when some of them came to see me, they were just going through the motions, and same when their wives came to console my wife."

"It's curious, though," Harrington put in very cautiously, "one would've imagined those guys rooting for you all the way."

Steiner kept gazing at the floor, cornered, ill at ease.

"I don't know why," he finally raised his voice. "I don't know, but there were exceptions."

"You can say it again," Harrington joined in elatedly. "Group Sergeant Korovitz never wavered in his belief you were completely innocent and were framed by the German bastards, and I can add a name or two."

"Good ol' Leroy," Steiner muttered, a little less dejected now.

Harrington resumed his seat on the bunk. "There will be a lot of paperwork, and we'll be coordinating closely with German police and their D.A. Office . . . but if everything goes according to plan, why, the end may be in sight before too long." He was exuding confidence.

Steiner nodded, smiling bleakly, and Harrington wasted no time in tackling another subject.

"I had a number of meetings with your Group Commander, Sergeant, there were forms to be filled out, information transcribed, affidavits signed, etc., etc, and frankly, I am baffled."

"Sir?"

"Can you tell me something about Trainer's background? Who is he?"

"To tell you the truth, Captain, I know very little myself."

"Even so."

"Well, he's Regular Army, he's from Kansas, he was given battlefield commission in Korea while holding the rank of staff sergeant."

"Battlefield commission, eh?"

"That's right, you know what a battlefield commission is?"

"It so happens I do, thank you, Sergeant, but I appreciate the thought."

"You're welcome . . . sir."

Making a show of it, Harrington stretched out his arms, revolving his head and raising his shoulders by fits and starts. "It's against the crick in the back, I get it now and then," he explained defensively, continuing the exercise.

"Right you are."

"But to get back to Trainer, I didn't know we had officers like that in the Service; for crying out loud, man, he's an absolute moron, illiterate, totally incapable of thought, and on top of it pissed half of the time. I tried to explain to him the procedures we follow in the Judge Advocate Office, but even the simplest ones were beyond him. I quake in my boots at the thought of putting him on the stand. God only knows what he'd say, and we might lose just because of him. Why the hell does the Army make officers of such . . . such sub-humanoids? Do you have an answer?"

"But he knew right away it was a frame-up, didn't he?"

"This he did, I won't deny it." Harrington paused, and then writhed with hidden fury. "In addition he has the manners of a pig, he who by an act of Congress is supposed to be an officer and a gentleman!"

From the corner of his eye Steiner was observing the visitor, demure, faithful to his own beliefs, his own man.

But the visitor was as mercurial as any straw boss on the make. He leapt joyfully from the bunk, stooped, and pulled out from his briefcase an expensive-looking bottle.

"It's brandy," he whispered, "Napoleon brandy, and as we are close to the finish line I thought we might indulge in a little libation . . ." He chuckled to himself.

"Sir?"

"A drink for the road of success."

"I wouldn't say no to that," and seeing that no glasses were materializing in the visitor's hand Steiner reached for paper cups over the washbasin and handed them over.

"Watch that door," Harrington recited ceremoniously and in a stage whisper. "It's like the Prohibition."

"Looks like," Steiner agreed, and they raised their paper cups.

"To every possible success."

"To every possible success," Steiner followed suit. "Good stuff, never tasted the like of it before," and he set about inspecting the bottle.

"Noble brew to be imbibed on very special occasions," and Harrington set about refilling the paper cups.

"Say," he called out, "I know your hometown. We drove through it as newlyweds on the way to Niagara Falls . . . and honeymoon six years ago . . ."

"That's what some folks do," Steiner said non-committally. "Have you been there since?"

"No, I haven't. You see we were married six years ago, honeymoon at the Falls, and all that, and we were divorced three years later, which makes it three years ago."

"I see, well, that's also what some folks do."

"Yes," Harrington observed with a sigh, "some folks, many folks. Still divorce is preferable to perpetual misery."

"That's what many folks say," Steiner continued calmly with his refrain.

"Do you have pleasant childhood memories from Elmira, Sergeant?"

"Couldn't ask for no better. Both our parents were born there, and their parents too, and there were cousins, uncles, aunts, and the rest of the clan within a fifty-mile radius. It was kinda easy for Molly and me when we were kids to squeeze a free meal. Dad worked as guard at the reformatory, and we somehow scraped by. You're from Mass, sir, aren't you?"

"Born and bred in Northampton, and by the way we've known each other long enough. It's Julian, if I may call you Carl."

"Sure thing, sir, sure thing, Julian."

"I am afraid my childhood memories are not as idyllic as yours. Financial factors to be sure, my father was a postman, but also tensions within the family, my father's alleged philandering, my mother's alleged nervous condition, and so on. Just before entering high school I went to live with my uncle in Springfield who was a widower and had no children. My two sisters and a brother remained behind, and this is the last time I had any real contact with them. I did well in high school in Springfield and won a scholarship to Yale. After that I never looked back."

"Well, Julian, some folks stay close to the family and some don't, and that's all that can be said about it."

Harrington took a deep breath. "I've been meaning to look up my parents, my sisters, my brother, and Uncle Graham, who is really responsible for my going to college, but I never . . . found the time."

"You should, Julian, you should."

"I'll try."

"Don't try. Do it, write them, or go and see them the next time you're stateside."

"Right ho, Reverend Steiner. I'll do my best."

"That brew you brought with you, Julian, is mighty smooth on the palate. Might one have another drop? And I hope no squad of MPs will barge in here and find us red-handed breaking Army Regulations. That would never do, would it now?"

"I'll tell you a secret, Carl, which I tell only to the happy few, and on most infrequent occasions."

"Tell me, for my entrails is ready to jump clear outside its perimeter."

"Fuck the regulations . . . fuck 'em all the way," and while he was fuming Harrington could see Steiner sitting quietly at the end of the bunk, paper cup in hand, prim and very proper, the very model of decorum.

/   /   /

It was barely 0800 hours on a brilliant Monday morning right in the middle of May, but Major Fiorello was already behind his desk arranging into symmetrical piles the manifold papers, of divergent provenance, which had been conveyed to his office in one manner or another and with which it was his bounden duty to deal as Adjutant of 16th U.S. Army Engineer Group. Major Fiorello was a man of neat habits, and he would defend to the last coin in his pocket the virtues of orderliness, punctuality, and thoroughness. He had very little use for what he called the "intuitive" and "creative" approach to administrative work, and now he was smugly chuckling to himself as his desk was beginning to resemble a nearly finished plan, where each square and quadrangle, large or small, proudly proclaimed its own unmistakable identity—a precise disposition of the material at hand, but also an intricate design nearing completion. When the telephone buzzed he was for a moment put out because he did not want to speak to anyone so early in the morning, and besides he was enjoying what he was doing. Still he braced himself for the inevitable, and when he spoke into the receiver it was in a forbiddingly official tone.

"Adjutant's office, Major Fiorello speaking."

"Good morning, sir," the voice at the other end sounded warmhearted, "this is Korovitz. You sent word to C Company last week that you wanted to see PFC Hartmann, and he's here in my office. Do you want see him now, sir?"

Fiorello's official tone promptly melted away.

"Thank you, Sergeant. Yes . . . send him in, please."

When he heard the knock on the door, Fiorello was scanning the desk, his hand inside one of the drawers groping for Hartmann's folder. Presently he closed the drawer and blurted out: "Come in."

Private First Class Oliver Hartmann entered, drew himself up to attention, and saluted.

"Please sit down, Hartmann," Fiorello began in a comforting manner, "first of all I want to convey to you my condolences on the death of your father, it must've been a terrible blow for you and the rest of your family . . ." He stopped on purpose awaiting Hartmann's response before it would be proper to proceed. But the PFC's face was taut, frozen into a gloomy mask of intransigence. Fiorello leaned forward and smiled sympathetically. "I am sorry," he said trying to sound gentle and concerned.

"I thank you for your kind words, sir," Hartmann shot back, taut, stiff, and unfeeling as before.

Fiorello shifted in his seat, and his hands jumpily, nervously explored several desk drawers in search of the needed folder while he addressed the enlisted man.

"I am sure you are aware that your mother applied to the Department of the Army for your discharge." He smiled again making every attempt to catch the man's eye, but the man just stared into space.

"Anyway," Fiorello rose to his feet, placed himself in front of the desk, and leaned against it. "Anyway, everything's in the bag. Your mother's request has been approved with the full support of the Social Services and Red Cross, the Army endorsed it, and you will be getting your compassionate discharge."

"When will that be, Major?"

"Well, Army is presently cutting your orders, and then Red Cross has to be notified—it's all a formality—I'd say you'll be out of here in the first week of June . . . that's less than three weeks from now, and a day or two later you'll be sitting in your home in Milwaukee. The Army flies you right to your hometown."

"Does this mean I won't be able to enlist later?"

Fiorello was taken aback, and he could scarcely disguise it.

"Excuse me, Hartmann," he let fall carelessly, "I've got to fish something out." He dashed back to the drawers and let his fingers run through them frantically. But the folder was not to be found. Almost as an afterthought he pulled the front desk drawer wide open and there under a handful of folded travel vouchers lay a white manila folder marked *Hartmann, Oliver D., Compassionate Discharge*. Fiorello slid into his armchair and examined the pages.

"I doubt whether you could enlist in the Army until the home situation has been greatly improved." Once again he made his best to catch Hartmann's eye and establish visual contact but to no avail. The young man was staring silently into space with a determination that might make him a hard nut to crack in a POW camp.

"You were drafted," Fiorello continued, "but now you will be the man of the house and the breadwinner." He peered over the pages. "Your mother, who according to these reports is in poor health and who quite recently suffered another heart attack, as well as your brother Kyle who is only twelve, will be dependent on you. I think your main responsibility should be to look after your family and provide a measure of stability. No doubt social workers will be there to help you, but quite frankly enlistment is not an option because all parties agreed to compassionate discharge as the best possible solution."

"I didn't have much of a choice," Hartmann put in stonily.

"I understand, and I appreciate the blow you've been dealt, your father's sudden . . ."

"With all due respect, sir," Hartmann interrupted showing unexpected animation, "it would be best if you didn't mention my old man at all. He's out of my hair now, and let the son of a bitch fry in hell."

"As you wish," Fiorello concluded sadly, and he schooled his voice to softness. "You'll be leaving us soon, is there anything we can do for you?"

"I don't think so, I'm a trooper, I can look after myself . . . sir."

Fiorello nodded and let his gaze fall on the tips of his shoes.

"Best of luck to you, Hartmann."

He visited the chaplain in his office, chatted with him for a few minutes, and upon return found the bulky frame of PFC Vincent Quinn waiting outside the door.

"Major Fiorello, sir," Quinn was gasping, "I'd gone to the main office, but Group Sergeant is carrying on one hell of a long conversation with Army, and I need to speak to you urgent like."

"Isn't Vallejo in the main office?" Fiorello asked, a little surprised.

"Sergeant Korovitz let it be known Vallejo has a day off."

"Good for him," Fiorello laughed. "Well, now is as good a time as any. Come in, Quinn."

Once inside the Adjutant's office, Quinn came straight to the point.

"At last I got some good news."

"Good."

"As you know very well, Major, I've been applying to a hundred and one colleges for an athletic football scholarship and been training as regular as possible at Army and managing Little League there . . ."

"Yes, I am aware of your extracurricular activities . . ." and Fiorello's lean face began to look even longer and funnel-like, projecting extreme caution and suspicion.

"Well, I got accepted," and Quinn raked up a smile, "four-year athletic scholarship at Holy Cross College, tuition paid. I'll be on their football team, but they also want me to help out with other programs, wrestling, weightlifting, and such like. Their dean flew in to Stuttgart two weeks ago and interviewed me—I understood he interviewed a number of guys in different commands—and on Friday the telegram came, official letter of acceptance to follow by air mail."

"Congratulations, Quinn." Fiorello uttered the words with forced cordiality. "Congratulations, and what is all this leading up to?"

Quinn raked up another smile. "My enlistment ends September 4th, two years to the day, but Holy Cross wants me in the last week of August, and I thought I'd check with you, sir, if I couldn't be let loose a little earlier, two weeks earlier like?"

"Is that all there is to it?"

"Yes, that's all, sir."

"I don't see why we can't help you out." Fiorello sounded immensely relieved. "As a matter of fact we often discharge enlisted men before the actual discharge date; in some measure this depends upon coordination with the processing personnel at the other end. It's a complicated administrative process in which both ends have to cooperate."

"Absolutely, sir, absolutely," Quinn cried out.

"We send men home in large batches, some of whom still have a couple of weeks or less to serve, while others are right on the nose. Troop movements have to be planned with great care, but we never keep a man beyond his discharge date, not even by one day. This would be against the law."

"I am with the Major all the way, and I understand like great care gotta be exercised and dripping sweat taken with a forgiving heart so them troop movements can come and go to a tee."

"That's right," and Fiorello nodded with satisfaction. "I'll make a note of it, and we'll try to ship you out of here a week or two before September 4. No matter when you leave, this will fulfill the requirements of the two-year draft, so that the Army will not be able to draft you again"—he chuckled smacking his lips—"unless, of course, there is a war on."

"As the Major says, unless there is a war on, which I most sincerely hope no one will try to stir up, for my if for no one else's sake." Quinn was making ready to go, but Fiorello, completely relaxed now, threw his arm up.

"That college of yours, where is it?"

"In Illinois, some eighty miles west of Chicago."

"And the name?"

"Holy Cross. It's run by the Jesuits."

"Oh, I see. The Jesuits! There you have busybodies, always straining themselves to conquer more, to dominate more."

"They are putting me through school."

"Don't kid yourself, Quinn, they are going to work you to the bone for the greater glory of the Jesuit Order. You don't matter to them, you're just a peon, what matters are their own grandiose ambitions. Sad as it is, for the Jesuits the end justifies the means."

"You don't care for them . . . much, do you, sir?"

"No, I don't, and there's no reason I should." Fiorello looked commandingly around, and a thought flashed through Quinn's worn-out mind that perhaps after all the major was ready to dismiss him. But the major had other things in store for the future luminary of Holy Cross.

"D'you know, Quinn, a distant cousin of my wife's is a Dominican monk. A sterling fellow, and my only regret is we see so little of him, once or twice a year at Christmas, at Easter sometime." Having said this he rose to his feet and stood there straight and erect every inch of him, the thumb and middle finger of his right hand joined in a tight miniscule ring high above his head. "Ecce homo," he articulated with love and veneration, "ecce homo, my wife's distant cousin I mean. For me he is the personification of what is truly best and inimitable in Christianity."

"I've had little Latin and less Greek, so you'll forgive me, sir, if I ask you to translate." Quinn was all humility. But the invocatory mystical mood had deserted Fiorello, and he curtly informed the PFC that a translation of these momentous words would have to be obtained outside the confines of the Adjutant's office. Quinn stood to attention, saluted, and raised his voice high.

"Thank you very much, sir." His hand was on the doorknob, twisting it when Fiorello's voice made him start and mutter a couple of expletives in quick succession.

"Come back, we aren't finished yet, and you'd better sit down as this may take a little time." Quinn did as he was bidden.

Fiorello waved before him three single-spaced typewritten pages stapled together. "This came on Friday. I barely glanced at it then but read it closely over the weekend. It's the English translation of a complaint from the German police in Baden-Baden to us, and Army is sending English copies to all commands within the 7th Army. The complaint details the attempt on the part of two men, believed to be Americans and very possibly GIs, to burglarize Hotel Paradies in Baden-Baden or possibly do bodily harm to some of the guests or both in the evening hours of Sunday, May 6th. One of the intruders was very big, a football player type. Do you think it could've been your twin brother, Quinn?"

"I have no brothers, sir."

"Too bad for you. The other was small and scrawny, it puts one in mind of Hartmann's twin brother."

"Hartmann's only brother, Kyle, is twelve," and Quinn shook his head repeatedly in a slow deliberate motion in utter stupefaction. "Major Fiorello, for the life of me I don't have a clue what you're getting at!"

"Don't you play a dumb ass with me, boy!" Fiorello shouted, pounding the desk with his bare fist. "It was you and Hartmann, you answer to the description, but we have to find out the purpose of this expedition. Burglary, attempted murder perhaps, what did you plan to accomplish?" he went on shouting.

"First of all, sir," Quinn was speaking softly, giving the impression of wishing to engage in a rational discourse, "what is this Baden-Baden?"

"Come off it, and stop feeding me this Irish malarkey," Fiorello shouted again. "You know as well as I do it's a resort some thirty miles southwest of Stuttgart."

"I thought at first it was some gadget you put in the bathroom," Quinn commented innocently.

With difficulty Fiorello held his tongue and wagged an angry finger at Quinn. "You watch it, boy, you watch it!"

"What other proof is there of us being there?" Quinn asked again.

The major consulted the complaint. "The manager heard the two men speak in English and saw the small one climb a ladder to a second story window holding a small object in his hand. It could've been a weapon. The heavy one held the ladder."

"This ain't no proof."

"The manager called out to the two men asking them what they were doing, whereupon the scrawny one slid down the ladder with the skill of a cat burglar, and the heavy one tossed the ladder away. They both took off with breathless speed to their car parked some three blocks away and drove off like men possessed. The manager ran after them and employed his field glasses, but the license plate of the car was thickly covered with mud. The car, according to the witness's best guess was a small VW. You own a small VW, don't you, Quinn?"

"So does twenty thousand other guys within 7th Army."

"True, but we also have your descriptions, and when we put you and Hartmann in a lineup and check for fingerprints, we may come up with a very strong circumstantial case."

"These so-called charges are pressed by the Krauts, we are Americans," and Quinn added with heavy emphasis, "they got no jurisdiction."

"By Jove they do! The attempted felonies were committed on German soil, presumably against German nationals, and the Army will fully cooperate."

Now, having heard the bad part of the story, Quinn sat there absolutely quiet avoiding at all cost eye contact with the major. Enormous and brawny, his loosened up muscles puffing up the fabric of his tunic and trousers, he was a mass of gigantic energy, dormant for the time being, but ready to explode at a moment's notice.

Fiorello circled the desk like a prizefighter and placed himself next to Quinn, bending slightly, brooding and expectant.

"Might just as well make a confession," he advised off-handedly, as if he had no stake in it.

At long last Quinn raised his eyes and now the two men were locked in an eye-to-eye contest, neither of them blinking.

"Let me try a hypothetical: assuming that in a particular situation far, far away from here, two men were poking around some hotel or other and were chased away by the caretaker, and assuming there was absolutely no felonious intent present, no intent to do bodily harm to anybody or to steal anything, would the officer in charge be willing to grant immunity to these two men in exchange for the truthful account of what happened?"

As Quinn went on talking, Fiorello inched closer to him and his gaze became more and more intent, more and more prosecutorial, until he threw his arms up in the air, dashed round the desk, and sat down assuming a magisterial demeanor.

"You're pretty smart, Quinn, that big, sluggish football player all brawn and no brains, that's just an act, isn't it. But I can see through you, yes, I can," he hissed and continued hissing. "You talk of immunity, like some hit man changing loyalties and toying with the idea of turning state's evidence. It's only fair to say the good fathers at Holy Cross are getting more than they bargained for. Immunity!" he jeered. "Immunity. I don't have to give you immunity, I can force the information out of you, understood?" and Fiorello, his wrath unquenchable, pounded the desk again and again.

"I don't think you can force the information out of me, sir."

"And why not?"

"Because no one can be forced to testify against himself, it's in the Constitution."

"Aha!" Fiorello jeered again. "So now it's shyster Quinn telling the Army what it can and what it can't do." He was going to embark on further vitriolic summations, but Quinn jumped up from the chair, stood at attention, and uttered in a firm, level tone of voice: "Sir, request permission to go to men's room."

Fiorello nodded. "But come right back," he rasped out, "no Houdini tricks! Do you read me?"

"Loud and clear!"

When Quinn returned to the office, Fiorello was in a much better mood, his fury mostly spent.

"Pull up a chair," he beckoned to the enlisted man, "so we don't have to raise our voices, and tell me what happened. If this was a prank, we'll forget all about it, but I have to be fully informed, and I'll decide. You know I'm a fair man."

"I have to backtrack a wee bit," Quinn said calmly. "We're running a book on Sergeant Korovitz . . ."

"Illegal gambling again," Fiorello snorted, "court-martial offense!"

"There's nothing against gambling in Army Regulations, and this day, unlike the day before, everything's above board, honest to the core. Fully legit. We even have an oversight commission, and built into the ordinance is a clause about unscheduled audits."

"Go on."

"Well, story has it that Master Sergeant Korovitz and his fiancée, herself a sergeant, salute each other in the sack before they screw. Lots of men were laying bets but proper odds couldn't be set, if you know what I mean, sir."

"Go on," Fiorello murmured listlessly.

"Legend has it last month in a hotel outside Stuttgart Korovitz was so hell-bent on saluting Adrianne in the sack, on and on he went so when the time came he couldn't get a hard-on. One of our guys was taking pictures through the window but . . . as they say in court the evidence was inconclusive. All we wanted to get in that Baden-Baden joint was how many times the lovebirds were saluting each other in the sack before they got down to business, 'cause the men are betting on it . . . How many salutes before nature takes its course."

Fiorello buried his face in his hands and remained in that position for what seemed to Quinn an exceedingly long while. When he spoke at last it was droopingly but also with a mustering sense of shame as if he more than any other were responsible for the sad events.

"I assume the lady in question is Sergeant Adrianne Hurley, Group Sergeant's fiancée?"

"The same, she's at Army, works in Records."

"So the party at that hotel in Baden-Baden was the two sergeants, and the object in the man's hands who was standing on the ladder was a camera."

"You might say that, a super-duper one."

"Yes or no?"

"Yes, yes, sir, if you want every 'i' dotted and every 't' crossed."

Fiorello was now sitting on the edge of the armchair, his hands carelessly moving things on his desk, his bearing modest almost self-effacing.

"I am at a loss for words," he admitted gamely holding what was boiling inside him in check. "You and Hartmann invaded the privacy of another human being, in this case the privacy of a senior NCO and . . . and of his fiancée, members of the Armed Forces who traveled to a nearby resort in search of well-deserved R & R and who had every expectation their privacy would be respected. Shame on you! You behaved crudely, coarsely, violating the code of conduct and ethics which is expected of a U.S. soldier . . . If you took any pictures, I imagine they were promptly developed and are now selling like hotcakes for a quarter a piece."

"With all due respect, Major Fiorello, we was chased away before we could take any pictures, but if we did they'd be selling for a fin minimum. This is hot stuff."

Fiorello had recovered from his fit of modesty and self-effacedness. He got up and stood behind his desk, like a peacock on display erecting and spreading his feathers, appearing taller than he really was, his eyes flashing, his chin elevated and thrust forward, the very image of vanity, sway, and command.

"I have most of the evidence in my possession. I shall consider it very carefully, and I shall adjudicate," he proclaimed with dignity.

"Adjud . . . sir?"

"Yes, Quinn, I shall adjudicate, I shall render judgment."

"Well, praised be the judge, adjudicate, Major, adjudicate away all you want, but keep in mind, sir, we was just responding to what the customers called for," Quinn said, getting up.

Chapter 10

Whistling a merry tune Sergeant James O'Leary pushed the door leading to Group Office and immediately caught sight of Sergeant Korovitz shuffling papers at his usual post, a look of unredeemable boredom marring his entire physiognomy, and Colonel Trainer standing gaily by the window, puffing out circles of smoke from his cheroot as happy as any run-of-the-mill kid blowing out soap bubbles, if not more so. Every time Trainer puffed out a larger circle than the one before, still loosely conforming to geometrical restrictions, he would cheer roaringly and clap his hands. In this hullabaloo he was both the player and the cheerleader, the gutsy field and the applauding stand.

O'Leary waited till the latest ephemeral figure merged with the elements, stood to attention, and saluted.

"Good morning, sir."

Trainer recognized him at once. "Ah, Jim O'Leary. What's for dinner, Sarge?"

"Whatever the Master Menu decrees," O'Leary answered haltingly. "It isn't like the old days." Still saluting he turned to Korovitz. "And top of the mornin' to ye, Group Sergeant."

"Good morning, Jimmie," Korovitz smiled smugly, "the world still treating you fair and square?"

"That's a question, Group Sergeant, I am loath to answer as I stand here."

Korovitz followed the first delighted guffaw with another even more delighted, and the creator of magic circles in the air was quick in joining him.

"I know what you mean about the Master Menu, Sergeant," Trainer began after the laughter had subsided. "Hell, it surprises me the Pentagon hasn't drawn up a master latrine roster, ordering all of us to urinate and de . . . defecate at designated times only. 0700 hours first trip to the latrine, 0730 hours relieve yourself, if you can, and so on."

"Maybe a request should be sent to Department of the Army, recommending these very measures," O'Leary suggested with a mischievous twinkle in his eye.

"Sure," Trainer promptly concurred. "You write such a request, Jimmie, sign it, and out of the goodness of your heart let me glance at it."

"This is what I call a true give-and-take," Korovitz announced with dignified conviction.

Trainer sat down in the corner and picked up the thread. "Hell, wouldn't it be simpler if every unit could plan its own menu. To hell with Washington! Sergeant James O'Leary could regale us with delicacies every hour on the hour, and hell, every swinging dick would be happy."

"I thank you for your confidence in me, Colonel." O'Leary was conscious of the honor bestowed upon him and made sure the others noticed it. "Actually I came by to tell you, sirs, an old friend of mine will be dropping by before too long."

"Oh!" Trainer was intrigued. "What are her measurements? You wouldn't like to keep anything away from us, would you, boy!"

"It's a he, sir, and I'm sure you remember him."

Trainer's curiosity all but evaporated.

"A name would help, if it ain't too much to ask," he mumbled, inspecting his dirty fingernails.

"Ernest Tannenbaum, we were corporals and cooks together in '56 and same year he was sent to OCS. Well, the other day he graduated with honors and is now a fully commissioned second lieutenant."

Trainer was scratching his chin. "Yeah, I remember, a tall fella . . ."

"I remember him too," Korovitz joined in, "bright, tight-lipped, could take anything under the sun in his stride."

"That's my Ernie," O'Leary uttered with pride. "He'll be reporting to Army, and under the regulations he's got some leeway in choosing his first assignment."

"That's right." Trainer nodded. "That's right. So he'll be visiting you here at the 16th, Jimmie?"

"Right, sir, we stayed in touch all the time he was at OCS, and he'll be looking up others too 'cept that most of the guys who were here in '56 are gone."

"They certainly are, both officers and men." Trainer grew pensive and let his eyes roam disconsolately around the office.

"The one who helped Ernie one hell of a lot was your Group Clerk in those days, Dirk Donkers; he'd be advising him what college correspondence courses to take, how to study for the qualifying exams, and the rest. Ernie told me without Dirk he wouldn't have made it."

Trainer raised his head and cast a piercing glance at O'Leary.

"When Lt. Tannenbaum is on base, please ask him to come and see me."

"Yes, sir."

"The two of you might be interested to know"—his gaze shot towards Korovitz—"that without Donkers I wouldn't be a colonel and Group Commander today, without him and Hurstwood. Yes, that's right, they both helped me immensely." Trainer was very serious now, and a touch of nostalgia in his mien made his gravity easier to understand. "I had a couple of cards from Donkers"—he continued—"he's good, still in the graduate school, whatever that means."

"He's doing fine, fine," O'Leary added promptly.

"And Hurstwood." Trainer paused. "Why the hell did ye have to do it, Ted, why?"

"A terrible accident," Korovitz broke in sonorously.

"A terrible accident," O'Leary echoed the Group Sergeant.

"Those guys I knew in '56 are like ghosts now, haunting ghosts, creeping on you unawares and rising before you when you think you're alone. Bob Hastings, good ol' Bob, dead and buried, did ye have to go out on a limb, Bob, did ye? And Beryl, she's alive, but dead to me. Did I really deserve what you dished out, Beryl, did I?"

Korovitz was sitting very quietly behind his desk, but O'Leary standing in the middle of the office was noisily clearing his throat, giving every indication he was loath to leave the stage.

"May I add another name to your list of ghosts, sir?"

Trainer nodded.

"The one and only Captain Ronald Spelling."

"Oh, him," and Trainer was gazing absentmindedly at the ceiling. "I didn't keep track. What's happened to the little creep?"

"Well, you know he was attached for a while to G2 at Army, but that didn't last long. Also, that well-heeled dame he was going with, Claire something, a congressman's widow, she dumped him and married the guy who was chief of staff to her late husband's opponent in the primary, he's running for Congress in the fall."

"My, my," and Trainer began to fumble in his pockets for cheroots. He jumped from his seat, called to O'Leary not to leave, and disappeared into his own office.

O'Leary leaned towards Korovitz and spoke conspiratorially in an undertone, "I didn't want to say it before the colonel . . ." Korovitz pricked up his ears. "I heard it from guys who knew Spelling well, that broad he was going with was very demanding in the sack, apparently poor Ronie just didn't measure up, she wanted betta quality and infinitely more quantity, poor Ronie."

"You could've told Trainer about it," Korovitz mildly rebuked the Mess Hall Sergeant. "Why, he loves smutty stories, and the smuttier the better."

"Maybe so," O'Leary respectfully countered, "but not when they are told by a sergeant about an officer."

"You might have something there, Jimmie, you just might."

When Trainer returned, a brand new cheroot protruding roguishly from his mouth, his good humor was contagious.

"The past is always with us," he announced peering this way and that as though expecting a larger audience and resuming his old seat. "We can't get away from it . . . and we can't erase it, therein lies the rub."

"Wise words, Colonel," O'Leary commented at once.

"Can't say I'd disagree with you, sir," Korovitz put in between yawns.

"All those old faces from two years ago . . . they stare at me, keep staring at me. It ain't a good sign."

"I wouldn't pay too much attention to the phantoms of the past raising Cain once in a while," Korovitz spoke soothingly like a kindly physician confronted by a hyped-up patient.

"Those faces frighten me," Trainer stammered out. "I am afraid, I am afraid."

"Would you like a glass of water?" O'Leary asked.

Trainer shook his head. "Let me just sit here, and, Sergeant O'Leary, could you get me a blanket? I'm shivering."

"There's one in the closet," and Korovitz pointed a finger.

"I'll get one of the medical officers to come and speak to you, sir," Korovitz said firmly reaching for the telephone.

"No, no, don't, let me just sit here wrapped in a blanket. I'll be okay, I'll be okay."

He was still shivering even with the blanket snugly round him, but presently he smiled warmly.

"What's become of Major Hastings' widow?" he asked in a frail voice. "Does anybody know? What was her name? Courtney, I think."

"That's right, Colonel," O'Leary replied with conviction and alacrity. "Courtney married the major's brother Randolph who is a big-wig, investments, international trade, that sort of thing; I happen to know people in Boston who know them. She's very happy, both she and Randy are very happy."

"Good," Trainer smiled again.

"As for Captain Spelling," O'Leary went on imperturbably, "well, after the flirtation with G2, and several temporary assignments which didn't amount to a pot of piss, he was assigned to some place in Texas. Still there I believe. If the Colonel would like more information, I'd be happy to provide it. It so happens I have friends in different parts of Texas, and it would be a child's play to get the goods on the gigolo cap-tain."

"No need to," Trainer murmured, "but thanks anyway."

He sat there wrapped up in a blanket but still rubbing his arms to generate more heat, sheepish yet nosily sparkling when Korovitz and O'Leary pulled out something new from the past that caught his fancy—Hastings' prim and proper ways, Honigklausen's quick censure of anything that qualified however loosely as immorality, Spelling's well-advertised patriotism and his desire to save the Republic from the commies at least three times a week, Donkers' smart-ass antics, Hurstwood's backfiring common sense.

"There was a guy cut our hair," Trainer ventured, "a private, what was his name"

"Miller, Chuck Miller, sir," O'Leary promptly obliged.

"And then he disappeared. What happened to him?"

"Had a nervous breakdown, bad news from home. He's out on a medical."

Trainer nodded musingly.

"I'll have some lunch brought to your office, sir," O'Leary suggested solicitously. "You may not feel like driving to the Village."

"Thank you, Sergeant, but no. I brought a sandwich my housekeeper made for me. It'll keep my strength up."

Korovitz came up to Trainer and held a hand against his forehead. "You're not running any fever, sir, but I still advise seeing a doctor."

"This is nothin', nothing, temporary weakness, one minute riling up me bones gone the next."

"Say," and he looked pointedly at Korovitz as though dispelling the others' suspicions of his ill health. "Say, there was a guy a couple of years ago, chosen representative of the rank and file when it came to gripes, silver-tongued and all that but a damned good trooper . . . Billy something . . . ?"

"Billy Cadogan from West Virginia," Korovitz was quick in supplying the information. "I know the family well. Several generations of coal miners, but not Billy."

"Oh?"

"He got to be a paper boy, union official, sure still reads about what goes on in the pits but don't see them no more. He's doing very well, a rising star of organized labor."

"I'll be damned."

"There's another suggestion I'd like to make, if I am permitted." Korovitz was at his most dignified.

"How can I stop you?" Trainer complained.

"You ought to get married again, have someone to look after you."

"That's what Sam keeps telling me."

"Sam?"

"General Samuel Stebbins."

"That Sam!"

"Right. That very Sam!"

"And?"

"And what?"

"Well, will you take his advice?"

"Maybe, but now my stomach's kinda empty. I'll go after me sandwich." He got cumbrously to his feet and hobbled towards his office. With the blanket draped all around him and the cheroot squeezed between the teeth he looked like a great Indian chief in times past who had just cut a deal with the white traders for firewater, a hundred rifles, and whatever else was handy. By the door he stopped.

"I'm run down, need a little rest, that's all," he said meekly. They were watching him with concern.

"Thank you, guys, you take good care of yourselves, d'hear me?" and shut the door behind him.

/ / /

After lunch Trainer was a changed man. He laughingly dismissed reminders that he had had a debilitating spell, laughed off Korovitz's advice for a medical examination, and peered sternly into his eye when Group Sergeant began recounting the misadventures of an old acquaintance in northern Kentucky who had suffered from similar symptoms and was saved by doctors in the nick of time. Buoyant and on the go, he bounced on and off between Group Office, his own office, and that of the Adjutant immersed in day-to-day chores. When the telephone on his desk gave out that shrill alarming clang he so much disliked, he was busily inhaling as much smoke from the cheroot as his lungs would accommodate and then puff it in stages like patrols sent out at a few seconds' intervals on dangerous missions.

"Sir," Korovitz was saying, "it's Specialist Shelton for you on line one, he's calling from outside the base, says it's urgent."

"Yes, Shelton," Trainer broke silence cheerily, "what's up?"

"Sir, I'm on the way to base and am calling from a *gasthaus* roughly half-hour's drive. We haven't heard from Vallejo since 1400 hours yesterday, Sunday."

"He could be busy with his investigation."

"No, sir, the arrangement has always been that he calls both Captain Harrington's number at Army and my fiancée's number in Stuttgart every two hours. His last call was at 1400 hours yesterday. He said everything was fine and since then not a word."

"What is your conclusion, Shelton?"

"That Vallejo is no longer a free agent. He was told to report to Restaurant Dolores at noon yesterday. He called us at noon and then at 1400 hours, both times from the restaurant. Also he may not have been aware that the Moser brothers were taken into custody on Saturday night in Stuttgart as material witnesses and that yesterday morning an arrest warrant was issued for one Hans Ketterer on suspicion of murder . . . I'd say they've got Jesús and are keeping him prisoner, probably somewhere in Stuttgart."

Trainer thought for a moment. "I agree with your conclusion, get down here as fast as you can. Do you have any guesses or information where Vallejo could be kept?"

"I have some names and addresses, sir."

"Good! Report to me on the double!"

"Yes, sir," and Shelton rang off.

Without delay Trainer apprised Fiorello and Lieberman of what he had just heard and asked them to stand by in their offices. Then he sat down at his desk, deep in thought, drumming the cluttered desk with his stubby fingers. When Shelton arrived the five of them congregated in Group Commander's office.

"They have Vallejo," Trainer said, dispensing with preliminaries.

"We gotta get him back. I'm putting together a posse. Sol, John, Shelton, and myself will leave in one hour. Leroy will stay behind to coordinate, take messages, contact us if need be."

"Sir, I have a suggestion," Shelton blurted out.

"Go on."

"Our posse would be strengthened if you added two enlisted men, Vincent Quinn and Oliver Hartmann, sir."

Trainer snickered. "The three musketeers, eh. Pity we can't get the fourth one, what's his name?"

"PFC Frederic Bonsuer was transferred to 7th Army historical section a month ago. He helps write the history of the 7th U.S. Army," Korovitz explained pretentiously.

Trainer snickered again. "Right, we'll have to settle for just the three quarters of the musketeering body and not a single one more. Group Sergeant, give the order. Quinn and Hartmann are volunteering for a special assignment. They are to wear civvies and report here in exactly forty minutes." He turned to Shelton.

"I have civvies with me in the car, sir," the specialist matched Trainer's inquiring glance.

"Good thinking, Shelton." Trainer snickered one more time. "You might be going places," and he immediately addressed Fiorello and Lieberman. "Gentlemen, please change to something unmilitary, doing your damnedest to blend in with the Krauts. Forty minutes!"

"There is something you should know, Ed," Fiorello began biting his lip.

"What?"

"Quinn and Hartmann may be facing charges. I don't think it's a good idea to bring them along."

"Oh? What are the charges?"

"Trespassing, disturbing the peace, possibly intent to break in."

"Why wasn't I told about these charges, John?" Trainer boomed out the question.

"This is my beat, Ed, you've left all such matters to me, remember?"

"Not this one!" Trainer boomed out again. "Not this one!"

"Well?"

"I want all pending charges against Quinn and Hartmann dropped. D'you understand, John?"

"By what authority?" Fiorello called out defiantly.

"By order of Group Commander! And I want them to know about it before they volunteer for this very special assignment. I need their best, not their second best."

"Yes, Colonel." Fiorello's tone did nothing to hide his demur and vexation.

"Another thing, John. Issue side arms to all the members of the posse, including me. Revolvers and live ammo. At once."

"Is this wise, Ed?"

"Major Fiorello, I am giving you a direct order." Trainer spoke through the teeth. "If you refuse to carry it out, I'll find someone else, and I'll see to it that you spend many a moon in a cozy spot in my native state which answers to the name of Fort Leavenworth."

Fiorello shook his head sadly like a seasoned teacher confronted by a recalcitrant pupil responsive to the cane only and to nothing else and at once headed for the armory.

As soon as the major had left there was a knock on the door.

"Come in," Trainer roared.

A well-dressed civilian in his early thirties stood on the threshold.

"I am Detective Sergeant Paulus Gottfried Rickmeyer from Stuttgart City Police. I was sent here personally by General von Metzler to assist you, Colonel Trainer, in locating your missing Group Clerk, Jesús Vallejo."

"You are welcome, Detective Sergeant, and please convey my thanks to the general." Trainer crossed the room, and the two men shook hands.

"What are your precise orders?"

"Please? Oh well! To cooperate with you in any way and when necessary exercise my own judgment."

"Good orders." Trainer nodded approvingly. "You have the addresses of at least some of the houses used by Bund 45?"

"Yes, sir," and Rickmeyer pulled from his pocket a legal-sized sheet of paper. "This is the list of houses the Bund has been using in the last five years. The ones checked in red have been used in the last twelve months."

"I see. Let's spread it on the desk so that all of us can take a peek."

"By all means, Colonel." Rickmeyer went on explaining in some detail the use made of each dwelling as a planning office, storage center, safe house for the operatives, testing ground for small weapons, depository for files and promotion material, and so on. They all listened very closely and asked specific questions which Rickmeyer answered without hesitation. And now, as Trainer was about to speak, Fiorello returned carrying a large subdivided leather bag full of revolvers in holsters and boxes of ammunition.

"Come over here, John, and familiarize yourself with the locations," Trainer said. "We have to make some hard choices."

"Sir?" Shelton raised his hand, and Trainer nodded. "My fiancée did some checking for me. One of the addresses on Sergeant Rickmeyer's list, 47 Schumann Allee rings a bell."

"Go on."

"The house is owned by a Frau Schwämer, Natalie Schwämer, the lady Vallejo met at Restaurant Dolores. Also the house is leased to a German couple by the name of Gustav and Elise Hirsch . . ."

"That sounds familiar," Trainer muttered.

"It should. This is the elderly couple which was conveniently close to the Motor Pool on the night Dieter Hauch was killed and subsequently made a sworn statement that Hauch and Sergeant Steiner had been quarreling."

"What d'you make of it, Rickmeyer?" Glistening pearls of sweat were gathering on Trainer's forehead.

The detective sergeant bent over the list and was running over the names and addresses.

"We know the house, we searched it once, oh, eight or nine months ago. It's an old structure, built in the 1880s, not well kept up, and it has a large cellar. At one time it was a well-stocked wine cellar when Frau Schwämer's grandfather was still alive."

"Any other comments?" and Trainer looked inquisitively around.

"One more thing," Rickmeyer interjected. "The house is secluded, out of the way. There's a garden, and tall trees block the view from the street. The layout allows a lot of privacy, and it's close to the edge of the city."

"Just a place you'd want to keep a prisoner in," Lieberman commented, scrutinizing the list.

"Okay," Trainer said fiddling with his cheroot. "We go there first, surprise has its advantages. If we come out empty-handed, other safe houses will be alerted."

"I shall radio the Headquarters, they'll send a backup," Rickmeyer rapped out at once.

"You'll do nothing of the sort."

"At the very least I have to call the general."

"This time of day your general is sipping jasmine tea, you wouldn't want to interfere with an old man's habits, would you now? I'd call it heartless."

"What is the authority for this mission then?" Rickmeyer persisted, redder and redder in the face, his manner challenging.

"The authority is the U.S. Army, friend, and that's all you need to know."

"He's right, Detective Sergeant," Lieberman put in jovially, "dead right."

"Gentlemen, those of you who have not had the time to change into civvies will do so now. We are pulling out in thirty minutes. You'll draw your weapons then. Dismissed."

In less than thirty minutes they were back in Group Commander's office displaying a wide and colorful variety of civilian attire, Trainer himself sporting a much-worn darkish and crumpled suit which made him look like a clergyman recently defrocked. Quinn and Hartmann, who had arrived earlier, favored sports coats and brighter hues.

"I thank all you men for volunteering for this mission, and especially you, Padre"—Trainer spoke dourly—"our goal is to rescue Specialist Jesús Vallejo who's been kidnapped by a German fascist outfit. There's one addition to our patrol, Detective Paul, Gotty . . . Rickmer."

"It's Paulus Gottfried Rickmeyer," the German policeman cried in desperation.

"Whatever! Draw your weapons, revolver and holster, and two boxes of ammo for each man."

They all followed his instructions to a tee.

"Rickmeyer, you have your own gun, right?"

"Yes, sir, but I must warn you that American personnel are strictly forbidden to carry firearms on German soil unless they are in uniform and part of a military column. This is the law and the agreement between our two countries."

"Well, the law will have to be bent just a tad and the agreement between our two countries pruned a wee bit. Rickmeyer, as of now consider yourself inducted into the U.S. Army, and think of me as your recruiting sergeant. Any breach of discipline on your part will be severely dealt with, understand, soldier!!!"

"Sir, I don't believe what I am hearing," Rickmeyer murmured haplessly.

"Major Fiorello, you own a station wagon, we'll need to use it. Can the seven of us fit into it?"

"No sweat, sir."

"You are the designated driver, Major." Trainer paused and let a commanding eye travel from face to face. Then he thrust his arm forward, the palm held perpendicularly—a signal for the detail to advance.

"We are going in, follow me," he barked. He ran out of the office and down the corridor to the main entrance, the others running behind him. Outside he accelerated, the palm of the hand still held perpendicularly, and the others accelerated behind him. But as he ran, Trainer became aware of someone trying to catch up with him and of indistinct words gasped out. He turned his head and caught a glimpse of Fiorello gesturing and then calling out:

"Ed, Ed, stop."

In a huff he turned towards the Adjutant.

"What the hell d'you want, John?"

"Ed, we are running the wrong way."

"Hell, no! This is the shortcut to the parking lot."

Fiorello was still catching his breath. "But my station wagon is parked outside the Mess Hall. The parking lot was full when I got here after lunch, so . . ."

"You could've had the courtesy to tell me, John. I take it amiss." Then he turned round and thrust his eager arm forward again ferociously giving the same signal. "Forward, full speed!" he roared and ran like a man possessed, the others trying to keep up with him, all the way to where Fiorello's station wagon stood parked in dignified seclusion.

Few words were exchanged on the way to Stuttgart, but once they crossed the city limits they sounded off individually and in unison, exhorting and planning the attack, Fiorello at the wheel, Trainer next to him in the middle, and Rickmeyer to the right of Trainer by the window, Lieberman, Shelton, Quinn, and Hartmann glued to passenger seats in the back.

"We'll have to get the sense of the place first," Lieberman was holding forth, "drive by it several times, familiarize ourselves with the layout, find out how many guards there are, etc., etc.," and he went on outlining his tactics.

"Right!" Trainer joined in rowdily, "case the joint and hope Vallejo's still alive."

"If this would help," and Rickmeyer sounded as much in earnest as he could ever be, "I could pose as an insurance salesman, or any kind of salesman for that matter."

"Good idea, Detective Sergeant," Trainer agreed appreciatively, and then all of them burst out laughing.

"What's the joke?" Rickmeyer asked, shifting a hurt gaze from face to face.

"Nothing, nothing at all," Lieberman assured him, "and no offense meant."

"You should be able to explain rationally why all of you are bellowing with laughter," Rickmeyer persisted.

"It's hard to explain." Fiorello was being friendly and cagey at the same time. "I know I couldn't."

"Sergeant, this door-to-door salesman's gaff has a long history," Quinn's voice was heard from the back.

"Hell of a long history!" Hartmann added with infinitely more volume.

"Well, that's the beginning, go on."

But Quinn and Hartmann were now like two clams, and Rickmeyer shook his head disappointingly.

"John, can't you step on it!" Trainer was all impatience.

"There are speed limits inside the city, Ed."

"In fact, Major, you have been exceeding the speed limit the last several miles, please slow down." Rickmeyer was openly concerned.

"Hell," Trainer hollered, "this milk train routine wasn't part of the deal. German cops can't touch us, so step on it."

"German cops can touch you and will touch you, Colonel, I know precisely what they are empowered to do. And another thing. Your gun is sticking out from your belt. If we are flagged down for speeding or for some other reason and the cops see that you're armed it won't be child's play. There will be a dickens of a price to pay."

"Everyone hide your firearm under your coat or other piece of apparel. This is an order. And this goes for you too, Ed." Fiorello was not joking.

In response Trainer grumbled obscenely and spat out of the window. As the car slowed down they all fell back to planning the entry to 47 Schumann Allee, weighing pros and cons, anticipating the obstacles. They were now very close to the outskirts of town and presently they made a right turn.

"Number 47 is"—Rickmeyer rapidly consulted his notes—"the eighth building on the right-hand side," and in utter silence and at a reduced speed they plodded on. Soon a clump of tall, broadly-trunked trees came into view, their foliage opulent and drooping, and straining their eyes they discerned through the gaps in loosely interlocking branches and fans of fluttering leaves the contours of the old house, wide and low, stone steps jutting out from the base of the façade, and high above a broad, weighty portal with rusty handles standing guard. The house had three stories, and from what seemed to be its middle rose a circular addition, something like an attic, its measurements no more than a fifth of the area below. The outside walls made of stone were in a sad state of disrepair: small fragments were missing, everywhere the thick brown lacquer which had originally covered the well-fitting blocks had all but disappeared, and here and there tufts of grass shot out of the disintegrating rock, birds' nests perching between them. Paint was peeling off the shutters, and on the ground floor every dirty window had at least a portion of it covered with cardboard.

"This mansion has seen better days," Lieberman sighed when they had gone well past it.

"It was a handsome structure when it was freshly built," Rickmeyer declared with pride. "It was written up in newspapers, journals."

"Let's go past it a few more times," Trainer advised. "Is there an alley on the other side?"

"No, no alley, just a fence, and then new property begins."

They turned around and approached the old house from the opposite direction. Now they concentrated on the grounds, as unkempt as the dwelling itself, with refuse scattered pell-mell and bicycle wheels and chains half-submerged in oily puddles. Against the back fence an abandoned shed crouched precariously on yellow grass due to crumble at the slightest nudge. They slowed down and were going to stop when they saw the portal open abruptly and two well-dressed young men coming out. They lit cigarettes and were at once engrossed in an animated conversation. Fiorello accelerated, and they were soon out of sight.

Trainer leaned to the right. "Did you recognize them?"

Rickmeyer shook his head. "They must be new recruits."

"How many entrances are there?"

"Three, the main and the kitchen one at the other end. Also, there is a separate entrance on the right side to the cellar, which communicates with the rest of the house."

"I see." Trainer was musing. "It stands to reason there are more guards around than those two smoking dudes."

"It stands to reason," Fiorello concurred.

"This is what we're going to do." Trainer spoke calmly and with finality. "It's almost 1830 hours now, and it will be dark by 2000 hours. We'll effect entry then. There'll be a staff meeting beforehand, and everyone will know precisely what to do. Any questions?"

"There is a café a mile or so north of here, we could rest up and get ready there," Rickmeyer cautiously suggested.

Trainer wagged a finger. "Right. Can you navigate us, Paul?"

"Actually, sir, it's . . ."

"It's what?"

"Nothing, sir, absolutely nothing."

They remained at the café till 1945 hours, treating themselves to huge portions of sausages and french fries, washing it down with coffee or beer, and planning every move. Shortly before 2000 hours they parked the station wagon two blocks away in a side street, spread out like a patrol in enemy territory, and advanced towards the old house. Hartmann and Lieberman jumped the fence by the shed and pulled out a ladder from its littered floor.

"I kinda suspected this geezer of a shed would have a ladder in it, they usually do," Hartmann whispered grinning broadly. Trainer and Quinn made a zigzag line from tree to tree all the way to the side entrance leading to the cellar, and Fiorello, Shelton, and Rickmeyer congregated by the kitchen door. Dim light glimmered on the ground floor, but high above through two second-story windows glowing light could be seen fed by high-powered bulbs. Lieberman bent over and Hartmann climbed onto his shoulders.

"No one in, quiet as a graveyard," he whispered, "but overcoats are lying on the sofa, they must be inside the house." They put the ladder up against the wall, and Hartmann climbed to the second story. From the edge of the bright windows he was peering inside and spread out his right hand raising a finger from the left one. Then he held up two fingers of the right hand and four fingers of the left hand. Lieberman nodded and beckoned to him to come down. "Tell the others," he whispered. Noiselessly and lightly, as if he had no bodily weight to carry, Hartmann ran to the side entrance and whispered to Trainer and Quinn: "Six persons on the second floor, an elderly couple and four guys looking like guards or operatives." Trainer nodded. With the same noiseless ease Hartmann ran round the house to the kitchen door and repeated the message to Fiorello, Shelton, and Rickmeyer. Fiorello glanced at his wristwatch.

"Right! We are now going to phase two." Using a master key, Rickmeyer and Hartmann opened the kitchen door, and the four of them tiptoed inside. Rickmeyer led the way and pointed to the left. In a matter of seconds they saw the staircase leading to the cellar, and making every effort to be as quiet as possible they began to descend. But every second step or so creaked jarringly, and they presently began to run down the stairs and found themselves in the cellar with the outside door staring them in the face. Rickmeyer pressed the light switch, let Trainer, Lieberman, and Quinn in, and almost immediately they became aware of a commotion above the stairs, men running, agitated voices shouting at one another. Trainer touched Lieberman's shoulder and drew an "8" in the air. The latter nodded, moved away from the door, and disappeared down the main aisle towards the bays. Upstairs someone was frantically pulling the portal open, someone else was rummaging in the kitchen, and footsteps were clearly audible on the stairs leading to the cellar. Rickmeyer turned off the light, and they waited in semidarkness away from the door as one of the men smoking outside the house came down and was groping for the light switch. Trainer thrust his jaw forward in the direction of the stranger, and Quinn's right went into action, while Hartmann stood by with tape and rope.

Before they could do anything else, hoarse voices were calling from the top of the stairs to the now immobilized and speechless Bund operative. All at once Rickmeyer pierced the prisoner with a spiteful glint, smacked his lips, and called out in German: "Everything's fine, come down." Two men came down instantly, and the detective sergeant welcomed them by displaying his police badge and pointing his revolver at each man's belly.

"We are investigating possible kidnapping and various other offenses," he said in German. "My assistants will tie you up for the present and until the police van arrives. Empty your pockets and hand over your identifications." They offered no resistance while Quinn and Hartmann set about their business, laying on a chair the personal belongings of the two men and their revolvers.

"What are the names of the people on the second floor?" Rickmeyer asked. "I want a quick answer."

"Herr Gustav Hirsch and Frau Elise Hirsch."

"And the third person?"

"Lothar von Wellingen. He's just a kid, he likes to play cops and robbers. He's barely sixteen."

"Is he armed?"

"No, no," the two men protested. "He's here just for the fun."

"I hope for your sake you are telling the truth," and under

Rickmeyer's mild manner there lurked a note so ruthless and menacing that the two men sounded off in unison, "It is the truth!"

Rickmeyer turned to Shelton. "I am going upstairs to detain the couple and the young man. Please come with me. Quinn and Hartmann will remain here guarding the prisoners," and the two men mounted the stairs.

Fiorello's inquiring eye sought Trainer's.

"Where the hell is Sol? And is there any sign of Vallejo?"

Trainer gave the appearance of being unusually tense. "Sol's exploring the cellar, it's a hell of a place."

"Let's find him."

"Okay, and you boys take good care of them creeps."

"Yes, sir." Quinn and Hartmann stood to attention.

Trainer went down the main aisle with Fiorello at his heels. Broken down wine stands, tiny rickety tables, overturned stools with seats missing lined the way on both sides, and everything was covered with a thick layer of hardened dust.

"Hi there!" Trainer called out. They heard Lieberman's voice anon. "I'm coming your way," and as they hurried on they soon heard his advancing steps, and presently his tall figure stood before them.

"I checked all the bays and as much of the cellar as I could. In most places there's no sign anyone set foot here for a hell of a long time, except for one spot. It seems to have another compartment at the back, and it's all boarded up."

"There is something here I find very odd, Sol," Fiorello said. "This cellar's supposed to be derelict, and there hasn't been a bottle of wine in here for years, but look at the light, wire fixtures, they're brand new, could've been installed last month."

Trainer and Lieberman nodded. "Let's find that secret bay of yours, Sol," the colonel spoke up, "lead the way!"

"It's almost at the other end."

When Lieberman halted at last and pointed to the right, they saw just another empty, filthy bay with besmeared walls and a littered floor, but in the back new, heavy, close-fitting boards covered what should have been an assortment of bricks and plaster. Using iron bars and whatever tools they could find, they wrenched out the heavy wood, board by board. At once a heavy stench went up their nostrils that made it difficult to breathe. They threw to the side the last board and thrust their flashlights forward. In a bay much less spacious than the one where they stood, a man was tied to a sturdy shaft in the middle, his hands held together by thick rope high above his head so that he was forced to balance himself on tiptoes. It was Vallejo. He was stripped down to the waist, and his mouth was fastened by adhesive tape. He was barely conscious, but when the tape was gently pulled off he smiled wanly. "Mighty glad to see you, Colonel." As they were untying him, Fiorello pointed to his back. Deep lacerations extended horizontally, some quite fresh and others older by hours, starting at the shoulders and descending to the buttocks. On some, blood had already coagulated, but on others it was still in a liquid or semi-liquid state, and here and there it was dripping at short intervals, relentlessly, drop by drop by drop.

"I thought after Korea I'd never see anything like it again," Lieberman drawled out.

"They didn't even dress the wounds," Trainer muttered. "Bastards, they'll pay for this."

They covered him with Lieberman's sweater and Trainer's jacket and supported him on both sides.

"No fresh air was coming to that enclosed space," Fiorello rapped out. "My calculation is in four or five hours there wouldn't be enough oxygen for Vallejo to breathe, unless he died sooner of other causes."

With great care they carried him in an upright position in the direction of the door, but all of a sudden the earsplitting squealing of God knows how many police sirens made them stop.

"I think Rickmeyer's friends are here," Lieberman whispered, keeping an eye on Vallejo. "It won't be long now," and within seconds the house and the cellar were teeming with uniformed German policemen.

A little later the German police doctor was saying to Trainer: "Your boy is fine. Vital signs are all in order. He was dehydrated, of course, had no liquids in more than twenty-four hours, so we gave him lots of water. And he was hungry, not having eaten for the same period of time, so we gave him some hot soup."

"Thank you, Doctor."

"Another thing, Colonel. There was no window or opening of any kind where he was kept. I examined the room. In several hours' time all the oxygen would have been used up, and Specialist Vallejo would've been asphyxiated. You arrived on the eleventh hour. And, of course, we dressed the lacerations on his back. My estimate is that in the last twenty-four hours he received in excess of sixty lashes. But the lacerations will heal. Also, as Specialist Vallejo told me he is not allergic to anything, we gave him injections against possible infection."

Trainer ground his teeth. "When you have finished with him, Doctor, I'd like to take him to the Medical Center at 7th U.S. Army Headquarters in Weiningen."

"Of course, our ambulance will drive him there."

"Could I drive with him, Doctor?"

"Of course, and I wrote a very brief report on his condition. Please give it to one of your army doctors." He handed Trainer a sheet of paper.

The colonel straightened himself up. "I would like to thank you again, Doctor, for what you did for that GI. I am grateful, and the United States Army is grateful." And he saluted.

"You are very welcome, and the patient is in a satisfactory condition." The doctor smiled and moved away.

After some fumbling Trainer located the members of his party and addressed them collectively.

"Gentlemen, thank you for the job well done. I thank you all. Vallejo is fine."

"Where do we go from here?" Fiorello inquired, observing with keen interest the ceaseless activity of the German police.

"Please drive back to base, all of you. I'll accompany Vallejo to Army Medical Center and will probably spend the night there. I want to be with him tonight and when he wakes up in the morning."

Fiorello nodded with feeling. "Understood, Ed."

Just then Rickmeyer appeared out of nowhere.

"Colonel, I have a message for you from my headquarters."

"Shoot, Pauli!"

"My headquarters is advising you in the strongest possible terms not to speak to reporters, German or American, not to hold any press conferences, not to give out any statements about what happened in the last twenty-four hours. Complete silence is to be maintained. This is straight from the general."

The wrinkles on Trainer's forehead were jumping up and falling down spasmodically, and his grimacing face was shifting right and left. At last, his eyebrows raised, he turned towards the German detective. "Please tell the general and your headquarters their request will be complied with all the way. You're still conducting your search and investigation, Detective Sergeant?"

"We are, and we don't want the wrong people to know what we are doing."

"Understood," and then Trainer's countenance brightened. "Pauli, how the hell did you know how to imitate the voice of that guy we nailed to bring downstairs the other two?"

Happy as a sandboy, his nostrils distended, the chin pressed forward, and the head high in the air, Rickmeyer was gazing at the dark heavens above.

"At the Police Academy we had an instructor who had a theory on the . . . on the co . . . correlation between body build and vocal chords, and my own training as a singer . . ." He stopped abruptly, slightly embarrassed. "It would take hours to explain."

"We mustn't detain you, Detective Sergeant," Lieberman put in with studied politeness. "Your hands are full."

"Yes, very full, very full, Captain, and please excuse me."

"You did a great job, Pauli, and all of us are proud of you," Trainer called after him. "And I still want to know how you pulled that goddamn trick. Take care of yeself, Pauli, take care!"

Then Trainer turned again towards his own party.

"Thanks to your initiative and skill our mission has been accomplished, and at this time I wanna single out three of ye for distinction: Sergeant Shelton, Specialist Quinn, and Specialist Hartmann. I salute you men!"

Just then a German policeman was seen frantically waving his arms and shouting at the top of his voice.

"Colonel Trainer, the ambulance is about to leave, please come at once."

Trainer broke into a trot. "John, Sol, I'll see you guys at the base," he hollered without turning his head.

A little later when Fiorello and Lieberman had finished answering questions posed by the ranking German officer, the latter said, making indistinct noises with his tongue and lips:

"It was nice of Ed to promote the three enlisted men right on the spot."

"Damned nice," Fiorello agreed.

"What about us? Don't we deserve promotion?"

"The very same thought crossed my mind."

"Maybe Ed ought to be reminded?"

"Damned right, Sol, you do the reminding, and keep me out of it."

"Oh, I see."

"In every military enterprise there is the front line of attack and the quartermaster corps."

"So?"

"It can be warm and cozy in the quartermaster corps, warm and cozy and quiet, so long as no one is rocking the boat and everyone is minding his own business. Give it some thought, Sol, when your mind is free and easy, give it some thought."

"How could I not to," Lieberman answered pensively, "how could I not to."

/ / /

On Wednesday afternoon, two days after Jesús Vallejo had been forcibly freed from his airtight cell in the cellar of 47 Schumann Allee in the city of Stuttgart, a young MP lieutenant with more freckles on his cheeks than years on his back, in the company of two German civilians, entered the reading room and library at 16th Engineer Group. The young lieutenant had spoken to the librarian, Frau Gruber, on many previous occasions, asking her questions about recent German history, and soliciting her guidance in selecting journals and books about the causes of the two world wars and their painful aftermath. He knew her fairly well and always treated her with great respect. In fact, every time he left her presence he felt better educated, wiser, and more mature. As a mother figure she gave freely of herself but was also exacting and did not brook fools gladly. He was still smarting from one extremely lively encounter when full of confidence he was expounding to her the advantages of a particular economic policy in the early days of the Weimar Republic, only to hear his facts challenged one by one, his conclusions laughed out of court, and his intelligence impugned. He tried to bury the painful experience deep below the level of consciousness, but it had a curious way of surging to the surface when least expected, and twice he saw himself in a humiliating dream standing in the corner of the library wearing a dunce cap.

But now the lieutenant was ill at ease, still disbelieving what he had been told. He doffed his hat and tried to rake up a jovial smile.

"Frau Gruber, these gentlemen are detectives from Stuttgart and," his voice very nearly broke. "They are here to ask you questions."

Not a single twitch of emotion marred Frau Gruber's impassive countenance, and she watched the three of them for an unusually long time without making a sound, the lieutenant thought. Finally she rose to her feet, tall, stately, unapproachable.

"I've been expecting you." Her voice conveyed information and nothing more. "What I did was for the *Vaterland*. I regret nothing," and then pride and defiance were at last ringing out of her, pride and defiance as she threw dauntingly at them her last bullet, her last shot:

"Heil Hitler," and she gave the Nazi salute.

/ / /

On the same Wednesday afternoon, nervous and apprehensive, PFC Frederic Bonsuer was sitting precariously on the edge of the chair facing a grim E.E. Trainer in his office.

"Your section informed me you'd be here to interview me, PFC, if I consented." The colonel was hammering out his words. "What's the name of that section of yours at Army?"

"Historical Section, sir, 7th Army Historical Section."

"Oh, yes," Trainer mused, laboriously clearing his throat. And then for a brief moment his brow lightened. "You're the fourth musketeer, aren't you, Bonsuer?"

"It's nice of you to remember, sir."

"Well, what's up?"

"It's a new venture, sir, Colonel Teleman's baby you might say. Colonel Teleman . . ."

"Lieutenant Colonel Teleman," Trainer corrected Bonsuer in a hollow voice.

"Lieutenant Colonel Teleman has an utterly novel idea about the history of the 7th Army. I might add at this juncture that Lieutenant Colonel Teleman is a seasoned newspaperman with long years of experience in the trade, especially with what he calls 'more digestible' papers, not the *New York Times* or the *Christian Science Monitor* . . ."

"Oh, no," Trainer broke in.

". . . but with the dailies that speak to the man in the street, are understood by him, capture in print his cravings and desires." Bonsuer was warming to the subject and went on full tilt portraying the more easily digestible papers in vivid images, drawing comparisons, present-ing arguments, returning to base, and then daringly, his strength redou-bled, flying off to new images, comparisons, and arguments.

Trainer listened in stony silence.

"To come back to our muttons," the visitor continued smiling engagingly, "in the past the history of the 7th Army was a dismal affair; stuffy, desiccated, its record of engagements, deployments and redeploy-ments, cocky advances and tactical retreats withering on the vine, frightening the would-be readers, and chasing the dead back to their graves rather than being subjected to a single page of it. In short the old history is dead, and no sane person will come within a reading distance of it."

Here the speaker paused, tossed his head this way and that, and resorting to expressive gestures, jumped with both feet into his next argument.

"Hank Teleman, please excuse me, Lieutenant Colonel Teleman wants to change all this."

"Aha!"

"The new history will contain a human element, a human touch. Chief has high hopes for it, he wants it to be a bestseller. After all, times change, and U.S. Army can't stay in mothballs forever. Hank, Chief I mean, is looking forward to the day, not far removed if I may indulge in a prophecy, Colonel Trainer, when the *New History of the Seventh United States Army* will hold its own in the highly competitive market where different kinds of popular literature mingle freely, each of them brother or sister to all the others, because each of them can vaunt its unmistakable human element, its unmistakable human touch."

"Is the Army buying it?" Trainer again laboriously cleared his throat.

"At present, sir, our colonel is engaged in delicate negotiations with the top brass but," a saccharine insider's smile was forking Bonsuer's mouth, "a birdie told us the prospects are excellent."

"Okay, ask your questions, PFC."

Bonsuer leaned forward in his seat, and his bearing reflected a newly formed camaraderie with the colonel and a new bond between them, that of two devoted toilers in a common enterprise.

"The dreary catalogue of battles won, rivers crossed, prisoners taken, and the reverse of it all bores everybody to tears," he began, "but you and I, sir, and Hank, of course, we three march to a different drummer."

He leaned further forward, and now his manner was unmistakably conspiratorial.

"What can you tell me, sir, about the native women when you were in combat in Italy and later in Belgium? What was the going rate for a quickie? How was it arranged? I understand there were broads who followed the army all the way from Sicily to the Swiss border. How much did they charge? Were there other women for hire? How about the VD rate, did it fluctuate, or was it more or less constant? And the gays in uniform? How many have you encountered? How were they treated?" Bonsuer was now rattling off, elaborating, filling the gaps, answering some of the questions himself. "This will ginger up the text, Hank's words not mine, and the final generic question regarding the booze? How much was drunk on different occasions, was alcoholism rampant or incidental? Any stories you can tell me of men hopelessly drunk or so horny they couldn't hold a rifle until getting their rocks off, or smarting under VD and pitifully regretting not using rubbers, or stories of gay men shamefully exposed, all these would ginger up the page. Our readers will want to know everything and more, and this will keep our volume on the bestsellers' list for a damned long time; this human touch in no way detracting from the bravery and gallantry of our troops in the IIWW and in Korea, this being understood by all parties, I trust."

Trainer was strangely quiet during Bonsuer's voluble performance, but when the young man at last fell silent he raised his shoulders and clapped his hands.

"Private First Class, Bonsuer," he spoke in fatherly accents, "will you please stand up?"

"Certainly, sir."

"And now will you make a ninety degree turn to the left, you will be facing the door."

"Of course, sir."

What happened next was so outlandish and in fact so fantastic that Bonsuer's senses were feeding into his brain an irrational belief that he had been knocked unconscious and was now living through a horrible nightmare. Powerful boot kicks were landing on his posterior with deadly precision, right side, left side, right side, left side, and at last he recognized he was fully conscious and a victim of brutal abuse. Turning his head to see what lay behind him, he caught sight of Trainer, a savage grimace twisting his face, kicking him again and again as if nothing else in the world mattered.

"Stop it, sir, stop it, it hurts," he screamed at last, dashing towards the door and excitedly turning the knob but not before receiving two more painful blows. In the corridor he ran as fast as his legs would carry him, but his persecutor was on his heels kicking, and Bonsuer screamed again, "It hurts, I won't be able to sit down for days, let me go." It was not till he had reached the main entrance and cast a glance backwards that he saw Trainer standing nonchalantly some distance away, his malevolent eyes still fixed on him. Bonsuer gave the door a push and ran all the way to his car while Trainer sauntered back to his office, but not before Korovitz stuck his head into the corridor and asked, "Is everything all right, sir?"

"Everything's not only all right, Group Sergeant," Trainer answered with splendid self-assurance, "but as it goddamn ought to be."

Chapter 11

They had placed themselves incongruously far from each other in the living room in their house at the Village, she standing at one end by the passage leading to the kitchen folding their sons' shirts, pants, and underwear, and he sitting tensely on the couch at the other end, the whole length of a diagonal separating them and bisecting the large area; incongruously removed because normally they had always sat very close to each other or had reclined on the same love seat.

"So when do you propose to move out so you can be with your German slut?" Rachel Lieberman gave every indication of being wholly absorbed by the laundry basket, but presently she let her eye roam over the walls and shouted with rage. "When?"

"I don't know," Sol Lieberman answered quietly. "I don't know. I'll move out whenever you want me to move out."

"Will you stop being a rabbi, and will you also resign your commission?"

"I don't think I'll be able to continue as a rabbi after the divorce," he answered again in the same quiet, level tone. "As for the Army . . . well, I really haven't come to that bridge yet; I might go back into the Reserves."

Rachel pushed the laundry basket out of the way and was looking into his eyes, her arms akimbo.

"We are planning ahead, aren't we," she laughed maliciously, but her eyes were moist and she began to sob. He stood up and bent forward, his arms poised in her direction, but she wiped her face at once and hissed: "Don't come near me, don't touch me!"

He quietly sat down, and she went on raucously.

"You said 'after the divorce,' but how the hell do you know that I'll give you the divorce in the first place? Who the hell told you? Unless you lost all your marbles I never mentioned divorce."

He was silent for several seconds and then spoke firmly, not pleading with her but being impersonal and clinical.

"If the roles were reversed, I'd give you a divorce. I would do so because I'd understand that you need a divorce to start a new life with a man who means more to you than the whole damned world. This is called mutual trust, Rachel, this is called understanding, this is called common decency."

"Common decency!" she sneered. "When my husband of nine years who also happens to be a rabbi, that is a leader of the congregation, picks up a German slut half his age and wants to destroy our marriage and make our sons fatherless, I am advised to comply because it is common decency . . . I don't know if I should laugh or cry."

"I am asking you again not to call Nina a slut. She is not a slut."

"Such gallantry," Rachel sneered again. "I'm sorry, but there has been so little of it shown to me."

Sol looked beat now, beat and downcast because he was about to embark on the same monologue he had uttered several days before with very little success. He braced himself for yet another exercise in futility.

"Rachel, please listen carefully . . . We talked about it already, and perhaps after tonight there'll be no need to stir up the ashes, everything will be settled once and for all."

Her mocking smirk and the ill will that was graven all over her face assured him that in point of fact matters would remain unsettled for a long time to come. Still, he pressed on.

"I didn't decide one fine day to fall in love with Nina. My falling in love was not a conscious act. But having fallen in love with her I want to share my life with the woman I love. This is of paramount importance to me. Frankly, everything else dwindles in comparison. I am sorry, but this is the way things are. Rachel, I'd like to spare you discomfort and grief, but I don't know how, I don't know what to do. As for the practical arrangements, I'll agree to anything you stipulate . . . anything within reason."

"The boys stay with me, I'll have the custody," she snapped.

"So be it, but I hope I'll be able to see them from time to time."

"I don't know, have to think about it, I'm not certain you deserve it."

"The financial settlement will favor you."

"This is not about money, Sol, in case the obvious truth hasn't dawned on you."

"I know," he said sadly. "I know."

Rachel took a step to the left and sat down nimbly on a chair. She had regained her composure, and only her eyes red and puffy and smudges of the mascara round them testified to what she had been through.

"You think of this fling as the grand passion of your life, one and only, love at first sight, an unbreakable bond, something out of a medieval romance. Let me tell you, my good man, this is your early climacteric, you're nearly thirty-six, and you are bewitched by young flesh. The hots, your hots, are a classical medical case. They'll probably last for several months, and then you'll want to go back to the old ways and to the wife who is no longer a teenager. This is what usually happens, except that when you come back to your senses, I shall no longer be here waiting for you."

"This will not happen," he said firmly. "I mean my wanting to come back."

"I wonder! How old is the slut?"

"Nina is twenty-two, and I am asking you again not to call her by that name."

She shrugged her shoulders ostentatiously, nurturing that look of deadly contempt behind which an ironic, patronizing fillip lent her an added dose of self-assurance.

"So, what are your plans, scumbag?"

"We want to get married as soon as," he scanned her face searchingly, "I am free to marry. And then I am taking Nina to Kansas City.

I'd spoken to Dave, and there will be a job waiting for me at KC Printing. Both Dave and Ken understand."

"Lucky your brothers are in your corner."

"They are family, Rachel."

"So am I, Matt, and Sol, Jr.!" She countered with wanton bitterness.

"I haven't forgotten, Rachel."

"So you'll be joining the family business, good for you," she went on oscillating between blind fury and sardonic repartees, "and the slut, whatever her name, will she also have a perch somewhere within the city limits? After all, there are so many street corners and so many street-lights!"

"In the middle of June Nina will graduate from Tübingen University with a degree in urban architecture. After that she'll need practical experience before she gets her license. Dave already spoke to the people at Pembroke, Fisk, and Fein, and they will be glad to accept her as a matriculated apprentice as of September 1st."

"Pembroke, Fisk, and Fein?" Rachel placed her index finger on the tip of her nose and was being coquettishly inquisitive.

"The biggest architects in Kansas City. You must remember them, we met Tom Pembroke and Allen Fisk at parties, and Father entertained them on numerous occasions."

"I think my mind is going, which shouldn't surprise anybody, because my life is over. Do you understand what I am saying to you, scumbag?"

"Nina wants a career of her own," Sol continued, paying no attention to what Rachel had just said. "She balks at the very thought of being just a *hausfrau*. She is a liberated woman, and I am using this expression attaching the best possible meaning to it."

"You thought of everything, clever you. You take care of your slut. She ought to be grateful."

The big hand of the Swedish clock on the mantelpiece, with its angular design and thick brown pigment that glistened in the light, sidled tightly to eleven, and they sat in silence as the hours tolled by. The clock had been a favorite of Sol's ever since he spotted it at a Swedish bazaar in Kansas City years before, and he and Rachel took turns in extolling the correspondence of its straight lines and sharp angles with the shrillness of the toll. The clock was for them an inter-art marvel unifying sound and space.

"I have to check on the boys," Rachel said calmly.

"I'll go with you."

She hesitated for a moment and nodded assent.

"Don't get any wrong ideas," she laughed.

"I'll try not to," he whispered, following her.

When they came back to the living room, Sol held her hand.

"Could your sister come and stay with you . . . until it's all over? You need someone to be with. Perhaps both of them, Debbie and Trent?"

"Debbie possibly, but I am sure Trent couldn't find the time. He's just been nominated dental surgeon of the year, and he's too busy filling his pot of gold."

"Your parents?"

"Oh no, never . . . I haven't told them yet, and I dread the moment when I do."

He was caressing her hand and said, "You shouldn't be alone, you must have somebody to lean on."

"I have the booze," she exclaimed. "It will knock me out when I can't cope. In fact," and she looked him over head to foot, "it's time to get plastered. You can join me, Mister, misery loves company."

"No!" he shouted. "You mustn't, I won't allow it."

She was nonplussed and stared numbly into space.

"I know what I am doing to you is dreadful, but I'll spare no time or effort to help in any way I can. No, I won't give up Nina, I never will, but I'll do my utmost and more to make things better for you, to be there when you need me, to hold your hand when you want it held."

"I want a very large scotch and then another very large scotch." She sounded like a red-hot customer at the bar.

He winced. "No, this is not the way. It's time for you to hit the hay, young lady."

"But I lost my bearings, which way is our bedroom?"

"I'll point the way."

"Be gentle, Sol, no pushing, no shoving."

"I'll be gentle." He put his arm round her tender body and led her with great care across the house.

/   /   /

Even before the plane began circling over Baltimore, Lieutenant Ernest J. Tannenbaum was eager to set foot on solid ground, and although his seat was in the middle of the tourist cabin, he managed to be first in line when the stewardesses finally gave the signal for disembarking. He ran down several flights of stairs to street level and headed for the wide gate marked "Transportation, Limos, and Cabs." Once outside he hailed a cab and shoved a scrap of paper with the address scrawled out on it under the driver's nose.

"That's way out of town," the cab driver rolled the white of his eyes, "it will cost you the whole of six bucks, Lieutenant. Are you sure? There are buses going that way."

"Yes, I'm sure," Tannenbaum bawled. "I'll take the cab."

He was hardly aware of the splendor of the vegetation on both sides of the road as they hurried through the environs of Baltimore—thickets of shrubs and woody plants displaying the intense colors of the month of May, rolling grasslands with flowers springing up on all sides, majestic trees with foliage so impenetrable they created sanctuaries round them which the gods of willow, birch, and oak guarded jealously. As they had reached the edge of the estate where the enormous park full of flowerbeds, fountains, and statues encircled the De Brabantz mansion he could hardly suppress a chuckle. The structure was most imposing by any standard, but different parts of it reflected the changing styles of the last two centuries and the different tastes of its successive inhabitants. "Thank God, no additions were made in the last ten years," he muttered.

"Any particular place you want me to drop you off?" the driver asked, slowing down.

"Take me to the main entrance. You'll have to follow that winding driveway. It goes on forever."

"Right you are, sir."

As they were winding their way past countless bends and curves, Tannenbaum again let his eyes rest on the mansion itself growing asymmetrically before them. He knew its history well, having heard it from Mr. Carey De Brabantz himself and countless times from the redoubtable head gardener, Mr. Flint. When Isaac De Brabantz had come with sacks of gold to the American shores in the year 1736 and settled in what was then the Royal Province of Maryland, he had a house built some thirty miles away from the waxing burg of Baltimore in the high style of his native Andalusia. But Don Miguel, his eldest son, a classicist by association, had no patience with cloisters and winding balconies, and set his mind on enlarging the family seat by making it part of imperial Rome. Greek columns and bare granite walls now surrounded on three sides the Andalusian hearth and tiny windows let in little light. The mansion tripled in size was unbearably cold in winter and egregiously uncomfortable in all seasons, and members of Don Miguel's family complained endlessly of his inhumanity. He stood his ground, dismissed his family's laments as the whining of spoiled puppies, asserted whenever it pleased him the absolute authority of paterfamilias, and predicted on his deathbed, to everyone's utter disbelief, that Washington, the capital of the Great Republic, whose cause he had joined late in the day, would follow in the matter of official architecture the precepts of Imperial Rome.

His son George, wealthier many times over than his father and grandfather and embittered by prolonged waiting before he became lord of the manor, decided to bring a new broom to the thorny issue of the family seat. A frequent visitor to the British Isles and the toast of the literati of London and Paris, he developed an abiding interest in the Middle Ages, in the emotive and the spontaneous in literature, in ballads, and folklore. So far as architecture was concerned he prided himself on being a fearless advocate of the Gothic Revival, and without interfering with the existing structure he more than doubled its size in a decidedly Gothic manner building, turrets, and spiky roofs, constructing chambers with vaults and very high ceilings, and fitting stained glass in all the windows.

But this fearless artistic revivalist was also committed to comfort. On all four stories of the immense De Brabantz manor a host of fireplaces was built, new vents and chimneys installed, windows widened, new doors furnished. Not the least of the permanent innovations carried out with great skill, and at great expense was the entirely new furniture, which now filled all the rooms, new tapestries, carpets and rugs, and new bric-a-brac. Antiques were everywhere, but stress was also laid on the comfort the chairs, couches, and ottomans were expected to afford. George De Brabantz opined that conscious as he was of the execrable taste his father and grandfather had shown, he was at pains to show perfect taste with all the amenities of an up-to-date technology thrown into the bargain. The successive bearers of the illustrious name made some changes and improvements in the building itself, but these were essentially minor, except for their electric light, and efforts were mostly directed at the grounds, the swimming pools, new stables, and a golf course.

George De Brabantz—it was recognized—had looked ahead and had looked well. Without ever aspiring to the honor he became the family's favorite ancestor, his name being called out or whispered on all sorts of occasions. By the end of the nineteenth century as the De Brabantz mansion came to be revered both as an historical monument and a social and cultural center, the family itself could boast of its many distinguished public servants, soldiers who gave their lives for the Union and openhanded philanthropists equally adroit at amassing fortunes as at giving them away—among them Nathan De Brabantz, Carey's uncle, bosom friend and colleague of Senator Henry Cabot Lodge. The present occupant of the mansion followed the family tradition, enlisting as a very young man, seeing service in France in World War I and being awarded high American and French decorations; in later years a financier on a grand scale yet always willing to serve on crucial governmental committees to which he was appointed by President Roosevelt and President Truman.

Ernest pulled at the ornate bell, and a tall, silver-haired man dressed in black opened the door.

"I am Lieutenant Ernest Tannenbaum. I am here to see Mr. and Mrs. De Brabantz and Miss Vivien, of course."

For a brief moment the man was summing him up like an intelligence officer sums up in interrogation a prisoner or defector, always bearing in mind that a grimace or a sigh, or the way ash is tipped off a cigarette, may yield as important, if not more important, a clue as a reasoned, well-prepared answer.

"I trust you had a good flight, sir; De Brabantz family is expecting you in the small drawing room. I am Alfred, the butler, let me take your coat and hat, and please follow me."

"Thank you, Mr. Alfred."

"Just Alfred, Alfred will do, sir," and the butler smiled indulgently as one smiles at a child assuming an innocent appearance while hiding stolen candy under her blouse. They traversed at a quick pace several luxuriously appointed rooms and stood on the threshold of the small drawing room.

"Lieutenant Ernest Tannenbaum, sir," Alfred announced with easy dignity.

At once a man trim and of middle height whose age could lie anywhere between forty and sixty wearing checkered trousers and a cashmere sweater rose to his feet and advanced to greet him, holding out his hand.

"All of us are so glad to see you again, Lieutenant," he said smiling and doing his best to put the visitor at ease.

"It's my pleasure, sir."

A woman wearing a long, stylish skirt and a matching vest half-covered by radiant trailing scarves stood on tiptoes and implanted a peck of a kiss on Tannenbaum's cheek.

"Miss Sarah," he cried out exultantly. "How you doin'?"

"You were a good friend to Vivien, Lieutenant, when she badly needed a friend, and this will not be forgotten."

"It's Ernest, Miss Sarah, it's always Ernest for you and for you too, sir," Tannenbaum cried out again.

And now a slim, dark-haired woman in her early twenties very smartly dressed, her face and hair showing what marvels exclusive beauty salons and hairdressers can accomplish, stepped forward.

"It's been so many years, Ernest, too many years."

"Eleven to be precise, Vivien."

"You're tall and all muscles."

"This is very true, eleven years ago we thought of you as the fat boy," Miss Sarah added.

But Vivien was in no mood to exchange witticisms, reminiscences, or repartees. She ran up to Ernest and threw her arms around him, kissing him lovingly on both cheeks. She hugged him again and again, and finally she managed to let fall:

"Oh, I am so happy to see you, Ernest, I've got so much to tell you, we've got so much to talk about."

"We do, we do."

At this point Carey De Brabantz faced Ernest and congratulated him on receiving the commission, and the four of them gave free rein to small talk.

"Is the redoubtable Mr. Flint still around?" Ernest asked with a touch of malice.

"He's semi-retired, but his temper hasn't improved with years," De Brabantz informed him, chuckling.

"For some time now we've found him very bitter and unpleasant," Miss Sarah confided in Ernest, "and his social views verge on the tyrannical, fascist . . . I don't know if I am using the right word."

"I thought he was nutty the way he always put the blame on what he called the lower classes," Vivien said, pulling a face. "Another nutcase."

De Brabantz knitted his brow. "Flint is extremely conservative, furthermore he believes that one is glued to one's place in society from birth on. Consequently any notion of social mobility is anathema to him. Strange views for someone born in this country, as he was. He also served in the Navy, with distinction I understand."

"I'm glad he's going away," Vivien concluded.

"Our incoming head gardener, Jim Braddock, is a different kettle of fish altogether. He's a jolly kind of fellow, telling jokes and stories all the time and an excellent planner."

"You must've noticed all kinds of changes in the household, Ernest," Miss Sarah went on. "In your days our butler was Thomas . . . I am sure you remember him, but he retired six years ago, and Alfred took his place."

Ernest was silent, grinning and nodded his head.

"You remember Thomas?" Miss Sarah persisted.

"Actually, I don't, Miss Sarah. You see eleven years ago when I worked on the grounds, I never entered the mansion itself. I dealt only with Flint and . . . and his assistants, and it was always outside the house."

"How silly of us not to remember it," De Brabantz chuckled self-deprecatingly, "but since we are on the subject of grounds, let me show you what will be done to the park." He led Ernest to the window and began to outline and explain. "Do you see those two paths crossing by the large fountain at the back?"

"Yes," Ernest confirmed cautiously.

"Well, all that part of the park will disappear. New landscaping from here to well beyond the fountain. Instead of all those crisscrossing paths and lanes a new avenue will be laid out dividing the park into two equal parts for pedestrians and cars." He was infinitely more excited about the landscaping project than anyone else in the small drawing room, and he launched into the manifold advantages it would bring to all and sundry when completed. But a hand was laid on his shoulder, and he heard his wife's voice. "Carey, I think we ought to leave the young people to themselves, they have so much to talk about."

"Could I just finish what I began saying?" De Brabantz asked, put out. "I'm sure Ernest is keenly interested in the park."

"I am sure he is not," Miss Sarah put in very gently. "Let's sit in the library, I am inexcusably behind going over my favorite magazines."

"Of course," her husband agreed, "if the two of you will excuse us," and he looked pointedly at Vivien and Ernest.

"Certainly, sir."

"Thanks, Dad and Mom." Vivien was being brisk and appreciative.

"It's good to see you again," Vivien said stroking the sleeve of his coat. "I made such a mess of things."

"You couldn't foresee the marriage would fall apart."

"Perhaps not, but I was warned by friends and by my father . . . my close friends told me point blank he was just a playboy first and foremost and underneath not a very nice one . . ."

"And your father?"

"Well, I remember the long conversation Daddy and I had on the eve of our engagement. Daddy said, 'Kitten, if you think you'll be happy with Wendell there's nothing more to be said; you have my blessing and best wishes. But it's only fair to tell you once you take away his party spirit and that famous charm, there's nothing left. Wendell doesn't have a single thought in his head.' Well, Daddy was right. I found out very soon that beneath the smile and the laughter and the constant obsession to have one hell of a party there was very little really. And soon after the wedding he started seeing someone else. That was the last straw."

"And your mother?"

"She was the one who was pushing for the marriage. She told me afterwards she'd been hopelessly wrong, but it was way too late."

"Vivien, you told me in your letters Wendell's family moved in the same . . . social circles as your family?"

"Very true, and this is what made mother such an ardent advocate. They are immensely wealthy, and they are fully-fledged Sephardic Jews just like the De Brabantzes. Actually their family came from Spain to America—twenty years or so before my family. Ernest, aren't you getting bored stiff with all that pedigree nonsense? You should be!"

"This is part of you, and I wouldn't get bored with anything that's truly you."

She was radiant. "Another thing that has to be dredged out regarding the fast disappearing Wendell has to do with his being the only son, in fact the only child. So, you see, on paper it all looked most promising: an alliance of two mighty families, the only son marries the only daughter, and they will live in unabated luxury till death doth them part."

"I am sorry for your sake this didn't turn out the way you had hoped. Your letters when things began to go wrong were frantic."

"And your letters, Ernest, made it possible for me to get through it. Without you, I don't know where I'd be today." Her eyes were moist now, and all of a sudden she began to cry, tears trickling down her cheeks continuously, and the crying becoming uncontrolled, desperate. He took her in his arms and held her very close, her head resting on his shoulder, her cheek barely touching his. It was the embrace of the big, fearless brother protecting his helpless sister, seeing that no harm comes to her. And the embrace lasted and lasted.

"Your letters kept me going during the crisis and before they were always the source of infinite joy. How many times have we written to each other?" she asked airily. "It must be in the hundreds."

"Oh at least," he egged her on.

"Eleven years."

"Eleven years," he repeated. "I think your parents deserve credit for allowing us to write to each other at all, especially for allowing you to write to me."

"My parents are really quite enlightened, no matter what impression they may give."

"You know, when things were going from bad to worse with Wendell I could barely keep myself from calling you, but in the end I decided not to, because I didn't know how your parents would take it."

"Probably just as well you didn't. When you wrote I could read the letters again and again, and they always gave me strength. Calls would be different. You should be an M.D., Ernest, you understand the human psyche." She uttered the words with pride.

He smiled, and a touch of lightheartedness gladdened his mien.

"I am just a very junior army officer on the brink of a new career."

"But with heaps of intelligence and sensitivity that few others possess."

"Thanks very much, Vivien, I understand the ordeal will soon be over."

"That's right, as I told you in my last letter, as soon as Daddy had found out things were truly hopeless between Wendell and me, he set about organizing an amicable divorce."

"Go on, this is the part I know nothing about. Go on," he cried with fervor.

"The lawyers already reached an agreement. Wendell will not contest, he acknowledges adultery, there is practically nothing in the property settlement since he is not claiming anything, and I get the custody of Jocelyn with very loosely formulated visitation privileges for Wendell. Anyway he said through his attorneys he has no abiding interest in Jocelyn."

"It's a piece of work!" Ernest came out with after a moment's reflection. "A well-conducted campaign."

"We have to pay court costs, though," Vivien laughed. "But it's well worth it."

"I'll say!"

"Wendell's lead attorney told Daddy his client had behaved like a perfect gentleman, to which Daddy retorted 'the first and last time in his life, I'll wager.'"

They were immersed in laughter, and finally Ernest asked: "What is the time frame at present?"

"A month to the day from now, which will be June 21st, the final hearing will be held at the Superior Court in Baltimore. As is his custom, the judge will make one last appeal to both parties to reach a reconciliation. Failing this, the parties will be declared divorced, and I shall be a free woman again."

"Congratulations, Vivien, congratulations from the bottom of my heart."

"The best part of it, apart from getting rid of Wendell, is that I may keep Jocelyn. I love her, Ernest, even though Wendell is the father. I love her, and if I couldn't keep her it would be unbearable, truly unbearable."

"I know, and I loved the snapshots you sent."

"I'm sorry you can't see her today, the Wolverhamptons, our distant neighbors to the north, are throwing a huge party for their grandchildren—there are so many of them they're beyond counting—and Jocelyn was invited. She's there with her nanny. Her first formal engagement."

"How old is she now?"

"She'll be ten months old in a few days, ten months and I love her dearly."

Presently they fell silent, as if digesting all they had imparted to and heard from each other, all thoughts, feelings, suppositions and predictions, principal and subsidiary, those that tore their breasts apart, and others that were merely dimly experienced. Vivien had risen to her feet and stood there intensely alive and commanding.

"Oh, Ernest, you are now an officer, and you rose from the ranks, just like Daddy did from private to captain in the First World War. You've written to me lots and lots, but I want to hear what was happening to you in the last eleven years from your own lips, and mostly about OCS. Let's sit on another couch, over there"—she pointed to the far end of the small drawing room, which to Ernest looked most spacious indeed, belying its name—"this couch here I find curiously jaded."

They sat down on the other couch which for Vivien exuded a new and fresh quality, and she asked him question after question to which he gave exhaustive answers only to be interrupted now and then, adroitly doing his utmost to answer several questions all at once and warding off others. She wanted to know about his life as an enlisted man, about OCS, and about his plans for the future, about his family and his friends. He talked and talked, and so did she. In time they shifted to other topics and tried to do justice to all of them. When Vivien unintentionally glanced at her watch, she threw her arms in the air.

"What time is your plane?"

"8:35."

"It's almost 7:30, and all this time I offered you nothing to eat. What kind of a hostess am I?"

"You're a wonderful hostess, Vivien. Don't give it another thought."

She picked up the telephone and dialed the intercom:

"Daddy, we have to get Ernest to the airport! His plane takes off at 8:35!"

"I think we can do it, kitten," Ernest heard De Brabantz's collected voice. "Speak to Alfred and have Joseph bring the Rolls to the front of the house in five minutes. Can you and Ernest meet us by the front door in five minutes?"

"Yes, Daddy. I would gladly drive you myself, but they pulled my license for six months," Vivien explained sheepishly. "I was a wee bit under the influence."

"We really have lots of time," De Brabantz announced confidently, opening the car doors. "You kids had better get in the back."

On the way to the airport Miss Sarah conveyed to Ernest in simple words how happy she was to see him after all these years. "You must come again soon, promise?"

"I promise, Miss Sarah."

De Brabantz caught Ernest's eye in the rearview mirror.

"Be certain to come back. Now you're a friend of the family."

"Thank you, sir."

As they stopped in one of the non-parking zones in front of a main entrance, De Brabantz said: "I hate to say this, my boy, but you'd better run."

As Ernest jumped out of the Rolls, he turned to the three of them.

"Thank you for everything, Miss Sarah, and thank you very much, Mr. De Brabantz. Vivien, three cheers," and he blew her a kiss. Then he ran so fast they would not be able to see him for the dust had there been any dust in his way. At the airline counter, the slightly embarrassed agent, her eyes twinkling, said in an undertone, "I am sorry, but your flight has been delayed for forty-five minutes." Ernest sat down on a solitary bench far from the madding crowd and ruminated. The delay lasted not forty-five minutes but an hour and half, and when he finally stood in the terminal at the Newark Airport the walled-in clock was signaling 11:10. He obtained quarters from a coffee shop attendant who was closing up, found a public phone, called the operator, and began to insert the coins. Soon a familiar voice came up. He steeled himself to be composed and unhurried: "Alfred, this is Ernest Tannenbaum, I am very sorry to be calling so late, but could you patch me up to Miss Vivien? It's rather urgent."

"I think this can be arranged, sir. I know Miss Vivien has not yet retired for the night." Ernest was detecting a touch of conspiratorial bonhomie in Alfred's voice.

"Ernest, are you all right, or has there been a terrible accident?" Her voice was weighed down with worry.

"No accident, and everything's hunky-dory. I just wanted to say how great it was to see you."

"It was great to see you too."

"Vivien?"

"Yes, Ernest?"

"As I was saying . . ."

She waited without muttering a single word.

"The truth of the matter is I love you, and I have always loved you. Will you marry me?"

"Yes, Ernest," she cried with joy. "I love you too, and yes, I will marry you, I will, I will, I will."

He walked to the curb where a Fort Dix bus collected military personnel bent on entering or reentering the base after a night on the town, but the last bus had left only a couple of minutes before, and he was scouring the street for a cab when a large four-door sedan pulled up.

"Looking for a ride to base, Lieutenant?" a friendly sergeant behind the wheel called to him. "Hop in, and if you don't mind, please sit up front. I have some raw recruits in the back, mere kids, and they can't hold the booze."

Tannenbaum got in.

"Me and my buddies try to help all those who are new to the military. Some of 'em kids don't know what AWOL means."

"They should," Tannenbaum put in callously, "this is one of the first things they are taught in basic."

"This is absolutely true, sir, absolutely true," the sergeant was accommodating. "Still, some of 'em kids have short memories." They drove in silence, but very soon the sergeant spoke again. "We carry out those rides to and from base as part of a charitable effort, and the proceeds go into a fund for widows and orphans."

"Whose widows and what orphans?" Tannenbaum asked.

"It's kinda hard to explain in a single sentence, sir," the sergeant replied unperturbed. "But take it from me, it's in a good cause. We ask for voluntary contributions only, donations you might say."

Tannenbaum pulled out his wallet. "Will five dollars cover the time and effort of your driving me to base, Sergeant?"

"It will indeed, sir, and I thank you from the bottom of my heart. I can always spot an Academy man," he added with a quick smirk. Next he folded neatly the bill and took out a business card from his coat pocket. "This is for the future, and just in case," he said, pressing the card into Tannenbaum's hand. "We can help any enlisted man . . . and an officer too if need be, with AWOL, drunkenness, and other petty offences, but nothing heavy. I know most of the MPs around here, having been an MP myself at one time, and my buddies have their own connections. You have my army and my private number on the card, and either will do. Should a man under your command, Lieutenant, need a little help, you know where to turn."

"Thank you, Sergeant, I'll bear this in mind."

"It will be a pleasure, sir."

"I have only one request now," Tannenbaum said brusquely. "That you take me to my destination first before you attend to your benevolent and charitable activities."

"No problem there, and with all due respect aren't you a wee bit harsh on a simple guy trying to make an extra buck?"

"Drop me by Officers' Temporary Quarters, it's a block past the main gate on the right." Tannenbaum was being brusque again.

"Will do, and may I wish the Lieutenant a very happy, a very satisfying night."

Chapter 12

Long before the members of the tribunal were scheduled to take their seats, the Court-Martial Chamber at 7th U.S. Army Headquarters in Weiningen began to fill. The portion called affectionately or mischievously the Gallery where every Tom, Dick, and Harry could sit on a hard wooden chair, look wise and pitilessly survey men broken on the wheel of justice or on rare occasions set free, was already half-full. The visitors were mostly NCOs often accompanied by their families, enlisted men for the most part, recently graduated lawyers who would rather chew army cud as privates for two years than spend an extra day in the military even if it meant wearing an officer's insignia, and a sprinkling of junior officers associated with Judge Advocate. There were some dependents too, men and women alike, the curious or those wanting to keep abreast of current events, and others looking forward to a bit of drama, a contest of wills or statutes or both.

The first two rows in the Gallery were equipped with broader chairs sporting soft seats and arm rests. These rows were traditionally reserved for the brass, the top brass, or any other brass that cared to show its face. The rookies, men freshly shipped from the States not fully integrated into their units and therefore an easy prey for any cocky sergeant who got it into his head to put together a work detail to please his superiors, and who often dusted, rearranged, and guarded those lustrous chairs, had an indisputable explanation for the softness of the top layer. As the colonels' and generals' main occupation was to fart in their seats and as cushions and soft fabrics absorbed sound much better than bare wood, soft seats were expressly installed to allow the brass to fart at will and hear their farting muted. The putrescent smell would remain of course—there was no remedy against it—but its actual source was not always easy to locate, and besides when there were dozens of possible sources intermingling and interacting, charging anyone with responsibility was a dicey proposition. This explanation had gained wide currency and was seldom contradicted.

Among the public waiting impatiently for the session to begin there were some who knew what would happen, and their conversation focused on why, in the first place, this had been allowed to progress that far. But the majority had no prior knowledge and guesses, cries from the heart, speculations of all sorts, and even bets were the order of the day. While the minority retraced events, analyzed, and rendered judgment, the majority was in the throes of suspense, fired by a gut feeling that here the stakes were very high indeed.

As the massive hand on the wall clock above the table reserved for the members of the tribunal moved close to 1000 hours, there was a new gush of people pressing forward through the main entrance at the back. Simultaneously a side door opened, and General Ryan, flanked by two aides, entered the chamber. One of the aides whispered something in his ear, and the general stepped briskly forward, a benevolent smile rounding his face.

"Mrs. Steiner, I am General Ryan. We think we ought to sit in the front row."

"Thank you, General, and I'd like to introduce my two sons."

"Please do."

"Petty Officer Second Class Wesley Steiner and Seaman Tony Steiner." The two salts, their uniforms shining, snapped to attention and saluted.

"The three of you should be comfortable in the front row," the general spoke protectively, returning the salute, and he pointed the way.

Molly Steiner smiled. "Thank you again, General Ryan."

The general reeled on his heels, and in doing so he nearly collided with Colonel Trainer.

"Ah, Trainer."

"General!"

"Trainer, I want you to sit next to me, in the front row, of course."

"It's an honor, sir."

"You're a clever bugger, and you know how to strike behind the enemy lines. That's worth a lot. So I want you by my side when the Russkies take to the field, tomorrow, the day after, or whenever." His words were overheard, and at once an appreciate ripple of laughter rose in the immediate vicinity.

"Can you be more specific about the date of the attack, General?" a voice asked.

"Can't betray closely guarded military secrets. You boys try to get me in trouble . . . like always." He snickered and led the way to the center of the front row where he and Trainer complacently sank onto their soft chairs and tried to relax.

At this precise moment the side door opened again, and Sergeant Steiner, followed by Captain Harrington, carrying two bulky briefcases, entered the Chamber and sat down behind the table marked *Defense*; and on their heels Major Reginald Senko accompanied by two assistant trial attorneys settled down behind the adjoining table marked *Prosecution*. A few seconds went by before the imposing figure of Colonel Waldo Smithers, the Law Officer, was seen in the side doorway. Self-importantly he walked up to his designated seat, a chair and a desk mounted on a solid wooden stand some four feet above the floor level, stage left of the tribunal and with an easy view of the defense, the prosecution, and of the judges themselves. From this elevated perch Smithers, well versed in the law, was to make sure that the unfolding legal process was always flawless, the legal process of which he was steward and guardian.

Another minute of uneasy silence intervened, and then a captain acting as Clerk of the Court called out: "Please rise." A narrow door behind the judges' table was swung open, and in marched the President of the Court, Major General Samuel Stebbins, and in quick succession the four remaining members, two colonels, and two majors. They duly took their seats, and the Clerk of the Court called out to the Gallery, "You may be seated." General Stebbins let his eye rove slowly over the prosecution and defense tables, over the Law Officer, and finally over the assembled public now resting on pins and needles, an eye movement calculated to get perhaps a better sense of the occasion. Then he glanced sharply to the right and left as though making absolutely sure that all the members of the court were present and accounted for and addressed the defense counsel:

"Captain Harrington, it is the understanding of this court that you wish at this time to make a motion, and the Court awaits your motion."

Harrington stood up, with feather-light fingertips smoothed the uniform, and spoke in a firm, resonant voice:

"Mr. President, in view of the new and conclusive evidence which came to light only very recently, copies of which were dispatched to the Trial Counsel, the Law Officer, to you, Mr. President, and individually to the four remaining judges of this general court-martial, I move that all charges against Master Sergeant Carl T. Steiner, who stands accused before this court, be dismissed." Thereupon he read each charge in full: murder in the second degree, grand larceny, conspiracy to defraud the United States government, theft of government property, petty larceny, and then spelling out one specification after another in detail. When Harrington had finished, the President in turn addressed the trial counsel:

"Major Senko, how say you to this motion?"

"Mr. President, the prosecution fully concurs with the defense and supports Captain Harrington's motion."

"Mr. Law Officer, do you find the defense motion to be grounded in the law, to be consistent with the law, and to follow the law?"

"I do, Mr. President," Smithers answered accentuating each syllable.

Stebbins next turned to members of the tribunal:

"How say you to this motion?" he asked of each of them in turn. They all expressed concurrence with the defense.

General Stebbins' features contracted briefly as he momentarily gazed into space.

"Will the accused please rise?"

Steiner and Harrington stood at attention.

"Master Sergeant Steiner, as the new evidence, of which this court is fully cognizant, demonstrates without a shadow of a doubt your total and complete innocence, this court dismisses all the charges against you, as these charges appear in the indictment. We regret that the new evidence came to light so late in the day, but this could not be helped. I commend both the prosecution and the defense for their diligent and thorough work, and as for you, Sergeant, I cannot begin to tell you how happy I am at the outcome. You are a free man again, your reputation is untarnished, and I wish you Godspeed. Court is adjourned."

Pandemonium broke out. People were clapping their hands, leaping up, shouting for joy, stamping their feet, jumping over seats, running up and down the aisles. No one seemed to be calm, and the contingent of NCOs proved to be as vociferous as anyone else. To many who had heard the grave charges against the accused recited for the first time this was a providential victory of good over evil, a sure sign that God in Heaven would brook no injustice on Earth. Almost at once a line was formed to shake Steiner's hand—General Ryan placed himself at its head—and soon the feted family of four, Carl, Molly, Wesley, and Tony, the last of them driving his mother to despair by refusing to tell her what his duties were on the nuclear submarine, was crushed by well wishers. Harrington joined them for a while, and Steiner held his hand warmly in his.

Molly gave Carl a succession of passionate kisses and was the darling of the crowd, and Wesley and Tony clung to their father haranguing him with praise. For a long time high spirits showed no sign of abatement, and it was well after twelve noon when the ever-exultant public began to trickle out.

In a corner adjacent to the main entrance, Smithers noticed Harrington rearranging papers in his briefcase and beckoned to him.

"You did it again, Julian, you pulled yet another rabbit out of a hat. Is there no way of stopping you?"

"I rather expect the reasoned response in most places is that justice triumphed, justice which was in a very real danger of being perverted. But apparently not in Colonel Smithers' corner. Do you believe Sergeant Steiner should have been convicted of murder and other offences?"

"I was merely commenting on your personal role in the affair."

"My personal role is unimportant. What strikes me as infinitely more important is whether justice was served. If you think I suborned perjury to secure dismissal of all charges, you should advise Army to take legal action against me. In fact this is your bounden duty as an officer of the court." Casting a sideways glance, Harrington could not believe his eyes how uniformly and intensely scarlet Smithers' face looked.

"One of these days the gods will turn against you, Captain, the hat will be empty, no rabbit in it. And one of these days . . ." Smithers proceeded leisurely, savoring every word, but Harrington, all riled up, cut him short.

"One of these days, what?"

"We must have a drink, Captain."

"I think not, Colonel. I've had enough of your company to last me a lifetime. Go and jump into a lake; maybe the fish will be more compassionate towards you than the human species." He picked up the two briefcases from the floor effortlessly like the lord of the manor who picks up daisies off the edge of the moat and unhurriedly sauntered to a side exit.

/   /   /

"I still can't get used to the idea of our daughter Nina marrying you, Captain Lieberman. I know your intentions are wholly honorable, and I know the two of you are deeply in love, but it's all so terribly strange," Nina's mother was saying. She was speaking in German and the daughter, the sole object of this afternoon's tense meeting at the Günthers' spacious and well-aired house in Stuttgart, was translating word for word.

"And of course, there is a difference in age," Frau Günthers sighed and reached for her handkerchief.

"We've been over it before," her husband Klemens joined in, "we cannot change the facts. Sol is nearly thirty-six and Nina is twenty-two, we know that. Is it unusual, perhaps. Is it an impediment to the proposed marriage? Decidedly not." He stopped and looked round the large living room trying to divine what lay behind the frozen facial expressions of his brother Joachim, his sister-in-law Lenore, Sol Lieberman and his American attorney, and Nina herself. His wife's facial expression was the very reverse of frozen; it was like a moving camera photographing her every brainwave, and he wished at times that at least some aspects of her inner life would not be so flagrantly displayed.

"I suggest," he went on in a deliberately dry and official manner, "that we deal with the practical issues, the date of the wedding, prenuptial agreement if any, Nina's life in the United States, and so on."

"To what you have listed, Klemens, I must add one other consideration," his brother Joachim promptly pointed out, "and that is the religion in which the children of Sol and Nina, should they have any, will be brought up. This is of crucial importance."

Sol, who was sitting on a small sofa by the large Venetian window next to his American attorney, while Nina was roving hither and thither in her capacity as the translator, scrambled to his feet.

"Darling, let's sit together, so we can answer your family's questions together, and show them we are acting together, like husband and wife to be."

"Of course," Nina cried happily, kissing Sol on the lips.

They eased themselves onto a low couch facing Joachim and Lenore Günthers.

"I am always happy to meet with Nina's family," Sol started off directly and with little grace, "but I want to make it clear that all decisions with regard to our married life will be made jointly by Nina and me. You, her parents, and her uncle and aunt, will not be consulted. You may be informed, which is good manners, but you have absolutely no authority over our lives. I want to make it clear at the very outset so there will be no misunderstandings."

"That's right," Nina raised her voice, "this is our joint decision."

"Klemens, would you please translate for the benefit of others?" Sol asked in a softer tone.

"Of course."

"I want you to know, Captain Lieberman, that Nina is our only daughter, and naturally we want the best for her. We had such plans for her . . . such plans." Gisele Günthers cried with much emotion, "You should understand a mother's feelings."

Lenore Günthers came over to where her sister-in-law was sitting and put her arm around her. "Everything will be all right, Gisele . . . Nina is in no danger," she said gently, and then she faced Klemens. "A mother's feelings ought to be respected," she poured forth, her eyes flashing with anger. "You only understand what goes on inside a courtroom. Try to be human at least one day in the year, Klemens. If you're capable of it, that is."

He held up his hands in a conciliatory gesture. "Lenore, please, no histrionics."

Pastor Günthers now clambered to his feet noisily, and without addressing any particular person spoke forcefully and with a kind of bitter determination. His brother translated sentence after sentence.

"When my niece announced she would be marrying Chaplain Solomon Lieberman on active duty in the United States Army and about to be divorced from his wedded wife, I did not object. Why should I? Young people ought to have much freedom in selecting their marriage partners, and I am opposed to undue family interference in such matters. But now something else is staring us in the face: Solomon Lieberman is of Jewish confession, in fact, he is a rabbi. Our Nina was born and brought up in the Christian fold by which I mean the holy and eternal Lutheran Church, and what is at stake here is the future of Protestantism in the entire Günthers family and by implication in the state of Baden-Württenberg."

Red-faced and tense, he stopped and blew his nose, his eyes resting questioningly on Sol and Nina.

"Marriage is much more than an institution," he went on, "much more. Preeminently it is a sacred institution, and we the Günthers have been pastors in this part of Germany for generations. As the current pastor I want an assurance from Rabbi Lieberman and Nina that their children will be brought up as Christians, will have all the benefits of Lutheran upbringing and teaching."

A strange silence now descended on the parlor, a silence that augured ill for what Pastor Günthers had just finished saying and avowing that those assembled would have been far happier if the pastor had held his tongue.

"This is something that can wait," Klemens Günthers dismissed the matter off-handedly, pulling a face, "and besides the whole question of dictating to parents regarding . . ."

Then he saw his brother's index finger going up and up with apostolic zeal.

"Yes, Joachim?"

"We are confronting the sacred matter of the true religion; do you want to play havoc with our immortal souls?"

The pastor stood ready to charge further and on with his argument, his brother the counselor being poised for a quick repartee, but both were thwarted by Nina and Sol's giggling. "You tell him, darling," Sol pressed her on. "Oh, no, you start, and I'll have lots and lots to say later." "All right," he whispered while the two brothers gazed at him and Nina with mounting impatience.

Sol was on the point of offering his and Nina's response to the pastor's request when Gisele Günthers' sobbing made him stop in his tracks. It had started as a brief succession of half-suppressed cries, but almost at once Nina's mother began to weep loudly with utter abandon while tears streamed down her cheeks, and her hands dashed here and there in tragic fatalistic gestures.

"For Heaven's sake, Gisele, pull yourself together," her husband called in a schoolmaster's voice.

This made matters even worse. She was in hysterics now, wailing, lamenting, shedding profusions of tears, falling back on the ottoman, and gripping her throat as a sign that she had difficulty breathing. Her sister-in-law stroked her arms and tried to dry her tears, and her daughter attempted to hold and console her between spasms. But Gisele Günthers was inconsolable.

Sol remained in his seat, Joachim stood about at a loss as to what he should do, and Klemens, unrestrained disgust contorting his countenance, crossed over to where Willard Kerman, Sol's American attorney, was sitting.

It was a full ten minutes before Gisele calmed down, and Nina rejoined Sol on the small couch.

"You ought to tell Uncle Joachim," she whispered conspiratorially.

He embraced and kissed her passionately.

"Pastor Günthers," he began summoning as much joviality as he could, "you asked about the religion our children will be brought up in, if we have any children, that is."

"I did, Chaplain Lieberman, I did, because the question is of the utmost importance to our family."

"Well, then, your church is part of the long Christian tradition which goes back to Jesus Christ himself, because it did not really begin with the Reformation."

"You are right, Chaplain. The true Christian church has always been there, but as time went on it became overshadowed by hostile forces which had nothing to do with Christianity."

"Quite so. Hence you are the legatees of a tradition that is nearly two thousand years old."

"Without a doubt."

"As a Jew I too belong to a long religious tradition which goes back to at least the tenth century B.C."

"But of course!"

"So as things stand, Nina and I carry on our backs at least five thousand years of ritual and faith."

"This is so, Chaplain." Joachim slowly bent his head left and then right in deep reflection. "You put it in a very bizarre way, if I may say so, but that is right."

"Well, Nina and I are thinking of giving our children a fresh start and bringing them up as Zen Buddhists. We haven't quite decided, but this is the turn in the road we are very likely to take."

"Buddhists, Zen Buddhist children," Joachim repeated in utter stupefaction.

"That's right, back to the Buddha," and Sol grinned from ear to ear.

In front of them Gisele began to sob again but was promptly comforted by Lenore, while Joachim took a step back and stamped his foot.

"There are jokes that are proper and amusing and others that are simply in bad taste. If this was a joke, Chaplain, then it was in the worst possible taste."

His face was beetroot red and his eyes protuberant and flashing with anger as he swiveled them from one person to the next.

"But it wasn't a joke, Uncle Joachim," Nina chirped in innocently. "Sol and I feel that young people, our future children included, deserve to have their intellectual horizons broadened. Mankind ought to be one large family . . . a family joined by understanding and love. No divisions, no stuck-up convictions that some of us are better than the others. There is no chosen people, there is no chosen race; there is no true religion, because all religions, worldwide or confined to a few acres of land, are equally true and untrue. This planet could be a paradise for everybody but, of course, the bigots, the plutocrats, and the false prophets stand in the way." Nina threw her arms high in the air and tossed her head back. Vibrant with the disgust for the world and with her idealistic ardor she looked radiant, bewitching. Then she raised her voice and let out scornfully, "There are still some of us left who believe this stinking world of ours can be improved."

"We had such plans for Nina, such plans . . ." Gisele was heard sighing and weeping. "Why is God punishing us in this terrible way, I want to know why?"

Joachim paid absolutely no attention to his sister-in-law's lament. Instead he took a few steps forward, and presently he and Klemens were brushing the lapels of their coats. An unfriendly smirk marring

Klemens' dignified face was getting more and more unfriendly with every second as the older brother was looking his younger brother over, missing nothing.

"Congratulations, Brother Klemens. In addition to your other accomplishments, you are also a master parent and a master educator. You and Gisele have brought up your daughter in a manner which will become the envy of the civilized world, and who knows of the unciv-ilized world as well! Congratulations again."

Parrying his brother's intrusion best he could, Klemens made an energetic pooh-poohing gesture and through half-closed lips raked up a repartee.

"I beg of you, Brother Joachim, I beg of you." Then he took up a position by the fireside, a public speaker ready to field questions, while his brother sat down quietly next to his wife.

"What was all this about?" Sol nudged Nina. She waved a hand.

"Nothing important, just the usual family crap."

But Sol was not the only curious party. At the other end of the par-lor Willard Kerman had leaned forward and stood up as soon as Joachim's lapel brushed that of Klemens', pricking up his ears. His German was still in diapers, but now and then as he listened attentive-ly to a conversation he could understand an odd word or two, usually a simple short word, on the order of table, chair, stove, lamp, bed, and similar ones denoting everyday objects. But of the exchange between the two brothers he could not make head or tail, and not a single word sounded familiar. Besides, he felt neglected. After perfunctory introduc-tions he had been left to his own devices, and even though Sol had insisted on his coming over to the Günthers' house in case there were questions to be answered, no one had paid any attention to him. So far it had been one of those awkward family reunions on the eve of a momentous event when different family members are free to vent their predictions, pet theories, and carefully nurtured mental reservations. No one had spoken to him, and his opinion had not been solicited. Moderately irked, Kerman stood up, stretched out his arms, and sent a broad, self-assured smile in all directions.

"After an early sprinkling this may still turn out to be a nice day," he ventured, making it clear his opening gambit was also an invitation to others to say whatever they pleased. It worked. Klemens began to discourse on the many silver linings that shot through the dark clouds of the month of May in this part of West Germany, and Lenore in her faltering English extolled the May weather, its warmth, its absence of gusty winds, and the long hours of gentle, endearing sunshine. Nina and Sol offered their own personal thoughts on the subject, and suddenly everyone was in his or her own element chattering about the weather and about nothing else, save the stone-faced Joachim and the gasping Gisele still inquiring of the Almighty why she was being so terribly punished.

Klemens rubbed his hands with gusto and announced that the chiming afternoon hour was ideal for drinks and light refreshments and turned to Nina. "Could you bring the wine and the glasses? You know where everything is."

"Of course, Father."

"Didn't your mother prepare a tray of sandwiches, pretzels, and cakes for this afternoon?"

"I imagine she did."

"Find it and bring it here. It's no use asking your mother. She is . . . indisposed."

"Shouldn't Mother see a doctor?"

"Nina, apple of my eye, your mother has been seeing doctors from the moment she emerged from your grandmother's womb and wet her first diaper. Doctors can't do anything for her, she is past medical science, past medical art, and past any medical stratagem, invented or uninvented."

"Daddy, really!"

"And if you can't find the tray, no harm's done. We'll just step up the booze."

"You begin to sound more and more like an American."

"Why not, our destiny is inextricably bound to America. We are still under her tutelage. It's going to be different in twenty, thirty years, maybe; but not now."

While Nina and Lenore were arranging trays—the ones prepared by Gisele were quickly found—glasses, and napkins on side tables, and Sol was uncorking wine bottles, Klemens pressed the magic button on the mahogany bookshelf, and a well-filled liquor cabinet rose from between the tiers of learned volumes.

"I fancy the ladies will choose wine, including my rebel daughter," Klemens said, "and the gentlemen . . . well *chacun à son gout.*"

"Just a drop for me," Nina put in hastily. "I am on the way to becoming a teetotaler and a vegetarian."

"Well, I certainly am not," Willard loomed behind Nina. "Counselor, I wonder if I could have a scotch."

"Please help yourself, Mr. Kerman." And as Willard was helping himself to a large drink, he asked, "You practice in my country, I believe, but mostly before American military tribunals."

"That's correct, I represent our boys at courts-martial for the most part, but I also handle divorces, marriages, pre-nups, etcetera. This usually takes place at U.S. Embassy in Bonn, on American soil."

"Quite," and Klemens nodded, sipping scotch.

"And your specialty if any?" the now gregarious and voluble Willard was persisting.

"I am afraid I am strictly what you call a corporation lawyer. My clients are corporations, very large businesses, institutions."

"Yes, yes, I have heard of you." Willard was visibly impressed, pouring himself another large scotch. "Let me give you my card." He pulled one out of his breast pocket and handed it to Klemens who pocketed it without so much as a glance.

"Back in the States your home base was exactly where, if you allow me to inquire?"

"Jefferson City, Missouri."

"Oh, yes."

"Two years ago, when the ink wasn't yet dry on my divorce papers, I blew in here to 7th Army Headquarters."

It was clear at this juncture that Klemens had very little interest in prolonging the conversation with Willard beyond what was the host's obvious obligation, and he began to spar gently with all three, Nina, Sol, and Lenore, adroitly not allowing any one of them to get in the way of the others. But amidst levity and banter he felt a heavy hand clamping his shoulder. He peered sideways and heard Willard's voice of heavy fellowship. "I'd like to invite you to dinner at the Officers' Club in Weiningen, Counselor. We got one hell of a place there. What's a good evening for you next week, eh?"

"Let's talk about it some other time," Klemens shot back without turning his head and immediately launched into a serious conversation with Lenore about his brother's health. They were sitting in twos and threes now, gaining a face or losing one, as the law of social demand and supply dictated, changing places often, holding forth, and absorbing ad nauseam. Willard made a point of telling the two Günthers couples as much about himself as he could squeeze in before being told to stop, and Joachim mingled with the others, at one point facing his brother in silence, their arms interlocked. Gisele, to whom wine and her favorite refreshments were brought by each member of the family in turn, put them politely to the side, her eyes red, her breathing irregular.

Then as the merry intercourse began to flag, Nina exclaimed to Sol, "We have to tell them more about the children's education. We were interrupted."

"Can't it wait? I don't think they are exactly in the mood for radical speeches."

"Oh no, we have to. Forgetting about it won't do."

He shrugged. "Have it your own way, but don't say I didn't warn you."

Nina stood up gracefully, pressing her hands to her breast, exuding sympathy for all those now congregated in her parents' parlor and addressed them in enthusiastic tones. Just before she opened her mouth, Sol touched her waist again and whispered, "Nina, this is not the time or place," but she paid no heed to him, and her mission bloomed in her mind.

"A little while ago I told you that Sol and I are considering bringing our children up as Zen Buddhists; this course of action has a good deal to recommend itself because in this way we shall be forging closer bonds with the rest of mankind outside—to use that terribly hackneyed phrase—the Judeo-Christian tradition. Conversely we hope that our counterparts in different parts of Asia will be bringing up their children as Methodists, Lutherans, or Orthodox Jews. This is a noble endeavor, and it is my fervent hope that millions of hands will be reaching out for one another across the seas. Still, there is something else under the same rubric which is equally important, and more fundamental, and I am simply bursting to tell you all about it." She paused and let her eyes wander to the ceiling, keenly sweeping it this way and that and as before avoiding eye contact with anybody.

"At our study group 'Humanitas' at Tübingen we devoted a great deal of time to the rights of children in the world who, because of outdated ideas, are not properly represented politically or legally and who at best enjoy the very dubious status of second-class citizens. Action is urgently needed, and to let things stand as they do now is criminal." Nina again fixed her gaze at the ceiling, as if the ceiling had something earthshaking to tell her or were nurturing her thoughts to perfection.

"We formulated an advisory memorandum called der Funke, 'spark' in English, which will be sent shortly to educational institutions, newspapers, and humanitarian organizations throughout the world. And now it is my great pleasure to give you a preview of the proposed reforms and answer questions, if any." Once more the ceiling was the sole beneficiary of Nina's glancing attention.

"To give children from age of three to age fourteen rights analogous to those enjoyed by adults we advocate:

1) that every child as early as possible be given the right of choosing his or her own Christian name or simply first name and that this be enforced by the law. Parents ought not to have a say in selecting names for their children—this should be left exclusively to the children themselves.

2) that every child as early as possible be given absolute freedom in choosing the religion he or she would like to be a communicant of. Once again, parents' own religion ought to have no bearing on the religion chosen by the child, and parents' wishes in this respect ought to be immaterial. If a child refuses to practice any religion whatsoever, belong to any particular church, or be affiliated with any religious organization, his or her wishes ought to be respected, and this ought to be enforced by the law.

3) that every child ought to have the right in the broadest possible sense of planning his or her career in adult life, preparing for it while still a minor, and engaging in activities which lead up to and shape his or her future career. And that this be enforced by the law.

"We advocate these measures to free the child from the yoke of cruel and inhuman tyranny under which he or she has suffered for centuries and give him and her back freedom and dignity to which every human being is entitled."

Nina bowed slightly in the direction of each group of guests and then in the direction of her father who pensively sat alone, like a seasoned actress conscious of her striking talent who yet considers politesse the most effective manner of asserting her own superiority.

To everyone's surprise Lenore was the first to break silence. She lauded Nina for her concern for the children, her idealism, her courage.

"I've seen many a case in our parish of parental abuse of children, not physical or sexual abuse—I don't mean that at all—but of the father's authority being so unquestioned, so absolute that the child was stumped and scarred. I don't know, Nina, if what you propose is the solution, but at least you recognize the problem."

"I think you exaggerate parental abuse in our parish, Lenore," her husband commented curtly.

"I most certainly do not!"

Gisele, who was wailing anew, sobbed out again, "The plans we had for you, Nina, the plans we had for you," and then she added in an indignant tone, "It always amazes one how those who have no children set themselves up as authorities on upbringing, education, and God only knows what else."

Klemens was politely silent and so were Sol, Nina, and Willard, but Joachim spoke sadly and from the heart.

"It is a matter of constant regret to us that God did not bless us with children."

"Are you at it again, Joachim?" There was anger in Lenore's voice. "Why open an old wound? Come to your senses, my dear."

Willard, to whom the gist of Nina's speech was translated, gave every appearance of being impressed. "Counselor," he proceeded cautiously, "Fräulein Nina argues her case with skill, though of course one could find fault here and there. But your daughter is a live wire, sir, a real Portia, yes by golly, she's got it . . . highly intelligent . . . I'm sure you're proud of her."

Klemens made it his business to completely ignore Willard and helped himself to some more refreshments. Then he smiled at Sol, a gentle understanding smile, and Sol replicated his future father-in-law's gesture.

"I understood very little of what my niece presented to us this afternoon, very little indeed," Joachim let out, "and I have nothing to say on the subject. Absolutely nothing."

"You should at least try to understand her position," Lenore joined in. "Pride of one's ignorance hardly becomes a rational human being."

Nina looked around the room disappointingly. "Does anyone have a question? Do you want me to elaborate, clear up something?"

As no one spoke, her gaze fell on her father.

"Daddy, how does the legal aspect of the matter strike you? Please say something," she added nervously.

"I would have to study the matter in depth, I would need time."

"I understand, but what is your general reaction?"

He laughed. "I need notice of this question, for the time being I can say nothing."

Nina stroked Sol's hair. "And you, my darling, what do you say?"

"Your position is far too extreme. It'll have to be modified."

"How? Tell me, tell me."

"Another time, my love. Another time."

Unable to catch her mother's eye, Nina waved to her and called, "Mother, tell me what you think?"

Taking temporary leave of her weeping grief, Gisele rearranged herself on the ottoman and hoisted herself up. She looked clear-eyed and self-possessed.

"If this is what you do in your spare time, my child, I can only say you have my deepest commiseration. You left your home because of this extraordinary marriage, but you also left your home because of the extraordinary views which were hammered into your head and because of the extraordinary company you keep."

Joachim leaned forward towards his sister-in-law. "Well spoken, Gisele. You spoke for all of us."

"Not for me. You did not speak for me, Gisele." Lenore's voice was unusually loud, as if she wanted to underline every single word. A cloud of sadness swept over Nina's beautiful face, and she sat down next to Sol lost for words, shut up in herself, still eager to hear from the others but realizing she was championing a lost cause. Sol put his arm affectionately around her, and she lay her head on his shoulder, her heart beating fast, tears welling up in her eyes.

Klemens was observing everybody's reaction from the corner of his eye and then shifted vigorously on the chair.

"There's too much gloom hanging over this company. Let's remember the good things. Sol, I understand Nina already has a job in the States waiting for her?"

"Absolutely. My brother Dave already spoke to the old man Pembroke at Pembroke, Fisk, and Fein, and Nina has been accepted as apprentice architect. The university had sent her transcripts and references, and it's in the bag."

"I'll tell them I want to work on dwellings, houses where people live, not on official buildings."

"You'll do nothing of sort, Nina," her father cautioned her. "You'll do what they tell you to do."

"This is good news, Captain Lieberman," Gisele said unctuously. "I thank you on behalf of our entire family."

"Good news indeed," Joachim followed suit. "Our Nina will continue her highly prized professional development."

"I know the outfit," Willard broke in noisily. "It's first-rate, highly respected, highly recommended, and all that and," he sneered more to himself than to the others, "they charge through the nose."

"Why shouldn't they, if their services are of high quality?" And Klemens cast yet another icy glance at Willard.

"I am in complete agreement with you, Counselor."

"Well, now," Klemens began in a lighter vein. "What is the agenda, Sol?"

"Well, Klemens, things seem to be moving at a giddy pace. I understand the divorce could be final next month, in a Kansas City court, and then the way will lie open for the civil wedding to be performed at the U.S. Embassy in Bonn. Mr. Kerman can tell us more."

"That's right." Willard felt the sudden allure of self-importance, and like a chameleon adapting to the color of the soil he went on adapting to the circumstances of his new role. He was now in command, and he spoke with authority.

"Rachel is not contesting the divorce, in fact in many respects she is very accommodating. I have here the draft of the property settlement, which I got from Bernard Loewenstein, who is representing her. We agree to it."

"Willard, could you hand it to Klemens for his perusal?"

"Of course."

"This is the settlement between you and Mrs. Lieberman."

"There is no need for us to see it," Lenore commented matter-of-factly.

"I don't mind, in fact, I'd like Nina's family to see it. She saw it, and I'd like her parents to see it. It's simply the way I see things. I like things up front." Sol spoke briskly.

His forehead puckering, Klemens was scanning the proposed settlement. "This is hardly my province as a jurist, but I would say it's most reasonable."

"Yeah." Sol pulled a face. "Rachel comes from a wealthy family. She doesn't give two hoots about money. But turn to page four."

"Custody of the children," Klemens read aloud. "She wants custody, surely you expected that."

"Read further down."

"Visitation rights? Oh, I see." Klemens read on. Then he turned a compassionate eye on Sol. "You have no visitation rights as such, except at her pleasure, and she can refuse every time." He whipped the paper with the back of his hand.

"Does she have you over the barrow, darling?" Nina asked merrily.

"Not yet," Willard declared with force, directing his words and savoring his commanding role even more eagerly than before. "Not yet. We are still negotiating, and besides Bernie owes me one."

For a little while Gisele had been looking healthier. The wailing and the sobbing ceased, she was no longer an eremite among the revelers, her spirits rose. Choosing the moment when no one would interrupt her, she tossed a question across the room in her high resonant voice:

"And what plans do the young people have for after the wedding? Is there to be a honeymoon?"

"Of course, Mother," Nina cried exultantly, and at once expectancy hung in the air. "We are going to Italy, spending most of the time in Florence and Venice and then down to Rome and Sicily."

"I hear there are still highwaymen in Sicily, better cross into France."

"Certainly not, Mother, besides I have a real man to protect me, isn't that so, Sol?"

"Why, of course, darling."

"You have helluva lot to live up to, pal," Willard muttered to himself and was not overheard.

Now Sol picked up the thread. "From Sicily we'll cross to Tunis and proceed west to Algiers and Morocco. In fact we are planning to spend a good deal of time in North Africa. We'll rent a car and drive inland. We want to see the country, the way those people live, avoiding tourist spots like the plague."

"For me what the two of you are planning is fraught with danger.

You will be among savages, the worst can happen." Gisele was not taking any chances.

"Sol is fluent in French," Nina said with pride. "He can handle any
situation."

"Indeed? I didn't realize." The concerned mother made no attempt
to hide her disbelief. But the prospect of a honeymoon first in Italy and
then along the North African coast made a strong appeal to everybody
else. Joachim hugged his niece lovingly and exclaimed this was a grand
idea. Lenore was blowing kisses to Sol and Nina and telling them lusti-
ly to follow their hearts' desires and pay no attention to what the others decree, while Klemens, the proud father, stood in the middle of the
room ready to receive more encomia about his daughter and future
son-in-law's travel plans. Willard too took part in the general merry-
making: he stood on a chair and hollered, "You kids have heaps of fun,
and don't do anything I wouldn't do, ha, ha, ha!"

When the jubilant voices had died down, Gisele faltered, "Our
honeymoon was also in Italy, Klemens. Do you remember at all?"

"Dearest, how could I forget?"

"And so was ours," Lenore spoke up.

"We went from Hitler's Germany to Mussolini's Italy," Gisele rem-
inisced. "Everyone seemed to be in uniform. And that perfectly darling
little French restaurant we discovered on Capri, Chez Tibère, what was
the name of the owner? And we passed the information on to you. You
loved it too."

"My dear Gisele, Joachim and I discovered Chez Tibère during our
honeymoon some ten years before yours and still during the days of the
late lamented Weimar Republic. The restaurant staff was very nice to
the Germans, unlike in many other places where the Italians were making it plain they would rather the Germans betook themselves with all
their money elsewhere and not come back."

"No wonder." Joachim looked grave. "The owner was a French fascist, as I recall, very thick with the Duce."

"And with Hitler."

"Dearest Lenore, of course we remember the French owner of the
establishment and his fascist snippets between courses, but you've got it
hopelessly wrong. Klemens and I were the ones who unearthed Chez
Tibère. And it was on our advice that you went there when you visited Italy again in '38."

"Dearest Gisele, I truly fear for you. You are hallucinating. You should learn to respect facts, yes facts, dearest Gisele. This cute little restaurant, where service was excellent and political opinions expressed very suspect, was our discovery, long before Hitler became master of Germany though the Italian peasant was already in the saddle."

"Lenore, you are talking utter nonsense. You should be ashamed of yourself."

But before Gisele had the time to rally her forces, Lenore turned to Klemens. "I am afraid we have to be going," she said firmly. "It was very sensible of you to have this family gathering . . . I think everything is on the right track."

"I hope so," and Klemens put his arms around Lenore.

"We have to be going too." Nina smiled cheerfully in the direction of her father. "Sol has a terribly busy schedule tomorrow, and I have to see to it he gets a good night's sleep, and with the Memorial Day practically upon us we have hundred and one things to do."

Other adieus followed, and Sol took Gisele's hand. "You really ought to begin calling me Sol, Captain Lieberman and Chaplain Lieberman have taken a flight to parts unknown."

"I suppose I ought to," she said without conviction. And as Lenore and Joachim were disappearing into the hall, she exclaimed boldly, "Stuff and nonsense. I didn't realize how forgetful Lenore has gotten to be, poor dear, she is showing her age."

Chapter 13

They were smart-looking to the point of incredibility, and everything they wore and carried had that defiantly new look, the summer
uniforms tightly pressed and the buckles shining, the shoes with so
much spit and polish imprinted on them that they reflected the sun like
stripes of glossy silver, the M1 rifles, stocks zealously seasoned with oil
and the barrels burnished—every bit of it bearing inaccurate testimony
of having come the night before out of the storehouse, from the assembly line, and the men themselves lifted from the eighth continent and
then hassled through immense shower chambers and barber chambers
and personal hygiene chambers and dropped antiseptically on the
parade ground of 16th U.S. Army Engineer Group in Kirchenberg, West
Germany. But in fact their provenance was the North American continent, their uniforms not new but freshly laundered and starched, their
M1 rifles tested on the range and in combat, and their super neat
appearance due to the ape-like grunting and bellowing of the hordes of
NCOs who had nothing better to do.

It was the Memorial Day Parade, on the military totem pole topped
only by the Fourth of July Parade, and immense effort had been
expended to make it a grand and unforgettable occasion. All the four
companies marched before the reviewing stand in perfect order, and

each company drew a straight vertical line of rifles held and another horizontal one of four rifles blending into one. The precision was amazing and hundreds of hours of training and training again made it possible. The general public, both American and German in large numbers standing on both sides of the marching route, gaped at the troops in wondrous appreciation. On the reviewing stand Colonel Trainer, surrounded by his staff and high-ranking officers from 7th Army Headquarters, watched with pride how well his group was performing and saluting each passing company's guideon. Some of the visitors were already whispering their congratulations to him, and he acknowledged them with a quick nod. As C Company approached, the wiry figure of Specialist Fourth Class Oliver Hartmann could be seen marching daringly just behind the Company Commander and the First Sergeant, his countenance frozen but flinging ferocious glances in all directions, his fighting spirit crouched in every pore in every muscle of his body.

After the parade the four companies arranged themselves lengthwise in the middle of the parade ground, and the military band played "The Star-Spangled Banner." The official part of the program thus disposed of, the band began to play merry tunes, songs of the day, excerpts from musicals and operettas, while the entrance flaps of the four immense tents were being thrown to the side. Trainer, already far away from the reviewing stand and a loudspeaker in hand, roared to the assembled crowd: "I am Colonel E.E. Trainer, Commander of the 16th U.S. Army Engineer Group. You are all invited to the reception which is about to begin on this momentous day, Memorial Day, when we Americans remember the war dead. Let me say a word about logistics: tent number I thus marked," and he pointed to the tent farthest away from him, "contains illustrations and displays marking the evolvement of the Corps of Engineers in the United States Army, their history, and the engagements in which they proudly took part. Tents II and III," and he pointed again, "offer food and drink for the hungry, Tent II serving hot dishes, entrees, sandwiches, and soft drinks, and Tent III desserts, coffee, and tea; and Tent IV displays some of the weapons we use today, weapons which at any hour of day or night can be used to defend the free world against communist aggression, and in particular the German Federal Republic, our staunch friend and ally. I hope you will enjoy the reception, and thank you very much for paying us a visit. Our base is always open to you." Trainer repeated the same announcement in

German, reading from a scrap of paper, and when he had finished an almost mystical sense of gratification shimmered from all his features—not a cat that swallowed a canary but a hundred cats that swallowed a hundred canaries!

Waves of Army personnel, of American and German civilians, swept through the tents, the former folksy and the latter on their best behavior, pouring over the charts and maps and delightedly helping themselves to the lavish displays of GI cuisine; and in the last tent German children and teenagers were avidly examining the automatic weapons, judging their effectiveness by the similarity they bore to what James Cagney or Humphrey Bogart fired with so much skill in the gangster films. Trainer, Fiorello, and Lieberman circulated in the crowd, welcoming visitors, introducing themselves, explaining, and being ably assisted by three enlisted men "borrowed" from Army who spoke German. The visitors showed a healthy appetite for food and drink, and now and again a middle-aged man, a German veteran of the last war, would buttonhole one of the hosts and, pointing to a chart or map, ask informed questions. By the table laden with apple pies, chocolate cakes, and sweetmeat Molly Steiner unburdened herself once more to Carl.

"I am worried about Tony," she said.

"Looks as healthy as can be," he assured her.

"No, no, he doesn't look healthy at all. Have you noticed his eyes?"

"Didn't see anything wrong there."

"His eyes are dull, listless. Before he joined the Navy they were live, sparkling."

"You exaggerate."

"No, I don't. And did you notice how he squints and keeps his eyes half shut?"

"Maybe he needs glasses."

"No, it isn't glasses he needs." She paused and then threw all of her into the fray. "He's been brainwashed, as God is my witness. That's what it is. Those Navy doctors, those bloodsuckers in white coats! They brainwashed our Tony."

"Come off it, Molly."

"I'll see General Eisenhower. I will."

"He ain't Navy, so he won't be able to help you."

"Listen to me, Carl," and Molly got hold of her husband's upper arm and held it fast. "Listen to me. When a boy can't tell his own mom

what he's getting paid for . . . then there's something wrong
. . . something very wrong."

"For cryin' out loud, it's security, Molly, security! Tony's serving on
a nuclear submarine."

"Security, my ankle! When the government sees fit to destroy the
family and incite a child against his mom, then something must be done
about it. This is the United States of America, the greatest country in
the world, not Redland or some banana republic. Something must be
done about it! Something must be done!"

Carl bussed Molly and put another piece of chocolate cake on her
plate.

"D'you like it?" he asked affectionately.

"It's fine. It's almost as good as the one I make."

"That's praise indeed."

"I spent several hours trying to find out what Tony's duties are, and
all he could say, poor boy, was 'I can't talk about it, Mom, I can't talk
about it.' Security, my ankle!"

The time designated for the Memorial Day open house and reception was twelve noon to 1500 hours, but already around 1430 hours
many visitors began to leave. Most of them walked away with happy
faces eagerly expressing their appreciation of the hospitality extended,
and at one point a line was formed by those who wanted to thank
Trainer personally. He stood there with his interpreter, twice as big as
life, suave and canny, telling all and sundry to return soon. Shortly after
1500 hours work details appeared on the scene, pulling down tents and
carrying whatever had rested in them to safer quarters, the conveyance
of everything which had been brought from the kitchens being personally supervised by James O'Leary, the loquacious and mercurial Mess
Hall Sergeant. A great event has come and gone, but it made a dent and
augured well for the future.

Quinn and Hartmann were sitting on their bunks, bitching to each
other and to anyone else who would listen about the hardships of the
day.

"The worst drag was not the damned parade itself, but all the
chicken shit we had to put up with. Why, it lasted for weeks," Olie ranted on.

"That's right, friend," Vince agreed, "and you know what's behind
it?"

"What?"

"Trainer is bucking for promotion, it's all over the camp, he wants to be addressed as Brigadier General Trainer."

"No shit!"

"And I'd say," Vince went on in the same deceptively silky manner, "that jaunt after Vallejo and today's fireworks may have put it in the bag."

Olie winced. "So Trainer is getting to be a general by breaking our backs."

"Something like that. Though we shouldn't forget he promoted all three of us, Hal, you, and me, in the field like, no questions asked."

"That was nice of him," Olie started to nod. "Very nice."

Vince snickered, "Man, you looked good this morning, real good," giving Olie a mock punch in the belly.

"Maybe I did. What of it? That was my last hurrah."

"I hear they'll be shipping you out next week."

"That's right, ten days tops," and as Vince was strangely quiet, he hollered, "out with it, Quinn, what the hell's the matter with you! Out with it!"

"I was just going to say . . ."

"Well say it, damn it, or I'll break every bone in your overfed body!"

"Take it easy, man. Take it easy."

Olie made an expansive gesture of extreme impatience.

"Well?"

"Maybe you'll find a way back into the Service."

Olie grew pensive. "Maybe, time will tell." Then his spirits rose. "You heard the latest, Vince?"

"What's the latest?"

"Korovitz is getting hitched."

"To one Adrienne Hurley, personnel sergeant?"

"The same. Big Teats Hurley, they call her."

"Well, well, well."

"I'm sorry I won't be here to lay a bet."

"One can be laid for you, boy, and results sent to your home."

"That would be nice."

"No problem, Olie. We'll take care of it."

Olie scratched his chin. "That will be his third walk to the altar."

"You don't say!"

"Right. His first two wives left him without as much as whispering good-bye. The first ran off with a strolling player—Vince, you're bound for college, what the hell is a strolling player?"

"Never mind," Quinn barked back. "Give us the rest."

"And the second with a photographer who was Korovitz's best friend."

"My, my, my, I see here a patch of land pregnant with possibilities."

Later in the afternoon, as Quinn was strolling towards the Group parking lot he saw Fiorello coming straight at him. It was too late to retreat, and the only recourse was to adhere punctiliously to the rules of military courtesy. Quinn slowed down and saluted sharply.

"Ah, Quinn." Fiorello brought the words out as if there was something pressing on his mind.

"Yes, sir," and Quinn stood to attention.

"At ease, Specialist." For what seemed to Quinn an unnecessarily long time Fiorello just stood there staring vaguely at the sky.

At long last he snapped his fingers. "I remember now why I wanted to speak to you."

"Sir?"

"C Company did very well on the parade ground, we were proud of you."

"Thank you, sir."

"But I noticed yours was the only company that didn't have the soldier of the month marching behind the C.O. and the First Sergeant. Instead, Hartmann was in his place."

"Specialist Hartmann?"

"Yes, Specialist Hartmann, Quinn. You know Hartmann? Why, you're bosom buddies."

Quinn grinned confidentially. "Major Fiorello, everyone went along with it, and we cleared it with Captain Bohn. This was our send-off to Olie, marching at the head. You know he will be out of here in a matter of days on a compassionate discharge."

"Yes, I know that, Quinn," Fiorello cackled, infuriated. "I'm processing his papers."

"In that case the Major knows all there is to know . . . sir."

"Let me try once more from the very beginning, and I expect straight answers." Ominously Fiorello moved very close to Quinn, and his face turned scarlet. "Where was the C Company soldier of the month, or did he defect to the Russians?"

Seasoned football player that he was, Quinn decided in a split second that the smart-aleck approach led nowhere.

"Sir, I want to be absolutely honest with you," and he became at once painfully aware of the Adjutant's narrowed eyes fixed on him maliciously and practically rolling in suspicion.

"You'd better be," Fiorello hissed out.

"The truth of the matter is, in April C Company singled out no one as soldier of the month."

"Why?"

"No one earned enough points. We are doing much better this month. Sorry, sir."

"'Sorry, sir,' is this all you can say?"

"What else do you want me to say?"

Fiorello bounded back, began to flex his muscles in a most spectacular manner, then bounded forward precisely onto the spot where he had previously stood.

Dear God, a thought flashed in Quinn's brain, *has he too gone stark raving mad?*

A basilisk gaze kept him under surveillance. "Different army units are in constant competition, Quinn. We are constantly rated and evaluated, and the ratings determine our standing in the Command and impact individual promotions, including those of officers."

"Aha." Quinn's brain was working double fast. "So that's his worry."

"While other companies were engaged in the pursuit of excellence, C Company preferred to chase skirts and get drunk. But the day of reckoning may be closer than you think. Much closer, Quinn!"

"Yes, sir."

Fiorello paused, sizing the specialist up, and then continued in a milder tone.

"16th U.S. Army Engineer Group is a team, one big team, with the C.O. as the quarterback, and all of us players. I want you to think of an immense field, Quinn, a field so immense that you can't see the end of it, and all of us from the lowest private to the colonel himself being players on this field as a well-disciplined team." He paused again, and the anger came back with a vengeance.

"But you people let down the team, you turned your backs on the team, and worst of all you betrayed the team. Your teammates will not forgive you. Where was your espirit de corps, man, your loyalty to other members of the team? Where was it, I ask?"

"Sir, I find it hard to visualize such an immense field and a team made of thousands. If you can't see the end of the field, where are the goal lines? And what are those thousands of guys supposed to do?"

"Don't be insolent. I was speaking figuratively, driving a point home which should've been obvious."

"Well, sir, there are times when a unit, a small unit, a platoon let's say, acts as a team, in a combat situation most likely, and then team spirit rules all, or should rule all. But if you take a much larger unit and in peacetime then . . . well . . . very often there's ain't no team spirit at all in it, as I understand it. But then, sir, I've never been in combat so I can't judge."

"You have an answer for everything, don't you," Fiorello sputtered the words out, not even bothering to look at Quinn.

"C Company's remissness has been duly noted, and an appropriate action will be taken." Then he glanced at his wristwatch and strode away.

Later in the afternoon Olie accosted Trainer outside his office.

"Colonel!"

"Yes, son."

"Ain't there no way to keep me in the Service?"

Trainer pressed his lips together, and his facial muscles contracted.

"We can't do it, I wish I could say different. Red Cross made a very strong case, Army approved it, and your mom expects you to come back and be the man of the house."

Olie smirked. "That bitch did nothing for me except bring me into the world nor did my old man." His voice grew harsher as he went on. "He had his bottle and his gambling, and she had her bottle and her boyfriends . . . though some folks"—and he snickered knowingly— "called them clients. They paid no attention to me, for them I was just excess luggage. I owe those two scumbags nothin'! Nothin', Colonel! Why do I now have to work my butt off to keep her and that little monster of a brother of mine alive? It don't make no sense."

Trainer leaned over Olie and spoke with infinite patience. "I understand what you're telling me, Olie, I understand full well. Maybe it don't make no sense, and I'm willing to take your word on it, I am . . . But the crux of the matter is we at this end can't do nothin' for you, our hands are tied. It's all been decided by the powers that be."

"And you call it justice, Colonel?"

"I wouldn't call anything justice, son, unless I knew the ins and outs, was two hundred percent sure and heard the testimony of twenty honest men of my choosing yapping aye."

"I understand, sir."

Despite the unexpected tension of the occasion and Olie's cocky demeanor, Trainer was not trying to cut the interview short. Instead he straightened himself up—as he did so Olie followed his example—and assumed a commanding posture.

"I want to say two things to you, Specialist Hartmann. The first may be of some help to you in the future, and the second contains the highest praise I can bestow on anybody. When you get home check with your draft board and find out what the reenlistment regulations say. Also make contact with the Wisconsin National Guard and if they let you, join the Guard. It so happens, units of the National Guard are activated now and then, and this would be a prompt way of getting back in.

"Secondly, you already proved yourself in our raid on Bund 45 in Stuttgart, and it was a real pleasure to see you march in the parade, I want you to know you have the makings of an excellent trooper. I would be proud to lead you and men like you into battle any day. Best of luck to you, Hartmann," and a ghost of a roguish smile licked Trainer's features. "I hope to see you again before too long." He extended his hand.

"Me too, sir, me too," and Olie shook it vigorously.

As the hapless specialist who, unlike many others, was being yanked out of the Army against his wishes marched away, Lieberman came up to Trainer.

"It's a sad case, I know the circumstances, they made a patsy of him. I reviewed the entire case with the Red Cross."

"I sympathize," Trainer said, "but his mother and brother are still his family."

"A pretty rotten family, if you ask me."

"I don't want to sound like Pontius Pilate, Sol, but there's nothing we can do."

"I know," and for a minute Lieberman was lost in deep meditation.

"I have a good rabbi friend in Milwaukee, Stanley Sussman," he said at last. "He knows everybody who counts not only in Milwaukee but in the whole state. I'll speak to Stan, he'll keep an eye on the boy and may be able to help."

"That's very kind, Sol. Olie will need friends. By the way, does he have a religious affiliation?"

"None that we've been able to unearth, though one of his grandfathers was baptized Methodist."

Trainer nodded. "Let's go give Korovitz a hard time, he's been holding out on us."

"How?"

"You'll find out."

They found the Group Sergeant immersed in stacks of papers of all sizes, all of them looking terribly important. Trainer tiptoed forward and let the words fall in a quaintly syrupy way.

"Dudes who hold out on their buddies run the risk of having their whoopsies chopped off and fed to the hogs."

"Sir?" Korovitz's head shot upward as high as his neck would allow.

"There's that big event coming up in your life, Leroy, and you shut us off. It ain't nice, friend, it ain't nice."

Korovitz uttered a sigh of relief. "Today being Memorial Day and everyone being busy, busy, busy, I thought waiting till tomorrow or the next day might be just what the doctor ordered."

"He's stalling," Lieberman adjudicated.

"He's trying to make fools of all of us," Trainer cried. "Your honor, the prisoner in the dock shows contempt for the bench."

"Penalty for such offense being hanging head down until death."

"Hanged till death, feet up," Trainer replicated rapturously and then broke into an uncontrollable horse laughter.

When the laughter stopped and Korovitz, recovering from so much excitement, was still eyeing the pair of them guardedly, Trainer stepped forward.

"Group Sergeant Korovitz, Captain Lieberman and I would like to offer our warmest congratulations to you on your forthcoming marriage," and there was a shaking of hands.

"Who is the lady in question?" Lieberman asked.

"Sergeant Adrianne Hurley of the Personnel Division at Army. Adrianne's divorce came through recently and mine some time ago, so we are ready and willing."

"Wonderful news for all of us," Trainer exclaimed impulsively.

"And for the two of us," Korovitz put in modestly.

"Stateside?" Trainer's countenance was really asking the question.

"That's right, stateside."

"Kentucky?" Lieberman queried.

"As a matter of fact the wedding will take place in Arkansas where the bride is from. Adrianne has a large family, her parents are still alive, and there are brothers and sisters with their families, kissin' cousins, nieces, nephews, and so on. My own family is rather depleted so we signed a treaty to please her folks."

"It sounds like one of those uninhibited Jewish weddings."

"Church wedding, of course!" Trainer pounded in with regal assurance.

"Right you are, sir. The Episcopal Cathedral in Little Rock."

"I thought you were a Methodist?"

"I am, and Grandpa was an elder in the church . . . but we try to please those we love."

"Understood."

"And the date, if one might inquire?" Lieberman liked to have all the relevant information in the palm of his hand.

"August 24th, and we are synchronizing it with our three-week leaves beginning on the 19th."

"Sounds super and leaving more than two weeks for the honeymoon." Trainer sounded more excited than the bridegroom.

"You should try it sometime, Colonel."

"Try what?"

"Getting married again."

Trainer shook his head resignedly. "No broad would have me."

"Ooohhh. This is not the spirit!"

"I am decidedly of the same opinion as the Group Sergeant." Lieberman broke in. "Getting married would be in your best interest, Ed. In fact, the sooner the better. You'll be a new man."

"You guys can be of the same opinion decidedly or undecidedly or any other goddamn way you please. The thought crossed my mind, yes, but I need time to mull things over."

Trainer was going to extemporize further, but the door was swung open and Fiorello ambled in.

"Any messages for me, Group Sergeant? Dropped in on the way

home." He glanced pointedly at Trainer. "Congratulations, Ed, on a highly successful parade and reception. My spies inform me there was much praise bestowed all round. A PR coup, if you ask me!"

"Thank you, John, things gone off well. And thanks again to all of you who worked with me."

Fiorello exchanged small talk with Lieberman and Korovitz and returned to Trainer.

"When is our hero coming back? What's the latest?"

Trainer blew his nose noisily and looked disconcerted.

"I'm sorry, I meant to tell you. It slipped my mind. Vallejo will be released in a few days, the leeches are satisfied he's completely recovered, the wounds on his back healed, and he's ready to be returned to active duty. They kept him under observation for some time just to be sure. And no aftereffects."

"That's a good prognosis. I'll say this, when it comes to a difficult case our Army doctors can be very thorough." Fiorello's appreciation was all the more telling because of its understatement.

Trainer belched. "Yeah, very thorough. He told me the only part of his body the leeches didn't stick their needles in was his prick. At least the creeps showed some decency, they ought to be commended."

"It will be nice to have Jesús back. He's quick as lightning, and he knows the ropes." Korovitz brushed his moustache and made a vague gesture as if he were contemplating burying himself again in his papers. But there were other things Trainer wanted to unburden himself of.

"This morning in my home I received an update on how the Krauts are progressing against Bund 45. Apparently they are moving slowly but surely. Hans Ketterer has been indicted on the charge of murder and the Moser brothers as accessories. Frau Gruber, our esteemed librarian, you all know about: she is held together with that elderly couple which gave false testimony—I forget their names—on charges of conspiracy to commit murder. Frau Schwämer, who owns the house where Vallejo was held captive, denies all wrongdoing, and her lawyers are making one hell of a fuss. The Kraut prosecutors are confident they have enough evidence against the actual perpetrators, the ones who wielded the knife or pulled the trigger. So far so good. But the higher-ups in the Bund whom Vallejo had encountered and whose names he passed on to the authorities eluded the dragnet."

"That's what usually happens when you deal with organized crime.

Greenhorns and foot soldiers are easy enough to catch. But when it comes to the higher-ups, the capos if you will, they are insulated, they have alibis and a hundred ways to beat the rap." Korovitz began to brush his moustache, exercising great care, and peered from face to face.

"Contrary to what you say, Sergeant, substantial progress has been made in some parts of the country, notably in New York. Are you abreast of Congressional hearings on organized crime?"

"I am, and it's a drop in the bucket, Major."

"I'd say it's a matter of opinion, Sergeant."

"Eh, you guys, get off your high horses, this is not a debating society." Trainer was dead serious.

"No offense was intended, Major Fiorello." Korovitz spoke first.

"And none was taken, Group Sergeant Korovitz."

"That's better," Trainer muttered.

Korovitz grinned and turned to Trainer. "Last week when Sergeant Rickmeyer came here with those papers for you from the German police headquarters . . ."

"Yes, yes, I remember."

"He and I had a nice long chat."

"Oh!"

"An interesting guy. He told me his fondest hope was to be an operatic singer. But his parents thought he was not good enough and so . . . alas thought his teachers. So he became a cop instead."

"But he still sings, don't he?" Trainer interjected.

"He does at various private and official functions, and he's much in demand."

"He's the one who can imitate a guy's voice by sizing up his body. During the raid I asked him how he does it, and he answered it would take too long to explain. Pauli's quite a character!"

"Sure is. As our friendly chat took us well past the afternoon, I invited him to dinner. We spent a very pleasant evening together."

"That was good of you, Sergeant. The Group appreciates it."

Korovitz waved a hand. "My pleasure."

"I spoke briefly with Carl Steiner and his wife at the reception. He seems to be his old unperturbed self," Fiorello remarked.

"He's fine," Lieberman added, "and it was a great comfort to have his two sons standing with him at the acquittal. This is what he had hoped for."

"His two sons and Molly." Trainer spoke with a twinkle in his eye.

"Oh yes, Molly," Korovitz was quick in joining in. "It's hard to imagine Carl without Molly."

"I guess we are all grateful for the happy ending," Fiorello announced unhurriedly and waxing a tad philosophical. "We are all grateful."

"Hear! Hear!"

"And it was another famous victory for Julian. That fella's going places." Lieberman was very nearly successful in suppressing a chuckle.

"What gives?" Trainer asked.

"Well, legend has it Julian sold his soul to the Devil for worldly success. After all, he's had a most extraordinary record of victories as defense attorney. For some he's become a reincarnation of Faust, or better still a new Faust for the twentieth century."

"Faust?" Trainer questioned.

"You know, the sixteenth century German magician."

"Oh, that Faust," Trainer concurred with a knowing wink.

As Fiorello gave every sign of being on the point of leaving, Trainer caught his eye.

"John, there's something else I forgot to tell you. Jessup, Captain Bohn, came to see me yesterday. April was not a good month for the soldier of the month selection. Some companies just scraped by, but C Company didn't make it. It's your decision, John, but the men worked their butts off to make the Memorial Day shindig a success. Let them rest on their laurels."

Chapter 14

He did not expect to be chaired through the marketplace but had hopes that at least some of the guys from A Company would remember him. They did not. Trainer, Korovitz, Fiorello, and Lieberman welcomed him with open arms, but to much of the base he was just another newly promoted sergeant who had been shipped out or was being shipped out or shipped in. "Eh, Sarge," called the new chaplain's assistant, "how long will you be with us?" And in the Mess Hall only Jim O'Leary knew what he had accomplished. His spell of glory had lasted less than twenty-four hours, from the time the news of his rescue hit the bush telegraph till noon of the next day. While standing by his desk as Korovitz kidded him about the countless trays of papers it would now be his bounded duty to sort out, Fiorello came to shake hands, mumbling a few banal words, and Lieberman was euphoric on his behalf but so jumpily preoccupied with other business that the fleeting minutes he spent with the returning hero were inconsequential. Vallejo felt a profound and unexplainable sense of letdown, and only Trainer understood what he was going through. As he was facing the Group Commander and shifting uneasily in his seat, Trainer's words struck a chord Vallejo did not know was there.

"When I got my battlefield commission," Trainer began, "why, guys patted me on the back and everyone was hollering 'Well done, Ed,' and of course the brass was going out of its way to be super nice to me, but I can tell you this, Jesús: those few days I spent with my old unit with a brand new bar on my collar were kind of eerie. The men were tripping and stumbling with their tongues all the time at a loss how to address me, the senior NCOs were building a wall between themselves and me, and by golly it was a real wall, and the officers were sizing me up curiously like I was a strange animal from another planet . . . and bein' very economical with words. I felt like I didn't have a single friend in the world and like I didn't belong nowhere. But, bein' a bit of a lone wolf by nature, I got through those miserable few days and started a new life in a new unit as a second john on the make." Trainer swiveled his head to the left as though he wanted to stare out of the window and cast oblique glances at Vallejo. "I hope you're not going through something like it."

"As a matter of fact, sir, I am going through something exactly like it," and Vallejo went on talking.

"This will pass, and I'd say you're tough enough to brave it through."

"I probably am, but I was never confronted by a similar situation."

Trainer grinned. "Fate don't fire blanks, boy. It don't, it never did, and it never will."

"Right you are, sir."

Trainer reached for a cheroot. "Soon you'll be moving to pastures new, but I'd appreciate it if you could stay with us, in your present capacity, for another spell, let's say two, three months tops. It's now what, the very beginning of June? Leroy will need a helping hand with all the crap that comes from Army, and this is the time for evaluations, reports, promotion recommendations, and whatever else our Pentagon masters dreamt up. It must be the stench of the Potomac that drives their minds to distraction! Major Fiorello tells all and sundry when it comes to Army paperwork he's got the bull by the horns. It ain't so. He too will need a helping hand."

"You can count on it, sir."

Later in the day Vallejo ran into Quinn.

"I never had the chance to thank you for rescuing me, Quinn."

"Well, Colonel Trainer conveyed your thanks as you was lying on a hospital bed to all of us who was crazy enough to volunteer."

"This was a brave and well executed operation."

"What you did, Sergeant, was much braver."

"Knock it off, Quinn. It's Vallejo or Jesús."

"Well, I don't know," Quinn intimated, fetching up a defensive smile. "Those who win new laurels don't want to be treated like plain ordinary humans."

"Take it from me!"

"I heard this one before, but we'll give ye the benefit of the doubt."

"By the way, where's Hartmann? He's shipping out any day now?"

"In three days, on the fifth. He's in town saying good-bye to a girl."

"I hope things will go well for him. One can't help but like the little guy."

"Don't call him the little guy. Vallejo, he's liable to turn himself into a fighting cock, no holds barred."

"I'll remember. Did the Bund 45 affair qualify for a nod from the Gambling Corporation?" Vallejo asked, a very cynical, very complacent smile forking his mouth.

Quinn made a belittling gesture and spat on the ground. "We did a little business mostly relative to the length of your stay at Army hospital. I want you to know no one lay a bet on anything that had to do with your wounds, the medical treatment you was getting, the general state of your health."

"Oh!"

"The Commission spoke with one voice."

"I am flabbergasted, gentlemanly code before profits."

"Listen to me, Sergeant," and Quinn lugged forward not in a menacing way but simply to assert his rights. "We are businessmen, not hyenas, skunks, or vermin. We are bound by a code of honor and decency, and our standards of conduct—in case you are curious to find out—are just as high as those of other segments of society: teachers, priests, educators, civil servants, and the like."

"Okay, okay!"

"To take unfair advantage of your weakened condition and let grubby fingers run up and down your noble wounds, tote up the odds would've been gross, Vallejo, yes gross! There are certain things that simply are not done!"

"I'm glad you put me on the right track."

They chatted for a few minutes about this, that, and the other, and then Vallejo asked: "You won an athletic scholarship to a college in Illinois?"

"Yep."

"And you are leaving when?"

"End of August, unless that asshole Fiorello forgets his promise."

"I'll be there to remind him, this is the least I can do."

"That will be dandy, Jesús. Thanks."

"Brigitta and Hal invited me to dinner tonight at their apartment. Any messages for them? After all, you and he were musketeers serving shoulder to shoulder on more than one occasion." He looked sharply at Quinn squinting to his heart's content.

"No need to," Quinn let fall with dignified phlegm, like a CEO turning down an unwelcome offer. "We have a direct line to anyone we wish to contact." And Quinn let his eye wander lazily to the right and left and glanced behind him. "Anytime you want to lay a bet, Jesús, you know where to find us. We keep long hours. Everything's on the up and up." He smiled reassuringly. "Don't be a stranger, fella . . . and keep your pecker up."

He reeled on his heel and was gone.

/   /   /

Later in the afternoon Trainer was sitting gravely behind his desk peering into several folders marked *Ernest J. Tannenbaum, Second Lieutenant,* while the subject of these folders, wearing a newly pressed, newly starched summer uniform, was facing him in respectful silence.

"Your record is excellent, Lieutenant, your instructors at OCS are saying all kinds of nice things about you, and prior to that while you were still a corporal and then a sergeant, your 201 was brimming with praise and niceties. No wonder 7th Army is interested in you . . . and you got interviews there?"

"Yes, sir, several this week. I also have an interview or two back in the States."

"Man of the hour, what!" Trainer was crouching over the complimentary pile. "I appreciate very much this courtesy call on your part. After all, this is your home base, and I remember well signing all the papers that sent you to OCS and on the road to success."

"Thank you, sir."

"Any preferences as to your future assignment, Lieutenant?"

"Well, sir, at OCS I specialized in automatic small arms and behind-the-enemy-lines tactics. I also took lots of courses in leadership, stress syndrome, and men under severe stress."

Trainer nodded. "These are areas I would've chosen myself were I in your shoes. You'll have no difficulty in finding an assignment to your liking, and feel free to mention my name whenever it can help."

"Thank you very much, sir. The geographical choice of the assignment will be made jointly by my future wife and yours truly."

"Congratulations again. Date's been set?"

"Oh yes, we'll be married on June 22nd at a registry office in New York City. You see, Vivien's divorce decree becomes final on June 21st."

"That's less than three weeks from now," Trainer cried out, swept away by the happy event. "Someone you've known for some time?"

"Right on the button, sir, for a very long time."

"Your first C.O. wouldn't be violently opposed to hearing more about the bride. . . if you catch my meanin'."

Tannenbaum began to talk, trying to minimize his future father-in-law's wealth and making cursory references to his own humble origins.

"Anyway, when I was still in short pants Mr. De Brabantz would employ some of us Jewish boys from the other side of the tracks to do a little work on the estate, raking leaves, fixing this or that, cleaning the garages. We were supervised by the formidable figure of Mr. Flint, the head gardener, who would tell us with a good deal of spirit he simply couldn't understand why Mr. De Brabantz bothered to employ such a shameless bunch of ragamuffins and that he would advise his employer in the strongest possible terms to send us packing. Mr. Flint was venting these threats every time we were working on the grounds, but maybe his employer had different ideas because our services were continually in demand. We always got a good meal in the kitchen—Mr. De Brabantz's direct orders—and we were well paid. During the break Mrs. De Brabantz, whom everyone called Miss Sarah, would arrive with a tray of lemonade and cookies, and she would talk individually to each of us, asking questions about our families and about what we wanted to do when we grew up and so on. I hope I am not boring you to tears, sir?"

"Just the contrary, Tannenbaum, carry on, and that's an order."

"Well, one day Miss Sarah did not appear bearing a tray of good-
ies—perhaps she was not feeling well or whatever the reason—and in
her place her daughter Vivien did the honors. I was fourteen or fifteen
at the time, and she was around twelve, I think. Even today, more than
ten years later, I can see her entire person very clearly advancing slowly with the tray, placing it next to a formidable marble statue, smiling
and saying very softly, 'Please help yourselves.'

"Something inside me snapped, I was floored, I was in seventh
heaven. Vivien—it was only later that I found out her name—was for
me a princess in a fairy tale, the embodiment of all the beauty and
charm and magic in the world. I was transformed, I was staring at her,
and I thought she was smiling and only at me, but not before another
guy gave me one in the shins blurting out, 'Wake up, stupid,' or something of the sort. In the months to come and later, I would see her from
time to time on the grounds of the estate, and a couple of times I
plucked up enough courage to speak to her very briefly, just small talk
and nothing else. She was always very courteous, very well bred. Well,
when I enlisted in the Army at seventeen and was going through basic
I said to myself why don't you write to her, you have nothing to lose,
if she doesn't answer so be it! So I wrote to her—I remember it took
me several days to compose the letter—and lo and behold ten days or
so later I heard from her. She wrote she had enjoyed what I had written, and she wished me all the luck in the world. She also said her parents wanted her to have as wide a circle of friends and acquaintances as
possible, and they didn't mind my writing in the least. After that I wrote
to her several times from basic, sweating it out to make my letters so
exceptional she wouldn't be able to put them down. In one of them—
I remember it distinctly—I gave her the new blueprint from recruit
training, namely the Army bringing hundreds of polar bears to base
which were half-starved and given special injections to go after anything that walked on two feet; and how they attacked us in a body—
this, I explained, was the survival test for the recruits and a way of
winnowing the chaff from the wheat—and how our ranks broke and
our men fell and the situation seemed hopeless, but lo and behold
Ernest J. Tannenbaum came to the rescue: he picked up from the
ground a diamond-studded sword belonging to a gallant officer whose
throat had been torn asunder by the bloodthirsty monster, led the
charge, pierced the monster several times with it, and when it fell bleed-

ing and lifeless to the ground, rallied the men, staged a counterattack, and chased the leaderless and disoriented polar bears away."

The wide-eyed and cackling Trainer clearly did not want him to stop.

"When I was in my second eight weeks of basic I sent Vivien a detailed account of the new test to which we were exposed. The C.O. had assembled an impressive array of robots newly shipped from MIT, programmed to kill anyone who opposed them. Once again we were in dire straits. We were being decimated, but I hit on a happy idea: leading a small band of patriots I broke into the Tech Office, overpowered the guards, and reversed the program. The robots were now poised against the Administration and Command Building, and we sent one simple message: 'No prisoners will be taken.' The enemy surrendered unconditionally in less than three minutes.

"On this and previous occasions Vivien wrote she didn't believe a word of what I was saying but loved each and every word of it, and a friendship was forged which grew with each passing month. We corresponded regularly, me telling her about the adventures and misadventures of Army life, she telling me about her studies, her friends, her travels. She was delighted when she heard about my promotions to corporal and later to sergeant, and I was thrilled to receive her gossipy letters from that fancy finishing school in Switzerland and later from Vassar. In due course our letters became serious and probing. Vivien was getting married to a very eligible young man of her own class, and it soon transpired the marriage was on the rocks. She turned to me as a friend, describing her unhappiness with candor to which even her parents were not privy. I tried to console her, restraining with great difficulty my natural instinct to wring the neck of one who treated her so badly. She told me later that without my moral support God only knows where she would've ended. I can tell you this, Colonel," and Tannenbaum shot a piercing unrelenting glance at Trainer, "the thought that I may have helped her, that I may have spared her further misery, invested me with the kind of happiness I had never known before. It was as if my entire life was merely one of waiting and preparation for the day when I could wipe her tears and lessen her pain. By this time I was already at OCS, and she was very happy for me, but our correspondence was mostly about her. Well, when I got my commission my first act was to fly to Baltimore and see her, and her parents, of course."

"And then like a good trooper you proposed to her, for what can be done today should not be left until tomorrow? Right?"

"Wrong. We talked for hours, but I left as a devoted friend. When I landed in Newark I called her and got it off my chest. She accepted."

Trainer's eyes sparkled with joy. "That's quite an account, Lieutenant, and quite a life. You're quite an original."

"Thank you, sir. There's one thing that is constantly on my mind."

"Out with it," Trainer hollered.

"I don't know how well Vivien can adapt herself to being married to a second lieutenant whose only income is his meager salary. She comes from a very, very wealthy family, and," Tannenbaum again shot one of his piercing unrelenting glances, "you will believe me when I tell you I am not after her money."

"I believe you, and as for your first question, she'll adapt if she has any sense. And you're ready to swear on a stack of Bibles she does have it."

"Oh, without a doubt."

"Then," and Trainer spread out his hands, "let's leave it to Father Time."

"Thank you for seeing me, Colonel."

"Thank you for coming to see me, Lieutenant. It was a veritable experience listening to you." He paused. "That bit about the polar bears and robots, no need to spread it among the higher-ups, is there?"

"No need at all, it's strictly for family consumption."

"Good."

Tannenbaum was collecting his coat and hat. "I was very sorry to hear about Sergeant Sampler. I knew him well. He was a very decent human being," he said in a different tone of voice.

"He was, and the good often suffer unnecessarily. His, I am afraid, was a long and painful death . . . You're staying at the Officer's Club at Army?"

"Tomorrow and next night probably. But tonight I am staying with Jim O'Leary and his wife. He and I have been friends for ever and a day."

"Good man, Jimmie," Trainer was speaking on the spur of the moment, "and you know what, folks are saying what they dish out in the Mess Hall these days is smoother on the palate than in months and years past."

"I wouldn't be surprised, Jimmie's wife is a pastry cook by training."

"Aha!" Trainer's raised eyebrows told it all. ". . . just a trivial question to satisfy my own inexcusable curiosity before you go?"

"Yes, Colonel."

"Your middle initial 'J', what does it stand for? Something simple I hope. John maybe? It's never spelled out in your records."

"No such luck. I suspect the record keepers didn't know how to spell it. 'J' stands for 'Jeremiah.' My full name is Ernest Jeremiah Tannenbaum."

Trainer assumed an official mien. "It's a very fine name, Ernest, and don't let no one tell you different. D'you hear?" he declared with emphasis, returning Tannenbaum's salute.

/ / /

Vallejo had decided to pay a visit to Restaurant Dolores on the first Saturday following Memorial Day. He left immediately after lunch and arrived at his destination shortly before 4:00 P.M. The place was merrily filled to capacity. As he made his way through the boisterous crowd, here and there a keen pair of eyes fastened onto him and several men in high spirits extended their hands uttering steadily, "*Ich gratuliere.*" Vallejo moved on, noticing now and again a familiar face, smiling and waving back. Honest Jasper caught sight of him at once, came out from behind the bar, and shook hands.

"We feared you might be a goner, Jesús. That Sunday and part of Monday there was little hope."

"Well, you know the story of a bad penny. It turns up again and again."

"There's something I want to say to you." Jasper sounded unusually solemn. "We knew members of Bund 45 patronized our establishment, but we didn't know who they were. We had no inkling what Ketterer, Vogelsee, and the others were up to. If we had known we could've warned you, but it is our policy not to pry into the customers' private lives."

"I understand, Jasper. What about Frau Schwämer?"

The bartender pulled a scornful face. "She denies everything, of course, and being a wealthy woman with high connections she's defended by some of the best attorneys in the Federal Republic. She was complicit, there's absolutely no doubt of it, but state prosecutors have to prove it . . . and this may take some doing."

"I see . . . Your dive is as popular as ever . . ."

Jasper laughed. "Actually, after what is referred to as the Schwämer Affair, business picked up considerably. In the days immediately following the arrests lots of people came here to inveigh as loudly as they could against the new Nazis. It was almost like a demonstration for democracy and public decency, and they were brassy." Jasper led Vallejo to the bar and filled two glasses with French brandy.

"This is to honor you on your timely reappearance, Jesús. May you have eight lives left like the proverbial cat."

"Thanks very much, Jasper. I'll keep you posted as each successive life is snuffed out," and they sipped the precious brew.

"You don't know about my new job?"

"No, how could I?"

"The truth of the matter is I've been offered the post of the head bar steward at the Kaiserin Hof, and I accepted."

"That's the swanky place near Schiller Platz?"

"Very swanky and now under new management. They are trying to make it the undisputed number one in Stuttgart." Jasper chuckled irreverently. "Catering to only the best people and those who are not averse to behaving like the best people."

"Congratulations. Higher salary, higher status?"

"Oh yes, much higher salary. There are three bars at the Kaiserin, and I'll be in charge of all of them. Most of the time I'll be wearing tails, supervising and dealing with an inordinate amount of paperwork."

"I am very happy for you. Son of a gun! And when does Herr Direktor take up his new duties and responsibilities?"

"July 1st, just what the doctor ordered." Jasper commented smugly. Then he added, "You're a sergeant now. How does it feel?"

"I haven't noticed any changes deep inside my psyche, but maybe I didn't look deep enough."

Waiting till his friend had a free moment between serving drinks, Vallejo asked: "How are Stephan and Frida? Has her family relented?"

"No, and they are not going to. There was a time not long ago when the father had second thoughts, but he was overruled by his wife and his two daughters. Not a penny for Frida."

"I'm sorry," Vallejo muttered more to himself than to Jasper. "I'm truly sorry."

"But there is a silver lining."

"Let's have it, for crying out loud!"

"Patience, my friend. Social Services have determined the two love-birds deserve support in furthering their education. They have been awarded a small grant, scholarship if you like, to attend a trade school and work only part time. Their tuition is paid, and they will be receiving living expenses. This is for six months with the possibility of renewal."

"That's great news," Vallejo cried out, "just great!"

"I agree. I think Frida wants to do dressmaking and Stephan TV repairing . . . You see, Jesús, our social services are really up to scratch. Many of our social workers suffered under Hitler or their families or parents suffered. Many of them supported our great socialist leader Kurt Schumacher . . . many of them are socialists. They fight for social justice, for better working opportunities for everybody, for redistribution of wealth, for reorganization of our educational establishments, for creation of more trade schools. We want better justice, more social mobility, new means of bringing everyone into the mainstream, particularly those who have been underprivileged and dispossessed."

"I would never disagree with those goals."

"In the States you have this expression 'the American dream.'"

"Yes, but at times it's no more than an expression."

"Still at other times . . . ?"

"It's an ideal that is realized."

"My point precisely. We in our fatherland deserve to have what I'd like to call 'the German dream,' a society in which every German, man or woman, can rise as high as his or her own ability and initiative permit."

"This is worth fighting for."

"Yes it is," Jasper said very slowly, very deliberately, busying himself with drinks urgently requested. During a lull he turned again to Vallejo.

"To come back to our muttons . . ."

"What goddamn muttons are these?"

"Frida and Stephan."

"Aha."

"It's nice of you to show interest in them."

"It's purely a matter of my liking them. In fact they'd invited me to share the evening meal with them . . . tonight, I'll be seeing them tonight."

An unspoken suggestion was distending Jasper's features, but Vallejo did not allow himself to be caught off guard.

"I've come to know the quaint customs of your country, friend. I am taking flowers for Frida, and a bottle of wine as my contribution to the meal."

"Excellent. Flowers are *de rigueur*, wine is optional, but it's a nice gesture. You're learning fast, boy."

Vallejo scoured the scene around him. "You haven't been to our base, have you? Would you like to come? I'd be happy to show you round."

"I'd like that very much, thank you."

"I'll be in touch in the next couple of days, and now I'll park myself in the lounge and try to regain my strength before the social exigencies of the evening."

"You do that," Jasper burst out laughing.

Ensconced comfortably in an armchair, Vallejo closed his eyes and tried not to think, not to remember, not to anticipate. But the human mind is a funny kind of gizmo. It can turn itself off when it pleases, but when its ostensible owner and overseer tries to blank it or unexpectedly throw some heavy duty right across it, it may welsh, take umbrage, refuse squatting rights to the intruder, or tell the owner to take a hike. It is the first alternative that is pertinent here. Effortlessly, Vallejo's mind traveled back several years, to his last semester in high school when on the advice of a much-respected counselor he registered for a world literature course entitled "Romantic Nature and the Beautiful People in It." The instructor, Dr. Wilberforce, a man of broad intellectual interests and much feared on the premises of the school, was in the habit of expressing himself temperamentally and not infrequently cholerically on a variety of subjects. His voice could be heard at the other end of the hall no matter how many walls stood in between, and as several students put it quite independently of one another, "Old Will makes such a racket it isn't decent, one can't get a wink of sleep." Fondly the memories of the luxuriant nature and of the handsome and refined beings resting insouciantly on its bosom flowed into his consciousness. They were like billows flowing onto a sandy beach and then breaking into froth and foam, all transparence and light. The remembered became the real. He saw the graceful and pure Paul and Virginia against a breathtaking exotic landscape, the comely Typees possessed of every private and public virtue, in their beautiful paradise of the South Seas, the innocent Atala surrounded by "a thousand grottos, a thousand alcoves . . . and . . . trees of every shape, of every color, and of every perfume." He saw other gorgeous children of nature, and he heard Dr. Wilberforce's deafening roar demonstrating the genius of Jean-Jacques Rousseau to the class, analyzing him, explicating him, spending hours on "Musings of a Solitary Stroller," and ending each class period with a war cry and a challenge: "The noble savage, and every other hero and heroine in the primitivist writing, derives not only the outstanding physical attributes from nature, but what is far more important, the outstanding mental attributes as well; goodness, empathy for others, compassion, honesty, proper sense of decorum, understanding, and wisdom all come from nature. For nature is the mother who nurtures us, and she is the horn of plenty. She is infinitely good, she is perfection."

Vallejo cast his mind back but to a more recent time. What of Frida and Stephan? They both showed that delicacy of feeling, good breeding, a wonderful sense of decorum. So who were their teachers? They certainly did not grow up in an earthly paradise like Paul and Virginia. Stephan was the son of a Berlin blue-collar worker and a *hausfrau* much given to drink, and both were killed in an air raid when he was three years old. Frida came from the upper echelons of German society, but her bearing had little to do with that of her class. There was a simplicity and grace about her that transcended social barriers and moved her far away from the self-conscious comportment of the German *haut monde*. Stephan had an easy manner about him, an easy manner and spontaneity that made him treat others, whether they be socially high or low, in the same open and courteous manner. His egalitarianism dispensed with social classes and divisions and set new rules, and Vallejo wondered where this happy egalitarianism had come from. If nature was responsible for Stephan and Frida's rare gifts, it must have been nature effectively disguised behind Berlin rubble and uninviting orphanages and behind the shabby lodgings to which a rich girl who refused to give up her lover was relegated. Vallejo wondered and tried to find an answer.

Once behind the wheel he drove straight for several blocks to a

corner where earlier he had espied a flower stand. He bought the flowers, double-checked his friends' address scribbled on a scrap of paper,
and drove on. A carefully chosen bottle of wine was lying on the back
seat, and he was full of anticipation. He was eagerly looking forward to
the evening.

Epilogue

In which what had been brought out and what had not been brought out in the earlier chapters is at last concluded.

It was now the end of June, and the loveliest June in many a man's memory. Trainer was sitting in his office tossing folders and papers all around him after a most perfunctory inspection and looking out of sorts when Korovitz put his head through the half-open door.

"Sergeant Shelton is here to see you, sir."

"Send him in," Trainer sounded off merrily, sailing the last folder like a Frisbee to the far wall.

"I've come to say good-bye, Colonel." Shelton saluted and smiled.

"Oh?"

"My enlistment runs through July 2nd, and Army wants me for a few days before my fiancée and I take off on July 3rd from Frankfurt . . ."

"Of course I remember now, Sergeant," Trainer interjected hastily, "and the wedding is on . . . ?"

"July 18th."

"That's right, I distinctly remember that date." He lapsed into a silence, then looked sharply at Shelton.

"We did some good work together, and it'd be a goddamn shame if it was forgotten. I won't forget it, nor should you."

"I won't, sir, you can bank on it. That may have been the most famous posse in history."

Trainer beckoned to the sergeant to sit down and, noticing his concern, bellowed, "Just kick those papers down to the floor, they have no business being in the way. Kick 'em off. Yes," he continued in a more restrained tone of voice, "that posse made some of us feel we were troopers again, not lousy paper pushers, and you, Hal, pointed the way."

Shelton made a slight self-deprecating gesture.

"Yes, you pinpointed where the enemy was, and it was my distinct honor to lead you guys on this very important mission."

Trainer reached for a cheroot, smacked his lips, and asked in a sly kind of way, "Big wedding? As I recall, in this celebrated vanity town of Alexandria where the dead are more than ghosts, folks like big weddings."

"Something like that, and yes a big wedding with all the trimmings."

Trainer was grinning from ear to ear.

"As Cousin Woodrow put it, half of the Sheltons will be there, but the other half, being behind bars, will not be able to attend."

"Who's Cousin Woodrow?" Trainer asked eagerly.

"He's my cousin, Dad's brother's eldest son and older than me, but everyone calls him 'Cousin Woodrow.' He's a prankster."

"Any truth in that behind bars bit?"

"None. The only Shelton who was behind bars in recent times, stateside that is, was Grandpa Shelton who served a brief prison sentence on the charge of bootlegging. That was back in the twenties."

"Only one in such a large family?"

"We were not more law-abiding than the next family, but I guess, cleverer."

"I take my hat off to you, Hal, but what kind of pranks does Cousin Woodrow go in for?"

"A wide variety. Some are funny, some are not. To give you an example: at the break of dawn he would steal into the racing stable and tie the horses' tails together. One time the stewards were already waiting for him and were going to give him the pasting of his life. But being swift of foot he got away. He's still boasting about it."

"Lowdown trick," Trainer deposed gravely, like a county judge pronouncing sentence on a poacher.

"Another time, it was last year when I was home on leave, Mom and Dad gave a party for a dozen or so people, some family and some friends—it was really for Dad who had just had a successful hernia operation and was fresh out of the hospital—and Mom decided it might be easier to take all those people to a restaurant for dinner rather than cooking at home. We'd gotten a tip about a brand-new place, which was highly recommended, and we all trooped in there, Dad leading the charge, and somehow Cousin Woodrow managed to be in attendance. Anyway, we all sat down, and Cousin Woodrow said he knew the headwaiter and could expedite matters, so we gave him our orders, and he disappeared and then disappeared for good. But twenty minutes later a waiter brought in an enormous tureen full of cream of wheat. Cousin Woodrow had told the headwaiter all of us had ulcers, but there would be generous tips etc., etc."

"That ain't funny at all," Trainer thundered. "Lowdown . . . so and so!"

"My mother would agree with you. That same evening she sent word she wanted to see him, and he came sheepish and begging to be forgiven. Well, Mom didn't forgive. She gave him a talking-to that lasted a good half hour or more, and later she told Dad, her breast heaving with pride, she had used a most unlady-like language to the little twerp."

"Someone ought to teach the little twerp a lesson," Trainer thundered again.

"It's been done, but Cousin Woodrow is like a duck diving and then shaking off the water. He swears he's a reformed man, and there are tears in his eyes; then he goes back to his prankish ways."

"Son of a gun," Trainer muttered through his teeth, "the twerp has all the marks of a North Korean."

"Maybe so," Shelton laughed, "but the funny thing is he's married to Betsy, one of the sweetest, kindest, and best-liked women in our entire family and, I'd wager, in the entire Commonwealth of Virginia."

"And Betsy can't teach her man how to behave?"

"Apparently no one can. However, I read in Mom's last letter she and Dad had a heart-to-heart talk with Cousin Woodrow and Betsy and informed them if there is any monkey business at the wedding cops will be called in at once, and furthermore Dad and Mom will never speak to them again; whereupon Betsy quietly assured Mom nothing untoward would happen, and Cousin Woodrow swore up and down he was mortally offended at the mere suggestion that he might sabotage his cousin's wedding, go against his flesh and blood, and so on and so forth."

"So they are coming to the wedding?"

"It took a lot of persuading, but Mom finally consented. He's on a short leash, though."

"Maybe the advantage of having a large family is one learns more about how we all tick. There were seven of us kids, four boys and three girls, and with the relatives added up we too produced a couple or more unbelievable characters. God have mercy on their souls!"

"I didn't mean to bore you with my family history, sir."

"You did not, Hal, you did not. Besides," Trainer added with a smirk, "it isn't everyday that one is introduced to Cousin Woodrow. How does the bride feel about going to a new country and the rest of it?"

"Brigitta's all excited about it, she wants to live in America, she wants to be an American."

Trainer nodded with approval.

"And do you actually have jobs to go to?"

"We've been very lucky. Both of us were hired by George Washington Hospital in Alexandria, Brigitta in obstetrics, me in radiology."

Trainer drew himself up.

"Sergeant Shelton, my compliments to the bride and Godspeed to both of you. Let's keep those memories alive. It isn't often that we are called upon to do something that is right and noble no matter what the others may say. And we were called upon to do just that."

After Shelton had left, Trainer went back reluctantly to his pastime of playing Frisbee with folders and official papers. But pain reeled in his stomach; he was constipated and grouchy. His housekeeper was away for a week, and for four days now he had been preparing his own dinners, throwing together into a pot whatever he had found in the icebox, mixing it, seasoning it with ketchup and steak sauce, and fortifying it with canned meat. He would have been at a loss in giving those dishes of his even the most generic names, but the results were concrete and indisputable: he felt much worse after each successive dinner than before it, and after two days of fending for himself constipation set in. He could not relieve himself; he could not even break wind. What felt like rocks blocked his alimentary canal, nothing was churning, nothing moved. He was utterly miserable, and he half-grumbled and half-hissed out to himself, "She better be back on time or else, or else," snatching another folder from a pristine pile to sail it high in the air, an easy prey. But fate had something else in store for the colonel, and he saw Korovitz looming over him.

"This came for you by special messenger, sir, direct from General Ryan," and he handed Trainer a slender envelope and a large, bulky one.

"Army likes to waste gas when they got nothin' else to do; special messengers my ankle, this makes them feel important, doesn't it, Leroy!"

"I would open these babies right away, Colonel, if you forgive the liberty."

"Yeah, yeah, yeah, all in good time," Trainer grumbled, the cramps making him squirm.

When he was left alone he ripped the slender envelope open. It contained his promotion to brigadier general effective immediately. He played for a few seconds with the bulky envelope, holding it against the light and pressing it at the corners to determine what was inside. He decided it was a thick wad of paper, and he slit the envelope carefully with the paperknife. Twenty-five single-spaced pages stared him in the face entitled *Preliminary Instructions, Objectives, and Goals for the U.S. Army Commission Charged to Explore Geographic, Climatic, Social, and Political Conditions in Vietnam with Reference to the Possible Activity of the U.S. Army Corps of Engineers*. Trainer pulled a face and found the line immediately underneath the title much more gratifying, *Head of the Commission: Brigadier General Edward E. Trainer, United States Army*.

As he was smugly admiring his new rank on the front page of the mammoth memorandum, he at once felt a slight loosening inside him, a little slack in the innards. "Gee," he thought, "maybe I can evacuate gas-like." And making sure the door leading to Group Sergeant's office was shut tight he began to break wind with great force, creating a putrid and highly offensive smell. This lasted for several minutes, and in the end he was almost a new man.

"Now, if only I could fire away a pound or two of solid-like substance, I'd be standing tall." He swung a window open, crossed into the adjacent office, and told Korovitz and Vallejo the news. They were incredulous but warm in their congratulations. He took the measure of every object, big or small, that stood in his line of vision and turned to Jesús.

"Sergeant Vallejo, please report to my office in five minutes precisely."

"Yes, sir."

Korovitz waited till the third party was out of sight and stepped closer to the Group Clerk.

"Watch yourself, boy. His housekeeper is away visiting her son and daughter in Munich, so he's not getting it regularly these days. He's as jumpy as a prima donna and as touchy as a defrocked preacher."

"Thanks, Leroy. I'll remember it."

Much more agile now, Trainer was dashing around the office gesticulating, carrying on an animated dialogue with himself, and occasionally singing the praises of fresh air.

"Sit down, sit down, Jesús," and he handed him the twenty-five-page text. "Please read it very carefully, make an outline, and focus on the highlights. I need to be briefed in no more than forty minutes. I'll read it with extreme care at home tonight, but your analysis will be damn valuable." Vallejo made an attempt to say something, but Trainer led him to the door, his arm swung fraternally around the Group Clerk's torso. "See you in forty minutes," he snapped, pushing the Group Clerk out.

In less than forty minutes Vallejo was again sitting in front of Trainer's desk, the memo and his own notepaper in hand.

"Let me give you the gist, and I wrote everything out in great detail."

"That's my boy."

"The purpose of this commission is to find out how well U.S. Army engineers can perform on the foreign terrain of Vietnam; is our equipment equal to the task? Are the men who will be sent there in need of additional training, and what kind of training? How are we to assess the attitude of the native population in the event of armed conflict and so on and so forth. You are to select three or four officers who are well-trained engineers for this mission and an NCO. The Pentagon will provide one or two of their own men, and the State Department will add two interpreters and two experts on Southeast Asia."

"Who are those experts?" Trainer asked sharply, ". . . peace-lovin', long-haired pro . . . fe . . . ssors?"

"It doesn't say. They could simply be State Department officials."

Trainer was sucking his thumb. "Anything else?"

"Yes. You have a three-day briefing at the Pentagon beginning August 1st, and your estimated stay in Vietnam is ninety days. The commission leaves on September 1st."

"So, as I understand it, they want me to bring along engineers who'll get down to the nitty-gritty, and I already made my selection: a major, a captain, and a lieutenant, all three within 7th Army Command. As for the NCO," Trainer studiously avoided watching Vallejo and instead let his eyes roam lightheartedly over the ceiling, "as for the NCO," he repeated more pointedly, ". . . would you like to volunteer, Jesús?"

"You know, sir, I want to go to OCS."

"But that's not till next year . . . right?"

"Right, I'll be through with my college correspondence courses in February, after that the sooner the better."

"We ought to be back way before then, and this little jaunt to whatever you call that place will strengthen your application."

Vallejo thought for a moment. "Colonel, I'd like to be considered for the post of the NCO on the commission you'll be heading."

"Sergeant Jesús Vallejo, your application has been duly reviewed, and you've been selected for the post in question. Consider yourself part of the team."

Left alone, Trainer strode to the bookshelf and made an effort to locate the atlases and a stack of maps he was convinced ought to be lying there. As he bent over, a piercing, jabbing pain in the belly made him wince and catch his breath spasmodically. The pain did not stop, and his fingers were still groping for the atlases and maps. Next he gave out a great yell, and Korovitz and Vallejo came running.

"Someone has filched my maps, my maps . . . they're my maps," he was screaming, biting his lips, and holding one hand by the abdomen. "They're my maps . . . catch the thief . . . do you understand . . . catch the thief!"

Korovitz stepped forth casually to the bookshelf and from the lowest rung lifted five bound atlases and a stack of maps.

"They've always been here, down at the bottom, no one filched them," he said brusquely.

"I need a map of Vietnam," Trainer growled.

Korovitz opened one of the atlases and was going to place it in front of his C.O., but the latter wrenched it out of his hands and flung it down on his desk.

"It ain't right," he howled, "it ain't right! What's happened to the Indian Ocean and to that damned peninsula?"

"You're holding the pages upside down, sir." Korovitz was as brusque as before.

"Oh, I see it now," Trainer muttered and beckoned to the two sergeants to remain where they were. He then began to flip through the pages of the different atlases, scrutinizing the world map and the maps of Asia and the United States, locked in thoughts of his own. When at last he pushed them aside, a shrewd, no-nonsense look crept upon his face.

"I've been doin' some calculatin', that Vietnam stretch or whatever they call it is one hell of a long way from Kansas. We got no business goin' there."

"We are just sending a commission to find out the lay of the land," Korovitz joined in.

Trainer drew in a deep breath. "That's the way fireworks start. We send men on a reconnaissance mission, and then before you can say Jack Robinson we rush in combat troops and more combat troops." He paused and fixed his eyes on each of them, pitilessly as if he wanted to dredge up and hold up to the light their deepest, their most intimate thoughts. "Ike ain't behind it. He's got horse sense. It's those goddamn armchair generals and the politicians . . . it's their doing, they gotta keep the ball rolling."

But Trainer's fury had all but evaporated.

"I'm sorry about the outburst, truth of the matter is my insides acting up real bad."

"In that case, you should go to the Infirmary forthwith and see a medical officer, sir," Vallejo advised in a flat voice.

Trainer gave out a high-pitched deprecatory laugh. "No way! I don't hold with them guys. No way!" But a kinder look was now transforming his features. "Thank you for your advice, thank you for finding the maps."

Once within the confines of their own office, Vallejo wasted little time.

"When is that housekeeper of his coming back?"

"In three days."

"Group Sergeant, do you think you could find a way of putting a three-day pass in my pocket, effective immediately?"

"There might be a slight problem, Sergeant, as I myself am in dire need of one and am racking my brains who can sign it except you know who."

"What a coincidence!"

/   /   /

Four days later Trainer, fresh as a daisy and exuding unabashed good fellowship and that particular kind of joviality which makes such an indelible impression on audiences large and small, was in his office bright and early long before the first GI reported for duty at the Command Building. His stomach was in perfect condition, and the rest of his body displayed healthy vigor, all its needs fully satisfied. He greeted Korovitz and Vallejo cheerily, and at once got down to business. "Well, I have my team all assembled and ready to go, and I can only hope the Pentagon and State guys will not be total losers." As Vallejo was leaving to confer with an MP sergeant about a recent drunk and disorderly case, the colonel buttonholed the Group Sergeant.

"I'm sure you must've figured it out by now, Leroy, once I return from that Asian plot of land I'll be reassigned. There will be a new Group Commander maybe even before I leave; it depends on how fast Army wants to move with it."

"Yes, I realize, sir."

"Do you want to stay on? I'll be recommending Major Fiorello as my successor. Will you want to work under him?"

"I have nothing against the major . . . but there's something else, and I meant to tell you as soon as the dust settles, so to speak. Maybe I should've spoken earlier."

"Let's have it now."

"Adrianne likes her job so she'll not want to be transferred, and we'd want to live together in a place without long commutes."

"Right!"

"So I've been making inquiries about openings at Army. There are several, but one caught my eye."

"Yes?"

"Casper Bullock is finally retiring . . ."

"I've heard this one ten years running."

"But this time it's true. Now his wife is all for it so he can fix things round their new home in Oklahoma."

"Aha, well, that certainly adds a pinch of seriousness to the matter."

"Anyway, I threw my hat into the ring, Bullock's job but also a few lesser shots. You told me I can count on a recommendation from you, sir."

"Sure, sure." Trainer retreated a step and stood there guffawing, but his posture made it clear he was impressed.

"So, before long it may be Sergeant Major Leroy Korovitz, Headquarters, 7th United States Army."

"Don't let's count our chickens before . . ."

But Trainer interrupted him flamboyantly: "I'd say you have a better than fifty percent chance, and I'll do anything to help."

"Thank you, sir."

Vallejo reentered the office, and Trainer patted him on the back.

"Since we are telling each other secrets, I have one for both of you. I had a letter from Ernie, Lieutenant Ernest J. Tannenbaum"—he pronounced "J" with emphasis amid chuckling. "He and Vivien were married in New York City on the 22nd of June, happy couple. And what's more he got assigned to 7th Army Headquarters, guess what section? Planning and Coordination. Ernie must have a lot on the ball since they took him; maybe more than any of us ever suspected."

"That's the brain of the Headquarters," Korovitz said trying not to make too much of it.

"Right! And Vivien apparently can't wait to get to Weiningen and Stuttgart. She's a well-traveled young lady, but not in Krautland. Britain, France, Italy, Switzerland, Spain, that was her beat."

"I remember Tannenbaum," Vallejo put in, "a regular guy."

"And bright," Trainer added.

"Yes, very bright."

Trainer's index finger was doggedly scratching his chin, and this was apparently to aid his memory, which in this instance was sluggish.

"Hell, there was somethin' I wanted to tell ye, but for the life of me . . . for the life of me I can't . . . I can't bring it to mind."

"We have the whole day," Vallejo observed coolly.

But in a flash the colonel had brought it to mind.

"I got it," he hollered triumphantly, slapping his knee. "It concerns Sol and Nina."

"We are all ears," Korovitz informed him

"They're getting married on July 22nd in Bonn at the U.S. Embassy, and I'm Sol's best man. His divorce will be final by then."

"Isn't she under age?" Korovitz assumed a serious expression.

"It all depends what you mean by 'under age,' Leroy. If in your book a girl of twenty-two is under age, you have a case."

"I heard she was much younger."

"Oddly enough, I heard the same," Vallejo said flatly.

"My, my, my," Trainer exclaimed, throwing his hands high in the air, "how tongues wag; gossip, gossip, gossip. And malicious gossip too. So you're telling me half the base believes the chaplain has been molesting a girl of twelve."

"No, no, no," Korovitz and Vallejo remonstrated at once.

"The talk of the town favors her being fifteen."

"Fifteen or sixteen at the most," Korovitz confirmed.

"For cryin' out loud," Trainer exploded. "This month she's graduating from college. How the hell can she be fifteen?" When he had finished hollering, Trainer became acutely aware of Korovitz and Vallejo watching him inquisitively in a curious guilt-assigning disbelief.

"There is no offense intended, Colonel," Korovitz spoke in an easy, accommodating manner, "but are you sure you've gotten all the facts right?"

Later in the morning as Trainer, with undisguised distaste, was doing battle with the mounting piles of papers, a rap came on the door leading into the corridor.

"Come in," Trainer shouted, and Fiorello stood in the doorway.

"I believe you wanted to see me." He spoke with caution and reserve, closing the door behind him.

"I did, John, and take the load off your feet."

Fiorello was hardly settled on the chair when he leaned forward and sputtered out: "Congratulations are in order, Ed," and he vigorously held out his hand.

"Thank you. Let me go straight to the point. I've recommended you for Group Commander, and Sam Stebbins says there should be no difficulties. In fact, it's in the bag, and it's only a matter of time when you assume command. I shall be in and out in August, and that hike to Southeast Asia"—Trainer smiled indulgently—"starts September 1st. When I return I'll probably report straight to my new unit. I was given to understand you will be promoted to Lt. Colonel when you assume your new Command, and it shouldn't be long before you make full bird."

"Thanks, I mean, thank you for recommending me." Overcome by the good news, the Adjutant was groping for something original to say.

"You're welcome, you'll make a good Group Commander."

"Eunice will be overjoyed," Fiorello stammered out at last.

"Does this mean you won't?"

"No, no, but I just wanted to bring her into the conversation."

Trainer blinked several times. "Why not. I understand."

"I'll follow your example." Fiorello's voice grew stronger and his manner more aggressive.

"You should keep your own counsel, John, this will be your show, no one else's. But a word of caution. Don't ask for perfection from the men seven days a week."

"Not perfection, but pursuit thereof. This should be every officer's motto."

"Within reason! Let the men breathe and wallow in their own filth before you put them on display. Save your petrol for what ain't run of the mill."

/ / /

It was a ravishing Sunday afternoon of early July, and Trainer was entertaining at home his old friend Dr. Inge von Treschkow and her fiancé, Dr. Konrad Bender, a heart specialist. As soon as he saw Bender unceremoniously jump out of the car and saunter up the path without even a ghost of self-conscious formality, Trainer's heart went out to him. Why was this man in his middle thirties, tall, blond, and lithe, with a lick of a thin moustache pasted over his upper lip which made him look like one of those dashing cavaliers in the employ of Charles I, why was this man so different from the other men of similar appearance, Americans, Germans, or Brits he had known? At first, Trainer had absolutely no clue. But when he found out that Bender, a Hamburger by birth, had spent the last two years of the war on a German torpedo boat mostly in the North Sea rising in 1945 to the rank of commander, that he came from an old naval family, his father being a captain and his grandfather a rear admiral, he began to put two and two together.

Inge's fiancé was a sailor, an old salt by experience and family tradition, and the sea marks her men for infinity. These markings are embedded in the very psyche of the individual, they cannot be discovered even by the most sensitive instruments, and they defy the crushing juggernaut of technology. A sailor will know another sailor, no matter what part of the globe he hails from, but in all likelihood, will not be able to tell how he came to that conclusion. Some things remain forever unexplainable, imponderable, and unexplainable! If one were to hazard a guess, the very aspect of the open sea which confronts the sailor for hours on end, an expanse devoid of bridges, suburbs, gas stations, and supermarkets, infuses calm into him and awe takes the place of cheap distractions. Whether most sailors love the sea is a moot point—the overpaid idiot from the media who once opined that the sea is to a sailor both mother and sweetheart, undoubtedly derived his knowledge of the waves and of those who sail them from dipping his foot and other parts of his offensive anatomy in a residential swimming pool—but it is true that most sailors respect the sea, in a way that no landsman respects the land; and this gives them intimacy with what lies beyond, recognition of the veiled order of things. They shape the sailor's soul, but in a manner so subtle as to deceive nine landlocked dudes out of ten.

The afternoon had gotten off to a good start. Conversation was easy, spontaneous, and each of them talked a great deal. Konrad told Trainer about his service in the Navy and then rattled on enthusiastically about his two years of post-graduate studies at John's Hopkins and the charms of Baltimore, old and new, while Inge and the host asked innumerable questions; Inge outlined to them the important educational reforms her ministry was boldly advocating and then chatted about her mother, her friends, her co-workers. Trainer talked about everything under the sun, including Kansas and was struck by the way Konrad and Inge understood each other without uttering a single word, their minds being happily attuned, and their opinions often identical about topics of which they had had no prior knowledge. It sadly reminded him of how Beryl and he in years past could read each other's thoughts and anticipate what the other would do.

Konrad spoke English like a native, but Trainer was a little puzzled by his guest's very pronounced New England accent, as though he had been flown in on a magic carpet from another planet or straight from Boston. He also noticed that Inge, whom he had always seen in the past dressed like an executive, was now dressed differently, very differently—like a woman in love. The new Inge brought her femininity to every gesture and turn of hand. The wedding plans were discussed, and Inge reminded Konrad his divorce would not be final until November 1st. Yes, he sighed, they simply had to wait; nothing could be done about it. And both of them were warmly complimentary about the refreshments which awaited them. Trainer's housekeeper had surpassed herself: canapé's, sandwiches, various salads, caviar, meatballs, marinated fish, and other delights. She had been spurred in her efforts by the fact that the general would be entertaining two German doctors, head of section at a ministry and a heart specialist, and she was duly impressed. She had always been in favor of Trainer getting to know socially her compatriots, so long these compatriots were of the right kind, as she put it, and Trainer followed her instructions to the letter.

When Inge and Konrad heard about Trainer's promotion, they were jubilant. Konrad told him with disarming candor that the highest-ranking American officer he had ever encountered was a studious-looking first lieutenant in Baltimore with a passion for seventeenth-century harbors in the New World, and his fiancée made appropriately polite noises. There was only one unavoidably unhappy moment when Inge let it be known her brother Wolfgang's health had deteriorated to the point it was now a matter of weeks at the most, or even days. Inge's eyes were moist, and Konrad at once put his arms around her and held her close. *She needs him now, and he is there,* Trainer thought, and a conviction bore through his mind that Konrad would be there whenever Inge needed him. Soon a note of gaiety was struck again, and they talked, kidded one another, agreed, disagreed, contradicted one another, and laughed individually and in unison as if there was no tomorrow.

When Konrad announced he would like to wash his hands and disappeared down the hall, Inge came up to Trainer. She was very still and deep in thought.

"Yes, Inge," he said very gently, "what is it, I'm here?"

It took her a while before she opened up.

"What do you think of Konrad?" she asked.

"He's great, just great."

"Yes, he is. You must know no one will ever take Ted's place. But I'd like to live again. I think Ted would want me to live again."

He clasped her bonny hands in his, huge and rough, full of blisters and calluses.

"I'm sure Ted would want you to live again," he murmured soothingly. "I damn well know he would."